"Do they

"Oh, Kate
determine

Kate leaned forward, her eyes wide and earnest.
"Don't you think it's odd, considering the amount
of time Patrick and I spent in Belfast, that he never
once took me to one of its finest restaurants, one
that he frequented often?"

"I'm not sure that is important."

"Patrick was a conversationalist, Maeve. There
wasn't anything he didn't say or describe in great
detail. It was very uncharacteristic of him not to
even mention the name of a restaurant where the
maître d' knows his name, enough to offer me
condolences six years later."

Maeve's mouth, lovely, sultry, deliciously curved,
tightened. "Leave it, Kate."

"What if I can't?"

"What good will come of it?"

"The truth."

Maeve snorted. "Truth, always the Holy Grail.
What if it tears your family apart?"

Kate looked at her friend incredulously. "Look at
my family, Maeve. Can it get any worse?"

The green eyes were very bright and filled with
pity. "Don't test the waters, Katie. Leave this one
alone. You've your children to think of. Patrick was
a man, not the best, but certainly not the worst.
Accept that and move on."

"Is that what you would do?"

"It is."

MIRA Books is proud to present

THE DELANEY WOMAN

by
JEANETTE BAKER

Available June 2003

JEANETTE BAKER

BLOOD ROSES

MIRA®

ISBN 1-55166-910-2

BLOOD ROSES

Copyright © 2002 by Jeanette Baker.

Visit us at www.mirabooks.com

Printed in U.S.A.

Author's Note

Northern Ireland—or The Six Counties, as the Nationalist/
Catholic population calls it—is a land long divided by
economics, tradition, religion and bloodshed. Almost five
hundred years ago Henry Tudor, surrounded by Catholic Spain,
France and Ireland and convinced that England could never be
ruled by a woman, was desperate to establish a dynasty, and he
decided that Ireland would be his first colony. Displacing the
Catholic population, banishing and executing the Catholic
aristocracy, and transplanting Englishmen and Scots to lands
long held by Catholics, he, and later his daughter, Queen
Elizabeth the First, systematically attempted to eradicate the
Celtic/Catholic tradition in Ireland. Land, residences,
employment, political appointments and education were
reserved for Protestants. The Penal Laws became the birthright
of Catholics, as did civil rights violations, discrimination, torture
and false imprisonment. Even so, because of the fierce nature of
Irish independence and the strength of the Catholic Church in
Ireland, Henry was unsuccessful at the grassroots level.

Not until forty years ago, when television brought to the world
the civil rights movement then taking place in the United States,
did the oppressed Irish of the Six Counties find their voice. Out
of the ashes of Bloody Sunday and the Belfast and Derry riots
rose the Provisional Irish Republican Army. These men and
women, most of them not yet thirty years old, were determined
that "the croppies of the North" would no longer accept the
status quo. As a result, years of bloodshed, murder and martial
law ensued, culminating in the Good Friday Agreement, a
power-sharing proposal supported by 70 percent of the Irish
population. Among the dissenters were the militant, splinter,
paramilitary groups on both sides.

At the time of this writing, the Peace Accord hangs by the
slimmest of threads. As a result of the IRA's refusal to turn over
their weapons, David Trimble resigned as First Minister. Ireland,
Britain and the United States scrambled for terms. The IRA
relented and agreed to place their weapons beyond use. Loyalist
groups, claiming the terms were too nebulous, have refused to
accept them. Shortly after, the IRA rescinded the agreement to
turn over their weapons, claiming their statement, issued in
good faith, was not met by Loyalist decommissioning nor by
integration of the Royal Ulster Constabulary, the police force of
Northern Ireland, which is 90 percent Protestant—another
sticking point of the agreement.

Meanwhile, red, white and blue paint coats the curbstones of
Loyalist housing tracts, while Nationalists raise the Irish flag

and sport its colors of green, white and orange. July, the marching season, continues to be a time of tension in the North and, despite rabid disapproval on both sides, the bloodshed, although sporadic, continues.

On a more positive note, opportunity for Catholics has increased dramatically in Northern Ireland. Young people are educated together in universities, work together in businesses and, occasionally, live together in the better communities. Violence is frowned upon, as is the discrimination of the past, and the infamous prison, Long Kesh—or the Maze—has become almost obsolete.

The world is aware of the resources to be found in Ireland, not only its enormous economic potential but the charm and resourcefulness of its people. The Irish are like no other population in the world. Cheerful, warmhearted and intelligent, they continue to delight travelers from all over the world with their wry wit, their ability to tell a story and their wonderful toe-tapping, foot-stomping music.

Kate Nolan, her children, her father and Neil Anderson are purely characters of my imagination. Their actions, conversations and opinions are compilations of countless numbers of people I have come to know in the north and west of Ireland. Because all novels have an element of truth, because I am a mother, because marriages do not always run smoothly and because all human experience bears a resemblance to others who share this planet, this novel is based in reality. Although it has political overtones that cannot be ignored in a novel set in the North of Ireland, *Blood Roses* is primarily the story of a family struggling to come to terms with loss and change.

This book would not have its flavor were it not for Father John Forsythe of Belfast, who put aside his extremely busy Easter week schedule to educate me on the current situation in the North. I am also indebted to Paula Murphy, a teacher in Belfast, who offered her opinions over lunch in a charming restaurant outside Derry, and Patti Greiner of the Ohio Ulster Project, who graciously offered names, addresses and phone numbers of contacts in the North.

In addition, I would like to thank Patricia Perry, Jean Stewart and Stephen Farrell for their careful critique of my manuscript, their thoughtful comments and their willingness to drop everything and absorb themselves, once again, in my story.

Jeanette Baker

January 2002

Glossary

Democratic Unionist Party (DUP)	Right wing, Unionist, anti-Catholic party formed in 1971 by Ian Paisley
Irish National Liberation Army (INLA)	Established in 1975 by breakaway elements from the official IRA
Irish Republican Army (IRA)	Name given to original Nationalist physical force group who fought the British for Irish independence
Loyalists	Working-class Unionist Protestants who remain loyal to the union with England
Nationalists	Working-class Catholics who want to see the six counties of Northern Ireland unite with the twenty-six counties in the Republic of Ireland
Orange Order	Powerful Protestant society whose annual marches touch off Protestant-Catholic clashes
Provisional IRA (Provos)	Militant wing of IRA that broke away from IRA in 1969
Royal Ulster Constabulary (RUC)	Armed Northern Ireland police force made up of Protestants
Sinn Fein—"We Ourselves"	Political party and wing of the Provisional IRA, mainly supported by working-class Catholics
Ulster Defence Association	Largest Unionist paramilitary organization in Northern Ireland

Ulster Freedom Fighters	Pseudonym for Ulster Defence Association death squads
Ulster Unionist Party	Official and largest Unionist party in Northern Ireland
Ulster Volunteer Force (UVF)	Paramilitary body established by Loyalists in the Shankill Road area of Belfast
Unionists	Protestants loyal to the union with Britain and opposed to a united, thirty-two-county Ireland
Unionist Party of Northern Ireland	Power-sharing wing of the Unionist Party

Prologue

The prime minister of England frowned at the woman seated before him. He was having second thoughts. Kathleen Nolan looked younger than her forty years, and much too attractive to take on the responsibility of the position he offered. Ireland was not a progressive country. A woman's voice was quickly silenced, drummed out by generations of violence, by men emasculated by unemployment and poverty. Politics, particularly politics in Great Britain, was still very much a man's world.

Still, she was Patrick Nolan's widow. That would give her automatic credibility in the Nationalist community. She also came highly recommended by the first minister, a Protestant Loyalist who never recommended anyone. Quite simply, despite his doubts, there was no one else.

He summoned his most charming grin. "The policing commission is a step in the right direction, Mrs. Nolan. It's the first step in a force for all of Northern Ireland. I can't think of anyone better suited for the position of police ombudsman than yourself."

Kate Nolan wasn't easily intimidated nor was she prone to flattery, thanks to a mother who considered her most important role in life to expunge all signs of vanity in her oldest and loveliest daughter. Kate had learned her lesson well. It would take a great deal more than party manners, an engaging smile and a compliment to win her compliance, even if the compliment did come from the prime minister of England.

She smiled politely. "I appreciate your confidence, sir. I shall consider your offer carefully and report back to you by the end of next week."

He blinked, swallowed a gasp and recovered quickly. "I had hoped to welcome you aboard a bit sooner."

"How soon?"

"Today."

Kate tensed. "That's impossible."

"Are you familiar with the Patten Report, Mrs. Nolan?"

"Not intimately, although I understand the basics."

"Tell me what you understand."

She was silent for at least a minute before speaking. He watched her gather her thoughts and carefully form the words. It was a good sign, a woman who spoke thoughtfully, carefully, a woman not given to impulse.

"Chris Patten and other nonpartisan members took fifteen months to craft a document spelling out how the Royal Ulster Constabulary, the Six Counties illustrious police force, should be restructured."

He noticed she said *the Six Counties* rather than *Northern Ireland*. Her bias was Nationalist, no matter what Trimble said. But perhaps that was to be expected, considering who she was and what her husband had been.

"Do you disagree with the findings of the report?"

"Of course not," she said shortly. "No sane Catholic could possibly disagree considering where we are now."

"But you have reservations."

"Yes." Because she knew he would ask and because it needed to be said, she told him, ticking each one off on her fingers. "There is no prohibition of plastic bullets as there is in the rest of Britain. These are lethal weapons and have been used time and again against innocent Nationalists of Ulster. Secondly, there is no mention of the RUC's human rights violations. In fact, Chief Constable Finnigan is in charge of human rights violations, a conflict of interests if there ever has been. I object to the roles of Chief Constable Finnigan and Secretary of State Peter Mandelson. All accountability still rests with them." Her lip curled. "Your police board has very little power. I'm not convinced I wish to be part of a committee that has no ability to enforce, particularly when it comes to overseeing Robbie Finnigan.

"Besides—" the corners of her mouth twisted bitterly "—everyone knows that in Ireland the most dim-witted man knows more than any woman."

He allowed her the full strength of her emotions, saying nothing. He wished this Catholic-Protestant thing would fall into the ocean. Not that he had anything against Catholics. His own wife was a Catholic, although not the rabid, bitter kind found in the North of Ireland.

"What if I said you had the power to enforce?"

"I would ask you what that means."

"Provision fourteen in the report allows for the board to call upon the chief constable to retire in the interests of efficiency and effectiveness."

"Subject to the approval of the secretary of state."

Her response was quick, loaded, definitely not the response of a woman who knew only the basics. He smiled pleasantly and changed the subject. "Is the investigation of your husband's murder progressing to your satisfaction, Mrs. Nolan?''

Her lips tightened and a thin white line appeared around her mouth.

''Six years have passed,'' she said slowly. ''*Progress* isn't the word I would use.''

He had the grace to look embarrassed. ''I'm truly sorry it hasn't been resolved.''

She relented. He watched her soften with more than a little relief.

''The delay isn't your fault,'' she said. ''I realize you haven't been prime minister for long. I deeply appreciate your interest and efforts, for my sake and for my children. For us, this must end sooner rather than later.''

''It must end with a conviction, Mrs. Nolan. The worst we can do is arrest someone without evidence enough for a guilty verdict. The eyes of the world will be on us through this one.''

''Patrick would have laughed to think he was worthy of so much attention.''

He pressed her. ''Your husband would want you to take this position.''

''Yes,'' she said evenly. ''He would. But there are other considerations now.''

The prime minister stood and held out his hand. Kate took it. ''Please, make your decision quickly,'' he said.

Without using her arms, she rose, gracefully, from the wing chair. ''Have you anyone else in contention?''

Once again, he grinned. He looked absurdly young and carefree for a man who'd inherited a powder keg. ''Not a soul. I'm counting on you.''

''I may fail miserably, you know.''

He laughed, a boyish man with a ready smile, a head full of wavy dark hair, a wife he loved with regularity and three young children. "Have you ever in your life failed at anything, Mrs. Nolan?"

She stared at him astonished. "Of course."

"What was it?"

Kate thought a minute. "I'm sure I have as many failures as the next person. Perhaps I've blotted them from my memory."

"Perhaps." The most powerful man in the kingdom winked at her. "I'm sure it will come to you. When it does, be sure and ring me up. I'll be anxiously waiting."

Kate smiled politely. "Good day."

"Good day, Mrs. Nolan."

Two days later he finished signing his name at the bottom of a page of his official stationery, folded and stuffed it into an envelope, all the while allowing his phone to ring six times. This was new for him. At the beginning of his term he couldn't wait to find out who was on the other line. Confidence came with experience. He picked up the receiver. "Yes."

"Neil Anderson is here to see you, sir."

"Send him in."

The door opened. The prime minister rose, walked around the desk and held out his hand. "Welcome, Neil. Thank you for coming."

Neil Anderson smiled briefly and shook the prime minister's hand. He did not sit down. "I'm not sure you'll thank me after you've read my investigation on Patrick Nolan."

"It doesn't signify. I told Mrs. Nolan our report would be completed." He laughed nervously. "Good Lord, I practically gave her my word. I had no choice in the matter. Whatever you've found, we must give it over.''

Anderson held out a thick manila envelope. ''This is everything. I trust you'll know what to do with this, sir. It's not a pretty picture.''

''You're a good man, Neil. I don't know what we would do without you. I understand you've taken on the Belfast situation.''

''Only the drug trade, not the bloody holy war they've been in the middle of for generations. I'm due for a bit of a break.''

''Shall I offer you tea or perhaps something stronger?''

''Nothing, thank you. I'll leave you to your reading.''

''Very well. I'll ring you back when I've finished.''

Four hours later, the prime minister looked out the bay window of Number 10 Downing Street. His face was pale and his hands shook. The contents of the envelope Neil Anderson had given him lay scattered across the floor where he'd tossed it in a rare fit of temper. ''Damn it,'' he muttered to himself, ''damn it, damn it, damn it.'' There was no way in all the world he could keep his word to Kate Nolan.

Kevin Nolan answered the phone on the second half of the double ring. ''Hello.''

''Kevin?''

''Aye.''

''How much for a B?''

''Who is this?''

''Eddie.''

Kevin thought a minute and then remembered. Eddie was from Ballymurphy. He'd dealt with him once before. ''A bill twenty-five,'' he said.

"All right. I've a friend who wants it."

"It has to be a ball. I won't work with anything below that."

"Is it good?"

"Do you have to ask?"

"Where shall I meet you?"

Kevin hesitated. Belfast was four hours away and he had school. He couldn't be there before the end of the week. "In the house behind the square on Friday," he said. "Don't bring anyone else and don't lag because I can't wait."

"I'll be there."

"Come alone."

"Aye."

Kevin heard a click and then the line went dead. Carefully he replaced the receiver and picked up his textbook. History was a bugger. He hated school, history in particular, and he hated that his mother made him attend a *religious* school. Plenty of lads he knew were at the National School. Why did she insist on all this religion stuff? It wasn't as if she was particularly devout, not like Mrs. McCarthy or Johnny Gallagher's mum. Those women preached every day of the week starting with family meals and ending with nightly prayers. At least Kevin had been spared a mother like that, but barely. Christ. He was sixteen years old. Why did he have to attend a bloody religious school? If it wasn't for that and his mother, life would be bearable, especially now that he knew how to take away the hole in his heart.

One

Blood roses. Patrick's favorite. Kate Nolan pressed the last of the potting soil around the roots, sat back on her heels and read, once again, the inscription she had so painstakingly composed six years before:

Patrick Nolan
1955–1994
Beloved husband and father
He died as he lived, with no regrets

Dropping the trowel into her bag, she wiped her forehead with the back of her hand. Patrick would have liked it. She knew that, just as she knew he'd liked his tea weak, his meat rare, his house uncluttered and his newspaper with his breakfast. Over time she'd learned it all, right down to the way he tensed when she pulled the lobe of his ear through her teeth. It was a signal, theirs alone. It meant she wanted him, sometime soon, very soon, just as much after seventeen years of marriage as in the beginning.

Love, Kate decided, was details, built over a lifetime of private moments. Sometimes, for the fortunate, love lasted forever, beyond skin grown slack, crow's-feet and laugh lines, beyond stretch marks, faltering steps and fear-sharp words born of worry and pain.

Love? Had she known even the smallest measure of what could be between a man and woman when she'd decided in her ignorant youth to choose Patrick Nolan. By the greatest of miracles he'd loved her back. How did a woman explain the ache in her heart that comes from losing the kind of man who comes only once in a lifetime?

Her love was like that, so absolute and uncompromising that for years she lay awake at night trying to remember the exact phrasing of her husband's sentences. Patrick had been so good with words, much better than she ever was. When friends asked her why it was so important to remember, she had no answer for them except *It just is.*

Patrick was a rarity. His dreams were simple, yet profound; to be happily married, to produce healthy children, to earn his own way, to provide for his family, to be blessed with good friends, to see his country at peace. How did one explain Patrick Nolan to those left behind in this land torn by war and religion, polarized by suspicion and politics? Kate could tell them, but no one would believe her.

Slowly, gracefully, she stood and brushed the dirt from her knees. Then she gathered her belongings, stepped around the head stones and made her way to her car.

It was late spring. The days were longer now. Deirdre would be home for spring recess. Kate frowned. Kevin might be home, too. She hadn't seen much of him lately with her late hours and his school and sports schedule. Tonight she would make a point of waiting up to ask him where he had been. Too many boys without fathers lost their way.

* * *

Deirdre's compact wasn't in the driveway. Kate unlocked the door and called out into the silence. No answer. She frowned. The house was quiet, too quiet. Shaking off her looming depression, she walked to the sink, washed her hands and automatically opened the refrigerator door. She would make dinner. Surely by the time it was ready, one of her children would be home.

Kate referred to herself as spaghetti thin. Slender was the term preferred by her friends and the more generous of her acquaintances. Eighteen-year-old Deirdre and sixteen-year-old Kevin shared her body type. Both were born weighing a respectable amount and gained steadily until their first birthdays, at which time they terrified their mother by stubbornly refusing to be fed. Whatever sustenance they ingested was through the laborious, frustrating and often unsuccessful process of curling awkward baby fingers around bite-size morsels of food and negotiating them in the direction of their mouths.

By age four Deirdre tipped the scale at a slight two stone. Her brother, two years younger and six inches taller, was a bit heavier. Miraculously they survived, their wiry, too-thin bodies amazingly resistant to illness or fracture. By the time they reached adolescence, Kate allowed herself to believe in the possibility of their reaching maturity and stopped bribing them to clean their plates.

Oddly, or perhaps in reaction to her children's disinterest in food, Kate kept two refrigerators, a side by side, subzero, sixteen-cubic-foot-size in the kitchen and another, not quite so large or so modern, in the basement near the freezer. Both were filled to capacity with containers of chicken divan, shepherd's pie, lamb stew, homemade trifle, brownies, gingerbread and scones, all precariously perched on top of containers of gravy and jars of homemade preserves, loaves of bread, tins of fruit, gallons of milk, three dozen eggs and several rolls of cookie dough, enough food for a regiment, much too much for three people, none of whom weighed enough to qualify as a blood donor at the Royal Victoria Hospital.

Kate needed to feed people. She didn't understand nor could she explain her compulsion but there it was, an overwhelming desire to sate the appetites of anyone and everyone who came to her door, to share the fruits of her home, her prosperity, her well-stocked larder. Over the course of her life she'd prepared hundreds of dishes: fish fries and pot roasts, roasted chickens and legs of lamb, wrapped casseroles and meat patties, blanched vegetables and fruit, baked cakes, pies and puddings, all the while sealing, labeling and storing her own private version of security through abundance.

Patrick had laughed at her. But the truth of the matter was he could no more pass by a hand outstretched in need without filling it than Kate could refuse a hungry body a hot meal. They were well matched. Bleeding hearts people called them. Philanthropists. A man and woman who, at the end of their lives, would not approach St. Peter and the pearly gates in vain.

Yet, for all Patrick's goodness they had killed him, at home while eating dinner, in front of his wife, his children. Black-masked men carrying guns had burst through the door, dragged him from his chair, pushed him hard against the wall and, without a word, murdered him.

That scene, called up from the dark days of Ulster's violent years, rolled once again through Kate's mind. As always, she focused on the contrasts. The peaceful aura that surrounded their weekend home. The golden afternoon light of Sligo, Yeats country. The gleam of polished wood. Copper pots hanging from the island in the kitchen. Food smells, hearty, rich. Wine, ruby-colored, filling deep, long-stemmed glasses. The comfortable bickering of her children's voices. And then the world exploded.

Heavy boots pounded into the dining room. Cruel eyes, slits behind anonymous masks, stared at them. Kate inhaled the sharp, feral smell of fear, sensed her own rising panic, heard the muffled rat-a-tat of shots through a silencer. *Why a silencer* she'd wondered. *Who was to hear the shots way out in the country?* She saw her husband's blood spurt, watched his body slump to the floor. Deirdre screamed and Kate's terror heightened. *"Please,"* she'd begged, *"don't hurt my children."*

And they hadn't. As suddenly as they'd come, the men were gone, melting into the golden dusk of County Sligo as if they'd never been. Kate had looked at the clock. She'd called her family to dinner at six. It was twelve minutes past the hour. Twelve minutes to snuff out a man's life. Twelve minutes to destroy a family, a man, a woman and their children.

"Katie," a familiar voice called through the front door before stepping inside. "Are you home?"

She shook her head to clear the ugly picture, turned on the flame under the pot of water and waited for her father to find his way. "In the kitchen, Da."

"I was hopin' you'd be up to some company for dinner," he said, filling the doorway with his sturdy frame.

She smiled. "You know you're always welcome."

"Will Deirdre and Kevin be joining us?"

Kate nodded. "I think so."

John O'Donnell sat down at the table, glanced at the newspaper headlines and frowned. "They'll never settle it, not in my lifetime."

Sliding a pat of butter into a frying pan, she rummaged for the kitchen sheers, found them and began to snip slivers of dill into the melted butter. "Don't be such a pessimist."

"A pessimist you say." He turned disapproving blue eyes on his daughter. "And hasn't our country been at war for eight hundred years?"

"Actually it's more like four hundred." She pointed to a spud-filled bowl on the counter. "Can you manage to peel the potatoes or are you here only to discuss politics?"

"Very funny. I can peel and talk at the same time."

Kate kissed her father's balding head. "I was afraid of that."

"Will you take nothing seriously, Katie? The hoodlums are gathering to march as we speak. Every year, nothing changes. I would have thought after Patrick—"

Kate's hands shook. She turned around and leaned against the counter, crossing her arms. She took several deep breaths and uttered a short prayer for patience. "I take a great deal seriously, Da. That's why I sold our country house in Sligo. I believe in what I'm doing. It isn't easy to convince these people to compromise and it doesn't help me to hear that nothing will ever be settled. Besides, it isn't true. We've come a long way in a very short time. It will work. Give it some time and have a bit of faith."

"I don't like you crossing over the border as often as you do," John O'Donnell grumbled, "and I don't trust David Trimble. It's best to say nothing to those people."

"I trust him. He's an educated man and the best possible choice for his party." She ignored the reference to the border. They both knew her job required regular visits to Northern Ireland.

Although the second birthday of the April peace accord had come and gone, Northern Ireland's future was still unstable. Hope, fragile as spun glass, hung in the air, suspended by broken arms agreements, hard-line paramilitaries with nowhere to go and a population suspicious of all but their closest neighbors.

Despite it all, peace was moving forward in the Six Counties. The Sinn Fein delegation had taken their seats on the representative council as had the Social Democrats and David Trimble's Ulster Unionist Party. Government services were slowly becoming integrated with a proportionate number of Catholics and Protestants and the IRA had agreed to release their weapons. Kate wasn't naive enough to believe that every location would be divulged. But she recognized the gesture for what it was, a step in the direction of peace.

It was her lack of naiveté, her ability to settle on a resolution, and her subtle but logical progression toward a goal that had resulted in her appointment to the civilian police council as ombudsman. All government-subsidized institutions had been mandated to integrate work forces with equal numbers of Nationalists and Loyalists. Kate's job was to ensure that they followed the letter of the mandate and to mediate any disagreements arising from it. She had been remarkably successful in every area but law enforcement. The Royal Ulster Constabulary, Northern Ireland's police force, was disappointingly and predictably resistant to all forms of compromise. That she was Patrick Nolan's widow didn't help matters, either.

Kate sighed, slid the salmon into the pan, lowered the flame and began chopping tomatoes. Where were her children?

The familiar slap of the screen door reassured her. Deirdre's voice, cheerful, warm, followed. "Hello. I'm home."

"Hello, love," Kate returned. "Grandda and I are in the kitchen. I hope you're hungry."

"Starved." Deirdre breezed into the room, kissed her grandfather's cheek, smiled at Kate and opened the refrigerator. "Can I help?"

Kate reached out and affectionately tugged her daughter's casual ponytail. "You can set the table. Are you home for the rest of the week?"

Deirdre nodded. My last exam for the term was this morning. How many are eating?"

"Four," her mother replied. "Maybe Kevin will show."

Deirdre's lips tightened. "I doubt it," she mumbled under her breath.

Kate picked up a fork and pierced a potato, testing it for doneness. "What did you say?"

Deirdre flushed, closed the refrigerator without taking out the olives she'd set her mind on, picked up the silverware and turned down the hall toward the dining room. "Nothing. It wasn't important."

Keeping one eye on the clock, Kate managed to hold up her end of the conversation, finish her meal, rinse the dishes and stack them in the dishwasher, walk her father to his car and wave until he disappeared from view, bid her daughter good-night and watch the last of the late night news before she gave in to the panic that was slowly working its way up from her stomach to her chest, closing her throat. The dreaded asthma that debilitated her on rare occasions raised its ugly head. She fumbled for her inhaler always within reach. Where was her son?

It wasn't the first time Kevin had stayed out all night or even the second. Despite her threats, there was little she could do to discipline a sixteen-year-old boy. Kevin towered over her by nearly a foot and outweighed her by three stone. Kate knew he wasn't really a bad boy. The moody, sullen side of him wasn't really Kevin, neither was the simmering rage she'd seen unleashed recently, nor the sense of entitlement that so disturbed her. She brushed aside his defiance as nothing more than normal teenage rebellion. It was her fault really. She'd indulged him because he'd grown up without a father and because the real Kevin, the gregarious, sensitive, sweet son she adored, still showed himself often enough for her to overlook the new, dark side of his nature.

It was nearly three and she had a ten o'clock meeting in Strabane with Robbie Finnigan, chief constable of the RUC. She threw several more pieces of peat into the flame and walked to the window. A car turned down the street. The headlights dimmed. Kate tensed. Relief flared in her chest and then died as she recognized her neighbor's car. Another car passed and then another. Breathing deeply, Kate unclenched her fists. She would make a cup of tea. It would relax her and use up a few minutes.

The familiar ritual, boiling water, scalding the pot, shaking in loose tea leaves, pouring the milk, adding the steeped tea and two well-rounded teaspoons of sugar served its purpose. After methodically sipping two cups and pouring herself a third, she was able to analyze the matter of her son's habits with a relative degree of objectivity. Kevin was spoiled and willful. Her reluctance to discipline him had led to this act of disrespect toward his family.

Rinsing her cup and teapot, she wiped them dry and walked back into the living room, curling up on the couch. Anger pushed against her frantic fear, igniting the faint pressure in Kate's temples into a throbbing pain. Pressing her fingers against the sides of her head, she leaned back into the cushions and closed her eyes.

The piercing double ring of the telephone woke her. Automatically she looked at the clock. Five o'clock. No one called at five in the morning. Her mind was slow and thick with sleep. She picked up the phone. "Hello."

"Mrs. Nolan?"

"Yes."

"This is Neil Anderson from the Ormeau Road Station in Belfast. We have your son, Kevin, in custody."

Adrenaline shot through her veins. "On what charge?"

Deirdre appeared at the top of the stairs.

"In the interests of professional courtesy, Mrs. Nolan, I would rather discuss the matter with you here. Will you come?"

"Of course. I'll leave immediately." She remembered her appointment. "Please tell Constable Finnigan that I'll have to reschedule our appointment."

"I'll do that."

Kate stood up quickly and nearly fell over. Wincing, she bent to rub the feeling back into her right leg. Every movement seemed agonizingly slow. Belfast. What was Kevin doing in Belfast? She needed to see him, to touch him, to assure herself that he was safe.

Deirdre's voice broke through her thoughts. "What happened?"

Kate hesitated, then decided on the truth. Deirdre wasn't a child. "Your brother is being held by the police in Belfast. Have you any idea why?"

The girl was silent for too long.

"Deirdre, if you know anything, please tell me."

"I don't know anything except that Kevin is—" she stopped to search for an appropriate word "—troubled."

"What does that mean?"

"It means you should probably call a lawyer."

Speechless, Kate watched her daughter disappear down the hall into her bedroom. A lawyer. How ironic. Resentment, illogical and pointless, gathered in her chest. When had the Nolans last needed a lawyer? Never in Kate's memory. And now that they did, he was six feet under the ground.

Two

The country roads of Donegal were all single-laned, narrow and rutted, typical of rural Ireland. In the bone-chilling dark, at five-thirty in the morning, traffic consisted of hay wagons and tractors, slow moving and difficult for Kate to overtake because of poor visibility on her right side.

Her headache, her fear for Kevin, the snail's pace at which she was forced to travel and the terrifying sensation of sinking deeper and deeper into a bog from which there was no escape kept her grip on the wheel clawlike, white-knuckled, desperate.

The roads were better in the Six Counties but Kate kept to the Republic for as long as she could, crossing the winding roads of the Blue Stack Mountains hazy with mist and fairy light, marking off the miles through small towns, Ballybofey, Killygordon, Castlefin, until she reached Strabane, the border and checkpoint that, under the terms of the Peace Accord, was scheduled for demolition at the end of the month.

Kate had never known a united Ireland but the sight of British uniforms and guard towers surrounded by barbed wire never failed to raise the bile in her throat. It wasn't her battle, she reminded herself. The boy in uniform was Deirdre's age, another mother's son a long way from home.

Wordlessly she handed him her papers and waited for the inevitable wave through. Was it taking longer this time or was her imagination playing tricks with her mind? She was about to ask if there was a problem when he motioned her past. Out of sight of the checkpoint, she pulled over to the side of the road and fumbled in her purse for her inhaler. Steadying her shaking hands she covered the mouthpiece, sealing her lips around the plastic and breathed in, once, twice. Leaning back against the headrest, she waited for the tightness in her chest to ease. Two hours had passed since she'd left Ardara. Another two would take her into Belfast. What was Kevin doing now?

Minutes later her lungs had cleared. Kate followed the signs to the B47. She would enter Belfast from the north, through Antrim, catching the M2 toward the City Centre, merging onto the West link to the Falls and the Ormeau Road.

At nine o'clock she maneuvered her Volvo into the left lane and rounded the corner. The lights of the RUC station loomed before her. Kevin was in there. Her son. Her sixteen-year-old son.

Kate pulled into the car park, turned off the engine and swallowed hard. She'd walked into the RUC barracks of Belfast countless times, alone and with Patrick. She'd seen other women's sons handcuffed, brutalized, locked away in cells behind bars. She'd offered solutions, sympathy, Patrick's legal services, and occasionally, as a last resort, tea and biscuits. But never once, until tonight, had she truly understood.

The red-cheeked boy at the front desk couldn't have been much older than Kevin. He straightened when he saw her. "Good morning, Mrs. Nolan."

"Good morning," she managed politely. She felt

vulnerable, exposed, as if she had intruded into enemy territory, an ordinary Catholic without the trappings of her job or Patrick's position walking into an RUC station. "I've come for Kevin Nolan, my son."

"I'll tell the constable you've arrived."

Kate slid down onto the wooden bench and stared at the clock. The hands and numbers blurred. How long since she'd last slept? Twenty-three hours? Twenty-four? What could Kevin have done? Should she have listened to Deirdre and called a lawyer? Surely not. Kevin was only sixteen years old.

Neil Anderson, chief criminologist for British Special Services recently down from London, prided himself on the accuracy of his first impressions. He looked through the glass window of his office intending to briefly glance at Kate Nolan and found that he couldn't look away. She wasn't what he expected.

Black hair, fair skin, clear light eyes, small delicate bones. Very Irish. A cross between classic and elegant. Lovely was the first thought that leaped to his mind. Young was the second. Too young for the responsibility Northern Ireland's new government had thrust upon her, too young to be Kevin's mother, much too young to be Patrick Nolan's widow.

What he knew about her, he'd gleaned from the files: Catholic, social worker by profession, university graduate, middle class background, no affiliation with the Nationalist cause before her marriage, personal invitation from the prime minister to serve on the civilian police council.

He felt a twinge of sympathy. A woman like this, a woman who'd driven across Ireland at a moment's notice because her son needed her, didn't deserve the news he was about to give her.

After a few brief words with the officer at the desk, Neil removed his jacket and tie and rolled up the sleeves of his shirt. Informal seemed better, less threatening. Kate Nolan would prefer informal. He crossed the room to the receiving area and addressed her. "Mrs. Nolan?"

She looked up. Her eyes were blue flecked with green, ocean-colored.

"Yes."

He held out his hand. "I'm Neil Anderson."

Unsmiling, she took it. "I'd like to see my son."

Direct, uncompromising, a woman with priorities. He liked that. Once again, he regretted his role. "In a minute. First I'd like to discuss a few things with you."

"What things?"

He motioned toward the glass-lined wall. "In my office, please."

"I'll follow you." She stood, poised, in control. Perhaps he'd underestimated her.

Neil led the way into a neat, well-organized office and motioned her into a seat across from his desk. His orders were completely clear but they didn't set well with him. "Would you care for some tea, Mrs. Nolan?"

She brushed away his suggestion with an impatient hand. "Please, come to the point, Mr. Anderson."

"Very well." He looked at her and knew that he would tell this woman nothing short of the truth. Neil spoke deliberately. "Your son has been charged with the selling of an illegal substance."

"What kind of illegal substance?"

She wasn't as innocent as she looked.

"Cocaine."

Kate paled and gripped the edge of his desk. Images, raw and painful, flashed through her brain. Kevin bathing in the sink, chubby and naked, chewing on a washcloth, Kevin blowing out candles on his birthday cake, Kevin accepting a citizenship award at school, riding his bike, playing with the hose, digging in mud. Kevin couldn't go to jail. "That's impossible," she said flatly. "Children don't sell cocaine. Drug dealers do that."

"Your son was caught with an amount too large for personal consumption."

"He's sixteen years old," she whispered.

"The prosecutor will be Richard Dunne," Neil continued. "He will ask that no bail be set and that Kevin remain in prison until his trial date. Should your son be convicted of such a charge, it will cost him several years in prison. Kevin is sixteen. At his age, it's customary for such a crime to be tried in an adult court."

She wet her lips. "Do you know who he is?"

Neil's brow wrinkled. "I beg your pardon?"

"Kevin is Patrick Nolan's son. He can't go to jail. He won't survive."

This was the part of the job he hated, playing the game, pretending ignorance in order to manipulate her into agreeing to what he had in mind all along. "You're exaggerating."

She shook her head. "No."

"I don't understand."

"Surely you know of my husband's reputation."

Neil knew more than he'd ever wanted to know about Patrick Nolan. "That was a long time ago."

"Not long enough for Kevin. Patrick put quite a few people behind bars, Mr. Anderson, mostly Protestant paramilitaries from illegal organizations. They would like nothing better than to get their hands on his son."

He frowned. "Kevin has committed a crime, Mrs. Nolan, a serious crime. Are you suggesting that I look the other way simply because of his father?"

"There must be some other way besides prison."

Neil drummed his fingers on the table. Tension was thick in the small room. Suddenly he stood. "I'm going to bring Kevin in. I think we should hear what he has to say."

Kate was confused. Something didn't make sense. "I was under the impression that you'd already spoken to him."

"I have. I'd like you to hear him as well."

"Where is he?"

"In a holding room."

She nodded and watched Neil Anderson leave the room, walk down the hallway and disappear around a corner. The wait was no more than five minutes but it seemed much longer.

Suddenly Kevin was there, in the room, and she was standing with her arms tight around him. "Oh, Lord, Kevin," she murmured, "what have you done?"

He pulled away, a wounded look on his face. "Nothing. I've done nothing. I've no idea how it got into my jacket. It was just there and they arrested me and brought me here. Everyone else left." He was babbling, the words coming too quickly for coherence.

Keeping a tight grip on his arms, Kate held him away from her and looked, really looked at her son. Kevin wasn't lying. He couldn't be. She knew, just as she knew the color of his eyes and the wave in his hair. Keeping her eyes on her boy, she spoke quietly. "You've made a mistake, Mr. Anderson."

Neil sighed. If he had a pound for all the mothers in

denial, he would be a rich man. "Kevin's drug test was positive, Mrs. Nolan." He hesitated. "I'm sorry."

Kevin's face was flushed. Kate lifted his chin, forcing him to look into her eyes. "Have you anything to say, love?"

"I wasn't *selling* it, Mum," he mumbled.

"Were you using it?"

He nodded briefly and hung his head.

Kate kept one arm around her son and turned to face Neil. "Possession for personal use isn't the same as selling."

"Our informant claims that Kevin was there for the purpose of distributing."

"He's lying," Kevin shot back. "How does he know what I was there for?"

"Our informant is a she."

Kevin flushed and turned away. "What does she know?"

The man's steady gaze never left Kevin's face.

Defeated, the boy collapsed into a chair beside his mother. "It doesn't matter anyway. I've already agreed."

Kate frowned. "Agreed to what?"

Kevin pointed to Neil. "He'll tell you."

"In exchange for dropping the charges, Kevin has agreed to help us," Neil explained.

Her face closed. "How?"

"We need an informant, a trusted one."

Kate's eyes narrowed and it seemed, to Neil, as if all the blue in her irises had concentrated into a thin, brilliant line.

"Don't be absurd," she said. "Kevin is still a child. I don't want him to have anything to do with this. Besides, why should you trust him? You don't even know him.''

"The situation is very serious, Mrs. Nolan. I wouldn't suggest this if there were an alternative.''

"What are you saying?''

His jaw hardened. He leaned forward. His eyes were gunmetal gray, hard, piercing. English eyes. His voice was grim, determined. "This country's peace accord is hanging by the slimmest of threads. There are those who would see it completely destroyed. Black market trade has come out of nowhere, along with an infiltration of illegal drugs into the working class communities of the Shankill, Ardoyne, Andersonstown and the Falls. I believe the same people who brought bombs and terrorism into Northern Ireland are responsible for the drug trade. They have the support of their communities.''

"If you're referring to the IRA, they've complied with all articles of the agreement.''

"The Irish National Liberation Army has not.''

"They're a terrorist group," Kate protested. "They have no political representation and they have nothing to do with the majority of the Catholic community.''

"I believe they operate with their full approval.''

"That isn't true," she whispered.

"I've been through Andersonstown and the Falls, Mrs. Nolan. How many Catholics there agree with disarmament?''

The argument was an old one, stinging her into a defense she did not entirely approve of. "They're waiting, Mr. Anderson, to see if this brave new government has a place for them, equal to the place it has for its Protestant citizens. They're waiting for the RUC to conform to the terms of the Patten Report.''

His fingers formed a pyramid on the desk. "We are at an impasse because neither side will agree to go first."

"Why must it always be those of us who are Catholic, the ones with the greatest amount to lose?"

"Because your stake in the outcome is higher."

Unconsciously she rubbed her fingers across Kevin's hand. "What do you want from Kevin?"

"Locations, names of dissenters, drug dealers, details of conversations." He ticked them off on his fingers. "Even a report on the general mood of the organization would be helpful."

Her hands shook and her cheeks were very white. "You're asking my sixteen-year-old son to risk his life. Have you any idea how dangerous it would be?"

"Not as dangerous as it would be for anyone else."

Her heart dropped. It would be too much to hope that this Englishman hadn't done his research.

"Kevin has two uncles who have connections," he continued. "I doubt if they would allow him to come to any harm."

"Blood won't mean a thing if they find out what he's doing," she argued. "Informants aren't tolerated."

"It isn't pleasant for prisoners in Long Kesh."

She stood. "I'm sorry, Mr. Anderson. I won't allow this."

Kevin looked up in alarm. "I could do it, Mum. I don't want to go to prison."

"You won't go to prison," she promised. "This is your first offense. No one goes to jail for a first drug offense. I'll find a lawyer. You'll be home by morning. Don't worry." She smiled bracingly. "If I might speak with you alone, Mr. Anderson?"

Their eyes met and held. He saw air-light bones,

straight, smoky hair and sharply honed Celtic features. For a moment his resolve wavered. He forced himself to remember who she was, who her husband was.

He stood, walked to the door and opened it. "Mr. Laverty," he called out to the man behind the desk. "Please take our prisoner back to his holding room."

Kevin blanched and turned frightened eyes to his mother. "Mum?"

"Is that necessary?" Kate asked.

Neil's reply was clipped, impatient. "You tell me."

Kate's voice changed and the temperature in the room seemed to drop. "It won't be for long, Kevin," she said through thin lips. "Whatever happens, I'll see you again tonight."

She waited until her son left the room. Furious, she turned toward the enemy. "You can't intimidate me, Mr. Anderson. I'm no poor, uneducated croppy. We both know you've nothing on Kevin. It's his word against your informant's who, I'm fairly sure, isn't a police officer. Am I right?"

"Almost."

"Almost?"

"This is Northern Ireland. Do you really want to take a chance on Kevin's freedom?"

"This is a *new* Northern Ireland," she shot back. "Illegal arrests and confessions obtained under torture no longer exist."

"People are still dying, Mrs. Nolan. This is marching season. Belfast is a powder keg. I need someone."

"You're not getting Kevin."

"I have no one else."

Her reserve broke. "That's what you all say," she said bitterly. "You Protestants think nothing of risking one more Catholic life. You know nothing about us or what we've had to endure.''

He straightened and she noticed that his hands were balled in his pockets. ''You're mistaken. I'm not a Protestant. I'm an Englishman down from London and I don't give a bloody damn about your absurd religious vendetta. I do care that people are dying on my watch and I'll do whatever I can and use whomever I can to stop it and that includes your son.''

Kate slung her purse over her shoulder. ''I don't think so. I'll say good day for now but tomorrow I'll be back, with a lawyer.''

He held the door shut with his hand. ''That won't be necessary. Credit me with enough experience to know that the charges against Kevin wouldn't hold up, however, I believe you're forgetting something.''

She waited.

''Kevin wasn't set up, Mrs. Nolan. The charges are real. Your son has a drug problem. This time we've no proof. The next time we will and I won't be so easy on him.''

''There won't be a next time.''

He sighed. ''Believe it or not, I hope you're right.''

''May I take my son home now?''

He opened the door and walked beside her to the front desk. ''Release Kevin Nolan, Mr. Laverty,'' he said quietly. ''The charge against him has been dropped.''

Three

Kevin leaned his forehead against the cool glass of the window and closed his eyes. God, he was tired. The cocaine rush had left his body, leaving him drained and heavy. His mouth was dry and his tongue felt so thick it nearly gagged him. He was thirsty but forming the words to ask his mother to pass one of the water bottles she always kept in the back seat was too much effort.

"Kevin." Kate's voice pierced the fog shrouding his brain. "Tell me what happened."

Nausea swept through him, waves of it pressing against his throat, rising from his stomach. Weakly he shook his head.

Relentlessly she persisted. "How long have you been doing this?"

"What?" he mumbled, keeping his eyes closed.

He heard her speak again but the words were jumbled. He couldn't make them out. If only he could lie down. He would feel better after he slept. He would think of answers, well-crafted, dishonest answers that would satisfy her, answers that would stop her questions and wipe the pale, haunted look from her face. He hated her when she looked like that. No. Hate was too strong a word. Kevin didn't hate his mother. It wasn't possible to hate Kathleen Nolan. What he hated were her probing questions. He hated the worried frown between her eyes and the pain in her voice whenever she spoke to him. He hated the way she chewed her lips raw and the hesitant way she asked him to take out the garbage. He hated the beautiful, nourishing, abundant meals she insisted on cooking even when he wasn't hungry. He hated that she never swore or cried or lost her temper.

He hated other things, too, more and more with every passing week, things that had nothing to do with his mother. He hated the quiet of the house in Donegal, the boring drone of his instructors at school, the tight, disapproving look on his sister's face when he walked through the door long past dinner hour and, most of all, he hated the empty, too-large rooms that screamed out for the laughing, playful, complete family that had once been his.

Kevin missed his father. Six years had passed but his memories were as vital and whole and detailed as if they had taken place the day before. Patrick Nolan was the kind of man lesser mortals created legends around. Strong and competent, brilliant and charismatic, he was fair to adults and children alike. The very thought of him and what he'd lost closed the air passages in Kevin's throat and brought on the despised asthma inherited from his mother.

"Kevin," his mother's voice intruded again. "I need an answer from you. The charge was a serious one."

He stared out the window.

"For God's sake, Kevin." Her voice broke. "This isn't a game. Please, talk to me."

He couldn't look at her, couldn't manage the hurt in her eyes.

"I'm all right, Mum," he mumbled. "You don't have to worry about me."

"What were you doing miles away from home, with those people?"

He kept his eyes fixed on the bogs framed by the car window. Hacked open like a newly exposed wound, half the marsh lay dark, rich and wet. The paler half was home to stacks of dun-colored turf drying in the open air. *Ireland's energy source,* his father had told him.

"Kevin?"

He remembered his mother's question. "They're not so bad." Out of the corner of his eye Kevin saw her hands clench around the steering wheel, her bones white beneath her skin. "I'm tired," he said, hoping to ward off further questions. "They didn't let me sleep all night."

"I'm tired too, Kevin," she said, showing an unexpected flash of impatience, "and I never want this to happen again. I drove four hours through the dead of night to pick you up. You owe me some answers."

"I said I was all right," he said sullenly. "I've done nothing wrong."

"You tested positive for an illegal drug. For—" she stumbled over the word "—for cocaine, for God's sake. How can you tell me that isn't wrong?"

He clenched his fists, but he didn't answer. There was no answer to such a question. By whose standards was it wrong? Was anyone worse off because he'd snorted a line? Or was it two? He couldn't remember.

She wasn't leaving it alone. "Who were the people you were with?"

He felt the blood rise in his throat. *Leave me alone. Please, just leave me alone.* "I don't know."

"Do you really expect me to believe that?"

His fists slammed down on the dashboard. "I don't

fuckin' care what you believe,'' he shouted. "Leave me alone.''

Kate slammed on the brakes. Kevin felt the back end of the car fishtail across the road. It leveled out again and rolled to a jarring stop. Two red spots of color stained his mother's cheeks. He watched as she carefully, without speaking, set the emergency brake, pulled out the keys, opened the door and began to walk back down the road.

A bevy of emotions rolled through Kevin's chest, anger, fear, shock, horror. In his mind the breach he'd just committed was nearly as great as the one that had landed him in a jail cell. Never had he used bold language with an adult. That it was his mother upon whom he'd inflicted such a perversion was more than he could bear. She had probably never heard such a word in her entire life. He was a misfit, in far too deeply to reverse himself. What was to become of him? If only he could turn back time. If only he could have stepped in front of the bullet that had taken his father's life. Patrick would be alive and his mother would be happy. Moaning, Kevin dropped his head into his hands and wept.

Kate looked at her watch. Ten minutes. Ten minutes had passed since she'd left the car and still the rage consumed her. *I will not retaliate,* she promised herself. *I will not scream nor swear nor verbally shred this child I've created.*

Her own mother had given her a deep-rooted terror of irrational anger. Eileen Connelly had none of Kate's scruples regarding corporal punishment. Without exception, she'd raised her seven children as she'd been raised, with an acerbic tongue and the back of a hairbrush. Kate, the oldest, had felt the sting of that brush more often than the others, more likely because of her birth order than her level of defiance. Even Eileen, short-tempered and filled with displaced anger over the disappointing sameness of her life, had balked at raising welts on the legs of a child younger than five. Kate's recollection of her home life was of an unhappy woman who had screamed and slapped her way through the lives of her children.

Eileen wasn't unusual. Only a handful of mothers in the Ireland of previous generations concerned themselves with what Kate considered rampant child abuse. The blatant use of the rod on her generation of children resulted in Kate's rabid desire to do differently. She would, she resolved, apologize to her children. She wouldn't raise her voice, refuse to listen or randomly dole out punishment that bore no logical relationship to the crime. She would, however, say *no* when necessary. She would establish boundaries and she would let her children suffer the consequences of inappropriate behavior. But how far and in what direction was a mother to allow those consequences to lead? Kevin was a child. Could any sensible mother allow her child's life to be endangered?

Keeping to the side of the road, she walked rapidly, her back stiff, her eyes straight ahead, missing the igloos of golden wheat, the stacks of drying turf, the boiling clouds, shaping and reshaping themselves, the pale yellow of a reluctant sun.

Damn, damn, damn. Who did he bloody well think he was? Had there ever been a child so indulged, so spoiled by parents and grandparents? How dare he speak to her so?

Five more minutes passed. Clouds lined with light broke away and floated across a sky that would soon be blue. Kate's stride slowed, faltered. She felt better.

Exercise always helped. Her rage began to dissipate. She was in control once again. Control was essential. Control was the way she lived her life. Control was power. She breathed, felt the sting of cold air deep in her parched lungs, coughed, and turned around. She'd forgotten her inhaler. Praying that she would make it back to the car before she fell into the throes of a full-scale asthma attack, she measured her pace. How could she have been so stupid?

Don't panic, mustn't panic. Forcing herself to remain calm, Kate concentrated on the road, on the air flowing into and out of her lungs, on the rise in the road, on the herbal smell of wet turf. Gradually her tension eased, her air passages cleared and her mind found a focus outside of the physical.

Kate thought back to the day she decided to have a second baby. She'd debated for a long time before coming to the decision. Children were a serious matter and she was naturally cautious, an observer rather than a participant. She took her lessons seriously, relegating firsthand experience to intrepid risk-takers like Patrick. Not for her the casual, take-it-for-granted notion that a married couple should automatically procreate. Children were investments in emotion that one couldn't begin to imagine before becoming a parent.

Until Deirdre was born, the words pain and pleasure conjured up dreamlike, surreal, polite images. From the day she'd given birth, terror, joy and heartbreak had been her constant companions. The color and heat of her love for her children consumed her, thrusting her forward, forcing her to grab on to life, to wade through the pain, to soar with pride, to be stronger, wiser, deeper than she really was.

Would she do it all again, knowing what she knew?

Guiltily she pushed aside the thought. Hindsight was absurd. She would never deny her children. They enriched her, lifted her to heights she would never have reached. Where would she have been without them, after Patrick? Who would have kept her sane and given her life back to her? Kevin needed her. To be needed was balm to her spirit.

Even with the promise of sun, the morning was cold. Shivering, she shoved her hands into her pockets and increased her pace. She wasn't a trailblazer, not now, not ever. That had been Patrick's role. How often had she harangued him, begging him to step back, to allow someone else to lead, to be the martyr, the hero? He'd laughed at her. *Where would Ireland be?* he'd admonished her, *without the likes of Eamon de Valera or Michael Collins? What if they'd stepped back?*

Kate never answered, but she'd wondered about Michael Collins's fiancée, Kitty, the one who had never become his wife. What were her sentiments when they told her an assassin's bullet had found its way to the heart of her beloved? Was she grateful he'd died a hero's death or would she rather he'd been an ordinary man who came home at night and contented himself with telling his children stories beside a warm peat fire?

Her steps were slower now, her anger completely gone. It was safe to go back, to sit beside her son on the long drive home, to try to reach him somehow, this child she loved unconditionally and yet had lost somewhere along the way. If only she could pinpoint the exact moment he'd looked around for direction and in the looking found her wanting.

The wind came from the west, a cold stinging wind that reddened her cheeks and brought tears to her eyes. Her shortness of breath had completely disappeared.

She began to run. She hadn't the shoes for it, but she ran anyway, the balls of her feet finding the grade of the road as they always did. She found her stride and her hands left her pockets, her arms swinging smoothly, alternating with the bend of her knees and the steady pound of her feet on the pavement.

Running was her drug. She'd taken it up after Patrick's death, her anger and pain diminishing in direct proportion to the miles she ran every day in the soft beauty of an Irish dawn. She'd kept at it over the years, challenging herself, five miles, seven, ten, until the euphoria peaked and her body toughened and she was able to manage one day and then the next and the one after that. Years passed, holidays, holy days, birthdays, she and Deirdre and Kevin, the three of them in a world without Patrick. It was bearable now, not easy, never easy. The sharpness had muted, the awful throat-closing tears that rose unexpectedly at the sound of his name or the accidental uncovering of a family photo were gone now, leaving instead a dullness, a hollow ache that nothing was quite able to fill.

She made it back to the car in half the time. Kevin's eyes were closed, his head thrown back against the headrest, his mouth slightly open. Kate opened the door carefully so as not to wake him and slid into the driver's seat. Then she looked, really looked at her son and her heart broke. All that was left of her chubby-cheeked baby was gone. In his place was a beautiful, too-thin, sharp-cheeked, square-jawed boy, a boy who would soon be a man. Where had the years gone and how had she managed to do such a dreadful job of raising Patrick's son?

She felt a burst of irrational anger. This would never have happened if Patrick had lived. And Patrick would still be alive if only he'd been more careful, if he'd cared for his family as much as he cared for his country. Instantly she was ashamed of herself. Patrick Nolan hadn't a selfish bone in his body. He was a barrister, not a henchman privy to the secret plans of the opposition. How could he have known terrorists would seek him out in his own home and murder him in front of his wife and children?

Kate turned the key and maneuvered the car out on to the road toward Donegal, Ireland's most beautiful county. Kevin slept on. She slowed the car at the Strabane checkpoint. The guard looked in the window, saw her sleeping child and waved her on. Grateful for the reprieve, she negotiated the roundabout and turned northwest toward Ardara.

Her spirits lifted. To the right pink-tinged clouds settled on the peaks of the Twelve Bens. To her left the River Eske, silver under the gray sky, wound its way to the sea. On both sides of the road green hills dotted with longhaired sheep dipped and rose against the horizon. She was nearly home. She would put her son to bed, turn off the ringer on the phone and catch a few hours of much needed rest for herself. Patrick's Ireland could wait. It would still be here tomorrow. Today she would take care of her son.

Four

Deirdre pushed the rack of dishes inside the dishwasher, added detergent and closed the door. She looked at the clock. It was past noon and her mother still wasn't home, nor had she called.

Biting her lip, Deirdre reached for the telephone, hesitated, changed her mind and pulled her coat out of the hall closet. She would walk down the street to her grandfather's house. He would know what to do.

The wind stung her eyelids and the sensitive skin inside her nose. Bending her head, she crossed High Street and waved to a stout woman sweeping the street in front of the tearoom.

"Good afternoon, Mrs. O'Hara."

"Good afternoon, Deirdre, love," the woman replied cheerfully. "I thought you'd be gone by now. When is it that you'll be returnin' to school?"

Deirdre stopped. "Not for a bit. I'm still on holiday."

"Lucky girl." Una O'Hara smiled. "An education's a grand thing, lass. Don't be forgettin' that."

"I won't."

"You always were a clever lass. Your mam was, too, if I recall." She leaned on her broom. "Learnin' comes more easily to some."

Deirdre nodded politely, shifting from one foot to the

other. Mrs. O'Hara would talk all day if she wasn't diverted.

"Have you seen my grandfather?" Deirdre asked. "I really want to talk to him."

"You'll find him at the bookmakers." The woman pointed to a small shop down the street.

"Thank you," said Deirdre. "Goodbye, Mrs. O'Hara."

"I've never seen such a man for the horses," Mrs. O'Hara called after her.

Deirdre waved and hurried down the street.

She found her grandfather in a friendly argument with the bookmaker. "Seamus, lad, you've got rocks in your head," complained John O'Donnell. "That horse will never make a winner. Better to place your money elsewhere."

The bookmaker shook his head. "Since when have you had a winnin' purse, John O'Donnell?"

"I've had a streak of bad luck lately," John agreed, "but that doesn't mean I don't know horses. I'm tellin' you that the colt is too short in the withers and too thin in the rump. He'll never make it past the first pole."

"Grandda." Deirdre tugged at her grandfather's sleeve. "I need to talk to you."

John's eyebrows rose. "What are you doing here in town at this time of day, Deirdre, love?"

"I need to talk to you," she repeated.

"And so we shall," he promised, "as soon as I settle with Seamus, here."

"I need to talk now."

Surprised, John stared at his granddaughter. "What's gotten into you, Deirdre? It isn't like you to be so cheeky."

Her sleepless night and worry for her brother had

taken its toll. She was close to tears. "Please, Grandda."

"I'm not goin' anywhere, John," the bookmaker said. "See to the lass and we'll take this up later."

Concerned at last, John nodded, tucked Deirdre's hand inside his arm and led her out the door. "Shall we go home, love, or back to my house?"

"Home," Deirdre said immediately. "Maybe Mum and Kevin will be back by now and they'll worry about me."

"Isn't your mother workin' today?"

Deirdre shook her head. "Kevin's in trouble. The police called last night and Mum drove to Belfast."

John groaned. His grip on Deirdre's hand tightened. "What's he done?"

"I'm not sure," Deirdre hedged.

"Come now, lass, out with it. There isn't much I haven't seen."

Deirdre wasn't sure, but she had no choice. "He's lost, Grandda," she confessed. "Kevin doesn't care about anything. He skips school and takes drugs. I think—" she bit her lip "—he might even be earning money by selling them. He's never with any of his old friends. The phone rings all the time and he gets mad if I answer. The voices scare me. They're old voices, too old for Kevin. Sometimes he doesn't come home at night." Her voice dropped to a whisper. "He's so skinny and mean. I don't even know him anymore."

"Does your mam know any of this?"

Deirdre shrugged. "Mum isn't stupid. If I can see it when I'm home on holiday, she must know. She lives with Kevin every day."

John's face was grim. "Sometimes people only see what they want to see. Kate refuses to see wrong in those she loves. It's her most endearing and, at the same time, most infuriating quality.''

"She's not home yet and she left at five this morning." Deirdre's voice cracked. "I'm worried. They won't arrest her, will they?"

"No, love," John O'Donnell assured her. "Your mother's done nothing."

Tears welled up in her eyes. "Neither did Da and they killed him."

John swore under his breath. He took a minute to control himself. "Times have changed, Dee," he said. "Think of it. It's only one o'clock now. The drive to Belfast takes four hours on a good day. Your mother isn't in any danger. If every woman with a delinquent son was arrested, the streets of Belfast would be empty. Lads sow their wild oats. Kevin will come around. A few years from now you'll laugh about this together. You'll see."

Deirdre was doubtful. They'd rounded the curve of the rise that led to her house. She couldn't see the driveway. Her heart pounded. Please let her mother's car be there.

It was. She broke free of her grandfather's hand and ran up the steps to open the door. "Mum," she called out, "where are you?"

John followed more slowly. He stepped into the living room in time to see Kate walk out of the kitchen, holding her finger against her lips. She took one look at her daughter's face and folded the girl into her arms.

"Everything's all right, love," she said, stroking the smooth dark head buried in her shoulder. "Kevin's sleeping and I've decided to take the day off." Over the girl's head, her eyes met her father's. "I'm making lunch. I hope you're hungry."

John shook his head. He knew that look. Kate's relationship with food was a puzzle he'd never pieced together. He would get nothing out of her, not until she'd fed them all to satiation.

Over outrageous helpings of shepherd's pie and green salad, John quizzed his daughter. Her answers were hesitant and too brief for satisfaction, as if she were reluctant to reveal a confidence.

"For Christ sake, Kathleen," her father exploded in frustration. "Kevin's dearer to me than my own sons. Deirdre and I want nothing but the best for him. How can we help if we don't know the truth?"

"I don't know the truth, Da," she replied in her patient, low-pitched voice. "All I know is what Mr. Anderson told me. Kevin has a different story. I'm not blind nor am I naive. It's possible that Kevin is involved in something very serious."

"Why did they let him go?" Deirdre asked.

Kate shrugged. "Most likely the witness wasn't reliable and they had no other evidence. Kevin hasn't been in trouble before." She fell silent, her brow furrowed.

"What is it?" her father asked.

"Mr. Anderson is a professional from London."

"So?"

"He said—" She stopped.

"Aye?"

"It's ridiculous, of course."

"What is?"

"He thinks Kevin is heavily involved with drugs."

Deirdre slumped in her chair. Suddenly her food tasted like sawdust. Someone had finally put the horrifying fear she'd carried around for months into words. But would her mother believe her?

"What do you think?" John demanded.

"I'm not sure." Kate stirred the meat and potatoes with her fork. "I hardly see Kevin anymore. I have no influence over him. He comes and goes as he pleases. His friends are different. His marks in school are lower, but not seriously so." She blinked back tears. "Somewhere, I lost him."

"He's angry all the time," Deirdre volunteered.

Her mother nodded. "I know, love." She lifted her head and looked directly at her father. "But that doesn't mean he's criminally involved enough to profit from selling narcotics. If he needs help, he'll have it."

John searched his daughter's face. She was very like her mother in coloring and feature, but not at all in demeanor or temperament. He saw something behind the clear, lovely eyes that he hadn't seen in quite a while, since the first years after Patrick's death, a haunted empty look that twisted his heart. "Is there something else, Katie, something you haven't told us?"

Kate chewed her lip, a nervous habit she'd passed on to her daughter. "Mr. Anderson tried to use Kevin as an informant."

"What is he looking for?"

"It seems there's been unusual drug trafficking in Belfast. He thinks the IRA is involved."

John's lips tightened. "Even if it is, how is Belfast different from any other city? Dublin has its drugs. So does London. And if the IRA is involved, Kevin wouldn't fool them. They'd see right through him. It would be a death sentence."

"I don't think Mr. Anderson is overly concerned with the survival of one Catholic boy from the North."

"What is he concerned about?"

"Maintaining order, preventing unnecessary deaths, doing his job."

If she were anyone but Kate, he would have read sarcasm in her words. "There's nothing wrong with that, lass."

"Of course there isn't. He'll just have to do it without Kevin."

Deirdre cleared her throat. "What will you do with Kevin?"

Kate opened her mouth and closed it again without speaking. "I don't know."

"He'll be awake soon," Deirdre persisted. "Are we going to go on as if nothing happened?"

"I haven't really thought it through," said Kate. "He's not the easiest person for me to talk to."

"Let me talk to him," offered John.

"Thanks, Da. But he's my son. I'll handle this."

Deirdre interrupted them. "Kevin's gone beyond talking, Mum. If Mr. Anderson is right and Kevin is involved with drugs, it's going to take more than talk. You may have to insist on some kind of rehabilitation or counseling program. Kevin won't like that. How will you make him go if he doesn't want to?"

"I'm not going anywhere."

Collectively John, Kate and Deirdre, froze.

Kevin, thin as a deer rifle, stood at the entrance to the kitchen. His eyes were bright with anger and two spots of red colored his gaunt cheeks.

His mother was the first to recover. She wet her lips. "Sit down, Kevin. I'll fill a plate for you while we talk."

"There's nothing I want to say."

Kate's temper, slow to rise, flared. "Then you'll listen because *I* have a great deal to say."

Kevin crossed his arms against his chest and didn't move. "I suppose you've told Grandda and Deirdre everything."

"I don't know everything. This is a perfect opportunity for you to tell us your story."

The boy's lips remained mutinously sealed.

Deirdre spoke. "For pity's sake, Kevin, be reasonable. We're your family. We only want to help you. Do you think this is over? What happens the next time you're arrested? Mum can't help you forever."

"There won't be a next time."

"How can you be sure of that?" his mother asked.

"I won't go there again. Those chaps are nothing to me."

"Why were you there last night?"

Kevin's sigh was a mixture of anger and impatience. "There was a party, that's all. Leave it alone, will you, Mum?"

Kate stood and walked to the counter. Her hands shook. She willed herself to relax and began dishing man-size portions of meat pie and salad onto a plate. "Sit down, Kevin," she said again. "You must be starving."

"I'm not hungry at all."

John spoke for the first time. "It's time for me to be leavin'. Walk with me a bit, Kevin. I can use the company."

"He hasn't eaten, Da," Kate protested.

"One missed meal won't kill him. Besides, he said he wasn't hungry."

Kate gave up. "I'll keep the food warm. Don't be too long."

Wisely John O'Donnell refrained from saying a word until they'd passed the long road leading to the ancient Norman castle, now a ruin by the sea's edge.

"Do you know I've never been up to the castle?" he began conversationally.

Kevin stopped in the road and stared at him. "You've lived here all of your life."

His grandfather nodded. "Still, for all that, I've never seen it."

"Why not?"

"I can't say. I suppose it never interested me, a rubble of broken stone." The two walked on again. "Sometimes, what's right there in front of a man escapes him. It takes someone new, an outsider, perhaps, to give him a different perspective."

Kevin rested one hand on his grandfather's shoulder, a gesture he'd assumed two years before when he'd overtaken the older man in height. "Is there a lesson in that, Grandda? Is that why you wanted me to come with you?"

"Don't consider it even for a minute, Kevin, lad. I wanted my grandson's company, nothing more."

They continued for a few more minutes in silence. Then Kevin spoke. "Aren't you going to ask me if I did it?"

"No."

The words ratcheted out, one at a time. "I have problems, Grandda."

"You and the rest of the world, Kevin, lad."

"I can't manage them the way everyone else can."

"Why not?"

Kevin shrugged. "I don't know. I'll think about something and it gets bigger and bigger. Then my head hurts and my stomach heaves and I can't stand it. That's when I need the drugs."

"What kind of drugs?"

"Mostly weed."

"The man said it was cocaine."

Kevin colored. "Sometimes it is."

"That won't take away the pain, lad. It only postpones it for a while and then it comes back just as strong as it ever was. That's when you'll need more and more because you never give yourself a chance to heal."

"I'll stop."

"How?" John paused in front of the long, grass-rutted driveway that led to the home he'd lived in for more than forty years.

"I'll just stop, that's all."

"That isn't the way it works, Kevin. You can't do it alone. You're goin' to need some help."

"I don't need help. I just need everyone to leave me alone."

John considered arguing with the boy and decided against it. Was there ever a sixteen-year-old lad in the world who didn't think he had all the answers? It was only after years of living that a man knew how much he didn't know.

"Well, that's all right then. If you need a bit of help along the way, be sure and let me know. I've had a few of my own demons to work out and I don't have all that much to occupy me these days."

Kevin grinned and John's heart twisted. That wayward mischievous turning of the mouth was Patrick's legacy, not Kate's. John wished, more than anything in the world, that the boy had turned out more like his mother.

He gestured toward the house. "Will you come up for a spell?"

"I can't. Mum will worry."

"We'll call her."

"Not this time, Grandda."

John pulled the boy into his arms for a brief, hard hug, then released him. "Go home, Kevin. Take care of yourself."

Again, the quick, magnetic smile, so like his father's. Then he turned and walked away.

John watched him until he disappeared around the bend. He had other grandchildren, a slew of them, but Kate's children tore at his heart. Patrick's death had made them vulnerable, he told himself. But deep down he knew it was more than that. He'd kept silent about so many things. He was sorry for it now, but wisdom comes with hindsight and he wasn't so sure he would have done it any differently if he had to do it over again. It was too late to say anything. Kate and the children had their memories. They were all that was left to them.

John O'Donnell could have told his daughter that no man is perfect, that they all have their troubles as well as their secrets. He could have told her that love comes in many shapes and what a man means when he tells a woman he loves her may be not at all what she's hearing or expecting. He could have told her that love sometimes paints a mask over the facts and blinds a woman to the truth beneath and that, rarely, is a man worthy of the kind of regard that dries up a woman before her time.

But he did none of those things. He hadn't done them when it mattered and up until now he'd seen no point in changing his mind. But six years was long enough and his family wasn't healing. They lived in the shadow of a man whose memory threatened to squeeze the very life from them all.

Five

Deirdre looked around the room she shared with her roommate, Maggie Drummond. Something felt out of place and yet nothing really needed to be done. She hadn't really settled into life at Queen's. It had the best physical science department in all of Ireland, she reminded herself frequently, it wasn't all that far from home and the campus was truly lovely. Yet, there was something uncomfortable about living in her father's native city.

The truth of the matter was, Deirdre lived in a state of perpetual turmoil. No one, looking at her smooth features and composed expression would have guessed, but the truth of it was her current state had existed for so long that nothing else felt normal.

She knew there must have a been a time, long ago in the hazy past, when morning seeped into her consciousness heralding nothing more than an empty contentment, a mild curiosity over what the day would bring: sounds of the world awakening around her, a milk truck lurching across broken pavement, church bells signaling early Mass, tractor fumes, the sweet smell of unearthed peat bogs dark and loamy in the morning mist, car engines roaring to life, friendly greetings between neighbors who'd lived alongside one another from birth, her mother's bread rising in the kitchen, bacon and sausage sizzling on the stove, the sweet predictable flow of a life she had taken for granted.

It had ended abruptly, cut short by an act so heinous that her mind erased all memory of the details, leaving her with an odd secondhand awareness, as if she'd never been there, never seen the masked men who'd snuffed out her father's life before its time. Her therapist told her it was normal for a child to blot out painful memories. Humans were instinctively programmed for survival and she could not have survived the horrible truth of that day and still retain a hold on her sanity.

Deirdre had come to terms with the random horror of it all, but she'd developed a litany of worries. She worried about her mother crossing the checkpoints. She worried about her brother and his nefarious nightlife. She worried about her grandfather and the new slowness in his step. She worried about the sudden bend in the M32 and what the swerving cars meant for vehicles traveling in the other direction. She worried about her classmates at Queen's and whether the friendly banter carried messages she couldn't understand. Leaving her room at night to attend a study group at a neighboring dormitory required great gulps of air, several turns around the floor and recitation of a meaningless mantra that wiped her mind clear of the terrifying thoughts never far from the surface.

Deirdre was afraid of dying and, more than anyone, she understood how quickly the life force could escape the living. One could bear death. She knew that. She'd done so once already and lived through it. But she didn't think she could bear it again, not yet anyway.

Dreams interrupted her sleep, one in particular sending her to the edge of a panic that left her trembling and weak with nausea. Blue-and-white parakeets lived in wire cages in the middle of a courtyard more typical of tropical climates than of Ireland. Lurching unsteadily through the maze of cages, Deirdre managed to tip them over, freeing the birds and sending them to the four corners of the courtyard. Three cats, larger than life and predatorial, crept out of the corners toward the domesticated birds. Despite every effort to contain the cats in her arms, three of them were too much for her. Inevitably they wriggled out of her grasp and stalked the birds. She woke terrified, just as a feline paw reached out to embed its claws into the breast of an innocent bird.

Deirdre no longer met with her therapist. She felt odd and more than a bit embarrassed sharing her intimate thoughts with a stranger. She'd begged her mother to allow her to stop attending the sessions. Kate had spoken with the doctor and then reluctantly agreed. For the most part Deirdre was relieved, although she would have liked the woman's opinion on the bird dream.

Just now she was in a bad way. It was the end of the term. Exam results would be posted, blue papers with black marks, flapping in the wind, secured to a flat wall behind the gothic spires, Queen's pride, announcing who had matriculated. Scores were numbered, of course, but by this time everyone knew whose number belonged to whom.

It wasn't the marks Deirdre was afraid of, it was the crowds. She hated the press of wool-damp bodies leaning into her, hot breath against the back of her neck, harsh voices in her ear, insistent arms pushing her aside, propelling their way to the front of the queue. Americans called it *invading one's sense of space*. Deirdre rather liked that phrase. There was no sense of space in the common areas of the university. Students jostled one another, shared tables and blew cigarette smoke into each other's faces with cheerful regularity. No one else seemed to mind, just Deirdre, and yet she said nothing.

Steps sounded on the stairs. She held her breath. It wasn't her roommate. Maggie's shift was over at midnight and it wasn't much past six o'clock. A sharp rap sounded on the wooden door. She slid off the bed, crossed the room, opened the door and breathed a sigh of relief. "Uncle Liam." Her voice was a raspy whisper. "You scared me."

The crease in Liam Nolan's forehead deepened with his frown. "It's early yet, love. Surely you're up to entertaining a visitor or two before dinner."

Deirdre forced a smile. "I wasn't expecting anyone. What are you doing here?"

"I'm for takin' you out to a decent meal and a bit of the *craic*. Are you agreeable?"

The bubble of worry inside her chest dissipated for the moment. Liam was family. She reached for her coat. "Where shall we go?"

Liam stroked his chin. "The White Swan has a good Irish band playin' tonight."

Tucking her hand inside her uncle's arm, Deirdre stepped out into the hallway and locked the door behind her. "I've never eaten there. Is the food good?"

Liam grinned. "As good as Irish food gets."

Deirdre punched him playfully. "You know perfectly well that the best food anywhere comes from Mum's kitchen."

Liam shortened his steps to suit hers. "How is Kate?" he asked casually.

A full minute passed before Deirdre answered. "Well enough."

"That sounds a bit evasive, lass. Come now. We're family. Out with it."

Deirdre sighed. "It's Kevin."

"What trouble is the lad into now?"

"He was arrested."

Liam's face stilled. "On what charge?"

"I don't know if Mum would want me to tell you."

"Tell me anyway."

Deirdre closed her eyes and blurted out the ugly words. "Possession of cocaine."

Liam exploded. "Sweet Jesus! Where did he get that? Did they let him out?"

"They never kept him. Mum said they had no real evidence."

"That's never stopped them before," Liam said grimly. "Is the charge legitimate?"

Deirdre nodded miserably. "I think so. Kevin has acquired some new friends with bad habits."

"What does your mother say?"

"I don't think she knows he's as bad as he is." Deirdre fought the tears forming behind her eyelids. "She's in some sort of denial. I don't understand it. It's almost as if she's afraid of Kevin."

"Kevin would never hurt your mother."

"Of course not. But Mum doesn't like arguments and Kevin is very good at arguing."

"Is he now?"

"It's been hard since Da—" Her voice broke.

Liam squeezed her arm encouragingly. "I know, lass. Perhaps I should drop by a bit more, make my presence known. A half-grown boy is too much for a woman with no man in the house."

"We have Grandda."

Liam's bottom lip tightened. "He's old."

"Kevin loves him, and I do, too," she added, anxious to make her uncle understand.

"He's no part of your father, Deirdre."

Deirdre kept silent. The words that sprang automatically to her lips should not be voiced. No one could replace her father, not Grandda and not Liam. There was no one in the world like Patrick Nolan and the thought that she would never again experience that exquisite lightness terrified her. That the memory of one person could bring with it such a mix of joy and pain, lifting her spirits and at the same time freezing the blood in her veins, sucking the air from her lungs and pounding in the hurt over and over again, was a mystery to her.

People lost family members. Deirdre didn't know many in the Six Counties who hadn't. What was wrong with her family that they couldn't manage like everyone else?

She wouldn't think of it now. Her uncle had come to keep her company. Pasting a smile on her face she asked, "How is the antique business, Uncle Liam?"

Liam chuckled. "Well enough to buy you a decent meal."

"Thank goodness. I was afraid you were going to make me pay."

"Not on your life. That kind of thing isn't done by a good Irish croppy."

Deirdre laughed. "It happens more than you think. Boys don't have any more money than girls. We can't be expecting them always to be paying for us."

"I suppose not. Times are changing even in Ireland. Is it for the better, do you think?"

He grinned. He was charming her and Deirdre was grateful. This was her uncle, her father's younger brother, and she loved him.

The food was everything he'd promised. Over a glass of foaming Guinness, spring lamb, potatoes and peas, she relaxed, leaned into the flickering candles and gave herself up to the mournful notes of the Irish pipes. She'd heard them infrequently during the last few years. The whistle, fiddle and harmonica were preferred instruments. But the Uileán pipes were rarely heard outside of the remote coastal towns of the Gaeltacht. Only a true musician could coax the sweet, haunting, melancholy notes from the odd amalgamation of reed, leather, bellows and drone.

The last time she'd heard the pipes Uncle Liam had been there, too. Both sides of the family had gathered for Kevin's tenth birthday. Endless numbers of aunts, uncles and cousins as well as most of the town of Sligo descended upon their home. Da loved company and he loved music, fast, lovely, heel-clicking music that filled the air and moved the long grass and set the tree leaves swinging.

He invited everyone who crossed his path to Kevin's party. Mum did all the cooking herself. Banquet tables fairly groaned with roast beef, carved ham, baked chicken and fish, salads, potatoes, cabbage, turnips, beans and peas. Desserts were Mum's specialty but she'd outdone herself with Kevin's cake. He'd been fascinated with fire lorries ever since he'd been a baby. Deirdre remembered how he would run out of the house to see one pass by. He would stand in reverent silence, mesmerized, until the singsong sound of the siren had completely died away. For his birthday, Mum baked a cake, a full meter high in the shape of a lorry, frosting it with fire-engine red icing, even going so far as to painstakingly design the ladders, the wheels, the hoses and the slicker-coated figures of men at the wheel and in the back.

Kevin had been ecstatic. Only when Da assured him that he'd taken several pictures of the monstrosity had Kevin allowed Mum to cut the cake and serve the guests.

Deirdre remembered the cars parked along the road that day. Most belonged to relatives who'd come from various parts of Ireland. There were other cars as well, more than she'd ever seen on the narrow, country roads of Sligo, even during tourist season. The picture was as clear in her mind as if it were yesterday. She hung on to it. Small, dark, innocuous cars carrying only men, driving slowly past, not quite stopping. Da would go out to them. Windows would roll down. He would walk beside the cars. Sometimes he would lean into the window, sticking his head all the way inside.

For all his gregariousness, he never invited the men inside the cars to join their party. At the time, Deirdre was twelve, old enough to notice but not curious enough to wonder why. Now she did and it was too late to ask.

Da had long since satisfied her curiosity about his work. He'd explained in great detail about the law and a person's right to a fair trial. He'd explained that a fair trial in the North of Ireland meant one thing for Protestants and another for Catholics and he was meant to balance the difference. Never once had he alluded to the risks involved. Deirdre hadn't known about the men in the black cars. It was her mother who told her, later, much later, when she'd demanded to know why.

Kate had reluctantly explained it, understanding her

daughter's need to make sense out of what had seemed a random act. Oddly enough it helped, knowing there was a reason, that men in ski masks didn't just walk through doors and snuff out a life without cause.

Liam struck a match, bent over the flame and lit his cigarette. "You're quiet tonight. What's on your mind, lass?" he asked. The flickering light from the match illuminated his features, the sharp jawline, the arched nose.

Deirdre was struck by the resemblance to her father. Words that sprung to her mind stuck in her throat. She shook her head. "Nothing, really. The music is lovely."

"Aye," agreed Liam, inhaling deeply. "It is." He drummed his fingers on the table. "Tell me more about Kevin," he said at last. "Who made the arrest?"

Again Deirdre shook her head. "I don't know. Mum spoke with someone named Anderson."

Liam's nostrils flared and his eyes narrowed. "*Neil* Anderson?"

"I don't remember." She thought. "Maybe. Who's Neil Anderson?"

Liam composed his features, calling up the crooked Nolan smile. "A man I wouldn't want to tangle with. I think I'll pay a visit to your mum."

"If you wait until the weekend, I'll go with you."

"I'll see what I can do. If you don't hear from me, we'll make it another time."

Deirdre nodded. She was accustomed to plans set aside. The Nolans were all unpredictable, a family flaw, her mother said.

Kate Nolan was nothing if she wasn't predictable. Deirdre could set her watch by her mother's familiar routine. Only once in all the memories of her childhood had her mother faltered. She wouldn't think of that now.

"It's time I was seeing you home, lass," Liam announced, throwing a twenty-pound note on the table. "You need your beauty rest and I'm for bed."

Deirdre slid out from behind the table and walked toward the door and the row of coats on hooks along the wall. She found hers and was slipping her arm into the sleeve when someone jostled her from behind.

The young man from her political science class smiled down at her. "I'm sorry, miss. It's Deirdre isn't it? How are you?"

"Well, thank you."

"Are you coming or going?"

"Going."

"May I walk you back?"

Deirdre shook her head. "I'm here with my uncle."

He pulled his cap down over his forehead. "That's all right then. I'll see you tomorrow."

Liam's voice interrupted them. "Are you ready, Dee?"

She took his arm and addressed the boy. "This is my uncle, Liam Nolan. I'm sorry but I don't know your name."

"Peter," he said after a brief pause. "Peter Clarke."

Liam extended his hand. "Pleased to meet you, Peter. How do you know my niece?"

"We have a class together. We had a few last term as well."

Deirdre stared at him. How had he remembered that? She'd barely recognized him. He was rather decent looking in a normal sort of way, not bad at all, but nothing that would make him stand out in a crowd.

"What are you studying?" Liam asked.

"Archaeology."

Liam looked impressed. "An ambitious lad, are you?"

Peter grinned and Deirdre's eyes widened.

"Not ambitious enough for my father," he said. "His preference would have been law or business."

"Those are every father's preferences." Liam lifted an eyebrow. "Shall we walk back to Queen's together or are you staying for a bit?"

"I came for the music. Michael Flynn plays a grand whistle."

"That he does," Liam agreed.

Deirdre studied the boy's face. "Do you live at Queen's, Peter?"

"Not this year. I did last term." His glance moved beyond her. He nodded and waved. "Pardon me," he said, his eyes on her again. "I've friends waiting."

"Do you live in Belfast?" she persisted.

"Aye. But that's another subject. I've kept the lads waiting long enough." Once again he shook Liam's hand. "A pleasure meeting you, Mr. Nolan."

Deirdre watched him walk away.

"He seems a pleasant enough lad," Liam said thoughtfully.

"I suppose."

"He's taken with you."

Deirdre frowned. "How do you know?"

"He was nearly incoherent whenever he looked at you."

Ordinarily she would have been pleased, or at least embarrassed. But for some reason she wasn't. Instinct told her that her uncle's observation wasn't entirely accurate. Peter Clarke had been coherent enough before Liam had joined them.

After her uncle dropped her at her door, she pushed Peter from her mind, checked over her French essay, showered and called her mother. Kate's voice, serene, predictable, warm oil on chapped hands, never failed to soothe her. It was only when Deirdre mentioned Liam that she detected a small change, a hesitation, as if Kate were holding her breath. Then she smoothed over the silence.

"Does he come around often?" her mother asked casually.

Deirdre thought a minute. "Every few weeks. He doesn't want me to be lonely."

"Why should you be lonely, Deirdre? Surely you have friends your own age, friends who would be more suitable companions than Liam."

"They aren't family, Mum."

"I see." Again Deirdre sensed a brief holding back, a small microscopic note of disapproval. Her stomach tightened. Her mother's acceptance had always been unconditional, as unrelenting and sure as spring rain. She hurried to fill in the gap, grasping at the first thing that came to her mind. "We met someone at dinner, a boy from school. His name is Peter Clarke."

"How nice." The warmth was back in Kate's voice. "Tell me about him."

"He's nice enough. Liam said he was taken with me."

Her mother's musical laugh relaxed the knot in Deirdre's stomach and her words dissolved the last of it. "Of course he is. How could he not be?"

"You're biased, Mum."

Again that delicious gurgle, Kate's laugh. "I should hope so."

Deirdre closed her eyes and gripped the phone. She

was luckier than most. No one had a mother like Kate. "Good night, Mum. I'm going to bed now."

"Deirdre?"

"Yes."

"Be careful, love."

Deirdre's forehead puckered. "Why?"

"We've come a long way but things still aren't all they should be, not even in Belfast."

"I don't understand."

Her mother hesitated.

"Tell me."

"I don't think Clarke is an Irish name."

The words slammed into Deirdre's stomach. She managed to end the conversation, replace the phone and crawl beneath her comforter. The possibility that she could have made such an error horrified her. She'd never had a Protestant friend. Protestants attended Queen's University although they were in the minority. She knew who they were, sat beside them in class and occasionally nodded to them in passing. She did not study with them, eat with them or share their conversation. The glass curtain separating Nationalists and Loyalists, Catholics and Protestants, was a way of life, solid, inflexible, permanent. The enormity of her mistake swept through her. She, Deirdre Nolan, daughter of civil rights attorney, Patrick Nolan, had introduced her uncle, a man who'd spent time in Long Kesh for Nationalist political activities, to a Protestant.

Everyone knew of Patrick Nolan and his untimely death. Everyone knew he was her father. Peter Clarke could be no exception. How dare he approach her as if they were the same, as if it made no difference. Deirdre's back teeth locked. She was coldly, furiously angry.

Six

Kate kept her hands on the steering wheel and leaned over to kiss her son's cheek. He stared straight ahead, through the windshield, barely tolerating her lips on his skin.

She swallowed and waited for the digital clock to move forward one digit. "It's time, Kevin," she said gently. "You'll be late for school."

He nodded, opened the door and stepped outside, all without saying a word. Not bothering to close the door, he walked across the grass to the entrance.

Kate sighed, released her seat belt and reached across the passenger seat to pull the door shut. Motherhood hadn't turned out quite as she'd expected. For that matter, nothing had turned out as she'd expected.

The nagging unease that rode on her shoulder whenever she had a moment to think resurrected itself. Life wasn't supposed to be this way. Everything had run so smoothly when Patrick was alive. She would never get used to the frightening sense of anxiety that never left her, or the pressure of knowing that everything now depended on her alone, a terrifying realization for a woman who'd never, before the death of her husband, balanced her own checkbook, called for an airline reservation or filled her car with petrol.

Turning back through town, Kate followed the signs

to the B47. Her lunch meeting with Robbie Finnigan was scheduled for one o'clock in Belfast, enough time for her to pass through the government buildings and finish her report on the dismal progress of integrating the police force.

Kevin ducked his head, avoided eye contact with the group of boys standing near the water fountain and walked quickly down the long hallway to the open door of his first class. If he moved fast enough, with purpose in his step, perhaps no one would stop him.

"Kevin," a voice called out from behind him.

Damn. He'd almost made it. Reluctantly he turned. A sandy-haired, freckled boy ran to catch up with him.

"I called you last night," John Gallagher said. "Did your mother tell you?"

Kevin stared straight ahead, maintaining his pace, making no concessions. "Aye."

"Why didn't you call me back? It's my birthday today. I wanted you to come for the party. Mam's making a cake and my sisters are home."

"I can't," Kevin mumbled.

"Why not?"

"I have schoolwork."

"How do you know? You haven't been to school in two days."

"That's how I know. Have you ever been gone and not had work to finish when you came back?"

John considered the question and then nodded his head reasonably. "I suppose so. Still, you'll have time to finish. No one will ask for it by tomorrow, not when you've been away two days." He clasped Kevin's shoulder. "Hold on a minute. Were you sick?"

Kevin shook his hand off. "Aye."

"What about tonight?"

"I don't know."

John stopped in the middle of the hall. "What's the matter with you?"

Kevin threw back his head and faced his friend, his expression defiant. "Nothing's wrong. Just leave me alone, will you?"

The other boy's face stilled. "I'll leave you alone, Kevin," he said quietly, "if that's what you want." Then he brushed by him and walked into the classroom.

Kevin groaned, leaned against the wall, and breathed deeply. *Why couldn't he ever get it right?* A minute passed. The bell rang. He waited another minute. Mustering a semblance of self-control, Kevin walked through the door, wove his way through the maze of tightly packed desks and students and sat down in the back of the classroom. Brother Andrew was writing on the board. Kevin's breathing normalized. Reaching into his pack, he pulled out a pen and notebook and focused on his paper.

The teacher turned. "Kevin Nolan." Brother Andrew's sonorous voice called out.

His stomach twisted. "Yes, Brother," he managed to reply.

"You're wanted in the headmaster's office. Take your belongings with you."

Kevin's legs froze. He tried to move them, but they wouldn't cooperate.

"Now, Kevin."

Shakily Kevin got to his feet. Swinging his pack over his shoulder he walked out the door and down the hall toward the administrative offices. What could the master want with him? Only the most serious of offenses was brought to the attention of the headmaster. He racked his brain. What could he have done that anyone here at St. Anthony's would know about?

Drawing a deep breath, he paused a moment before the intricately carved door, then pulled it open. He inhaled the smell of varnish and old dust. Thick books lined the shelves, their spines bare, titles worn away long ago. A counter separated the waiting area from the desks where two women typed soundlessly on late-model typewriters. Behind the desks were offices, one large and one small.

Kevin waited for several minutes. Finally he cleared his throat.

One of the women looked up. "Yes?"

"My name is Kevin Nolan. The headmaster asked for me."

The woman stood and walked to the door of the larger office. "Wait one moment, Kevin." She knocked, opened the door and disappeared inside.

Kevin heard the murmur of voices. The woman came out again. "He'll see you now."

Kevin, heart hammering, feet like lead, walked around the counter and across the floor to the office door. Wiping his hands on his trousers, he stepped inside. The man behind the desk had his back turned toward him. Two large wing chairs took up most of the floor space. Kevin glanced around the room and his eyes widened. James McKenna, headmaster of St. Anthony's Catholic School for Boys, was a master fisherman and from the trophies on the shelves, a proficient golfer. Framed pictures of dignitaries with their catches lined one wall and politicians holding golf clubs filled the other. Mounted on the wall above his head was the largest fish Kevin had ever seen.

Mr. McKenna turned around. His piercing blue eyes

settled on the boy and then on the fish. "It's a sailfish," he said, "caught off the coast of Mexico."

"Did you catch her, sir?"

"I did. Do you like to fish, lad?"

Kevin nodded.

"Have you done much?"

"When my da was alive. I've done none since."

"Hmm." The headmaster motioned toward one of the chairs. "Sit down and I'll tell you why you're here."

Kevin tore his eyes away from the sailfish and sat.

"Your instructors tell me your marks have slipped. You've been recommended for probation."

Kevin sighed with relief. *If that was all—*

"What have you to say for yourself, lad?"

"It's true, sir."

"Why is it true?"

Kevin's mind sorted through the possible replies. "I haven't been applying myself."

"Why not?"

The truth. Tommy Dougherty once told him that it was always better to stay as close as possible to the truth. "Because I don't see the point. I've no interest in attending university."

"Your mother is educated, Kevin, as was your father. I'm sure your da would have wanted you to follow in his footsteps."

Kevin stared at the headmaster. *Was the man mad?* "I think my father would have wanted me to do what pleased me, sir."

"I agree." The laser-blue eyes pinned him to the back of the chair. "What is it that you want, Kevin?"

He wanted the art school but that was a pipe dream. "I don't know yet."

"But you know what you don't want?"

"Sir?"

Mr. McKenna stroked his chin. "Tell me if I understand you properly. You don't want to attend school and you don't want to go to university."

"That's right."

"Have you given any thought to your future?"

"I have."

McKenna waited.

"I'll find work," began Kevin, "in Dublin or Belfast, maybe even London."

"What kind of work?"

Again Kevin shrugged and said, "I don't know yet."

"Do you have a propensity for anything?"

"Excuse me?"

"A talent, Kevin. Do you have a talent?"

The boy flushed. What kind of question was that? "I don't think so."

"Well then, it had better be university. Those without talent won't be succeeding in this world without an education."

Kevin nodded. "Yes, sir." He wouldn't win this one, not with Mr. McKenna. Better to take the easy road and agree with the man. Kevin knew from experience that agreement silenced an argument quite effectively.

"Are you happy here at St. Anthony's, Kevin?"

Kevin stammered and shifted in the leather chair. "Happy, sir?" Another one of those stupid questions. Dare he answer truthfully?

The headmaster waited.

Kevin threw caution to the winds. "Happy isn't the word I would use, Mr. McKenna."

"What word would you use?"

"Please, don't take this personally, sir. I wouldn't want to offend you."

Was there a softening of the man's expression or was it a trick of the light filtering in through the long windowpanes? "Duly noted. No offense will be taken."

"I don't dislike it here, Mr. McKenna. I suppose the correct word is *tolerate*. I tolerate the days. It has nothing to do with St. Anthony's. It's that I prefer not to attend school at all."

"I see."

Kevin doubted very much that he did. The conversation had turned decidedly uncomfortable and he had the sinking feeling that Mr. McKenna would be calling his mother. Kate didn't need another upset, not yet. Hastily Kevin scrambled to mend his fences. "St. Anthony's is a very good secondary school."

"I'm happy to hear that you think so."

"It would be best for me to continue here, in case I change my mind and decide to attend university."

"It would be best," the headmaster agreed.

"I'll raise my marks, sir."

"I have every confidence that you will, Kevin," the headmaster said dryly. "Because if you don't, I will inform your mother that this isn't the proper place for you. As it stands you are on informal probation."

"I understand, sir."

"Good. You may go back to class now."

Outside in the hallway, Kevin's legs gave out. He leaned weakly against the wall and closed his eyes. He was a wanker. If a small thing like low marks could leave him in this condition, he was a serious lightweight. He took another minute to collect himself, pushed away from the wall and walked slowly back to class. How had he come to this and how in bloody hell was he going to get himself out?

Robbie Finnigan was a toad. It pained Kate to think of him that way. She was a woman who tried to see the positive in everyone, but there was really no other way to see the chief of Ulster's Royal Constabulary.

"I don't understand what the problem is. You've had nearly a year to make this work."

"These things take time, Mrs. Nolan. I can't just fire everyone on the police force and hire Catholics."

Kate drummed her fingers on the table. "How many men have retired in the last nine months?"

"I can't say exactly." Deliberately he avoided her gaze. "Four, maybe five."

Kate's crisp voice cut him off. "Actually there were nine. Only three of the nine knew there was a large bonus and benefits due them."

"Nine?" The chief constable frowned. "Really? I hadn't realized there were so many."

"How many Catholics were hired to replace them?"

"I'm sure you know the answer to that as well, Mrs. Nolan."

"I do, Constable Finnigan. Not a single new recruit is Catholic."

"Is that so?"

"It is. Your hiring practices must change, immediately. You know that. Why aren't you operating under the terms of the Patten Commission?"

"I'm not running a charity operation, Mrs. Nolan. Our people must be qualified. There aren't many Catholics who aspire to join our forces. They're seen as touts, turncoats."

She ignored his last comment. "I'm sure there are

just as many croppies from West Belfast who can wield billy clubs, Constable.''

''But will they use them, Mrs. Nolan?''

''Probably not with the same alacrity but I won't be sorry. I'm sure a large majority of the population will agree with me.''

''I've already hired replacements for the retired men. They have families. Do you want me to sack them?''

''Catholics have families, too, Constable. You were precipitous in your hiring. I'm afraid you'll have to make your apologies unless you can think of another way to bring on nine new Catholic police officers. Fifty percent is the number we're working toward. You're hovering at a miserable eight. I'll expect everything to be in place by next Monday. Please, don't disappoint me or I'll be forced to go over your head.''

''I can't integrate fifty percent of my work force with Catholics by Monday.''

''Start with nine.''

''You're a hard woman, Mrs. Nolan.''

''Good day, Constable.''

Kate made it through the waiting area, out the door and across the parking lot before she began to shake. Managing her car keys, she unlocked the door, climbed into the car and rested her head on the steering wheel. Her lungs burned. She forced herself to relax, to breathe slowly, to wipe the conflict from her mind.

Minutes passed. What next? The ride back home and the appointment with the therapist she'd scheduled for Kevin. Groaning, she turned the key, felt the engine catch and backed out of the car park. Across the street at the primary school, children played on an ancient jungle gym. Directly ahead an empty guard tower, barbed wire still intact, hung forbiddingly over the treeless neighborhood. Young men loitered outside a *Catholics only* pub. Women held children by the hand, pushed babies in prams and gossiped outside half-open doorways. Ragged strips of green, white and orange, the flag of Ireland, hung from every doorway, black flags and green *H*'s, commemorating the twentieth anniversary of Bobby Sand's death by starvation in the H-blocks swung from street signs, a typical afternoon in Belfast, except that Belfast was never typical, not even now.

She hesitated at the light and looked at her watch. It was too late to swing by the university and hope that Deirdre was in her room. Even though she came home on weekends, Kate missed her dreadfully. Nothing was quite the same since Deirdre had left for Queen's in the fall. Because there were only three of them, her absence was all the more obvious.

Kate bit her lip. She wouldn't be one of those mothers who kept a stranglehold on her children, binding them through guilt, reluctantly obligating the carefree years of their youth. Deirdre deserved her freedom and a chance to live her life away from her family's troubles.

It was Kevin who needed her attention. With a cautious eye on the road, Kate concentrated on the meeting to come, on the words she would choose to maximize the hour they would have. Kevin was always her challenge. Kate was a fighter. She wouldn't back away from a challenge, especially when he was her son.

Seven

It happened so quickly, Kate had less than an instant to react. She had barely turned left from Grosvenor Road to the Westlink and the M1 when a nondescript compact hurtled across the divider, spun out of control and crashed into the passenger side of her car. She felt the impact, a wave of dizziness and then the loss of orientation as her Volvo tilted sideways, careened for terrifying seconds and then rolled over. Imprisoned by the seat belt, Kate hung upside down for what seemed an eternity before the car rolled again landing on the embankment. She closed her eyes, breathed a silent prayer of gratitude and waited.

Minutes passed. Her heart shuddered. Gingerly she touched her head, stretched her muscles. She wasn't hurt, probably not even bruised. Breathing deeply, she sucked in as much air as her rapidly constricting lungs would allow. She needed her inhaler. Where was her handbag?

Voices blended together outside. Help had arrived. Thank God. A large fist knocked on the window. She pressed the automatic control and the pane inched down.

"Are you all in one piece, miss?"

"I think so," Kate managed.

His voice changed. "Mrs. Nolan, is that you?"

She looked at her rescuer for the first time. "It is, Mr. Anderson. You're a welcome sight. What are you doing here?"

"I pulled up just as you were hit. Are you injured?"

"I don't think so." She tried the door. "I can't seem to get out."

He grasped the handle and pulled. The door opened, he unlatched the seat belt and helped her out.

Kate gripped his arm. "I need my handbag."

"You need a hospital. You're pale as a ghost."

"I'm an asthmatic," she explained, between wheezes. "I can't breathe. My inhaler is in my bag. It was in the front seat but I can't find it now."

He took another quick look at her face, opened the back door of the car and ran his hands along the seats and the carpeted floor. "Here it is." Unzipping the leather side compartment, he handed Kate the inhaler.

Ordinarily she was self-conscious about her condition, but not now, not when her chest was so tight she felt as if she were breathing through a pinhole. Sealing her lips around the plastic she depressed the nozzle, drew the life-sustaining medication into her chest and held it there. Exhaling, she leaned weakly against the car.

Neil Anderson reached out to support her with his arm, but she waved him away and, once more, lifted the vial to her lips. Relief was still minutes away.

He watched the blue leave her lips. A hint of color crept back into her cheeks. Neil relaxed for the first time since he saw the small car leap over the divider and slam into Kate's Volvo. He hadn't known who she was until she'd rolled down the window. It was odd, the extent of his relief, considering who she was and, more to the point, who Patrick Nolan had been.

The singsong whine of an ambulance was very close. He hadn't even checked on the other driver.

"Wait here," he said and jogged over to the other vehicle. Already two police cars were positioned on either side of the blue car. The man inside was slumped over the wheel. "Is he alive?" Neil asked the officer standing nearby.

"I believe so, sir. The medics are on their way."

Neil leaned into the window and pressed his fingers against the pulse point in the man's neck. It was faint but steady. He straightened and nodded. "If he's treated quickly enough he might make it."

"What can have gotten into him, sir? Eye witnesses say the car ran right over the center divider."

"Most likely several pints of Guinness," replied Neil grimly. The inside of the car smelled like a brewery. "Is everything under control?"

"Aye, sir. We'll have him up the road in no time."

Neil nodded and sprinted back to Kate. She looked dazed and unsteady but no more than that. "I'd like you to see a doctor," he said.

She shook her head. "I've got to be back in Donegal by six o'clock. I have an appointment."

"You won't be going home in this car even if you were in any condition to drive."

"The appointment is for Kevin. I must be there." She gripped his arm. "Please. Will you take me?"

Keeping his expression carefully neutral, he studied her, wondering what it had cost her to make such a request of him, a woman like her, serious, almost prim, exuding the faintest scent of perfume, Irish skin, dark hair falling around her face, wide-eyed, utterly feminine, quietly fierce. It would be Kevin. For who else would she place herself under such obligation? "Of course,'' he said quietly. "Would you like to leave now?"

"Yes. Thank you."

"Where would you like your car towed?"

Kate shrugged, bewildered. "I don't know. I have no experience with this sort of thing."

Neil's mouth turned up in his first smile since he'd witnessed the accident. She was entrusted with the integration of Northern Ireland and yet she was lost when it came to towing her car. "I'll take care of it, but first I'll walk you back to my car."

She smiled gratefully and walked beside him, through the flare pattern in the street and around the stopped traffic to where his car sat on the side of the road. He opened the passenger door and she slid into the seat.

"Will you be all right for a minute or so while I see about your car and the chap who started all this?" he asked.

She leaned her head against the seat and closed her eyes. "I'm most grateful, Mr. Anderson. Don't worry. Take all the time you need."

He was back very soon.

"Is he badly hurt?" Kate asked, a stricken look on her face.

"He'll make it."

"Thank God."

She'd nearly died, yet her concern for the misguided young man in the blue car was genuine. Turning the key, Neil maneuvered the car out into the afternoon traffic. He was a very good driver, confident but careful. He pressed the power button on the radio hoping the steady hum of the engine, the smooth ride and the soothing music would work its magic on Kate's frazzled nerves.

His eyes never left the road ahead of him but he knew when her breathing deepened. Not for the first time did Neil marvel at the resilient quality of Irish women. Perhaps they were made differently, born with the quality of endurance and a resigned acceptance that life was not meant to be kind or equitable or fair. There could be no other explanation. An English woman, or any other he'd come across, would have been terrified after an accident like the one Kate had survived. She could have been killed and yet she asked for nothing, not even sympathy or a friendly ear to hash it out. She was Tony Blair's hope for the restructuring of Northern Ireland, she supported two children on her own, she'd suffered a harrowing trauma, her son was in serious trouble and her husband—Neil deliberately stopped his thought and continued in a different direction. Kate Nolan was unlike anyone he'd ever known.

She dozed through the lake country of Lough Neagh, the flat marshy bog land of Tyrone and the meandering road bordering the River Erne. Not until he breathed in the familiar smell of the Atlantic, tangy, saltier than the Irish Sea, did she fully awaken again. "We're almost in Ardara," she said, surprised.

"Yes. I was about to wake you. Shall I take you home or drop you somewhere?"

Kate looked at her watch. "It's still early. I have time to make dinner and drive back to Donegal with Kevin."

"How will you get there?"

"My father has a car. I'll use his tonight and rent one tomorrow."

"Grand."

Kate hesitated. "I appreciate this very much, Mr. Anderson. It's a very long way for you to go. I can't imagine what I was thinking.''

"You were thinking about your son.''

"Yes." Kate nodded her head. "That must have been it.''

"You're very close to him," he observed.

"I'm close to both my children. Deirdre is at Queen's.''

Neil knew that but said nothing. "When I pass the roundabout, where shall I turn?"

"Take the main road across the lake. We're at the end of the first street.''

Neil turned down a narrow street with no access that led to three homes, separated by a wide expanse of grassland, all with magnificent views of the sea. "This is a lovely neighborhood," he said. "Have you lived here long?"

"Patrick and I bought the house about ten years ago." Kate's voice was flat, her eyes empty. She stopped, bit her lip and started again. "I grew up in Ardara and my father still lives here. I wanted to be close to him." She pointed to the house on the end, a lovely, spread out gray-gabled home with a stone fence and large, diamond-paned windows. "Here we are.''

He pulled into the long driveway, turned off the engine and walked around the car to open the passenger door. "You might consider seeing a doctor. The accident was a nasty one.''

"All right." Kate walked beside him to the front porch. At the door she turned and hesitated. Courtesy warred with wariness. Courtesy won. "You've gone to a bit of trouble. May I offer you a bite to eat, Mr. Anderson? It won't be fancy, but at least you'll have a meal before you return home.''

"I think not," he said, frowning. "You can't possibly mean to cook a meal after what you've been through. You need rest, possibly a visit to a physician, if not a hospital."

Kate's eyes widened. "Of course I mean to cook. We have to eat."

He frowned. "I can bring food in."

Kate laughed. "In Ardara?"

"There must be something."

She folded her hands and looked up at him. "Cooking soothes me. Feeding people is extremely satisfying. Please, you've been very kind. Allow me to make you a meal."

Perhaps it would be best if he stayed. If she collapsed, he would be nearby. It was an excuse. He knew it as soon as the thought crossed his mind. Something told him Kate Nolan had never collapsed in her life. She was a survivor. But there was her son to consider. "What about Kevin?"

"Perhaps you'll get to know him better."

There was a motive behind her graciousness. He found it didn't bother him a bit. Smiling a slow, genuine smile, he said, "That would be grand. Please, call me Neil."

The door was unlocked. She preceded him into the entry. He was conscious of light, rich and warm streaming through colored glass, warm golden wood, greenery and comfortable furnishings. This was a home, a real home where people lived.

Kate stood at the bottom of the staircase, her hand resting on the carved railing. "Kevin," she called out, "are you home?"

"Aye, Mum. I'm upstairs."

''We have a bit over an hour before we leave. Call Grandda and ask him if we can use his car.''

''What's happened to ours?''

''It's in the shop. Come down and say hello. We have a guest for dinner. ''

Kevin appeared at the top of the landing. He peered over the railing and his face froze.

''Hello, Kevin,'' Neil said. He recognized terror when he saw it. The boy's hands trembled.

''Why are you here?'' Kevin asked.

Keeping his voice calm, Neil answered him. ''Your mother was in an accident. I happened by at the right time. She needed a lift home and she invited me to dinner.''

Kevin relaxed. ''I'm not hungry, Mum. You don't have to fix me anything.''

''Kevin—''

Neil interrupted her. ''Perhaps I should leave.''

Kate's beautiful manners prevailed. ''You'll do no such thing. I've invited you to dinner and you've accepted. If Kevin isn't hungry, he'll eat later.'' She smiled bracingly. ''Would you like a drink?''

''Only if you join me.''

Kate walked to the antique sideboard, opened the cabinet and poured out two glasses of Irish Mist, no ice.

He lifted his glass. ''Cheers.''

''*Slainte,*'' she returned. ''It was very nice of you to drive me all the way here. I hope you didn't have plans.''

''None that would be a problem to reschedule. I would like to make a phone call. Is there somewhere I can do that without disturbing you?''

''Of course.'' Kate led him into a beautifully appointed study with hunter-green walls, Persian carpets, thick white moldings and a couch and chair done up in burgundy leather. A natural golden light spilled across book-lined shelves filling every available wall and corner.

Confused, Neil looked around for the source. Kate pointed toward a skylight paned with yellow and amber glass. He wasn't a man to wear his emotions on his sleeve but the sight of streaming golden light filtering into a room that belonged in *Architectural Digest* took his breath away. His voice was reverent. "This is incredible. Did you do it yourself?"

"Thank you. I planned it but I hired someone to install the window and paint the walls."

"It must be difficult to leave in the morning."

"Sometimes," Kate admitted. "I'll leave you to your phone call and start dinner."

She had stuffed and browned the chops, torn the spinach, tossed the salad and started on the table when Neil returned to the dining room. "Is everything all right?" she asked.

"It's my once-a-month weekend with my daughter. She comes up from London," he explained. "My ex-wife and I don't always agree on how we should share her time."

"Strange, but I hadn't imagined you a father. How old is she?"

"Thirteen."

"Ouch." Kate smiled. "A difficult age."

"A lovely, responsible child who takes a great deal on her shoulders."

She changed the subject. "Are you hungry?"

"Starved."

''Good. We'll eat soon. Will it be water, fruit juice or wine with dinner?''

''Water, please. Otherwise I won't be worth much on the drive home.''

They ate informally, on the wooden table in the kitchen, sitting not at the head and foot of the table, but on either side, companionably. They spoke of the Peace Accord, of Belfast, of changes in the Six Counties. She described her job.

Neil listened attentively, watching the play of light around her mouth, the line of her throat. He was conscious of her femininity, a woman utterly serious, warm and poised, but businesslike, without a hint of coyness.

Her home, the home she'd created without her husband, reflected her, warmth, light, classically beautiful, highly functional. This was a woman with hidden reserves.

''You're very quiet,'' she said, after a lengthy pause. ''I've talked the entire time.''

He smiled. ''The meal was delicious, Mrs. Nolan.''

''Kate.''

''Very well, Kate. I don't often have anything like this.''

''How long have you been divorced?''

''Ten years.''

Her face was expressive. She was counting backward. He would make it easier for her.

''I left when my little girl was three years old.''

''I'm sorry.''

''Don't be. It's over. The mistake has been remedied and I have a lovely daughter.''

''Do you see her often?''

''As often as I can. At least once a month and every other holiday. She has school and friends in London.

Sometimes it's difficult for her to break away. I'm grateful for what I can get.''

''Of course,'' Kate murmured. She couldn't imagine a life without her children, watching them grow, waking them in the morning, sitting across the table listening to their good-natured grousing about the food, teasing them, hugging them, advising them. What would she be without them?

Neil's voice broke into her thoughts. ''I've taken up your time. It's nearly six o'clock.''

''It's all right. I'll leave the dishes to soak and finish up when I come back.''

Kevin stood in the doorway. ''Grandda's coming by with the car. He said he would give us a lift.''

''Does he know we're going back to Donegal?''

''I told him.''

Kate sighed and spoke to Neil. ''My father is a love but he can be relentless. Perhaps…'' Her voice trailed off.

Neil grinned. ''You don't want him interrogating me.''

''Yes.''

He stood. ''I'll be leaving now. Thanks again for the meal. I'll repay you whenever you're back in Belfast.''

''That isn't necessary,'' she assured him. ''You drove me home.''

He smiled and stood there for a moment looking down at her.

She pushed her chair away from the table and stood. ''I'll walk you to the door. Be careful going back. The roads aren't good this time of year.''

Mindful of who she was and the space she kept between them, he left her on the porch with a friendly wave. ''Goodbye, Kate,'' he said and walked to his car.

She hugged herself against the cold, a slight, straight figure standing on the porch rubbing her arms. "Goodbye. Thanks again for the ride," she called out.

He nodded, waved again and drove away.

Eight

They walked apart in stony silence, Kevin first and then Kate, keeping their distance, until they reached the car.

Kevin climbed inside, slammed the door and glared angrily at his mother. "What was that all about? Why did you bring me here?"

Kate's brow creased. Worry had become second nature to her. "I'm concerned. You've been different lately."

"No, I haven't."

"Kevin, the Belfast incident terrified me. Surely you understand that."

"I told you. It was nothing. It won't happen again."

"If I understood why it happened in the first place, I might have more confidence that you're telling me the truth."

"Are you saying you don't believe me?"

"No. I'm saying you can't possibly give me a guarantee unless you know what led you down that path in the first place."

Kevin groaned in frustration. "There is no path. It was just something that happened."

Kate snapped. "What happened isn't going to happen again. Not as long as I'm here. I'm having trouble trusting you and I don't like the feeling. I love you.

Deirdre and Grandda love you. Our family has gone through enough. We owe it to each other to make the best of what we've been given. Do you honestly feel you're doing that, Kevin? Does skipping school, earning failing marks and being arrested for narcotics possession make sense in light of all that? Do you think that's what your father would have wanted?''

''I don't want to spill my soul to a bloody counselor,'' Kevin muttered. ''Why do I have to do that?''

''Because there's nothing else to do, nowhere else to go. Something has to be done and if you think you've fooled anyone by insisting that you don't have any worries, think again.''

''I never said that.''

''Well, what are they?''

She saw the red rise in his cheeks. Irish skin. Patrick's skin. Her hands tightened on the wheel. ''You don't have to tell me, Kevin, but you must tell someone. That's why I made the appointment. I wanted you to feel as if you could confide in someone completely impartial. Can you see that?''

He turned toward her. ''Give me one more chance, Mum,'' Kevin pleaded. ''Please. I won't botch it again. I promise. Please, don't make me do this again.''

She was no match for the pleading look on her son's face but Kate was well into her second decade of motherhood and she'd learned a bit from the last one. One did not make decisions without thinking them through with a cool head. This was one of those times. ''I'll consider it, love'' was all she would give him.

Kevin changed the subject. ''When can I apply for my driving license?''

''I think you need to give it more time.''

''I'm a decent driver.''

"I know you are." Kate smiled reassuringly. "But there's more to driving an automobile than good reflexes. Others on the road may not be good drivers like the man who almost killed me today."

Kevin, in typical teenage fashion, ignored the reference. "How much longer do I have to wait?"

"A bit of practice every day for the rest of the month would satisfy me."

Kevin's face brightened. "Will you be home for me to do that?"

"I'll make a point of it," she promised, forcing a cheerful expression. *Kevin behind the wheel of a car.* The very thought of it sucked the air from her lungs. Her insides felt as if they were caving in. She didn't know if she could negotiate the short drive back to the small beachfront village that was home.

"Thanks, Grandda," Kevin shouted over his shoulder. "I'll have the car back to you by half past six."

John O'Donnell lifted his hand in farewell. "Be safe, lad."

Kevin was elated. It was a stroke of good fortune that he'd passed his driving test the first time. Few did, but then few parents were as exacting as his mother. The extra practice had paid off and now he was to be trusted alone in a car for the first time.

He adjusted the seat and then the rearview mirror. His grandfather was shorter by nearly five inches. After fastening his seat belt, he signaled and pulled out on to the nearly empty street. It was exhilarating at first, to control thousands of pounds, to merely touch the wheel and feel an immediate response. Kevin turned the corner past the chemist's shop leading to the road out of town. After passing the last residential street, he pressed harder on the gas. Signposts flashed by. The road leveled out. He grinned and pressed harder. The speed energized him. Peat fields and herds of sheep flew by. He ignored the No Overtaking sign and passed a tractor and two cyclists.

A stop sign on the Clifdon Road loomed ahead. Kevin pressed down on the brake hard. The car slowed to a complete stop. He looked at his watch. Twenty minutes had elapsed since he'd left his grandfather's house. The warm glow of his first solo drive had left him. Now what? He drummed his fingers on the wheel and considered his dilemma. What good were a license and a car if he couldn't show anyone? He thought of visiting Johnny Gallagher and immediately discarded the idea. He'd rejected his friend's birthday invitation. More than likely he wouldn't be welcome at the Gallaghers' anymore. Where could he go?

Slowly he pulled into the intersection, negotiated a three-corner turn and drove back the way he came. Tim Murphy wasn't really a friend and neither was Sean Payne, but they would admire his car. They might even want him to drive them somewhere. He could always count on the two of them to be close to home. They were older, out of school and on the dole. Kevin knew exactly where to find them.

Cleary's Pub was a fixture on the outskirts of Ardara. It was old, not so old as Nancy's or White's but old enough so that everyone within a fifty-mile radius knew of it. It wasn't quaint or charming enough to attract tourists, but for the native inhabitants it was a local landmark. Most stories had their roots strongly entrenched in the pitted wood and smoke-stained windows of Cleary's.

Just as he expected, Kevin found the boys bent over

a billiard table, each nursing a pint of foaming Guinness. They barely looked up when he hailed them.

"How have you been?" he ventured.

"What's it to you?" Sean, beefy and broad-shouldered to Tim's lean, emaciated height, chugged down half his pint. "You haven't been beating the doors down."

Kevin flushed. "You left me in Belfast and I got into some trouble."

"You weren't supposed to get jacked. You know that. Anyone who gets jacked is on his own."

"It was a setup."

"We heard," said Tim. "Are you all right then?"

Kevin nodded. "I think so. Nothing really happened."

"Of course not." Sean sneered.

Tim straightened and frowned at his companion. "Shut up, Sean. Did you have something to tell us, Kevin?"

"I've a driving license and a car."

The two older boys glanced quickly at each other. Tim spoke first. "That's grand, lad."

"Aye," said Sean. "We're on the lookout for just such an opportunity, aren't we, Tim?"

"We are."

Kevin felt the nervous tick on the edge of his eyelid begin to jump. "What did you have in mind?"

"We need a lift to Belfast."

"I can't do that."

Tim pulled a pack of cigarettes from his breast pocket and offered it to Kevin. "It won't take long," he said casually. "No one has to know."

Kevin shook his head. "I have to be back soon. I've my grandda's car."

Sean laughed. "We don't mean today. Wednesday is a good day. We could go on Wednesday."

"I've school on Wednesday."

"You could take a break," Tim suggested. "One day off wouldn't hurt you, a bright lad like you."

"I haven't done so well lately."

"One more day won't make a difference," Sean wheedled. "Plan on Wednesday. We need to get to Belfast on Wednesday. We'll be back in no time. The bus takes twice as long."

"I'm not sure I can get my grandda's car on Wednesday. He'll be suspicious."

"Ask him if you can drive it to school," said Sean. "No one will know. Our Tim will write you a letter and sign it. He has a clever hand."

Kevin frowned. "I won't say for sure. I'll have to let you know later."

Tim rested his hand on Kevin's shoulder. "You're not yellow, are you lad? Because if you are we'll have to let the lads know. It would be the end for you."

Kevin swallowed. "That's not it."

"What is it then?"

"There's a screw in Belfast. He's an investigator or something at the RUC station. He didn't want to let me go. I saw him in Ardara. I think he may be following me, waiting for me to do something wrong."

"What's his name?"

"Anderson."

Once again the two boys glanced at each other and then looked away quickly.

"Anderson, did you say?" asked Tim.

"Aye."

"Did he arrest you?"

"At first."

"On what charge?"

"Possession of narcotics."

"Is that all he wanted off you?"

Kevin hesitated. The need to tell someone of his near miss was strong but instinct told him to mind his tongue. "Aye," he said instead.

"Were you kept overnight?"

Kevin shook his head.

"Why not?"

"Something wasn't right with the evidence."

Tim whistled. "You're a lucky bloke."

Sean spoke up. "Luck has nothing to do with it. He's that posh lawyer's son. No one would dare arrest him."

"His da wasn't a favorite of the RUC," Tim said quietly. "He defended Catholics in Diplock courts."

Kevin stared at the lean, serious boy standing beside him. "That was a long time ago. How do you know so much about my da?"

"Everyone knows about Patrick Nolan, lad. He's a bloody legend." Tim bent over the billiard table and positioned his cue. "Now let us finish our game and don't forget to ask your grandda for his car on Wednesday."

From across the dinner table Kate watched her son mix his carrots and potatoes together into an unappetizing eddy and wished, not for the first time, that her Catholicism was less intellectual and more spiritual. It would be so reassuring to believe that God was sympathetic to the pleas of desperate mortals, that He actually listened to and answered the prayers of the helpless and muddled who couldn't manage their own lives without divine intercession. But she wasn't that kind of believer.

Kate had never been what the nuns called strong on faith. She believed in God, of course, and in the divinity of Christ and she would never be anything but a Catholic. Tradition and the sacrifices of her ancestors were too strongly entrenched in her history. But that was as far as it went. Even as a small child of seven, dressed in her first communion veil, she had known that something wasn't quite right. It had to do with her instinctive dislike of fairy tales. How could God listen to so many people who wanted different things and, more to the point, why would He want to?

She would have preferred the kind of faith her schoolmates had, unconditional, unquestioning, the kind that welcomed conflict, bolstered the faithful and took upon itself life's heaviest burdens. But somehow, that deep immersing of the spirit had eluded her from the very beginning and still did.

Watching her son struggle with his personal demons, she was once again consumed with frustration. Where had she gone wrong and why was Kevin paying such a dreadful price?

She forced herself to ask what she thought was a benign question. ''Grandda said you drove his car today. Where did you go?''

Kevin flung his head back. His eyes burned brightly. ''Where do you think I went?''

Kate's hand tightened around her fork. ''For pity's sake, Kevin, I was only making conversation,'' she stammered. ''It isn't important.''

Her answer incensed him even more. ''Why are we always talking about me?'' he shouted. ''I must be your favorite topic of conversation. Is there anyone in the entire town who doesn't know everything about me?''

Struggling for patience, Kate lifted her glass of water

and forced herself to sip it slowly. Mentally she counted to ten, set down the glass and wiped the corners of her mouth with her napkin. When she spoke, her voice was measured, controlled. "If you are the topic of anyone's conversation, it is your doing, not mine. You, of all people, should know me well enough to believe me when I tell you that I have never discussed your personal problems with anyone other than Grandda and Deirdre. If that bothers you, I'm sorry, but I'm not going to promise you it won't happen again. Sometimes I'm not the most impartial observer. I need the advice of people to whom you matter." She pushed away her plate. "Can you understand that, Kevin?"

"Aye," he said sullenly. "I understand well enough that it will take years before you trust me again."

Kate was silent for a full minute while digesting the accuracy of Kevin's statement. "I don't think it will take years, Kevin," she said at last. "But it may take more than a few weeks. I'm sorry."

He shook his head. "One mistake," he said bitterly. "One mistake and I'm cooked. Didn't you ever make a mistake, Mum? Don't you believe in second chances?"

"Yes, I've made mistakes and of course I believe in second chances. You're not exactly a prisoner, Kevin. You have quite a bit of freedom. All I asked was a simple question."

Kevin stirred the food on his plate. "I drove the Coast Road and then came back to Cleary's Pub to watch Sean and Tim play billiards."

Kate was familiar with Tim Murphy and Sean Payne. She disliked them both but decided to let her antipathy pass without comment. Kevin was touchy enough. Any criticism of his friends might alienate him completely.

Instead she smiled. "I hope they were suitably impressed with your new status."

He stared down at his plate. "I suppose so."

Kate recognized that they'd reached the point where nothing would improve either Kevin's mood or their conversation. She stood and picked up her plate. "Have you finished?"

"Aye."

She reached across the table and cleared his plate. "I'll finish up here." Refraining from asking about his homework, she walked into the kitchen, breathing a sigh of relief. Meals with Kevin, *anything* with Kevin, had become the most stressful part of her day.

The bleeping of the alarm stunned her into instant wakefulness. Groggily Kate fumbled for the off button, lifted her head to check the time, groaned and flopped back onto the pillow. Wednesdays, her one-day a week in Belfast, came too quickly. Allowing herself another five minutes, she stretched her toes and slowly worked her eyelids into the open position. It wasn't yet six o'clock, still dark, too early for anyone to expect a normal human being to rise. Still, Belfast could be as much as four hours away in morning traffic. Exercising all the discipline she could muster, Kate threw back the comforter, tested her toes on the floor and walked into the bathroom.

The showerhead was a new one, large and round with a myriad of spray sizes. Turning on the tap, Kate waited for the water to heat, stepped out of her nightgown and into the liquid warmth.

Ten minutes later, her head wrapped in a towel, she belted her robe and walked down the hall to knock on

Kevin's door. No answer. She turned the knob and looked inside. No Kevin.

Alarmed, she ran down the stairs. "Kevin," she called on her way down, "where are you?"

"Here."

The voice came from the kitchen. Kate turned on the light. Kevin sat at the table holding a mug.

"Why are you up so early?"

"Grandda said I could take his car today. I couldn't sleep."

She smiled. "I imagine it must be exciting to drive yourself to school for the first time."

He shrugged. "I suppose so."

She crossed the kitchen, bent down and kissed his cheek. "I'm off to dress. Drive safely, love. If I don't see you before you leave, have a lovely day."

"Thanks, Mum."

Humming to herself, Kate climbed the stairs. It was grand to see Kevin happy. Perhaps things could be normal again after all.

Nine

Liam Nolan scratched his two-day-old beard and squinted at the document on the table. He pointed to the location of a large munitions deposit on the north end of Ardoyne. "This doesn't look good, lad," he said to his brother. "Perhaps we'd better leave it alone. The risk of moving it in this climate is too great."

Dominick leaned back in his chair and shook his head. "We haven't a choice in the matter. This one is big. Special Forces is close to finding it. We'll smuggle it through the city and relocate it somewhere in Antrim. I'll ride along on this one."

Liam's expression turned skeptical. "I don't like it. Kate is in town on Wednesdays. She might see you and wonder."

"I'll take the risk."

"She could be blamed if anyone connects you to Patrick."

Dominick stared at his brother. Kate's reputation was irreproachable. The Virgin Mary would have more of a chance at blame than Kate Nolan. "Are you mad, Liam? No one in his right mind would blame our Kate for anything. She's pure as the Madonna. For Christ sake, look at what she's done for the country. They'll be genuflecting to her before this mess is over."

"Times aren't what they were, lad, not with Neil

Anderson in Belfast. We can't take anything for granted.''

''You've been an old woman ever since Deirdre told you he pulled Kevin in. Anderson wants nothing from us. He's in the drug business.''

''It's all one and the same. You know that.''

''The past is over, Liam. Kevin is safe at home. Kate is out to save the Peace Accord and we'll do what we must.''

Liam pulled a pack of cigarettes from his breast pocket, struck a match, lit the unfiltered end, drew in deeply and exhaled. ''Do you ever wonder what it would be like to end all this, Dom? We could go back into the antique business, travel the world, see New York City and Boston. I'd like to see America.''

''You've seen it.''

Liam shook his head. ''You know what I mean.''

Dominick's blue eyes narrowed. ''You aren't goin' soft on me, are you, lad? Have you forgotten Patrick?''

''Patrick lived in a different Ireland. There's little sympathy on either side for those who step outside the law.''

Dominick's thin, handsome face hardened. ''It's justice I want, not sympathy. When we're treated the same as everyone else, I'll live inside the law.''

Liam sighed. The conversation wasn't a new one and Dominick's mind was set on one goal. He wouldn't be swayed by anything less. ''The first minister's gone to Italy to study organized crime. Too many of the lads are falling into a nasty business, Dom.''

''They've nothing else.''

''Nothing but homes and families.''

''They've no cause, Liam. Nationalism was their

cause. Now that it's been taken away, what's left to them?''

''Are you sayin' what I think you're sayin'?''

''You heard me.''

''Are you tellin' me our lads are turnin' to crime because there's no longer any fighting to be done?''

''Aye.''

Liam stared at his brother thoughtfully. When had their roles reversed? Dominick was the youngest. For how long had he taken the lead? Liam couldn't remember. Somehow, after Patrick died, he'd stepped aside, comfortable with his subservience, relieved that Dominick had assumed the dominant role left vacant after their oldest brother's murder.

Liam knew he wasn't clever, not like Dominick, certainly not like Patrick whose brilliance had been obvious from the moment he could speak. Patrick had been a light never to be replaced. Liam's strength was his perseverance, his dogged relentless tenacity that saw a project through to the finish. That, and his die-hard belief in the Nationalist cause, a united Ireland, had earned him a reputation he was proud to carry, until lately. Liam saw no dishonor in breaking the law. Up until now it was a Protestant law, created and enforced by a Protestant police force against a Catholic population. Bad laws, he reasoned, were meant to be broken.

But recent events had raised questions in his mind. Since the Peace Accord sides were no longer so black and white nor strictly Protestant or Catholic. Everyone wanted peace and, oddly enough, the Loyalists had voted for equal rights for all citizens along with the Nationalists. It was perplexing, particularly for a man who'd never in his life called a Prod a friend.

Perhaps it really was different now. All factions were tired of war. Both sides wanted a fair sharing of power.

Dominick was poring over the document in front of him as if it were a treasure map. His younger brother was single-minded. Derry City's Battle of the Bogside was as firmly entrenched in Dominick's mind as if it had happened yesterday. At every opportunity he argued convincingly against compromise unless the Loyalists made concessions first. His logic was effective. Never again would Catholics of the Six Counties depend on British troops to help them against their antagonistic Protestant neighbors. Never again would they be forced to their knees, burned out of their homes, murdered in the streets while praying for the arrival of the Protestant-infested Royal Ulster Constabulary, Northern Ireland's police force. Sinn Fein could promise whatever they wished in the name of diplomacy, but Liam knew that as long as Dominick was in charge of munitions, there would be no disarmament, no turning over of weapons, until all of the terms of the Peace Accord had been met.

The sticking point was integration of the RUC with proportionate numbers of Catholics. Some believed it was impossible. Liam was not one of those. The single qualifying factor for his optimism was his sister-in-law's role in bringing about that very result.

Kathleen O'Donnell Nolan had qualities that normal women did not share. From the moment Patrick brought her home, Liam, renowned for the accuracy of his first impressions, could see that she was something out of the ordinary. Kate was intelligent, of course, and lovely in the black-haired, blue-eyed, creamy-skinned way of women who hailed from the far west of Ireland. He could not imagine Patrick with a woman either simple or unattractive. But Kate was more than either of those. One had only to engage her for the space of a few sentences before realizing that not only was she direct and dignified in a way that women no longer were, she was incapable of nothing less than absolute truth.

Liam was aware that this singular attribute had been the root of Patrick's many sleepless nights. During the turbulent seventies and eighties, frustrated Catholics, trapped by prejudice in British-dominated Ulster, supported Sinn Fein and the Irish Republican Army. Patrick was no exception. Because of his education and chosen profession, expectations for Patrick were high. What he'd intended to be minor involvement turned into something much more. During the final years of his life, the bulk of his law practice was confined to defending those convicted of terrorist acts against the government.

Kate knew all that. What she didn't know, what her husband dared not tell her, was the nature of his role in the organization most of the western world considered to be terrorists.

For Liam, what all the facts boiled down to now was confusion. He was no longer sure of anything. Where once he'd harbored no doubts at all about the propriety of his actions, he now had serious ones. His world was tilted at an uncomfortable angle and the righting of it would not be left to those who rowed against the popular tide.

Liam didn't approve of the new direction taken by the youths of Belfast's working class. In his day a lad had but three choices: emigrate to America or to the factories of Manchester and Liverpool or, more likely, live on alcohol and the dole like his father and grandfather, or join the ranks of the guerilla forces of the Irish Republican Army.

The latter allowed a man to keep his pride, stay home and win the respect and appreciation of his community. This had been Liam's choice and Dominick's and finally, Patrick's, although his education kept him on the sidelines for a very long time.

Their world had changed. Dominick was right. Today, lads had nothing to strive for or believe in, nothing to dull the edge of their pubescent tempers. And so, where once the IRA policed the Catholic communities of Andersonstown, the Falls and Clonard, keeping them free of petty crime, now drug dealers haunted street corners and every schoolchild knew where to find items sold through the black market.

As little as five years ago, elderly women could walk the streets without fear of purse-snatchers and muggers. Now, lads bent on mischief did what they would do, never mind that they stole from their own. Not that Liam had actually approved of the methods the IRA chose to emphasize their lessons. A bullet in the knee or banishment were a bit extreme but he couldn't deny they were an effective deterrent.

He could not see the point of gaining a say in the direction of a society if that society wasn't worth belonging to. His dilemma was further muddled by his late brother's wife.

Kate Nolan was, in Liam's mind, closer to sainthood than any human he had ever known. She was also a woman of rare insight. If she supported the Peace Accord, he had more than a slight suspicion that he should be supporting it as well.

''I'd leave this one alone, lad,'' he repeated. ''Let them find the weapons. Better yet, offer them up. It will put them off for a while and quiet the rumors that we won't decommission. It will also make Kate's job easier.''

Dominick lifted his head and quirked an eyebrow. ''What does Kate's job have to do with anything?''

''She's in a hard spot.''

''That's her problem.''

''Do you have something against our Kate, Dom?''

''She did nothing to smooth out Patrick's life.''

Liam stared at his brother incredulously. ''She was everything to Pat.''

''She didn't support his life, not like the other wives.''

''You can't blame her for that. He didn't tell her what he was.''

''And why couldn't he do that, Liam?'' Dominick shot back. ''If you ask me, there's something wrong with a marriage when a man can't be honest with his own wife.''

''She wouldn't have approved.''

''Why not? Does she think she's too good for us?''

Liam struggled to explain. Words didn't come easily for him. ''She didn't marry into it, Dom. She wasn't expecting it. Patrick wasn't involved when they married. He never told her when things changed for him. You can't blame Kate for that. The fault is Patrick's. In the end she and the children paid dearly for what he believed.''

Dominick frowned. ''Don't go putting Kate on a pedestal, Liam. She's a mortal woman, a fine one, but a woman all the same.''

''She's our family,'' Liam reminded him. ''She's Deirdre and Kevin's mother.''

"I'm not forgetting that. She may not want to be forgetting, either."

"What do you mean?"

Dominick shrugged. "It may be nothing." He stood and stretched, a tall black-haired man, lean, with the tight, ropy muscles of a boxer. "Go home now, Liam. There's nothing more to do here. I'll be along shortly."

"Will you leave this one, Dom?"

"Perhaps. I'll think about it."

Only partially satisfied, Liam walked through the back door and out onto the broken pavement of the car park. He decided to walk home instead of giving his car the usual tedious inspection for explosive devices, a precaution required for an automobile parked outside of Sinn Fein headquarters.

Kevin had never been to this part of West Belfast before. Until the Peace Accord, the Catholic ghettos of Andersonstown and the Falls were located behind the barricade. His mother considered these areas too unpredictable to allow her children anywhere in the vicinity, not even to visit Dominick and Liam.

"Turn here," said Sean.

"Park at the end of the street." Kevin obeyed, parking at the end of a dark close.

Tim clapped him on the shoulder. "Come inside with me. Sean can wait for us here."

Kevin followed Tim inside a house that looked fairly normal for a working class neighborhood, gray wood, peeling paint, a crumbling porch. But on the inside all semblance of normalcy ended.

There was no kitchen, no sitting room or bedrooms. All the walls had been gutted revealing rotting rafters and exposed electric wires. Boards were nailed across broken windows and over potholes in the floor. A single lightbulb suspended from the ceiling threw a feeble glow over a small aluminum table in the middle of the room. Filthy blankets, pillows and stained sleeping bags covered the floor. Herb, powder, colored capsules, drug paraphernalia, bongs, joints, clips, ashtrays and beer bottles cluttered the table, the floor, the corners. People came and went. Bodies in various stages of cleanliness and drug-induced haze lounged around, smoking, drinking, talking, sleeping in whatever space was available. The smells of urine and vomit permeated the air.

Kevin's stomach heaved. He tapped Tim on the shoulder. ''I'll wait outside.''

Tim gripped his arm. ''Not yet.''

''I'll be sick.''

Tim thrust something at him. ''Hold this and stay away from the door.''

The bag was light. Kevin looked inside and his eyes widened. ''I can't do this. Not again. They'll send me up this time.''

''No one's going to know.''

Kevin shoved the bag back in Tim's face. ''I can't risk it, not again.''

''Steady now, lad. Calm down. Just take it for a minute. Here.'' He pressed Kevin back into a corner. ''Sit down.''

Kevin pulled away. ''I'll wait outside in the car with Sean.''

''All right. Relax. Give the bag to Sean. I won't be long.''

Breathing a sigh of relief, Kevin turned and made his way toward the door. He reached out to turn the knob when a loud pounding sounded, followed by a crash and a splintering of wood. Men in green uniforms kicked open the door, pushing him back, filling the room. Another man in street clothes lifted a megaphone to his lips. "Police. Don't move. Everyone is under arrest."

A single shot rang out followed by a volley of sharp cracks. Horrified, Kevin watched a man in a green uniform fall to the floor. Panicked, he backed away, holding out his arms, eyes closed, pushing the entire ugly scene far away, beyond his reach. He wanted his mother and Deirdre and his grandfather. He wanted away from this place of drugs and death and filth and noise. He was Kevin Nolan of Ardara. What was he doing here?

Neil Anderson, his face expressionless, focused on the boy who sat across from him. The only furniture in the bare room consisted of two wooden chairs and a scarred desk that had seen better days. Two RUC officers manned the door.

Castlereagh Detention Centre, once proclaimed a torture chamber used by the RUC to obtain information from reluctant Catholics, had been ordered closed months before. Neil had never seen Castlereagh in its heyday. He had never been to the North of Ireland before his current assignment and he was very much looking forward to never seeing it again.

"Kevin," he began in his most reasonable voice, "tell me what you're on."

"Nothing."

Neil didn't need a confession. The boy had been caught with a large amount of cocaine, too large for personal consumption. "Who gave it to you?"

"I've done nothing."

"I'd like to help you, lad, for your mother's sake, but you're making it difficult."

Kevin deliberately turned away.

Neil took in the boy's flushed cheeks, the twitch in his left eye, the leg that wouldn't stop shaking and the involuntary clenching of his fists and drew his own conclusions. He tried once more. "I know you're not a regular supplier, Kevin. But you were caught with more than an ounce of cocaine in your pocket. A man was killed, a police officer shot. If someone put the goods there for you to take the blame, I'd like to know. There's no sense in your taking the fall for someone who wouldn't give you the time of day."

Kevin shook his head.

"They've arrested you for distributing. An ounce is too high for personal consumption. Do you understand what I'm telling you, Kevin? This is a serious offense. You could go to prison for up to three years."

"I don't know anything."

"That's not a convincing argument."

"Have you called my mother?"

"A message was left on her machine at home. We've had no answer yet."

"It's Wednesday. She's here in Belfast on Wednesdays."

Neil stood. "I'll ring her immediately. Until then, you can stay behind bars for the night and think about answering my questions."

Kevin looked around. "Here?"

Neil shook his head. "At the station. After that you'll go to prison until your sentencing." He called out in a voice loud enough to be heard by the policemen at the door. "Take the lad into custody."

Ignoring the boy's gasp, he walked through the door and out to the car park.

Ten

Kate pulled into the car park at the back of the Ormeau Road Police Barracks, set the brake, pulled down
the window shade where her hand mirror was fixed and
applied fresh lipstick. Not that Robbie Finnigan deserved new lipstick, but knowing she looked put-
together gave her confidence. It was past noon. Lunch
was over. The timing was perfect for a thorough inspection.

Stepping out of the rented car, she glanced into the
window at her reflection. Tucking the collar of her
blouse into place, she buttoned her navy jacket and
walked toward the entrance. *Keep it professional, Kate,*
she told herself. She rang the bell and listened for the
signal allowing her inside.

"Mrs. Nolan." A young officer behind a desk stood.
"May I help you?"

"Tell the chief constable I'm here to see him."

"Do you have an appointment?"

She smiled sweetly. "I have a standing one."

He punched three buttons on the phone line. "Mrs.
Nolan is here to see you, sir."

The silence stretched out between them. The young
man's face flushed a deep red. Carefully he replaced
the phone. "If you'll wait, Mrs. Nolan, Constable Finnigan will be out in a moment."

"First, I'll have a look around."

"I'm not sure—"

Kate had never seen anyone quite that shade of scarlet. "Yes?"

"Perhaps the chief constable would rather speak with you first," the boy managed to say.

Again Kate smiled. "Tell him I insisted on exploring and that you couldn't handcuff me." She smiled conspiratorially. "It will serve him right to keep me waiting."

The station appeared a hub of activity. She approached a man at his desk and smiled. "I'd like to interview a new recruit."

"We haven't any in at present," he said.

"No one here has been hired in the last three months?"

He shook his head. "No one here has been hired in the last six years."

Kate's throat closed and a fierce burning sensation traveled to the pit of her stomach. Damn Robbie Finnigan. He'd defied her. More importantly, he'd defied the prime minister of England. Keeping her face expressionless, she pulled a pen and notepad from her handbag. "Tell me your name, please."

"Garret Wilson," the man stammered.

"Tell me, Constable Wilson, how many police officers in this division make their homes in West Belfast?"

She could see the Adam's apple bob in his throat. "No one that I know of, Mrs. Nolan."

Her voice was crisp and clear and very cold. "Let me be sure I understand you. Not one officer, not a single one, lives in West Belfast and hails from a Catholic parish."

"No," he whispered.

"Is there anyone in this entire station who would know something that you would not?"

"I don't think so, Mrs. Nolan."

"I see." Apparently oblivious to the silent stares of the entire division of the Ormeau Road Royal Ulster Constabulary, Kate flipped her notebook shut, and marched down the hall to knock on the door of Robbie Finnigan's office.

Without waiting for permission, she turned the doorknob and stepped inside.

"Mrs. Nolan." Constable Finnigan did not stand. "I wasn't expecting you today."

Kate sat down, her expression cool, her eyes blue ice. "I'm surprised at you, Constable. You knew there would be unscheduled visits."

"I did."

"Why then, have I no progress to report on the integration of your police force?"

Robbie Finnigan's mouth twisted into the mockery of a smile. "I've answered that question in my report which I've already forwarded to the first minister. To be blunt, the Nationalist community does not encourage young men and women to join the RUC."

"I'm very sure the first minister will read your report with great interest, perhaps by next spring. Meanwhile, I've been assigned to take care of the matter. Therefore, I should like my own copy."

"I shall mail it to you immediately."

"I'd like it now."

"It isn't copied."

"I'll wait."

Finnigan's fingers formed a pyramid on his desk. "I'm surprised and quite touched that you would show such concern for your position at a time like this, Mrs. Nolan, when personal matters must be weighing on you considerably.''

Kate frowned. ''Excuse me?''

''You don't know?''

''Know what?''

''Your son, Kevin, has been taken into custody. The charge is a serious one. Weapons were involved. A man was shot.''

The room tilted and swayed. Kate clutched the edge of the desk for support. ''There must be a mistake,'' she whispered. ''Kevin is at school in Ardara.''

Robbie Finnigan shook his head. ''His grandfather's automobile has been impounded.''

Kate forced the darkness back. Swallowing, she wet her lips. ''Where is he?''

''The Castlereagh Detention Station.''

She couldn't have heard correctly. ''Castlereagh is closed.''

''Special Forces opened it again. The chief is with your son.''

Special Forces. Neil Anderson was the chief investigator. The blood drained from her face. She stood. ''Mail the document, Constable. I'll be waiting.''

Her hands shook. She could barely manage the keys. Backing out of the car park, Kate pressed the gas pedal and shot straight back into a pole. The metallic crunch of her bumper jerked her back into a semblance of control. Cautiously she shifted and the car moved forward. She breathed a sigh of relief. The body was damaged but the car was still mobile.

Kate's terror intensified with every stoplight. Robbie Finnigan's words echoed in her brain. *A man was shot and Kevin was involved.* The horror of it threatened to bring on another spell of the dreaded asthma. She tightened her hands on the steering wheel and deliberately willed herself into calmness, maneuvering the car through the familiar streets of Belfast on automatic pilot. Kevin was a child. He couldn't be involved, drugs perhaps, victimless crimes, certainly not violence.

"God help me," she prayed out loud. "This time, please help me and I promise I'll never ask you for anything else again."

Neil spotted Kate immediately. He waited for her to park her car in the lot and walk to where she stood.

She came directly to the point, no greeting, no pleasantries, as if their last meeting had never been. "What have you done with my son?"

"I've questioned him. He'll be taken into custody."

The poise for which she was renowned broke. "He's sixteen years old. You had no business speaking to him without my knowledge. I have a right to be with him at all times."

"Kevin is an adult in the eyes of the law," he began, sighed and started again. "This may be difficult for you to believe, but I'd hoped to make it easier on him."

"You're right. I don't believe you."

"Kate—"

She froze him with a look.

"Mrs. Nolan." He stopped and began again. "Kevin is deeply troubled. He's trafficking in drugs. A man is dead, a peace officer shot. Whatever you're doing isn't working. Unless he presents a very convincing argument for why he's carrying more than an ounce of cocaine, he's going before a judge." His voice gentled. "This isn't unheard of, Kate. A number of young people his age are going through the same thing. Kevin needs a mother who will help him, not one who sticks her head in the sand. Convince Kevin to cooperate with us.''

Waves of color flamed in her cheeks. "Where is my son?''

"He's under arrest. After the paperwork is completed, you'll be able to see him. It will go easier on Kevin if you can persuade him to tell us who is supplying West Belfast.''

"I shall be consulting an attorney.''

Neil shrugged. "I suppose that's the best way, if Kevin has something to hide.''

Kate laughed contemptuously. "You can't possibly believe I'll fall for that one. My husband was a barrister.''

"Your husband was a great deal more than that.'' The words burst from his lips, damaging words he should never have said, words he could never take back.

She whitened. Straightening, Kate brushed her hair away from her cheek with a shaking hand. "Yes,'' she said, "he was.''

Involuntarily he reached out. "Kate—''

She shrank back. He dropped his hand.

"Where will you take Kevin?''

"For now, he'll be detained at the Antrim Road RUC Barracks. Later, until his sentencing, he'll be in Long Kesh.''

He watched her turn and walk back to her car, a slim, straight figure who just now was functioning on the edge of her nerves. What was it about this woman that touched him so? He wasn't new to his job. Over the last two decades he'd seen hundreds of women, wives, mothers, daughters, all victims, all hanging on by a thread, all experiencing a similar devastation, tied together by a sense of frantic hopelessness, the same blank despair as they watched husbands and sons, brothers and fathers in colored jumpsuits, their hands and feet shackled, climb into armored transports destined for prison terms.

But they weren't like Kate Nolan. She didn't fit the profile. Neither did her son. They weren't uneducated, poor or living on the dole. What made a boy like Kevin with a mother who loved him, a designer home in the Republic and every other advantage a lad could want, go south?

Cursing under his breath, Neil climbed into his car, taking the turn into the traffic lane a bit too quickly. He didn't like this part of his job, especially the part that involved children. This was supposed to be a break for him, a change from the hard-edged, dangerous world of international terrorism. Instead he found himself wishing he were back again, in the world of unshaven men with wicked minds and hair-trigger tempers, men who deserved to be put away for whatever remained of their lives.

The Antrim Road RUC Barracks was a fortress like every other police facility in the Six Counties. One of the recommendations of the Patten Commission was to humanize the police structures, making them citizen friendly by hiring civilians, creating lobbies and friendly waiting areas. That was as far as it had been taken, a recommendation.

Kate pushed the bell. A voice spoke to her through the harsh metal. "State your name, please."

"Kathleen Nolan."

"You've been authorized to enter, Mrs. Nolan."

She pushed open the door and stepped inside. It was

cold, bone-chillingly cold. Kate shivered and raised her arms while a policewoman passed a wand down one side of her body and up the other. The woman stepped aside to let her pass.

"I want to see my son," Kate explained to the man at the desk.

"He isn't allowed visitors, Mrs. Nolan, not until he's brought before the judge."

She lifted her chin, prepared for battle. "What about an attorney? Surely you can't stop Kevin from seeing an attorney."

"Of course, as soon as his paperwork is processed."

Without another word, Kate turned and walked back out the way she came.

Dylan McCarthy was the best barrister that Belfast offered. A Catholic, educated at Trinity and Queen's, he was an expert on juvenile crime. Kate had seen him in action many times during her years as a social worker. Not in her wildest dreams had she imagined needing him personally.

She sat across from him in an office that barely escaped the description of luxurious; leather chairs, wooden bookshelves, plush carpeting. "Are you saying Kevin won't be released today? He'll actually have to stay there again tonight?" She was incredulous.

"He must go through the process, Kate. You know that. I can't do anything until he's charged. That takes time, as much as thirty-six hours."

Her eyes filled. She kept them wide-open and fixed on his face, attempting to keep the tears from spilling over. It didn't work. Embarrassed, she wiped them away with her hands.

McCarthy pulled a handkerchief from his pocket and

handed it to her. "It isn't as bad as you think, Kate. This isn't the seventies. We have rights. Kevin has rights. He'll manage."

She returned the handkerchief. He stuffed it back into his pocket.

"Besides," the barrister continued, "it might give him something to think about. We haven't addressed the issue of what will happen to Kevin once he's released."

"What do you mean?"

"He was arrested for narcotics possession. That doesn't go away. He'll have restitution to pay, a work program, counseling, recovery. You won't be able to just take him home to a happy ending. Surely you know that?"

She shrugged. "I hadn't thought that far ahead. Right now I want him away from that place."

"I recommend staying away from a trial. Kevin is a minor. This is a first offense. If he pleads guilty, he'll be allowed to make restitution under the penal code. A trial is dangerous. One never knows what the outcome will be. Drug issues can be inflammatory."

"What happens if he gets into trouble again?"

"Let's cross that bridge when we come to it, shall we?"

Kate shook her head. "I don't think so, Dylan. I need to know what Kevin's options are. It could be dangerous for him to plead guilty if his habits don't change."

"That part will be up to Kevin. You can't fix everything for him, Kate. He has to want to change."

She closed her eyes and pressed her fingers against her lids. "I can't believe I'm sitting here. How can this be, Dylan? What's happened to my family?"

Dylan McCarthy reached across the desk and patted

her hand. "You aren't alone, Kate. Many young people are troubled, especially here and now, in Belfast. Everything will come around. Some hard lessons will be learned but, in the end, most of our children turn out very much like us. I'm not sure that's a comfort, but it's the best I can do."

Kate smiled weakly. "Will you go to him, Dylan?"

He looked at his watch. "I'll make a call to the station. As soon as I know anything I'll call you."

"Thank you. I'll be at the Victoria. I've rented a room. But first I'll try to see Deirdre."

"Try to rest. Kevin will need you to be strong." He hesitated. "How is the investigation of Patrick's murder coming along?"

Kate shook her head. "I don't know. I haven't heard anything new and just now it's not as important as what's happening with Kevin."

"Keep your chin up, Kate. I'll do my best."

She smiled. "I know."

Deirdre pulled a chair up to the window of her dormitory room and waited until she saw her mother walking across the brick driveway. Jumping up, she opened the door and ran down the hall to the stairs where she met Kate halfway. She threw her arms around her mother and hugged her fiercely. "Have you seen him? Is he all right?"

Kate shook her head. "I haven't seen him yet. Mr. McCarthy said Kevin won't be allowed visitors until all his paperwork is processed, maybe not until tomorrow morning."

Deirdre pressed her hand against her mouth and blinked back tears. "What are we going to do, Mum?"

"Let's talk inside." Slipping her arm around her

daughter's waist, she led her back into Deirdre's dormitory room and closed the door. Then, with a weary sigh, she sat down on the bed.

Deirdre didn't think she could stand another moment without answers. She sat down in a chair across from her mother. "Mum?"

"We'll wait until we hear from Mr. McCarthy," Kate began. "He's our best hope right now. Depending on what happens there, we can plan for several possibilities."

"Such as?"

"If Kevin is released, he'll be required to participate in a recovery program. Mr. McCarthy believes he'll be sentenced to community service as well."

"Will the recovery program be an outpatient one?"

Kate looked surprised. "I don't know. Why?"

"If Kevin is a drug addict, there won't be any stopping him, Mum." The words rolled off her tongue, fast and furious and desperately sincere. "You can't make him do anything. It isn't really Kevin who's talking, it's the drugs. The only program that will work is one where he can't get out."

"Oh, Lord, Deirdre. Let's hope it hasn't gone that far."

"What are the other possibilities?"

"Kevin may have to serve time in jail. He was arrested with more than an ounce of cocaine on his person." Her mother's voice cracked. "His charge is for distribution."

"How could he do this?" Deirdre whispered. "What's the matter with him? Why doesn't he see what's happening to him and to all of us?"

Kate was losing control rapidly. She curled up in a fetal position on the bed. "Oh, Dee." Her words were thick and tear-choked. ''I don't know what to do. I can't bear this. I can't lose Kevin, too, not after all that's happened.''

Deirdre lay down beside her mother and wrapped her arms around her. ''We won't lose Kevin, Mum,'' she promised. ''Mr. McCarthy will come through for us. I know he will.''

Kate pressed her daughter's face against her shoulder. ''Of course, he will,'' she said. ''Mr. McCarthy is a wonderful lawyer. He knows exactly what to do. We'll put our faith in him. Meanwhile we should consider options for Kevin. I'll talk to people, check out recovery programs and counselors. People get through these things. Kevin isn't the only troubled boy in Ireland.''

''What if he won't do it? Kevin can be stubborn.''

''He won't have a choice. Perhaps this experience will have scared him.'' She stroked Deirdre's dark hair and pressed a kiss on her temple. ''Everything will work out. You'll see.''

Eleven

Promptly, at eight o'clock the following morning, Kate walked through the double doors of the courthouse where Her Majesty's justice prevailed. She had spent a restless night and the skin around her eyes was marked with dark, bruised circles. Otherwise, she was the picture of calm, her blouse crisply white, her tailored suit pressed, her hair straight and shining, not a strand out of place, falling like a smooth curtain to the tops of her shoulders.

She had been here many times before but always in a professional capacity. The large desk in the middle of the lobby would have the information she needed. With the ease of familiarity, she bypassed the information booth. On the counter lay the court's daily agenda. Kate flipped through the stapled sheets until she found Kevin's name and beside it the room where his case would be heard. She breathed a sigh of relief. Rodney Thompson was one of the more reasonable judges on the bench. His reputation for fairness had won him high marks in the Nationalist community. "Thank God," she murmured.

"Don't be too sure of that," said a voice behind her.

She turned. Worry lines creased Dylan McCarthy's forehead.

"Why do you say that? Has something happened?"

"Have you told me everything, Kate?"

"Why?" she repeated.

McCarthy frowned. "There is no bail amount set. It looks as if Kevin is being denied completely. That doesn't happen for a first drug offense. Has he been in trouble before?"

"Of course not."

"Then it must be a mistake and, if so, we'll fix it."

"What are you going to do?"

"He's scheduled to come before the judge this morning. I'll do what I can to see that he's released into your custody."

Kate wet her lips. "What if it isn't a mistake?"

"Kevin didn't murder anyone, Kate. No one sends a sixteen-year-old boy whose never been arrested to jail on a first-time drug offense."

"A police officer was shot and a man was killed. What if Kevin is blamed?"

"Unless he fired the gun, that's impossible. There's absolutely no evidence to suggest such a thing."

Kate swallowed. "I want to go in with you."

McCarthy nodded. "It's good for the judge to see a lad with the support of his family." He smiled encouragingly and motioned toward the door. "Shall we?"

She preceded him into the courtroom and sat down in the last of a row of seats near the front.

Patting her on the shoulder, the barrister continued past her, making his way toward a uniformed guard seated at a desk with several files in front of him.

Kate couldn't hear their whispered conversation. She looked around. Twelve rows of deep seats, ten and twelve across, were staggered on either side of two aisles running from the front of the room to the back. Separating the court from the spectators was a low wooden wall and two tables. An ornately carved door led to the judge's chambers and on one side of the room was a large wire cage with six seats inside.

A soft whisper startled her. "Hello, Mum."

Kate looked up to see her daughter slip into the seat beside her. Deirdre reached for her mother's hand and squeezed it.

"Did you clear your classes?" Kate asked.

Deirdre's lip trembled. "I didn't have time. But Kevin is more important."

The tightness in Kate's stomach eased a bit. "Thank you, love. You have no idea how I appreciate this."

"Has anything happened yet?"

Kate shook her head.

A door behind the cage opened. Deirdre gasped.

Kate tightened her hand over her daughter's.

Kevin, in a yellow jumpsuit, hands and feet shackled, shuffled into the cage and sat down. He looked tired and unkempt as if he'd been dragged out of bed without warning. Kate tried to catch his eye but he refused to look up. He sat slumped down in the chair, head down.

Another door opened and a man wearing a black robe and powdered wig entered the courtroom.

The guard stood at attention. "All rise for the Honorable Rodney Thompson, chief justice of Her Majesty's court in Northern Ireland."

Kate and Deirdre stood.

The judge sat down, slipped on his glasses and began to flip through a sheaf of papers.

"You may be seated," the guard said.

Kate shivered. She knew Chief Justice Thompson well enough from her years as a social worker in West Belfast. He was serious and conscientious, an advocate for the rights of children. But he had no patience for criminal acts. Behind the ill-fitting wig and wire-rimmed glasses was the power and weight of the English Crown, the hereditary enemy of all Irishmen. How would he see Kevin, as a victim or as the enemy?

The judge spoke. "Is Kevin Nolan represented by counsel?"

The barrister stepped forward. "Yes, Your Honor. Dylan McCarthy, here, representing the lad, Kevin Nolan."

"What is his plea?"

"I have had no chance to speak with the boy, Your Honor. May I request a stay until such time that I may discuss his case with him."

The judge lifted his gavel. "So ordered."

"May I also request that Kevin, in light of his age and the fact that he has no previous record, be released into the custody of his mother, Your Honor?"

Chief Justice Rodney Thompson looked as if he might say something but he did not. Instead he frowned. "Ordinarily the court would gladly grant your request, Mr. McCarthy. Unfortunately, because of the situation in West Belfast, I cannot allow it at this time." He looked at his calendar. "Because it is now Thursday and tomorrow is completely booked, Kevin Nolan will be arraigned on Monday." He looked out over the rims of his glasses. "Is that satisfactory, Mr. McCarthy?"

"This is without precedent, Your Honor. Kevin is a sixteen-year-old boy without any prior convictions. His record is clean. What harm is there in allowing him to go home? Kathleen Nolan is the boy's mother. Surely her word is good."

"Mrs. Nolan's character isn't in question, Mr. McCarthy," said the judge dryly. "If I could release the boy, I would. My hands are tied in this instance."

"May I ask why?"

"You may ask anything you please, however, I cannot give you an answer at this time."

"Where will the boy be taken?"

Again the man hesitated. He reached for the glass of water at his elbow and drained it. Then he cleared his throat. "He'll be detained at Long Kesh."

Kate gasped at the same time that Deirdre cried out.

"This is outrageous," McCarthy shouted. "He's a child."

"I'm sorry, Mr. McCarthy. My hands are tied."

Normally slow to anger, Kate didn't recognize the emotion that began at the back of her head and moved downward, heating her chest and stomach, awakening nerve endings in her arms and legs, fingers and toes. Only when she stood and walked down the aisle and lifted the latch and walked deliberately over to the cage where her son sat in dejected silence, did she identify the rage that consumed her.

"Kevin," she said softly, "I love you. I promise you this will go away."

From his seat on the bench, the judge spoke, ordering her back away from the prisoner. Kate ignored him.

"You'll be all right. Nothing will happen to you. Do you understand? I'll make sure nothing happens to you. No one will hurt you. Do you understand, Kevin? I won't allow anyone to hurt you."

The guard walked toward her. "Please, Mrs. Nolan," he said, "stay back."

Kate reached into the cage. "Speak to me, Kevin," she pleaded. "Say something."

Slowly Kevin lifted his head and focused on his mother's face. She smiled. Quickly, briefly, he reached out and touched her fingers. She stifled a sob.

The guard, about to move in, looked askance at the judge. He shook his head. The guard backed away.

Behind the cage a door opened. A man in green uniform stepped inside and motioned for Kevin to follow him. Kate watched the door close behind them and struggled against the panic rising in her throat.

Faintly she heard the solicitor speak on her behalf. "When will Mrs. Nolan be allowed to visit her son?"

"Long Kesh has regular weekend visiting hours. She should call ahead and arrange an appointment for either Saturday or Sunday."

Kate barely heard him. Her mind was racing forward, rejecting one solution after another. She felt a hand on her arm, heard Deirdre's question, the fear in her voice. "What happened here, Mum?"

Squeezing her daughter's hand, she shook her head. "I don't know. Let's go now."

Together they left the courtroom. Dylan McCarthy followed them outside. "Something isn't right, Kate. I don't like this. Can you influence anyone?"

Kate's face was the white of bleached bone. This was what Patrick had fought against, what Liam and Dominick were still fighting against. Nothing unusual had happened back in the courtroom, just business as usual. A Catholic boy had come up against a Protestant judge. The Queen's justice had prevailed in the same routine manner it always had. "I don't know," was all she said.

"I won't be able to get him out before the arraignment, not until I know what's happened and what we're up against. I'll find out," he said grimly, "but not before the boy is transported to Long Kesh."

She held out her hand. "Do everything you can, Dylan. We're depending on you."

"What will you do?"

She stared at him, blue eyes wide, defensive, furious. "I can't tell you."

He sucked in his breath. "Don't do anything rash, Katie. It won't help us in the end."

"I'm going to save my son, Dylan. None of this will matter if he's found with his throat cut."

"You're exaggerating."

Her raised eyebrows mocked him. "Am I? Have you forgotten what they did to Patrick?"

Embarrassed, Dylan apologized. "Forgive me."

She nodded. "Of course."

"Do me a favor, Kate. Be careful."

Again she nodded. "Goodbye, Dylan. I'll see you on Monday morning at the courthouse."

Deirdre waited until the solicitor left them. "What are you going to do?"

Kate was once more the professional, poised, in control. "I shall call in my markers." She smoothed her daughter's dark hair. "I'd like you to go back to Queen's. I'll call you later. We can meet and I'll tell you what's happening. Will that be all right?"

"Yes, of course. Are you sure you don't want me to go with you?"

"Not this time."

Deirdre's face reflected her emotions as clearly as a glass lake. The child was terrified.

Kate's heart broke. Would the sights and sounds of Sligo always hover, ever present, in her daughter's memory? "Don't worry, love," she said soothingly. "Nothing I do will be dangerous. I'm not at all brave, remember?"

Deirdre laughed. "You're the bravest person I know." Kissing her mother's cheek, she strode back to the car park, waving before she disappeared around the bend.

Kate waited a full twenty minutes before she made her way back to her Volvo. Inside the car she waited another ten minutes arguing the merits of what she was about to do. Then she pulled out into the street and turned the car toward the west side of the city.

The unmanned barricade separating East and West Belfast was an eyesore. All recommendations called for its complete demolition. So far nothing had been done. Slowly Kate drove past the brick and barbed wire. In her own mind, who she was had never been more clear. She was an Irish woman, a Catholic, in a land of English Protestants. Her husband's murder remained unavenged. Her children had no rights. Only here, in the Falls and the Clonard, in the streets of Andersonstown was she safe.

Passing the Peace Line that had nothing to do with peace, she crossed the Springfield Road into the Falls. Houses were small here, built back-to-back, directly on the asphalt, without yards. They weren't in ill repair, but they were too similar to be charming. Children's toys, tricycles and prams lay in haphazard disarray around doorways and front steps.

She stopped at the intersection of Glen Road and Whiterock to allow a group of schoolboys in parish uniforms to cross the street. They grinned and waved at her. She waved back. Her spirits lifted. In front of St. Patrick's Church a priest gathered his cassock and lifted one leg over a rusted bicycle. He pushed off, settling himself nicely. A woman called to him from the other side of the street. He answered her greeting with a friendly shout. In spite of herself, Kate smiled. She had forgotten that West Belfast was a community.

She passed through two more intersections and turned down Divas Street. They would be home, both of them. She'd called ahead to be sure.

Kate stopped in front of a white-framed house with a narrow porch. She set the brake but didn't bother to lock the door. No one in his right mind would disturb a car parked here.

Her heels sounded loudly on the wooden porch. Before she could knock, the door opened. Liam Nolan smiled at her and held out his hand. She took it. "Welcome, Kate," he said, when she'd stepped inside. "It's been too long."

"Thank you, Liam. It's nice of you to say so."

"Please." He motioned toward a shabby sofa. "Would you like a cup of tea?"

"That would be lovely."

"Dominick should be back soon. He knows you're here. Shall we wait for him?"

Kate nodded. She had never been on warm terms with Patrick's youngest brother.

Liam busied himself in the kitchen. She could hear the sounds of his movement, china tinkling, the kettle whistling, a drawer opening and closing.

"Shall I help you?" she called out.

"No, thanks." He appeared in the doorway carrying a tray. "I've managed to put it together."

The biscuits were the commercial kind, but the tea was hot and sustaining. She had poured her second cup when Dominick walked through the front door.

"Kate," he said coolly. "To what do we owe the honor?"

She came directly to the point. "Kevin is in jail."

''Where?'' Dominick asked sharply.

''Long Kesh.''

''That's impossible.''

Kate felt a tiny nerve throb in her temple. *Impossible* was the murder of her husband that had never in six long years been investigated. *Impossible* was her sixteen-year-old-son in Long Kesh prison on a drug charge. She couldn't bring herself to speak.

Liam broke in. ''What is the charge against him, Kate?''

''Trafficking in narcotics. They found an ounce of cocaine on him. A man was killed.''

''Was it a setup?'' Dominick asked.

Kate shook her head. ''I don't think so. No one knew he was there. Apparently the house had been under surveillance for quite some time. The police happened to go in when Kevin was there.''

Dominick frowned. ''Then what?''

''He was arrested and kept overnight. He saw the judge this morning.''

''Have you an attorney?''

''Dylan McCarthy.''

''Who presided?''

''Rodney Thompson.''

Liam's voice was kinder than Dominick's, patient, interested. ''He's the best Kevin could hope for. What happened?''

Kate bit her lip. She waited until she could be sure her voice was steady. ''Dylan asked to have more time with Kevin. The judge agreed but refused to set bail. Kevin has to wait for his arraignment in Long Kesh.''

''That makes no sense at all.'' Dominick stared at Kate. ''Is this his first arrest on a drug charge?''

''It's his first arrest ever.''

Over Kate's head, Liam's eyes met his brother's. "Have you heard anything, Liam?" Dominick asked.

"Nothing."

Dominick turned his attention back to Kate. "Give us some time. We'll have answers for you in a few days."

"What about Kevin?" Kate fought back her desperation. "He needs protection. There are people in prison with very long memories."

Liam poured her another cup of tea. "Why don't you go to your new friends, Kate? You're cozy with the prime minister and the RUC. Why not ask them to intervene?"

She looked at him steadily. "I'm still an Irish Catholic, Dominick and this is still Ulster."

Dominick grunted. "Don't worry about Kevin. We'll see to it that nothing happens to him."

Dominick frowned. "Who do we have in the Cage?"

"Danny Boyle is there and Fergus Feeney. They're the last of the political prisoners."

"Kevin won't be placed with them. We need someone else."

Liam thought. "What about Andrew Halloran?"

"What's he in for?"

Liam looked over at Kate. "You don't want to know."

Kate bit down on her lip. "Surely they won't keep him with adult felons."

Dominick stood and began to pace. "We can't be sure of that. First, we must find out why they've locked him up. It's unusual."

"Why is it unusual?" Kate's voice was bitter.

Dominick stopped his pacing and stood in front of her, tall, lean, a younger, angrier version of Patrick.

"British justice is relatively sympathetic to drug offenders, Catholic as well as Protestant. Only political crimes are given stiff sentences. This isn't coincidental. One thing is certain. Someone important wants something from Kevin." He stared at her, the message in his eyes unreadable. "Or else it's you."

"I beg your pardon."

"Perhaps it's you they want."

"What could anyone want of me?"

He smiled mockingly. "To see if it can be done."

"If what can be done?"

"If the saintly Kathleen Nolan is corruptible."

Twelve

Kevin, his hands hobbled, climbed into the bus and looked down the long row of seats. A dozen men, ugly men, all older and ravaged looking, sat sprawled, legs apart, heads thrown back, a challenge to anyone attempting to invade their space.

Heart hammering, Kevin sat down in the first empty spot and looked out the window. The worst, the unthinkable, had happened to him, to Kevin Nolan of Ardara. He was going to Long Kesh, the Maze, the Cages, a place so horrible even his uncles never spoke of it. How had he come to this? He was done with it all. He'd resolved to stay away from trouble, to settle in, to regain his life as it once was. One mistake, a single act of poor judgment and he was finished. The unfairness of it sickened him. He hadn't wanted to hold the bag of cocaine. He was only delivering it to Sean. It had been in his hand for less than a minute. He'd told Tim he wanted no part of it. Why hadn't he refused to hold it all?

He was paralyzed with fear. Even his tears were frozen. What would happen to him in a cell with men who'd robbed and murdered? Perhaps he could pray. He discarded the idea. God had given up on him long ago. His mother would help him. Never in his life had she let him down. She would move heaven and earth to secure his release. He relaxed. If anyone could get him out it was his mother. She was probably waiting for him even now.

He paid no attention to the twisting and turning of the bus as it passed through the wide streets of Belfast onto the Motorway leading to the outskirts of the city. He lowered one eyelid, the one closest to the window, closing out the brick town houses constructed after the Troubles, still little better than tenements, the red, white and blue curbs of the footpaths, the British flag, Loyalist territory. He wanted to sleep, to make it all disappear, but he was afraid.

The bus stopped in front of a chain-link fence. A man stepped out of the guardhouse and motioned it through the gate. Slowly it rolled down the rain-wet car park and stopped for a second time in front of a row of buildings.

As if on cue, the men in the bus stood. Kevin lurched to his feet. Systematically they all filed out of the bus and into the building where they lined up in front of a uniformed guard and a small, ordinary-looking man in street clothes.

When they were all assembled, the man spoke quietly to the guard who nodded and made notes on a small pad. Then the man cleared his throat and spoke. "I am the warden, Kenneth Edwards. You are here in Long Kesh. Today you will shower, shave and dress in prison uniform. Then you will be shown to your cells. Tomorrow you will be taken to your labor positions. If you behave and follow the rules, your sentence may be lessened, even commuted." He cleared his throat again. "Good luck."

Kevin heard only half of it. His mother wasn't here.

He would have to strip and shower in front of these men. His terror returned.

Slowly he followed the prisoners who shuffled through another door where a man in a mustard-colored jumpsuit handed him a towel, a bar of soap, underwear, a plastic bag and a uniform identical to his own.

Kevin watched as the prisoners began to disrobe. "What are ye waitin' for?" the man snarled.

Hurriedly, cheeks burning, Kevin began to take off his clothes. Low walls separated shower stalls. He stepped into one, lathered the soap in his palms and swiped his hands over his chest, once, twice, then rinsed and stepped out. He wrapped the lower half of his body in the inadequate towel and, somehow, managed to pull on the despised clothing. The plastic bag confused him at first but after watching the other inmates he stuffed his own clothing inside and gave it to the prisoner in charge.

Ten minutes later he was inside a cell, alone, seated on the bottom of a two-tiered bunk. He looked around. A single lightbulb dangled from the ceiling above an open latrine. The walls were gray and bare. Shoes were prohibited. Plastic slippers, gathered at the ankle were poor protection against the damp cold of the floor. Thank God he was alone. The tears that had eluded him all day threatened to spill over. He looked around for a clock. There was none. How would he survive here?

Neil Anderson tapped his pencil against his desk and frowned at the report in front of him. He was frustrated. For the first time he doubted his ability to resolve something he'd taken on. Perhaps his cause was an impossible one. Drug-involved crime was a way of life for city-dwellers. Certainly London wasn't exempt, nor was

Dublin, or any of the larger European or American cities. Belfast, once relatively drug-free in the Catholic areas during the active reign of the Irish Republican Army, should be no different. Why, then, the full focus on Belfast? Something didn't add up, something that had nothing to do with the manufactured explanations of those who'd recruited him.

Neil believed he had the answer and it had nothing to do with the cautious explanation afforded him. The explanation offered him was a reasonable one. The eyes of the world were on the peace process. Britain's reputation, as well as America's and the United Nations, was involved, the prime minister had explained. Censorship by Amnesty International was a terrible stigma. The Good Friday Agreement, the power sharing solution wrought out by the combined efforts of Ireland, England and America, was being held up and scrutinized by the world. Tony Blair, stung by the European Court of Human Rights who found Britain guilty of violations more times than any other signatory since 1950, wanted no mention of the rise of organized crime in Northern Ireland, nor did he want the RUC's policing efforts to be held up against those of the IRA and found wanting. The influx of drugs and the influence of drug lords in the city of Belfast must be stopped before they became entrenched. His arguments were appealing, idealistic ones. They were also hogwash. Neil resented the secrecy, the lies. He'd earned the right to know what he was dealing with, although if the truth had been presented to him from the beginning he would have flatly turned it down.

Neil's expertise was terrorist operations. He dealt with adults, criminals, men and women who knew the score, fanatics who expected to die. He had no experience with troubled children like Kevin Nolan, the children of confused parents who'd given their best. The horror of it all was that children would be sacrificed and he had no concrete knowledge of what he was dealing with, although an idea had wedged itself into his mind, an idea he couldn't shake.

His thoughts turned to Kate Nolan. What he was about to do to her son caused the bile to rise in his throat. She didn't deserve this. She hadn't asked for it. But Neil was a marked man. His timetable had been established long before he'd agreed on the Ulster assignment. At the moment Kevin Nolan was his best chance. His only consolation was that his work here in Belfast might ultimately spare the sons of many mothers.

The sick feeling worked its way down to his stomach. Somehow he didn't think Kate would be swayed by such an argument. From their brief acquaintance, he knew her children meant everything. Martyrdom held no allure for women like Kate. They were mothers before anything else.

Neil had never before been to Long Kesh. The tin, corrugated roofs of the outer buildings, the thin walls and the amateur nature of security surprised him. Since the release of nearly all the political prisoners, it stood half-empty, a brooding reminder of a dismal period in Ulster's history.

Because he was Special Forces, he was ushered into the warden's private office. Kenneth Edwards, a soft-spoken, serious man offered him a cup of tea.

''No, thank you.''

Edwards pulled a handkerchief from his pocket and meticulously wiped his hands. ''The prisoner is on his way. I can arrange for someone to stay with you if you'd like.''

Neil's eyebrow lifted. "For what purpose?"

The warden shrugged. "Protection?"

"The boy is sixteen years old."

"He could be dangerous. Desperate types usually are."

"I'm sure I can handle myself."

"As you say." Edwards walked to the door and opened it. "I shall be nearby if you need assistance."

Neil's lips twitched. Kenneth Edwards was a strange sort for a prison warden. He appeared bookish, studious, more the university professor type than a warden. The door opened and a burly guard entered the room with Kevin. The boy was cuffed and hobbled.

Neil stood and held out his hand. "Give me the keys."

The guard's eyes narrowed. "I've my orders, sir. No prisoner walks freely without permission from Mr. Edwards."

Keeping his hand outstretched, Neil spoke again, very softly. "I'll take full responsibility. Now, once again, give me the keys."

For a full minute the two men took each other's measure. Then the guard dropped the keys into Neil's hand. "That will be all. I'll call for you when I'm ready."

Without a word, the guard left the room.

Neil dropped to his knees and inserted the key into the center of the leg iron. It dropped away. He did the same with the cuffs. Finally Kevin stood before him, rubbing his sore wrists.

Neil stepped back, waiting for the boy to say something. Kevin remained silent, wary, arms at his sides.

"Are you all right, Kevin?"

"Aye."

Neil came right to the point. "Have you had enough?"

Kevin's lids dropped but not before Neil saw the light leap into his eyes. Again the boy said nothing.

Neil motioned to a chair. "Sit down, lad."

Kevin sat and Neil continued. "A large shipment of drugs has intentionally been allowed into Belfast. I need to know who in this city has the money to finance such an operation. I need an informant. No one will suspect you."

"No one will believe I'm in the drug trade on that level," Kevin offered. "I'm an amateur. People on that scale don't let people like me near them."

"These people will."

"Why?" Kevin looked up, freckled cheeks, eyes the blue-green of the sun-warmed Atlantic.

Neil cursed under his breath, jammed his hands into his pockets and began to pace. Minutes passed. Finally he collected himself and sat down across from Kevin. He spoke deliberately, tonelessly. "What I'm asking you to do isn't pretty, Kevin. If I had anyone else, I would use him."

"Go on."

"You know these men."

Neil watched the boy's jaw harden. He already knew or perhaps he only suspected. He pushed on. "Do you know who I'm referring to, Kevin?"

"No."

"I believe drugs are being trafficked into Belfast by high-ranking members of the Irish Republican Army."

Kevin's face whitened. He leaped to his feet, hands clenched, voice shaking. "You bastard! You want me to snitch on my own blood."

"I want you to save yourself and others like yourself. There's no good that can come of this. This isn't a cause, Kevin, it's a profit machine. A machine that thrives on the addiction of children, on the destruction of lives."

"I won't do it."

Neil stood. "Think about it." He waved his arm. "This can't be pleasant for you. I can make it go away. You'll be pardoned, under certain conditions, of course."

"What conditions?"

"You'll have to attend a program for drug offenders."

Kevin grimaced. "I don't need a program. I wasn't going to do it anymore. This whole thing is a mistake. I didn't want the bag. Tim told me to take it back to the car. I told him I wouldn't do it—" He stopped.

"But you did."

"You don't understand. It isn't like that. It was all a game. I did it because—" He stopped.

Neil waited but the boy had stopped talking.

"These are the facts, Kevin. If you had been where you were supposed to be, in Ardara, in school, you wouldn't be here right now. You were in the wrong place with the wrong people. That has to change or you'll be here again and again. Is that the kind of life you want?"

Kevin swiped the hair back impatiently from his forehead. "No."

"Will you help me?"

"I won't inform on Liam and Dominick."

"If they aren't involved, you have nothing to worry about. If they are, you have nothing to feel guilty about."

"I can't," Kevin repeated.

Neil moved toward the door. "Think about it," he said again. "You know where to reach me. Call me. It doesn't matter what time it is."

Kevin sat in the semidarkness of his cell pretending to sleep. The mattress was thin and the blanket meager warmth against the evening chill. His life had closed in on him. It wasn't supposed to be like this. He hadn't intended to become so involved. It had seemed easy at first, harmless, a way to earn extra money. His mother wouldn't allow him to work during the school year until his marks improved. Why shouldn't he earn a bit of extra cash just by passing on what someone wanted? By the time he'd realized the drawbacks, he was already in. To back out took a bit of planning. He knew what he had to do. He had been willing to do it, if only everyone would let him. It was too late now. He was stuck. Unless he went along with the police, he would be sent up for trial and, possibly, prison. He didn't like the looks of it. But to inform on drug lords, men who knew the ropes and had nothing to lose. Kevin shuddered. If they found him out, it was a death sentence. Liam and Dominick had nothing to do with drugs. Kevin was sure of it. But he was equally sure they couldn't help him. The reality of his predicament struck him. What could he have been thinking? He pressed his face against the pillow. Tears, hot and self-pitying spilled down his cheeks. Where was his mother? He wanted his mother. Exhaustion overtook him. His eyelids drooped and he slept.

Somewhere, in the cavern of darkness shrouding his cell, Kevin felt something pull him out of a sound sleep. On the edge of consciousness, he felt a presence. His eyelids flickered. A feeble finger of light pierced the gloom. Beside him, so close he felt the warmth of his breath, was a face.

A surge of adrenaline coursed through him and he jerked into instant wakefulness. Pulse pounding against his throat and temples, he stared in horror at the figure beside him.

The man grinned. "Take it easy, lad," he whispered. "I'm your cellmate."

Kevin's stomach cramped. His breathing was hard and labored. He swallowed, tried to speak, and couldn't. Nothing was worse than this. He wouldn't stay here. Nothing would make him stay here. Slowly he drew his legs up under him. Barely, he managed the words. "What do you want?"

The man's harsh, flat-planed face split into another grin. A huge gap separated his front teeth. "Well, now. Let me think on it. A friendly welcome, maybe? Are you up to a friendly welcome, lad?"

"Go away."

The man threw back his head and laughed. "Go away, the lad says," he jeered.

Kevin looked around. Where was the guard? Surely a guard patrolled through the night. "Get away from me," he said in a loud voice. "Get away or I'll call the guard."

"Easy, now." The man backed away. "I'll leave you alone. It's nearly mornin', now, isn't it?"

Kevin's breathing normalized. He waited until he heard the top bunk creak and the man's legs disappear over the edge. Then he climbed out of bed, grabbed hold of the bars and shook them, hard. "Guard," he called out, disturbing the quiet of the cell blocks. "Help! Guard!"

Two guards, one armed with a billy club, the other with a gun in full firing position, ran down the hall to his cell. "What's happened here?" one yelled out.

"Please," Kevin cried out. "I need to speak with Mr. Anderson."

The guard with the gun lowered it to his side. "It's the middle of the night. You can't speak to anyone in the middle of the night."

"He said to call him at any time, any time at all. Please, just take me to him."

The next afternoon, his mind drained of emotion, Kevin followed Neil through the front door of a run-down but comfortable-looking establishment on the corner of a long row of houses in similar condition. This was where he would live, indefinitely, until Anderson decided otherwise. The sign over the lintel read Tranquility House but Kevin wasn't fooled. He knew a halfway house for drug offenders when he saw one.

He didn't hear the mumbled conversation between Neil and the young man seated beside the phone. Content to sit on the lumpy couch across from the blazing fire, Kevin closed his eyes and dozed.

"Kevin." Neil shook his shoulder. "This is David Martin. He'll tell you how to go along. I'll be contacting you in a bit. Relax and settle in. All of this takes getting accustomed to. Don't worry about anything at the moment. You'll have plenty of time to adjust."

"Will you call my mother?"

"I already have."

Kevin wet his lips. "Is she—" He stopped and began again. "How is she doing?"

"She's relieved that you're out of prison. As soon as you're able to have visitors, she'll come."

Kevin nodded.

"I'll be leaving now," Neil said. "Call if you need anything."

David Martin had longish brown-blond hair and round, rimless glasses. He was very thin but his smile was pleasant. He held out his hand. "I'll need to see your bag."

"Excuse me?"

"Hand over your bag, please. I need to check it."

"Why?"

"Drugs."

Kevin gave David the bag and watched him search the pockets of his shirts and jeans, the linings of his jacket and the zippered compartments of the carryall. There had been no opportunity for Kevin to go home. The clothes were not his. They were new, of the basic variety, gratis of Neil Anderson and the Special Forces.

David Martin stood. "Welcome to *Tranquility House,* Kevin. Most of the lads are in class right now. I'll show you to your bed." He checked his watch. "It's nearly time for dinner."

"I'm not hungry."

"It doesn't matter. We all show for dinner and for classes. You'll get used to it. You may even come to like it. Most of us do." He smiled again. "Come along."

Kevin followed his new jailor down a narrow hallway to a small room with a slanted ceiling, two beds covered with cozy quilts and a window that looked out on a small garden.

David set Kevin's bag on the bed nearest the window. "We give all newcomers the bed with the view. It makes them feel better. Your roommate will join you in a bit. His name is Joe Sullivan. He's a good lad. You'll like him. Everyone does. I'll see you at dinner.''

Alone again, Kevin looked around the room at the peeling wallpaper, the buckled wood floors and stained lampshades. He thought of his bedroom at home, of the rich wood moldings and recessed lighting, the warm bookshelves filled with his CDs, magazines and favorite novels, the carved headboard and the scene lovingly painted on the ceiling by his mother, the solar system, planets circling the sun.

David Martin was a good sort. Kevin could see that. No doubt Joe Sullivan would be as well. Most likely he would grow accustomed to the newness of it all. But he was very sure he would never come to like it.

Thirteen

The small, grassy patch on the edge of the Crumlin Road bordering the Catholic Falls and the Protestant Shankill was empty that Saturday afternoon. Earlier that day there had been a street festival. It was understood by everyone living in the two working class communities that only Protestants were welcome. But now the field was deserted, food wraps, crumpled papers and bottles the only evidence left of the busy afternoon.

A boy somewhere around sixteen years old kicked his soccer ball against the side of an abandoned roadhouse and casually surveyed the empty field. It looked peaceful, but he knew from painful experience that appearances could be deceiving. Another lad, the same age, emerging from a house on the corner, gave him courage. He pitched his voice just loud enough for his friend to hear.

"Sean, will you kick the ball around with me for a while?"

The lad flashed him an impudent smile. "Haven't you had enough beatings, lad? Maybe your head hasn't healed yet."

"Come along," the boy urged him. "No one will notice. The prods are tired out from their day."

"They'll notice." His friend laughed and jogged toward the patch of green. "Let's give them something to notice."

Fifteen uninterrupted minutes passed while the boys played and talked, tossing the ball back and forth between them, eyes watchful and alert, always focused on the dismal row of roadhouses on the east side of the green. The sky darkened and for a time they believed their illicit venture would come to nothing. The first boy relaxed and began to enjoy the game. Then, out of nowhere, a sharp crack jerked him back to attention.

He turned toward the sound. On the broken pavement leading to the Shankill, a group of young men had gathered. Something dripped down the boy's forehead and into his right eye. He wiped it away and looked at his hand. It was covered with blood. All at once he felt searing pain. A well-aimed stone had found its mark on his head. The crowd from the Shankill moved forward purposefully.

His friend threw an arm around his shoulder. "Are you all right, lad?"

"Aye." He kept his eyes on the crowd.

"Let's go."

Both boys backed away. The Shankill mob broke into a run. The boys ran, too, separating at the edge of the Crumlin Road, disappearing down the maze of twisted streets into the Falls.

Emily Quinn, eleven years old and filled with the importance of her responsibility, had just crossed the street with her new baby brother. He was asleep in his pram. She gave Sean Dempsey no more than a passing glance as he ran by. Turning the corner that led to the patch of grass where no Catholic child had the nerve to play, she meant only to give the baby his first glimpse of green. The mob was upon her before she could scream.

Kate received the phone call in her government office on Donegall Square. It was a Wednesday. Her day had been unproductive, her mind filled with Kevin and the odd circumstances surrounding his release, circumstances that involved a certain Neil Anderson. She wasn't quite sure how she felt about the Special Forces agent and his involvement with her son. A week had passed since Kevin's release and she had yet to see him. It was difficult to concentrate.

"Kate Nolan speaking," she said into the mouthpiece.

"This is Maired Quinn," the voice said. "I'm callin' about an incident that happened last Saturday past concernin' my daughter, Emily, and my baby son."

Kate stifled a sigh. Another complaint. There were so many, most without evidence. "Go on."

"Can you come to us, Mrs. Nolan? I want you to meet my daughter and hear her story."

"Of course." Kate picked up a pencil. "Give me your location."

The neighborhood was a dreary one, treeless, with small houses set close to the road. The working class neighborhoods of Belfast, Ladybrook, Andersonstown, Turf Lodge, the Clonard, Ballymurphy were dismal in their similarity. Tiny, crowded Victorian houses made long rows down dozens of small lanes and streets leading off the main roads. Chimney smoke coated the sky with a dirty haze. Graffiti covered blocks of gray stucco flats. Broken pavement, convenience stores and pubs, off licenses, fruit stands and, occasionally, an empty

Laundromat and boarded up storefronts lined the streets, landmarks of a working class neighborhood, a neighborhood much like the one where her husband had grown up.

Kate found the house immediately. She pushed open the low gate and climbed the steps. Mrs. Quinn, a pretty, tired-looking woman, opened the door before Kate could knock.

"Thank you for comin', Mrs. Nolan. I didn't know where else to turn. Patrick Nolan was a great friend to us."

Kate was surprised. "I didn't realize you knew my husband."

Mrs. Quinn nodded. "Without his help, Davie, my son, would be in Long Kesh." She hurried on. "Davie isn't IRA, Mrs. Nolan. So many of the boys who are lifted aren't, you know."

Kate nodded. "Yes, I know."

The woman pressed a handkerchief to her nose. "It isn't Davie I called you about."

"You said you wanted me to hear your daughter's story."

Maired Quinn blinked back tears. "I never thought such a thing could happen, not to a young girl who never hurt anyone."

Kate's expression remained serene but her hands curled into fists. *Please don't let it be a child who was hurt.* She couldn't think clearly when the victim was a child. "May I sit down?" she asked.

The woman lifted her hands to her cheeks. "Oh for pity's sake, where are my manners? Please, come into the sittin' room. I've a fire goin' and a tray set out."

Working-class women in Belfast were, out of necessity, unfailingly practical. They refused to sit around nursing old wounds. There simply wasn't time for it. Maired Quinn was no different. Kate followed her into a cozy room with a couch, two overstuffed chairs, a coffee table and the inevitable floral-patterned area rug.

"Sit here by the fire, Mrs. Nolan, and take the chill off while I pour your tea. Do you take anything in it?" She waited until Kate was settled before handing her the cup and saucer.

"No, this is grand." Kate sipped the hot brew, mentally counted to ten, and plunged in. "Tell me about your daughter."

"I want you to see her."

"I shall," Kate promised, "but first I'd like you to tell me about her."

The woman's lips tightened.

Kate set down her cup. "This isn't my field, Mrs. Quinn," she explained. "I have a dreadful feeling that your daughter has been brutalized in some way by the RUC. If it were anything else you wouldn't have called me. I don't have the sense of detachment necessary to see your daughter's injuries and then to hear what happened to her. Most likely I won't remember a thing. It would be in your best interests, and in hers, to do as I ask."

The two women stared at each other in silence for several minutes. Then Maired began. "Emily was out walkin' her brother when she saw Sean Dempsey run past. Why the lad didn't call out a warnin' is a mystery, but he didn't. My Emily was about to turn the corner toward the green when the Shankill lads were on top of her. They threw the pram aside."

Kate pressed her hand against her mouth. "Was the baby hurt?"

"A miracle saved him, Mrs. Nolan. He wasn't even

scratched. The pram landed on its side but the baby was strapped in.''

Kate nodded.

''My Emily wasn't so lucky.'' She pressed the handkerchief against her nose. ''They were on her before she knew what happened. Maybe they didn't know she was a wee girl until they were finished with her.''

Kate swallowed. ''What did they do?''

The woman's voice cracked. ''They beat her and left her for dead. Even her own father wouldn't have recognized her.''

''I don't understand. Protestants have never followed anyone into the Falls.''

''They were drunk, Mrs. Nolan. There was a street fair that day, for Protestants only. Two of our boys waited until it was over and then tried to use the field. When they did, the Shankill mob came after them.''

''Did you go to the police?''

Maired's laugh was ragged and filled with the bitter rage of hopelessness. ''We did. Sean Dempsey recognized several of them. But it did no good. They cover up for each other. My child is bleedin' and broken and no one is punished. They won't even investigate for lack of evidence.'' She pointed toward the back of the house. ''If that child lyin' in the other room isn't evidence, then nothin' ever will be.''

Kate stared down at her hands. They were shaking. ''How old is your daughter?''

''My Emily is eleven years old. Can you help me?''

''Yes,'' said Kate. ''I can order an investigation and refer you to a lawyer. It may take time, but I promise you, something will be done.''

''We can't pay.''

''There will be no fee.''

Maired Quinn sighed and leaned back in her chair.
Her face caved in and the tears began to flow, accompanied by loud uncontrollable sobs. "My husband said,
no, you wouldn't be bothered, but I knew it would be
all right once you knew."

Kate's professional facade cracked. Maired was a
mother, a mother just like herself but with little education, few expectations and even fewer resources. She
walked around the coffee table, knelt down and drew
the woman into her arms. She felt her stiffen. Kate was
prepared for resistance. The Irish were not a demonstrative race. Outside of a handshake, displays of affection embarrassed them. She persisted. After several
minutes, she felt Maired's body relax and her weeping
subside.

Gently she sat back on her heels. "I'd like to have
a look at Emily now, if I may."

Maired scrubbed the last of the tears from her face
and stood. "Follow me. I'll introduce you. Don't expect
her to say much. Her jaw is wired shut and it's an effort
for her to speak."

Only Kate's innate poise acquired from years of marriage to a public figure saved her. The sight of the little
girl, thin to the point of emaciation, bruises fading to a
sickly yellow-brown, plaster casts covering most of her
head, both arms and one leg, unnerved her.

"There's someone here to see you, Emily," said her
mother.

"Hello, love," Kate said softly, covering the child's
two exposed fingers with her hand. "My name is Kate
Nolan. I came to help your mother." She watched the
little girl arrange her wired mouth to form the words.
"Don't try to talk," she warned. "I only came to say
hello."

The child settled back and tossed restlessly on her pillow.

Kate sat on the low stool beside the bed. In low soothing tones she spoke of small things, the end of Lent, the coming of long summer days, the baby who had miraculously survived.

Emily's eyes were clear blue slits behind the white plaster of the head cast. Kate watched them light with memory. She hoped there was a smile beneath the plaster. Finally the child's eyes fluttered and closed.

"She'll sleep now," said Maired.

Carefully, so as not to wake the little girl, the two women left the room. Maired closed the door behind her.

"Thank you for taking so much time with us, Mrs. Nolan," she said.

Kate smiled warmly. "I would love to come back and see Emily when she's well again."

"Please, do that. If you care to have a look at the green, I'll show it to you."

"Don't trouble yourself. I'll drive by on my way out."

"Have a care. Those hooligans won't know you from anyone else."

Kate parked her car on the south edge of the pathetic patch of weeds and dying grass that passed for a park in the Falls. She walked across and back twice, trying to imagine the conditions that would produce a mentality who thought nothing of nearly beating to death a little girl for no reason other than that she was Catholic. Who were these people, no more than children themselves, and who were their parents who'd fed their rage from infancy? Perhaps it wasn't fair to blame their parents. After all, she was Kevin's mother. How much had she known of her son's activities?

She climbed back into the car, looked at her watch and turned the wheel in the direction of the Ormeau Road Barracks. There was no reason to go home. Deirdre was at Queen's and Kevin was at Tranquility House with no access to visitors. She would stay in the city for the night and drive home in the morning.

It was late afternoon, but Kate didn't think Neil Anderson was the kind of man who clocked in. She needed answers and he hadn't returned her call. She picked up her mobile phone and punched in the number of the RUC Barracks.

"Neil Anderson, please."

"He is away just now. May I give him your message?"

"This is Kate Nolan. Tell him to reach me at the Stranmillis Guest House. I'll be here in Belfast." She gave him the number.

"I'll tell him, Mrs. Nolan."

Another turn in the opposite direction took her down the Malone Road with its lovely brick homes and well-tended gardens, into University Road. Just past Queen's, she made a sharp U-turn up the shopping area of the Stranmillis Road where pedestrians hurried to make last-minute purchases before heading home for the evening. Stranmillis was an upscale middle class neighborhood, lined with trendy boutiques, butcher and vegetable shops, restaurants and a wine store. Kate had chosen a small bed-and-breakfast just behind Stranmillis facing the Botanic Garden. The serenity of the neighborhood appealed to her. Here she could forget the evening news, Orange marches and children in body casts.

She picked up her message from the silver tray in

the hallway and read the name on the note. Neil Anderson. She climbed the stairs to the second floor, found her room, kicked off her shoes, picked up the phone and dialed his number. He answered on the first ring, just his name, no title. For some reason it pleased her to know that he required nothing more than that.

"Hello," she said breathlessly, "this is Kate Nolan."

A slight pause. "Hello, Kate. How are you?"

She found her balance. "A bit confused."

"How so?"

"Dylan McCarthy told me it was due to your intervention that my son was released from Long Kesh."

"Yes."

"You could have called me. I left several messages."

"We didn't leave each other on the best of terms. I thought it best if the news came from Mr. McCarthy."

"How is it possible that he was released?"

"I culled a few favors."

"I appreciate it, but why?"

She heard the release of his breath over the phone.

"I don't see prison as a cure for what ails Kevin. Where he is will be much better for him."

Kate's anger broke through. "Kevin is my son, Mr. Anderson. While I am grateful to you for bothering with him, you've placed him in a facility I know nothing about. I deeply resent that kind of high-handedness."

"Would you prefer that he be in prison?"

"Of course, not. What I prefer is that he be in a program of my choice, not yours."

"He's not a child, Kate."

"No," she snapped. "But neither is he an adult. I'm his mother and I know nothing about Tranquility House. How did you find this place and why am I not even allowed to visit?"

He ignored her first questions. "Kevin will be able to have visitors."

"When?"

"In three weeks."

Three weeks. Three weeks until she could see her son, touch him, learn the state of his mind. "That's a long time."

"Kate." She could hear the exasperation in his voice. "Why aren't you asking the important questions?"

"Such as?"

"Such as, how did Kevin arrive at this point and how can you be sure he doesn't fall back into it again?"

Was the man mad? Did he really know so little about the Irish, about children. "I don't know those things. Neither does any mother in the North of Ireland."

"I don't understand."

"Would you like to?"

"Yes."

"Then come with me, tomorrow. I'll show you what it's really like for us to live here."

"Do you think I don't know that?"

"Yes, Mr. Anderson, that's exactly what I do think."

"You won't shock me, Kate. I've seen parts of this planet that turned my stomach and that doesn't happen easily."

She was irrationally annoyed at his persistent use of her Christian name. Kate no longer wanted to be on a first-name basis with Neil Anderson. "You'll see a bit more if you agree to come with me, only this time it won't be a third world country. This time it will be your own, Mr. Anderson." She deliberately used his last name. "This time it will be red-haired, fair-skinned children who are the victims. Somehow, even though it shouldn't, that makes it harder to accept."

"Where and when do you want me?"

She gave him directions to the park.

"I'll be there at four o'clock tomorrow."

Minutes later, she was still staring at the phone, wondering what could possibly have come over her. The last thing she wanted was to spend the afternoon with Neil Anderson.

Fourteen

Deirdre stuffed her notes into her book bag, hoisted it to her shoulder and headed toward the exit door of her political science class. She'd seen Peter Clarke staring at her and deliberately waited until he'd filed out of the room. He'd approached her a few times since their meeting at the White Swan. She'd been pleasant but remote. He should have understood that she wasn't interested.

She wasn't doing particularly well in political science. She wanted nothing to do with government, history or politics. Those were national matters, not global ones. Deirdre was interested in numbers and science, in the large picture, the one in which all of mankind participated. Nationalism, petty boundary squabbles, haggling over territory and battle strategies held no appeal for her. Political science was a requirement, like composition and mastering an EU language. Nothing else would have coerced her into taking such a class if she had had a choice in the matter.

"Hello, Deirdre."

She froze.

Peter Clarke stepped in front of her. "We've an hour before medieval history. Would you like to go for a bite to eat?"

She shook her head. "I can't."

"Why not?"

"I'm meeting someone."

One eyebrow rose skeptically. "May I join you?"

"No." She'd said it too quickly. Now he would know there was no one. She wasn't sorry. He was too persistent. Anyone paying attention would know to leave her alone.

He grinned a brilliant, white-toothed grin that would have melted a normal eighteen-year-old girl's heart. But Deirdre wasn't normal. She'd been shaped by circumstance and the concept of letting anyone in left her wary if not jaded.

"Have I done something to offend you?"

She blushed and shifted the bag to her other shoulder. "No, of course not. We don't know each other well enough for that.

Without asking, he lifted the strap from her shoulder and effortlessly swung it over his. "We can fix that."

"No, we can't."

"Why not?"

Deirdre flipped her hair back over her shoulder and shoved her hands into the pockets of her denims. "I don't mean to be rude, Peter, but—"

"You remembered my name."

She stared at him. "We've had two classes together since the beginning of the term."

"Do you know everyone's name in your classes?"

"Generally, no. But I know everyone who is in *both* classes."

"You were saying?"

"It wouldn't work."

"What wouldn't?"

"Us."

"I'm not asking for your hand in marriage, Deirdre. I just want to spend a bit of time with you."

"Why bother?"

The smile faded. "To get to know you. Why does anyone bother?"

"Listen to me, Peter. You're probably a very nice person, but you're a Protestant."

"And?"

"I'm not."

He looked incredulous. "Are you telling me you can't have a meal with a Protestant? Do you think I'll curdle your food?"

She ignored his question. "Catholics and Protestants aren't friendly, Peter. Don't tell me you haven't noticed."

"Maybe out on the streets but not here. We're alike here."

"It's time you did notice. We're not alike at all. Look around you." She waved her arm to encompass the wave of students passing them by in twos and threes. "We sit in class together. We share meals and study areas. But we don't live together, pray together or recreate together. Only ten percent of our population crosses religious lines to marry and those who do are banned from political life and must accustom themselves to living in fear."

"I'm sorry about your father, Deirdre."

Her eyes narrowed. "How do you know about my father?"

"Everyone knows about Patrick Nolan."

"It was a long time ago."

"But you haven't forgotten it."

"It isn't something one forgets."

He looked down at the ground. "I promise to offer you nothing but tea or a Guinness. Will that do?"

She crossed her arms. "Why me? There must be others who would accept your invitation far more willingly."

"Thank you. I'm flattered."

"Don't grow another head or anything. It was just an observation."

He laughed and looked at the sky and wrinkled his brow as if deep in thought. "I like you. I like what you say when you answer questions in class. You're thoughtful and bright and compassionate. Intelligence appeals to me."

She stared at him. Whatever she'd expected, it wasn't this shy, sweet, vulnerable disclosure. Imagine a boy, a Protestant boy, saying such a thing to her. She felt herself wavering. It was only one meal. "I'll do it," she said, "but only this once."

"Really?" He looked elated. "You're serious?"

"Yes."

He held out his hand. "Come along then."

She hesitated. "I've agreed to a snack, Peter. That's all."

Deirdre could feel his disappointment but she wouldn't be bullied, no matter how nice he was.

They walked side by side, past the Gothic spires, the blue wrought iron gates with their gold posts, the cobblestones and iron gates, across the street to the Stranmillis Road.

"Have you always been like this or is it me?" he asked after they'd walked a block in silence.

"Like what?"

"Suspicious."

"I've already explained. Your religious persuasion makes me uncomfortable."

"Have you ever really known a Protestant?"

She shook her head. "I don't think so. There really hasn't been an opportunity or a need."

He stopped at a small tea shop with striped blue awnings. A cheerful-looking older woman with a broom in her hand waved them inside. "Hello, Peter." She stood on her toes to kiss his cheek. "How lovely to see you. There's a table all set by the window if you care to take it. I'll finish up here and be with you in a minute."

Deirdre settled herself in her seat. "Do you come here often?"

"Aye. I've been coming here since I was a wee lad. This is my grandmother's shop."

"That's your grandmother?"

"Aye. She's a character. My mum's nothing like her."

"You sound disappointed."

"Not really. It's just that Gran's such fun. Mum is the serious type."

"So is mine, but she's lovely just the same."

Peter nodded. "I've seen her picture. She's something of a celebrity."

"She's not fond of that part of her job."

"Tell me about her."

Deirdre was embarrassed. "There's nothing to tell. She's my mum, that's all."

"She must have enormous credentials to have the position she has."

Deirdre frowned. "Mum's actually quite shy, although no one would ever know it. She makes a very good first impression."

"Like her daughter?"

"I don't think so. Mum is actually a much more compassionate person than I am. She feeds everyone. It doesn't matter who it is. If you come to our door my mother will feed you, even if you're not hungry. She'll send you away with enough food to keep you for a month."

"Is she a good cook?"

Deirdre closed her eyes briefly and it seemed as if she could smell her mother's pot roast and potatoes. "Wonderful. No one cooks like Mum."

"Invite me, please."

She was saved from answering by Peter's grand-mother who bustled over with a pot of tea, a pitcher of milk and a basket of rich brown bread and butter. "Here we are, darlings, just the way Peter likes it."

"Gran, this is my friend, Deirdre Nolan. Deirdre, meet my grandmother, Mrs. Adrianne Richards."

"I'm very pleased to meet you, Deirdre. What can I get for you today?"

"Something sweet. What do you recommend?"

Peter spoke first. "There isn't anything like Gran's desserts."

"I've trifle today and apple cake with vanilla sauce," his grandmother said.

Peter glanced over at Deirdre. She shrugged her shoulders. "They both sound wonderful."

He decided for them. "Two apple cakes."

Mrs. Richards smiled again and her eyes disappeared into the folds of her face. "An inspired choice. It's really the better of the two."

Deirdre laughed out loud. "You should have told us that in the beginning."

The woman's eyes twinkled. "But I couldn't have,

love. It came to me for the first time when Peter ordered.''

''You're very funny, Mrs. Richards.''

''And you're very quick, a grand and necessary virtue in a woman.''

''Thank you.''

''You're very welcome. I'll be off now to dish up your apple cake.''

Deirdre waited until their hostess disappeared into the kitchen. ''She's lovely.''

''She likes you.''

''How do you know?''

''I can always tell when Gran likes someone. She teases them.'' He leaned forward. ''She's going to be very disappointed if you don't come again.''

''I'll come,'' Deirdre assured him, ''and I'll bring all my friends. This might become our new favorite haunt.''

He laughed.

''Seriously. Has she always run this shop?''

''Ever since my grandda died. She raised my mother on her own. Mum's an only child. She worked in the shop while growing up. Gran says she resented it. She doesn't come in at all now.''

''What about your father?''

''What about him?''

''Does he come in?''

''Sometimes, when he's not working. Gran always gives him a free meal.''

Mrs. Richards interrupted them carrying two generous, steaming bowls of apple cake, drizzled in thick cream.

Deirdre moaned with delight.

Peter grinned. ''I hope your appetite is bigger than

you are. It would be a shame to see you take two bites and fill up. Gran would be insulted.''

Deirdre picked up her spoon and scooped an enormous portion into her mouth. ''Actions speak louder than words,'' she said when the first delicious bite had settled in her stomach.

''Is that a challenge?''

''If you like.''

''All right, then. Would you care to place a small wager?''

''The terms?''

''If you eat one apple cake and a trifle, I'll take you to the cinema tomorrow night.''

''And if I don't?''

''You can pay for the cinema.''

Deirdre thought of her mother. What would Kate say? Suddenly Deirdre was no longer in the mood for sweets. She set down her spoon. ''I don't think so, Peter. I'm sorry. I really am. But it's impossible.''

Neil and Kevin sat across from each other in the shabby, but comfortable, sitting room of Tranquility House, a room similar to a thousand others in the working class neighborhoods of Belfast. The boy was silent and very pale. He looked thinner.

Neil wondered if he was eating and if the shock of his circumstances had taken a more serious toll than expected. After all, Kevin wasn't the normal criminal profile. His surroundings, while palatial to some, were most likely an unpleasant adjustment for the son of a famous lawyer.

The sympathetic direction of his thoughts shook him and he recovered immediately. He had a job to do and if Kevin had been innocent of wrongdoing he wouldn't be sitting across from him now. "Your mother is anxious to see you. If all goes well, you should be allowed visitors after two more weeks."

Kevin's glance, fixed somewhere over Neil's right shoulder, did not waver. He remained silent.

Neil cut to the chase. "Are you frightened?"

The barest flicker of an eyelash, nothing more.

Neil leaned forward. "I don't know the extent of the danger you'll be in, Kevin. For anyone else, I would say the risk is considerable. For you, it may not be. I'm here to make very sure you understand the possibilities."

"What's your point?"

"There are no guarantees. Are you sure you want to do this?"

"Do I have options?"

"One."

The boy's laugh was bitter. "No, thanks."

"Do you have any questions?"

"When do I start?"

"We'll wait a while. You're here to heal yourself. This is a chance to think about the life and friends you've chosen. All crime begins and ends with drugs, Kevin. The sessions here will help you with that."

Kevin waved his arm. "When I'm through with that, what will I do for you?"

"Behave normally. Listen. Avoid attention. Report what you see. That's all."

"I've never run in those circles. What if they don't accept me?"

"You were in deeply enough to make this a foregone conclusion. It was only a matter of time before you would have found these people yourself."

"They aren't stupid, you know. Everyone will know where I've been. Everyone will suspect me."

"I don't think so. You'll be just another boy from the Falls interested in making money without working for it."

The burning color was back in the boy's cheeks. "You don't know anything about it."

"Tell me."

Kevin's lips tightened stubbornly.

Neil shook his head. "You know nothing about it, either, lad."

"More than you."

"You won't find what you're looking for. One can only hope, when this is over, that you see the light and point yourself in another direction. Easy money isn't the answer, nor is the dulling of pain or whatever it is you're going through. You've a family and from what I've seen, it's a good one. Not everyone has that. Do them a favor and walk away from this."

"I would if I could."

Neil believed him. Unfortunately he needed the boy first. If Kate Nolan's son was the sacrifice for answers to the burgeoning influx of drugs into West Belfast, so be it. He stood. "Hold that thought. I'll be in touch."

"I can hardly wait," Kevin muttered.

"You're a cheeky lad, Kevin Nolan. Keep that part of yourself under wraps and you just might survive this."

Fifteen

They met at the corner of Falls Road and Northumberland Street. He was already waiting for her, leaning against his car; jacket slung over one shoulder in a relaxed pose. There was something about him, something she couldn't quite put her finger on, that separated him from the typical law enforcement agent, a harnessing of emotion, perhaps, beneath his pleasant manners and calm reserve, tension held back, simmering. In that, he was very like herself. She pulled up behind his car and parked.

Kate resisted the impulse to check her lipstick in the rearview mirror. This wasn't a social engagement, after all. She stepped out of the car and walked toward him. "Hello."

He turned and smiled. "You've brought the sunlight."

Kate laughed and looked at the faint rays of milky light struggling to pierce the cloud cover. "In a manner of speaking, although I can't say that I had anything to do with it."

"You're in a good mood this afternoon."

"I took a nap. Rest agrees with me. Can you give me any news of Kevin?"

"I've heard that he's progressing. You should be able to visit soon."

Kate drew a deep trembling breath and changed the subject. "This is the park. What do you think of it?"

Neil looked around. "Is this it?"

"I'm afraid so."

"It isn't much of a park, is it?"

"It's what they're accustomed to."

He nodded at the youths, all boys, kicking the football back and forth. "Who are they?"

"Lads from the Shankill."

"Protestants?"

"Of course."

"Do both sides share the park?"

"That was the agreed upon arrangement, however, it doesn't happen."

"Why not?"

Kate stared at him in amazement. "Surely you've been here long enough to know the answer to that. This is Northern Ireland, Neil. We don't share anything."

He let out his breath and waited for a full minute before replying. "What I meant to ask is is there an implied understanding as to which group uses the green at a certain time."

"No," Kate said shortly. "There is no time when Catholics are able to use the park safely."

"Why not?"

"Because the law here is survival of the fittest. The strongest will prevail and, for now, the strongest happen to be Protestants from the Shankill."

"Are you saying that if it were the other way around, things would be different?"

"If you mean to suggest that I believe Catholics are more compassionate than Protestants, you're wrong. Either way, bullies control the turf."

"Will they chase us off?"

Kate shook her head. "We're strangers. They have no grudge against those they don't recognize."

"It's an odd sort of life, isn't it?"

"I wonder if it isn't the rule rather than the exception."

"I don't understand."

Kate tucked her hair behind her ears and sucked in her bottom lip. She had the idea worked out in her mind and she wanted to explain it properly. "We're primates. We may be genetically predisposed to a pack mentality. Those of us who are educated and whose families instilled good manners have suppressed that instinct. But it's there. A bit of encouragement is all it takes to bring it out."

"Lord of the Flies?"

"In a manner of speaking."

"Why?"

"For most of them, there isn't anything else."

"I thought Protestants had more opportunity."

"Generally speaking, they have. But here, as in the Falls and other working class communities, there is no precedent for it. They simply aren't accustomed to thinking they have choices."

"Is this what you wanted to show me?"

The corners of her mouth lifted in the briefest of smiles. "No. I want you to meet Emily Quinn."

Neil's eyebrow quirked. "Why?"

"Humor me, please. I'll explain later."

He nodded. "All right. Shall I follow you or do we take one car?"

"Neither. It's a short walk."

Side by side, they covered the distance to the Quinns' small house. Maired invited them inside and led them down the hallway to the room where Emily passed her days and nights.

Neil was shocked at first. Kate could see it in the tightening of his jaw and the ridges that stood out on his neck. He was kind, warm and endlessly patient with the little girl. For the first time, Kate saw the father in him rise above the professional.

After refusing Maired's offer of tea, they walked back to the green, this time in silence.

"I imagine you'll tell me what that was all about in your own good time," Neil said at last.

Kate ignored the implied question and asked one of her own. "Are you aware that Robbie Finnigan is dragging his feet on Catholic recruitment into the RUC?"

He frowned. "It isn't my area, Kate. Truthfully, I hadn't noticed."

"It isn't exactly news," she said bitterly. "Nothing has changed. Crimes against Catholics have always been very normal here in Northern Ireland. Investigations have moved very slowly or not at all. My husband's murderer is still walking the streets. I'm no closer to seeing justice prevail than I was six years ago."

"What does Emily Quinn have to do with all of this?"

Kate pointed to the group playing on the green. "She's a little girl who barely survived a brutal beating at the hands of those boys simply because she was in the way. Nothing is being done. The police say there is no evidence even though two witnesses have come forward."

"That makes no sense."

"Oh, but it does. The witnesses are two Catholic lads from the Falls. Their accounting of the events is suspect because of who they are. Mrs. Quinn called me when she couldn't get satisfaction from the RUC. Her son and husband have been hounded, arrested and released a number of times on trumped up charges, but this time it was just too much. Emily is a little girl. She was taking her baby brother out for some air. She nearly died, Neil, and nothing is being done.''

"Have you filed a report?"

"Of course. I'm not passing this one off."

He looked at her, cheeks flushed, fists balled in the pockets of her jacket, voice choked with rage. "What is happening here?"

"It's simple," she replied. "In England if you're different, you're interesting. Here, if you're different, you're wrong and those who are right feel they have a moral obligation to change those who are wrong."

His eyes, clear gray and thickly lashed, searched her face. What was he thinking?

Finally he spoke. "This is really what you do, isn't it? It's what you were trained for?"

"It's what I've always done."

"What about your husband?"

"He did the same thing, in his way. We had that in common."

"Have you always worked with children?"

"Yes."

His voice went low and soft. "You humble me, Kate. I admire you very much."

She blushed. "You've given me a great deal of credit. This is what I do. Anyone else would do the same."

They had reached her car. The green was empty now. He reached for the keys in her hand. "Will you have dinner with me?"

"You needn't feel obligated to repay me, Neil. It really isn't necessary."

"Obligation has nothing to do with my invitation. Do you have anywhere to go this evening?"

Kate thought of Deirdre. The child had dutifully entertained her for several nights in a row. "Not really."

"Say, yes."

She hesitated.

"Please."

She laughed. "How can I resist?"

"Don't."

"Yes," she said. "I'll have dinner with you."

He grinned and years fell away from his face. "I'll follow you back and we'll take one car."

Kate slid behind the wheel of her Volvo, negotiating her way back to her guesthouse. He was a take-charge sort of man, like Patrick, the same type she was always attracted to. She reined herself in. Attraction had no place in her relationship with Neil Anderson.

She parked her car and waited for him to pull up beside her. He left the motor running, climbed out and opened the door for her.

"Have you a preference or shall we leave the choice of restaurants to me?"

"You decide," she said automatically, gratefully. Although she didn't shy away from responsibilities, she was no trailblazer by nature. The last six years without Patrick had been difficult. Her instinct was to allow a man to take the lead. Tonight she would relax, enjoy a glass or two of wine with her meal and dismiss reality for a few short hours. That it was Neil Anderson, a Protestant and an officer of the law awarding her this opportunity, did not escape her. She knew she was doing nothing wrong, but secretly she hoped she wouldn't see anyone she knew.

He turned toward the City Centre and Donegall Square where the better restaurants were located and pulled up in front of the Lime Tree.

Kate had never been here before. The drawing room was charming, dark wood, a cozy fire and deep, high-backed chairs arranged in conversational groupings.

The maître d' welcomed them. Kate ordered a gin and tonic, sank back into her chair and opened the menu. The prices startled her. Had it really been so long since she'd indulged herself at a fine restaurant? She glanced at Neil. He'd chosen the restaurant. Obviously he'd eaten here before. She relaxed and decided on the lamb.

"This is lovely," she said. "Thank you."

"Are you enjoying yourself?"

"Very much."

"Good." The drinks arrived and he ordered for both of them, a man in charge, comfortable with his position. "We'll start with the garden salad and then Mrs. Nolan would like the lamb. I'll have the prime rib."

"Normally those are prepared medium-rare," the waiter offered. "Is that acceptable, sir?"

Neil looked at Kate. She nodded.

The waiter hesitated. "It is Mrs. Nolan, isn't it? Mrs. Patrick Nolan?"

Kate nodded. "It is."

"I'm very sorry about your husband, Mrs. Nolan. He was a frequent patron of this establishment. He is greatly missed by all of us."

"How kind of you," she said slowly.

Neil waited until the waiter had gone. "You've been here before?"

"No," she said and looked directly at him. "I haven't."

Patrick had been here many times and she hadn't. The obvious was left, unspoken, between them.

Neil touched his glass to hers. "To friendship."

Friendship, with a Protestant police officer. Good Lord! What would Patrick think? She gave herself a mental shake. Patrick was dead and obviously there were a few things about him she hadn't known. She smiled. "I want to apologize for this morning on the phone. I'm very grateful for what you've done for Kevin. I was terrified for him. Now, at least I can sleep at night."

He dismissed her words. "No apology is necessary. I'm glad you're feeling better."

Kate settled back in her chair and sipped her drink. "Tell me about your family."

He looked surprised. "I have no family, just my daughter."

"Are you an only child?"

"I've a married sister in Wales and a brother in America. We lost touch after my parents died."

"I'm sorry."

He shrugged. "I suspect it's often that way with bachelors. Women tend to keep a family together. My brother never married and I'm divorced."

"I'm sorry. It must be difficult."

"It happened a long time ago," he said comfortably. "I've ceased to feel the wound, although it would help to see my daughter more often. That part is my fault," he admitted. "My work is hardly conducive to raising a child."

"My husband was the same," she offered.

Neil looked at her over the rim of his glass. "But he had you."

"Yes."

"I'll wager you never nagged or complained," he teased her, "not even when the children had the pox, your nanny didn't show and you had twelve appointments scheduled for a single morning."

She laughed. "I don't believe I nagged, but I did complain. It was completely unsuccessful, however. Fairly soon I realized that Patrick wasn't going to change. I either had to accept him or leave him, and that was out of the question."

"Why?"

She felt it again, the feeling she could never quite eradicate when Patrick's name was mentioned and the hateful, uncontrollable trembling of her lower lip. "Because I loved him," she said defiantly. "Whatever else there was between us, we had that."

"I know," he said quietly.

She reached into her handbag, searching for a tissue, found it and blew her nose. "How could you possibly know?"

"I know you."

Her mouth dropped. "You know nothing about me."

"I know you have taken on an enormous responsibility. I know you have suffered great tragedy. I know how you feel about your children." His smile lit up his face.

The tension left Kate's shoulders. Suddenly she felt enormously relieved. He was really a very good man. Look what he'd done for Kevin. There was no disloyalty in her sitting across from him, sipping a cocktail, enjoying his company. She would relax and allow herself this indulgence, this escape from the tangle that had become her world. "What is your daughter's name?"

"Erin," he replied.

"That's an Irish name."

"It's also a lovely name."

Kate jumped in all the way. "Was your divorce an amicable one?"

He looked surprised. "What an absurd question. How can divorce be amicable?"

Oddly enough, she wasn't offended. "Some are, I believe. However, I'm no expert. I've never known anyone who is divorced. We were only allowed it a few years ago."

"Perhaps some are amicable," he conceded. "Mine wasn't."

"Were you hurt badly?"

The corners of his mouth twitched. "That's a personal question, Mrs. Nolan. Are you quite sure you want to venture into that area?"

The impropriety of their conversation hit her, all at once, like an onslaught of spring rain after a frost. What would her father say, and Kevin and Deirdre? God! "I'm sorry," she stammered.

He reached across the space between them and took her hand. "Please, Kate. I wasn't serious. Don't back away now."

Her eyes were wide, horrified pools of blue in the bleached bone of her face. Her breath came out in short, shallow gasps. "I'm sorry," she repeated struggling for air. Where was her inhaler? "I can't do this. I shouldn't do this."

"Calm down." His voice was calm, reassuring, the voice of a parent soothing an unreasonable child. "We're two people, professionals, co-workers if you

will, sharing a meal. That's all.'' He glanced at the
floor. ''Is your medication in your bag?''

Fighting off her rising panic, she nodded.

''Would you like me to find it for you?''

He was so calm, so reasonable. Again, she nodded.

Within seconds the vial was in her hand. She closed
her lips around the head and pressed, sucking in the
life-saving vapor once, and then again. Kate closed her
eyes and leaned her head back against the chair. She
was safe. She could breathe. This man had no quarrel
with her. He was English. He was one of the Special
Forces but he was not the enemy. Kate began to relax.

Sixteen

Neil walked around the block leading to his City Centre flat for the second time. His nerves were paper-thin. Nothing felt right, not the stack of papers waiting at home for his review or the mattress that had been recommended for his back but was too hard for him to sleep comfortably. For the first time in the six months since he had given them up, Neil wavered at the entrance to an off license, fighting the urge for a cigarette.

Gritting his teeth, he passed by the door, resolving to put into perspective the mire he found himself in. Kate Nolan was a dangerous woman. He knew that. Neil didn't really believe in fate, but he'd seen enough unusual happenings not to discount it altogether and there was enough Welsh in him to believe that some choices are made before we're born. There was something about Kate Nolan that drew him in and terrified him at the same time. She was an attractive woman, damned attractive. Some, who liked their woman thin, serious and pale, might even call her beautiful. But it wasn't her appearance that pulled at him. It was her intensity, her belief that people were good and that one had merely to point out an error in order for it to be rectified. Quite simply, she gave him hope where he'd long been convinced there was none to be found. Neil had been alone for some time now, content to have the occasional fast and furious fling that went no further than the physical. He didn't need a woman like Kate in his life, a woman burdened with children and history, a woman who exuded goodness, a woman a man would find himself measuring others by. Where would he fit? How would he manage with her grown daughter and rebellious son?

He shook his head in disgust. His mind was moving in ridiculous directions, creating scenarios rooted in fantasy. Of all the women in the world, a relationship with Kathleen Nolan was the closest to impossible. Not only was she the police ombudsman for the Six Counties where personal relationships were strictly forbidden, but she was Patrick Nolan's widow and Kevin Nolan's mother. That alone ruled out anything other than civility and a polite handshake. Their meal together proved that more was impossible. After he'd calmed her down she'd become sensible again, the reserved companion, the concerned mother. He wanted more. He wanted to see how much fire was behind the cool courtesy, especially when it came to him. But his hands were tied. There was Kevin to consider and that was no small thing. Still, something told him that people were meant to pair up and a man kept searching until he found someone to love, somewhere to belong. Only then did he understand his place in the universe.

Neil's instincts regarding people were very good. He'd earned his position on the strength of those instincts. Growing up in the slums of Manchester, the younger son of a Welsh sheet metal worker and a frustrated, chain-smoking housewife who resented the duties of motherhood, Neil had steered clear of the drugs and the street gangs, the seedy pubs and the hated mills, surprised them all and done well enough on his A levels to qualify for university.

After a brief stint in the Royal Navy, he'd gone back for an advanced degree in forensics and criminology, earning himself a post as undercover agent with the Special Forces. Seduced by the danger of it all, the newness and glamour of the job, he rose quickly, first in the Middle East where he was responsible for the infiltration and exposure of criminals involved with the Libyan Freedom Fighters, the Palestine Liberation Organization and the African National Council and, later in Europe, with the disintegration of the Communist Block. Those in power were grateful to him. On those rare occasions when he was in England, they invited him to their country houses, their polo matches, their seasonal balls.

Somewhere, in the middle of it all, he'd managed to meet, woo and wed Lydia, a woman more interested in her appearance, her friends and the society pages than she had ever been in him. Not that he'd given the marriage much effort, he admitted to himself. Gone for months at a time, he didn't really blame Lydia for finding someone else. A woman deserved an attentive husband and he'd been far from that. Although he'd never technically been unfaithful to his wedding vows, he'd given up on his marriage before their second anniversary. Erin, his little girl, the sweetly scented softness of her and the incredible sweeping emotion that came over him when he looked at her, had kept him hanging on for longer than he should have, until the evidence of Lydia's affair was too humiliating to keep up appearances. Their divorce made the papers. Lydia kept the house in London, custody of Erin, a goodly portion of his retirement, and nearly all of their friends. Because she remarried immediately, Neil kept all of his salary, with the exception of the monthly stipend he paid toward Erin's support.

That was ten years ago. He'd buried himself in his work. The wound healed with a minimum of scar tissue. He would like to see more of his daughter. She was thirteen, nearly grown and he barely knew her. That was the primary reason he'd accepted his current position, something he would never have considered earlier in his career. His job description, which he now believed was a farce, was to expose the leaders of a black market drug ring that had the Special Branch of the Royal Ulster Constabulary spinning their wheels in ineffective circles. Since the peace agreement crime in the city of Belfast had increased by tenfold and the fragile truce, so painfully arrived at by men weary of living in fear, appeared likely to crumble. His mandate called for reducing the drugs and crime, thus preserving that peace.

Neil was a nonpracticing English Catholic. He had no patience for the tangled religion-culture conflict that had woven a stranglehold around Ulster for the last four centuries. Drugs did not interest him. He'd avoided them as a boy when they were peddled on the streets of Manchester as freely as roasted chestnuts at Christmastime and he wanted nothing to do with them now. Disciplined, responsible and compulsively neat, Neil didn't understand substance addiction. Even his occasional yen for a cigarette was immediately squashed. He had no patience for those who succumbed. Lads like Kevin Nolan, born with silver spoons in their mouths, spoiled from birth by doting families, had no excuse for their behavior. If boys from the projects of Manchester and Liverpool could manage, anyone could.

None of which reduced his dilemma. Kate was a devoted mother trying to raise two children on her own. She had the advantages of education and means, but it wasn't easy being both mother and father to an adolescent boy. The girl, Deirdre, appeared to be moving in the right direction. Girls weren't plagued by the same issues as boys. Neil was frustrated by his assignment. He wished Kevin had been anyone's son but Kate's. It had been hard enough at dinner to endure her pathetic gratefulness for Kevin's rescue from Long Kesh. Soon, she would find out the nature of his ulterior motive. Then she would excise him from her life as cleanly as skin off a potato.

Because Neil knew people, he knew what Kevin would do. It was the logical choice for a boy who'd grown up in a loving and loyal family. It was something Neil would have done himself if circumstances were otherwise. Kevin would confide in his uncles, preferring their counsel over that of a hated police officer. Neil had planned for that eventuality. It was exactly what he wanted the boy to do. He intended to rely on nothing Kevin reported to him, not until the inevitable occurred and the lad realized that in the criminal world, blood meant little at all. It was a strategy commonly used on inexperienced informers. Terror was an effective truth serum. Neil would know everything that Kevin knew, very soon.

It was a risk, fraught with danger. There was always the chance, although a slim one, that Kevin could lose his life. More likely he would be marked for execution, the sentence for informants. Ireland would no longer be safe. He would be an outcast, banished to England, away from family and friends. It wasn't unusual for a lad from Ireland to make his way elsewhere. Immigration was always an alternative for the Irish, although in most instances it was voluntary and rarely permanent.

Neil knew what Kate would do if Kevin left Ireland. The boy was sixteen years old, the age of majority by Irish standards, but a boy in all eyes but the law's. She would leave Ireland, make her home elsewhere, rescue her son. England would be an attractive choice for a woman with Kate's education and background. She would survive there, heal without the constant reminder of her past, and begin again.

The thought soothed him. He liked to think of Kate in London, enjoying the museums, the theater, the restaurants, the elegant shops. In his mind she fit there, much more so than in the war-torn and suspicious Six Counties or even in that charming village where she made her home. Ardara was a lovely town but Kate was a sophisticated woman. Did she have friends there and, if so, what did she find to talk about with women who had left secondary school for marriage and never traveled more than twenty kilometers from their homes?

Neil climbed the stairs leading to the flat he had rented in the heart of the city. He rarely thought about his surroundings but today they appeared more stark than usual. He looked around at the bare walls, the shelves empty of all personal mementos with the exception of the books he had purchased over the last few months. How long had it been since he'd really had a home, the kind Kate had made for herself and her children, a safe haven where a man could retreat and find the strength to regroup for his next encounter in an often antagonistic world?

His answer came instantaneously. Neil had never had such a sanctuary, not growing up and certainly not with Lydia. He drew the curtains against the night and walked to the liquor cabinet where he kept a bottle of ten-year-old Dewar's, a gift from the prime minister. Pouring himself a drink, he sat down on the couch and stared at the empty, cream-colored wall. Soon, too soon in his opinion, he would seek out Kevin Nolan and the game would begin.

Neil drained his drink. What was he doing here? He was dissatisfied in a way he hadn't been for years. Where was he going and what kind of life was it where children were sacrificed, used as bait in sting operations that made little difference in the big picture?

Liam Nolan glanced at his brother, a perplexed frown on his face. "I'm not following you, Dominick. Are you saying that we have no information at all on Kevin?"

Dominick pushed aside the papers on the table in front of him, stood and paced back and forth across the small space of the Divas Flats office in angry silence.

Liam sighed. He wasn't comfortable when Dominick was in a mood. Frustration did it to him, turned his younger brother into a tight-lipped, angry man. He watched him for a few minutes. "What do you plan on doing?"

Dominick pulled a cigarette and matches out of his pocket, lit up and inhaled. "I haven't decided yet."

"Is it really necessary to know? Kevin's out."

Dominick stared at his brother. "Don't be an idiot, Liam. We need to know why Kevin was released. His sentence was a harsh one for a first-time offender. It makes no sense. First he's in and then suddenly he's out? Something doesn't add up. No one has any news. It's as if one person is calling the shots, a person with a very closed mouth."

"Neil Anderson?"

"Possibly, but I'm not convinced of it. Anderson's specialty is terrorist operations. Kevin's small potatoes for a man like him."

"Does Kate know anything?"

"Our beloved Kate didn't even bother to tell us the lad was released."

"That's beside the point. We already knew that." He thought a minute. "Perhaps she didn't know."

Dominick's laugh was bitter. "She knew."

Liam stood and reached for his jacket. "I'll pay Deirdre a visit. Perhaps she can tell us something."

Dominick nodded. "Meanwhile, I'll look into the house where Kevin is staying."

The words Tranquility House were painted above the door. A man with long blond hair and rimless glasses answered Dominick's knock. "May I help you?"

"I've come to see Kevin Nolan."

"Kevin is in class now and he's already had one visitor today."

Dominick smiled. "I'm the lad's uncle. Surely you can make an exception for family."

The man shook his head. "I'm sorry."

Dominick's smile faded. "I'll come back tomorrow."

"Do that, but call first. That way Kevin will be available."

"When would be a good time?"

"In the morning around half past eight. We'll check with Kevin and mark your appointment. That way no one will take your place."

Deciding that the lad was merely following orders, Dominick shook his hand, walked down the street, crossed over to the Crumlin Road and found a sympathetic and nearly empty pub where he stopped to put together what he knew. Kevin was staying in a halfway house, an environment so substandard to his own home that Kate would be biting her nails down to the nubs. That ruled out his first suspicion. The Kate Nolan he knew would never in her right mind allow her son to spend a single night in such a place, all of which meant she had no choice in the matter. But, who did?

Dominick knew something about Neil Anderson and he wasn't ready to believe that a man with his credentials would depend on an unpredictable, half-grown boy for anything. The terrorism of the seventies and eighties was no longer a way of life in West Belfast. An investigator of Anderson's caliber wasn't required. Why, then, was he here? The rise of black market drugs was sudden and rampant, but no different from London, Birmingham, Manchester and Dublin, certainly no challenge for a man from the highest ranks of the Special Forces. Perhaps there was involvement that Dominick knew nothing about. He shook off the possibility. He knew West Belfast, every family, every political persuasion. There was nothing in the neighborhood that would have passed him by. He would have to rely on Kevin. If the lad knew anything at all, Dominick would pull it from him. Meanwhile he would wait. He was a Catholic from West Belfast. He knew something of patience.

Liam didn't bother to call before knocking on the door of Deirdre's room at Queen's. She was family, after all, and he knew her schedule of classes. She was free for the rest of the morning. Laughter greeted him, and a muffled, "You're early. Come in. I'm not quite ready."

"It's Liam," he said, turning the knob and stepping inside.

Deirdre poked her head out of the bathroom. "Uncle Liam. I wasn't expecting you. I'll be out in a minute."

He sat down on a chair and perused the bookshelves. His formal education was sketchy but, characteristic of his race, he was a reader. The greats were here, Yeats, Fitzgerald, Swift, O'Casey and Wilde, but there were new ones as well, O'Flaherty, Behan, Heaney. As much as Deirdre protested the requirements of her liberal arts education, she was well-read.

Sporting a hint of perfume, Deirdre walked out of the bathroom, hair shining and straight with a hint of red in the rich brown length. She kissed Liam's cheek. "Is everything all right?"

"Nothing's changed, if that's what you mean," replied Liam coming right to the point. "But I've a few questions to ask you, lass."

Deirdre looked surprised. "What kind of questions?"

"It appears that your brother's situation is something of a mystery."

Deirdre whitened. "Has something happened to Kevin?"

"You know that he's been released."

She nodded. "Mum told me."

"Did she tell you anything else?"

"What do you mean?"

Liam leaned forward. "The thing is, Deirdre, your uncle Dom feels it's a bit odd for Kevin to have been sentenced the way he was, without bail or exceptions, and then released so suddenly. What do you think?"

Deirdre's brow wrinkled. "I'm grateful. I haven't thought about that part at all."

"Do you know anything about his situation?"

She hesitated.

Liam sensed she was hedging. He smiled warmly, persuasively. "Your mother came to us and asked for help. It won't be easy if we know nothing."

Deirdre sat down on the edge of her bed. "All I know is that Kevin has been experimenting with drugs for some time now. I've tried to talk to him but he won't listen."

"He's not alone."

"I think it's more than that. I think he's been selling them."

"Why would he do that?"

Deirdre shrugged. "Money."

"Why does Kevin need money?"

"I don't think he *needs* money, Uncle Liam. It's more than that. Something isn't right with Kevin. Nothing's really been right for us since—"

A knock on the door interrupted them. Deirdre jumped up. Her cheeks were flushed. "It's my friend. We were going out."

Liam stood. "I'll be leaving."

Again the knock sounded.

Deirdre hesitated.

"Aren't you going to answer the door, lass?"

Deirdre opened her mouth and closed it again without saying anything. She crossed the room and flung open the door. A young man Liam recognized walked into the room. It was the lad from the pub.

"Hello, again," Liam said.

The boy reached out to shake his hand. "It's a pleasure to see you again."

''I don't recall your name.''

''Peter Clarke.''

This time the name rang a bell. ''Where are you from, Peter?''

''Belfast.''

''Where in Belfast?''

''Stranmillis Road.''

There were only a few Catholic families on the trendy Stranmillis Road and Liam knew all of them. ''Where did you go to secondary school?''

The boy's cheeks were as red as Deirdre's but his voice was firm and clear and exactly what Liam expected. ''The Benedict Academy.''

''Is your da Geoffrey Clarke?''

''Aye.''

Across the tension-filled room Liam's eyes met Deirdre's. She glared back at him defiantly. Maintaining eye contact with his niece, Liam spoke. ''I haven't kept up. Is your da still with the RUC?''

The Adam's apple in the boy's throat jumped. ''Aye.''

Liam walked out the open door. ''Enjoy your morning. I'll be seeing you soon, Deirdre.''

Neither Peter nor Deirdre answered.

Liam took the stairs slowly. He had much to think about. Deirdre was seeing a Protestant and Kevin was a drug peddler. It still didn't explain everything. He wondered how much Kate knew and, if it was as much as he thought, how she was managing. *Still waters,* Patrick had called her. The term was appropriate. What would Dominick think? Liam tried to imagine his brother's reaction. Dominick would reach conclusions that Liam would never consider.

* * *

Deirdre waited by the window until she saw her uncle crossing the green. Then she turned on the boy standing in rigid silence behind her. "Did you have to tell him?"

He didn't pretend to misunderstand her. "Did you want me to lie?"

"Yes."

"I'm not willing to do that, Deirdre, not for you or anyone."

Deirdre pressed her hands together to stop their shaking. "He knows. He'll tell my mother and then everything will be ruined."

"Why?"

Her eyes flashed. "Are you really that naive, Peter?"

"I don't consider myself naive at all. I'm just not willing to let this Catholic-Protestant thing rule my life."

"You're not just a *Protestant,* Peter. Your father is an RUC constable. He's probably arrested members of my family."

"I won't apologize for my father. He's a good man."

"Is he an Orangeman?"

Peter looked embarrassed. "Aye."

Her lip curled. "I thought so. All RUC arrests of Catholics are a sham."

"Do you think Protestant arrests are also a sham?"

"It isn't the same."

"Why not?"

"There is no reason to arrest Protestants unless they commit crimes. It's different for us. They hate us because we're Catholic."

His fists clenched. "You've been brainwashed, Deirdre. If you really believe that, and if you're typical of the Catholic population, there is no hope for us.''

She smiled sadly. ''In our eyes, there are no good men in the RUC.''

''I'm not my father, Deirdre. I have no control over what he does.''

She was very white and very resolved. ''This isn't going to work, Peter. I'm sorry. You'll have to leave now.''

He stared at her. ''What are we doing that is so unacceptable? We have fun together. We talk. We study. Is that so wrong?''

She wet her lips and wondered how to explain and whether it was even worthwhile to do so. Peter was kind and decent. He deserved an accounting. ''My father's murder was never investigated. The RUC said there was no evidence. My mother, my brother and I witnessed his murder.'' Her eyes filled. The pain gathered in her throat choking her words. ''They shot him down in front of us and then, for good measure, while he was bleeding all over the floor, they shot him again in the head.''

Peter groaned. ''I'm sorry. More than anything I wish it hadn't happened to you but I'm not responsible. The people I know would never do such a thing. They would want the murderers to be found.''

''The RUC don't want them found. They told us there was nothing we could do.''

''Don't do this, Deirdre,'' Peter pleaded. ''I thought we were friends.''

''No,'' she said. ''We're not.'' She stood there, a slight, straight figure, waging a battle with circumstances for which she was no match.

Seventeen

Kate drew on the lip of the inhaler, sucked the mist deeply into her lungs, counted to twenty and waited for the familiar rush to ease the tightness in her chest. It happened more often, lately, this closing of her air passages, the bands of tension tightening around her middle until she was forced to pull over to the side of the road or sit down in any available seat, scramble for her Ventolin inhaler, ignore the inquiring looks and simply wait until the episode was over.

A finger of light broke through the morning fog and flickered over the Twelve Bens, green with vegetation from spring rains. Perhaps there would be sun today. She stuffed the inhaler into the pocket of her windbreaker, pulled out her gloves and jogged down the sidewalk to the path leading toward the beach. She'd taken a break and returned to Ardara, hoping that a night spent in her own bed would work its restorative magic, her bed that no longer held any joy, any hope of love or sex or pleasure. She pushed the thought away. Her own problems could wait. Her priority was Kevin. She saw him every day. His visitation was no longer restricted and each time it was harder for her to leave. He was so pathetically grateful to see her. She couldn't bear to disappoint him. Today her father would be there. She had taken advantage of the opportunity and come home.

Wind whipped at her face reddening her cheeks, bringing tears to her eyes. She'd reached the sand now. Her calves ached. It was harder to move. She increased her pace, felt the bite in her chest, the sting in her thighs. The ocean was slate-gray, the color of the sky. Gulls shrieked and circled the pilings. Something brown leaped against the gray water, a sea lion. Waves crashed. The smells of sea and salt and fish mingled together.

She'd found her pace. Two minutes went by, three, four. She pushed herself steadily forward, lifting first one foot, heavy with morning fatigue and straining muscles, and then the other, forcing herself, harder and harder for the elusive feeling that had become her addiction. Despite the cold, perspiration gathered on her forehead, on the back of her neck, in the valley of her breasts. Then she felt it, first in tiny trickles, then a wave, rising, cresting, falling and, finally, a rushing stream of lightness, a wellness of being, a euphoria. It swept over her, through her, filling her, an affirmation, a reassurance that she would manage, that Kevin would recover, that Patrick's murderers would be brought to justice, that Deirdre would lose the brittle veneer that prevented her from trusting anyone other than those blood-related.

Kate reached the dock. Gasping, she slowed to a stop, pressed her hand against her side and bent over from the waist. Six miles. She felt empowered. Today she would return all of the calls on her voice mail. Today she would ring the prime minister and demand to be told exactly what was happening with Patrick's investigation. Another thought swam up out of nowhere. Today she would find out why her husband had regularly frequented a first-class restaurant in Belfast and why he'd never bothered to mention it, he who mentioned everything.

Dominick was a full fifteen minutes early for his visit with Kevin. The same man from the day before led him through a long hallway to a sitting room with two couches facing each other. A patterned area rug, a wooden mantel with carved animals and misty prints of spring in Connemara were the only decorative touches. Otherwise the room was empty.

"I'll tell Kevin you're here," the man said and disappeared down the hallway.

Dominick sat down on one of the couches and looked at his watch. One minute ticked by. He drummed his fingers on the small end table, his thoughts on what he needed to accomplish later that day.

Footsteps sounded on the floorboards. He looked up to see his nephew standing uncertainly in the doorway.

"Uncle Dominick?" The words came out like a question.

"Aye, it's me, lad. How are you doing?"

"I'm grand," the boy stammered. "What are you doing here?"

"Your mum said you were in a bit of trouble. I thought I'd come and see if you needed anything."

Kevin's face lit with his sudden smile. Dominick's throat burned. The resemblance to Patrick was remarkable, the same cleanly chiseled features, black hair and fair, freckled skin, the same lean height and flashing smile. The world had not deserved Patrick Nolan. Perhaps it was right that he had gone to a better place. Dominick had lost his religion long ago, even before his brother's bloody execution, but he was born and raised a Roman Catholic from the Falls. For generations his ancestors had fought, bled, died and buried their children under the limestone and in the bogs of Ireland for the privilege of practicing that religion. It wasn't something one could easily deny. Dominick understood that. His faith came and went with his moods and just now it had come back to him with a vengeance. What in bloody hell had Patrick's son gotten himself involved in?

Kevin settled in across from him. "I'm glad you came. I was wondering—" He hesitated.

"Go on."

Kevin looked around. "Do you think they can hear us?"

Dominick pulled out a cigarette and offered one to his nephew. Kevin declined. Dominick lit the end and slipped the matches back into his pocket. "I don't think so, lad." He leaned forward, elbows on his knees, and lowered his voice. "Is there something you're wanting to tell me?"

The boy swallowed and nodded.

"Start from the beginning."

Kevin looked at the clock. "We only have an hour."

"Do what you can." Dominick's voice was soothing, persuading.

The boy instinctively responded. "He wants me to inform," the boy blurted out.

"Who does?"

"Mr. Anderson."

"What's he looking for?"

"Drugs, I think. That's what I'm here for, selling cocaine. They put me in Long Kesh. It was the only way I could get out."

"Why you?"

Kevin's brow wrinkled, marring the smooth, young skin. "He said there was no one else who could get in, no one new besides me. He said no one would suspect me because of my history and who I was. He thinks the same people who were in the IRA run the drug trade in Belfast."

"He does, does he?" Dominick watched the flame-lit point of his cigarette and the curl of smoke drifting toward the ceiling. Everything had its own time, its own pace. Deliberately he gentled his voice. "Think very carefully, lad. Did he mention who it is that he wants?"

Kevin's eyes went blue and clear, Patrick's eyes. "He wants you, Uncle Dom, and Liam, too."

John O'Donnell watched his daughter cross the street at the signal and enter the restaurant. He stood and waved to her from his booth in the corner. She spotted him immediately. "Hello, Da," she said, kissing his cheek, taking the seat across from him. "Sorry I'm late. How is Kevin, today?"

"I wasn't able to see him. He already had a visitor this morning."

"Oh?"

"I waited to see who it was."

Her father was a storyteller. Kate had learned that long ago. There was no point in rushing him.

She pulled a piece of brown bread from the basket and buttered it. There was no brown bread at home. Deirdre and Kevin preferred white.

"He stayed the whole hour, and me shivering in the cold of my car. I started the engine a few times to give myself a bit of the heat."

"It's not even winter, Da."

"It's ten degrees, Katie."

She acknowledged the temperature and gently steered her father back to the point of the conversation. "Who was Kevin's visitor?"

"It was your brother-in-law."

Kate froze.

Gratified by her obvious surprise, John leaned closer. "It was Dominick Nolan, himself. Now what would he be wanting with our Kevin?"

She lifted the water glass to her lips with shaking hands and feigned a smile. "I don't know. He is Kevin's uncle. Maybe he's worried about him."

"If he was so worried about any of you, he would have shown his face at any time in the last six years."

"That's not fair, Da," Kate protested. "We haven't exactly made him welcome."

"He's an IRA man, Katie, even now when it isn't necessary and no one approves."

"My point exactly. Dominick knows we don't approve of him."

John sipped at his tea.

Kate noticed right away. Her father was the rare Irishman whose stomach rebelled at a second drink but he wouldn't refuse the first one. "Have you given it up completely, Da?"

He nodded. "Drink addles a man, makes him old and spent before his time."

"Good for you."

"Never mind about me. What will you do about Kevin?"

The barman called out to them. "The shepherd's pie is tasty today."

"I'll have fish," Kate replied.

"The same for me," echoed her father.

"Two fish plates it is," the man said disappearing through the double doors. He was both cook and barman when his wife shopped for supplies in Dublin.

Kate crossed her arms and looked at her father. "All I want is for Kevin to come home and be normal. I'm terrified that won't happen. Right now, he's where he needs to be. I can't imagine a better place for him. We have Neil Anderson to thank for that."

"The policeman?" John swore under his breath. "How can you even think that way, Katie?"

"Because it's true. We certainly weren't getting anywhere with Kevin." Her voice shook. "He was involved in a shooting, Da. He could have been killed or paralyzed for life. Our Kevin. Whatever I thought was bothering him was nothing compared with this. Isn't that ironic? I see children like Kevin every day and I couldn't recognize the signs in my own son."

He patted her hand. "Don't kick yourself, Katie. You've been a good and loving mother. This isn't your fault."

"It's someone's fault, Da. Not every child goes down this path."

"No, they don't. Deirdre didn't."

Kate smiled. "You're trying to cheer me up and I thank you. But Deirdre isn't likely to have Kevin's problems. They're completely different people. Besides, Deirdre has her own demons to shake. I wonder if she'll ever have a normal life."

"Because of what happened to Patrick?"

Kate nodded.

John turned his water glass around on the wooden table. "How is the investigation coming along?" he asked casually.

"It isn't."

''Perhaps it's better this way.''

His words stung. She turned on him. ''How can you say that? Anything is better than not knowing.''

''I'm not so sure.''

''What are you telling me, Da? Patrick's death destroyed my family. Do you think I should just give up without knowing why my husband was the target of an assassination team?''

''You already know that, Katie. Patrick worked with the IRA. He defended criminals, murderers, and he defended them successfully. More than a few wanted to see him dead.''

''He wasn't the only defense attorney for the IRA.''

John was silent. There was only so much he could say. Kate would find her way without him. She was closer than she'd ever been. He knew it would bring her great pain, but in the pain would come healing, for herself and her children.

Kate sat in the leather chair of what was once Patrick's home office and stared at the telephone. Hers was an old argument, one she had with Patrick too many times to count. He was loyal to his family while she wanted no part of Dominick Nolan's politics or the entire Nolan family. *You did ask him for help,* a voice in her head reminded her. Fairness demanded that she give him a chance to explain. She picked up the phone and dialed the number of the Sinn Fein office in Belfast.

''Dominick Nolan, please.''

''I'm sorry,'' a pleasant female voice replied. ''There is no one by that name here.''

''This is his sister-in-law, Kate Nolan.''

Instantly the voice changed. ''One moment, Mrs. Nolan. I'll see where he can be reached.''

Kate punched in the numbers the woman gave her. This time Dominick answered.

She came right to the point. "I understand you visited my son this morning."

"Good afternoon, Kate. It's grand to hear from you." His voice was cool, amused, superior.

"You haven't seen Kevin in years, Dominick. Why now?"

"I was concerned about my nephew. Don't forget it was you who came to me."

"The situation has changed. He's no longer in prison."

"Obviously." Now the voice was sarcastic, hard. "I wondered why you didn't bother to tell me of the change in his circumstances."

"There wasn't time." Even she recognized the pathetic nature of her excuse.

"There was time enough for other things, wasn't there, Kate?"

The pounding started in her chest and moved to her throat, her temples, the tips of her fingers. "I'm not sure what you're talking about," she stammered.

"Your job makes it difficult to understand which side you're on. Does being the police ombudsman mean you're required to break bread with them, even the one who set up your son, my brother's son?"

The ringing in her ears drowned out his words. "Are you having me followed, Dominick?"

"I'm not that interested in you, Kathleen. But you are something of a celebrity here in Belfast. When you dine at an expensive restaurant with an Englishman who makes his living as an expert in terrorist operations, you'll be noticed."

She swallowed. "Tell me how he set up my son."
Without sparing her any of the details, he told her.

Kate carried her teacup to the breakfast room where
the skylight picked up the last lingering rays of sunlight,
bathing the room in a lemony haze. The windows faced
the sea. The furniture was warm oak, the plants per-
ennially green, the temperature a lovely sixty-five degrees. She sat down at the table and stared out into the
late afternoon.

She knew better than to act on the emotions roiling
through her. Her first inclination had been to call Neil
Anderson, to vent on him her fury, her feelings of betrayal, contempt and, down there beneath it all, a small,
raw kernel of hurt. He'd used her, charmed her, soothed
her into believing he respected her, found her attractive,
even admired her work. It was all a lie to get to Kevin.
She'd woven fantasies around him, impossible, school-
girl fantasies that could never be, but nonetheless lifted
her to another place where possibilities still existed.

She hurt inside. Kate was no stranger to hurt and this
one was very small when taken in perspective. Still, it
hit her in a new place, rawer, because it had never been
touched before. Kate had loved only one man in her
life and he had never disappointed her, never given her
a moment's insecurity. He made her feel attractive, de-
sirable and feminine. Never once had she doubted that
Patrick loved her or that she was first in his life. She
was an amateur when it came to relationships, all kinds.

The blinking light on her message machine alerted
her to a new message. She hit the button and smiled
when she heard the voice. Maeve Murphy was her only
real friend. An artist from Dublin who sculpted glass,
Maeve was lovely, tall, full-breasted, long-limbed with

flowing auburn hair. She'd refurbished a mansion on the beach and held raucous parties with handsome European men who spoke in heavy, romantic accents.

Patrick had disliked Maeve, more than was warranted, Kate often thought. He'd barely known her, not enough for the vehemence of his feelings. *Selfish,* he'd called her, *and garish, loud and crass.* Kate hadn't seen any of those qualities. She'd seen only a generosity of spirit, a lack of pretentiousness, and a sensual charm she would very much have liked to cultivate for herself. Maeve was a breath of air blown in from exotic destinations. She had been Kate's lifeline in troubled times. She was the only woman she could truly call a friend. She lived in New York City for much of the year, returning to Ireland when there was the hope of a bit of sun. Kate missed her very much. They'd only had a few conversations since the trouble with Kevin. These had been satisfying, but not nearly as much as a regular visit, just the two of them sharing a bottle of expensive wine and a whole evening ahead.

If there was ever a time she needed Maeve, it was now. She checked her watch and decided against the call. Maeve was never home during the day.

There was no getting around it. Neil Anderson had hurt her pride. Kate was no longer young but she believed, in the recesses of her heart, that one day, when this was over and her obligation to Patrick fulfilled, she would love again. She had never considered Neil as a possible contender for her affections. She could never be with an Englishman from Special Forces, but there would be someone, a quiet man with no pretensions, no need for celebrity status, a man comfortable enough with himself to allow others to save the world, a man satisfied with a wife and stepchildren. Now, her dream felt tarnished around the edges, her confidence shaken.

Her tea was cold and still she'd come up with no alternative. She would have to confront Neil. Even now, Kevin might be in danger. Rationally she knew there was nothing she could do. Kevin was an adult in the eyes of the law and could make his own decisions. She wasn't even sure if the decision was a bad one. The alternative was Long Kesh. She wanted none of that for him. A niggling suspicion crossed her mind. Was Kevin's sentence a reaction to the trouble in Belfast or was it unduly harsh because Neil Anderson needed him?

The phone rang. Kate answered on the third double ring.

A female voice spoke. "The prime minister is returning your call, Mrs. Nolan. Please hold."

She waited for a full five minutes before she heard his voice. It always surprised her. One of the most important men in the world and he sounded like a schoolboy.

"Hello, Kate. How are you today?"

She was in no mood for pleasantries. "I'm concerned," she said bluntly. "My husband's investigation seems to be on hold. I haven't heard anything for a very long time and, truthfully, I've lost faith in the government's ability to resolve this issue."

She heard his breath catch and the hesitation in his response. "These things take time, Kate."

"I don't have any more time. Neither does my son."

"What's happened with your son?"

"Sources have told me he's being used by Neil Anderson in a sting operation in West Belfast. On the surface, it appears that drugs are the issue. But it may be a great deal more."

Again, the hesitation. Finally, "What can I do for you, Kate?"

"I'd like an appointment with you as soon as possible."

"When can you get here?"

"Tomorrow afternoon."

"I'll clear my calendar."

"Thank you."

Kate exhaled and replaced the receiver. One down, one to go. But that would be later, after tomorrow. She could only hope that Kevin could hold on until then. As much as she resisted the idea, she would have to depend on Dominick. Kevin was family. Dominick's sense of loyalty was strong. He wouldn't allow anything to happen to Patrick's son.

Liam Nolan brought up the subject casually, almost as if he'd forgotten it, an afterthought barely worth the trouble of conversation. "I saw Deirdre today."

Dominick nodded. He didn't bother to look up. The map in front of him was purposely skewed. In light of new developments with the Peace Accord, even Sinn Fein was wavering. He'd be damned if he turned over even one FN rifle to the bloody bastards. The arsenal would have to be moved. He didn't like exposing himself so obviously, but if need be, he would handle it himself.

"She's seeing a Protestant."

Dominick grunted. "Why doesn't that surprise me?"

"His name is Peter Clarke."

"It sounds familiar."

"His father is an RUC man."

Dominick lifted his head. "Are you thinking what I am?"

"I'm thinking it's a dangerous association."

"It can't go on."

"I'll speak with Deirdre."

"What good will that do?"

Liam looked surprised. "She'll know to stop seeing him. She'll have no choice."

"You'll have to tell her everything, Liam. Are you prepared to tell Patrick's daughter that he was an IRA man?"

"If I must."

"She'll tell Kate. We'll have the RUC on our backs in no time."

"Kate wouldn't turn in her own family."

"In case you haven't noticed, Kate doesn't consider us *family*. The last six years have made that plain enough. She's also involved with Anderson."

"One meal doesn't mean involved, Dom. She isn't seeing him socially."

"How do we know?"

"Someone would have noticed and told us. Be reasonable."

"I'm always reasonable."

Liam sighed. "If I'm not supposed to tell Deirdre, what else did you have in mind?"

Dominick's eyes narrowed to cold blue slits in his thin face.

"No, Dom," Liam protested. "Peter's just a lad."

"How many of our lads have paid the price, Liam?"

"For Christ sake, Dom. Times have changed."

Dominick snorted. "Some things don't change, Liam. If you're too softhearted for the game, perhaps it's time you got out."

Liam straightened and looked steadily at his brother, his eyes hard and bright and very blue. "Perhaps it is," he said quietly.

Eighteen

The British Midlands flight to Heathrow was nearly empty. As soon as the plane leveled, Kate pulled out her laptop and settled down to finish her report. As long as she had an appointment with the prime minister, she would bring him up to speed on the progress, or lack thereof, of the Patten Report. Damn Robbie Finnigan. Her cool disdain for the man had turned into something much more rabid.

London bustled with energy. Men and women in expensive tweeds, carrying briefcases and umbrellas, their eyes fixed on a spot over one's shoulder moved past each other, hurrying in the direction of an all important destination. Intimidated by the sheer size of the city and the grim, bland faces, she arranged her expression into one she deemed suitable and maneuvered her way through the airport crowds to the land transport queue. Inside the cab, Kate willed herself to relax and think about how best to approach the elected leader of Britain.

Neil Anderson, balled fists thrust deeply into the pockets of his trousers, looked out of the exquisite bay windows of Number 10 Downing Street and swore feelingly.

From behind his desk, the prime minister frowned. "I'm sorry, Neil."

Anderson turned. "How did we come to this?"

"It was inevitable."

"I didn't see it."

"Nonsense," the prime minister said. "What we didn't foresee was Patrick Nolan's involvement in the Irish Republican Army. It's most unusual. If I had known, I would never have asked Kate to stand as ombudsman."

"Your problem would be nonexistent, but it doesn't help mine much," Neil said bitterly.

"I don't understand."

"Kate's position as ombudsman has nothing to do with me. I'm still the man who investigated her husband. I'm also the man who has placed her son in an extremely dangerous position. Our relationship would be no different even if she weren't in the employ of the British government."

"I see." The prime minister cleared his throat. "Have you allowed it to become personal?"

Neil turned and continued to stare out the window. *Personal? What exactly constituted personal?* "No," he said shortly, "of course not." He heard the prime minister's sigh of relief. August. It was already late summer and yet the temperature was brisk and cold, more like early spring. He recalled his years in the Middle East where mornings dawned black and white, dogs slept in deep purple shadows, heat seared and the long, lazy days were smeared with gaudy color, when the mind-stealing dryness had done things to his brain and he had been so desperate he would have given everything that was his for one cold rush of wind rolling off the bogs, scented with heather and peat. He felt that same desperation now, when he was minutes from a confrontation he dreaded. She would think he had used her and she would be right. He had an overwhelming desire to make her understand it was more than that. Again he turned. Purposefully he crossed the room to where the prime minister sat behind his desk. Palms down on the polished mahogany, he leaned forward. "Tell me why I'm here."

"I've told you."

"Not all of it. Why are you paying me an enormous salary to do a job that any detective worth his salt could do?"

"Don't sell yourself short."

Neil no longer cared whether he kept his job. "Don't play me for a fool."

"Calm down, Neil."

"I asked you a question. I deserve an answer, an honest one."

The prime minister rose and walked to the window. "Is it my imagination or is the weather particularly bad this year?"

Neil headed for the door. He'd had enough. The man could handle Kate on his own. He reached for the doorknob.

"Wait, Neil. Don't go. You do deserve an explanation. The reason for my hesitancy is that by revealing the entire situation I'll dishonor a confidence, several of them."

"I'm not interested in names."

"In this case names can't be avoided."

"I don't understand."

"We, and I include myself, haven't behaved honorably with Kate Nolan or with this entire bloody Northern Ireland problem. In my own defense, it began long before my time. Thousands of people's rights have been violated in the last three decades. Thousands have died unnecessarily. People are still in prison serving sentences for crimes to which they confessed under torture. Amnesty International has cited Britain for more civil rights violations than any other country in Europe. I'm not proud of that. I'm trying to change it.''

''What has that got to do with me?''

''I wanted someone unfamiliar with this entire mess, someone unbiased. You're a Catholic from Wales and a Special Forces agent with experience ferreting out terrorist operations. I couldn't have chosen better if I'd created you myself.''

''What are we really doing there?''

''The Peace Accord under the terms of the Good Friday Agreement specifies a turning over of arms by both Loyalists and Nationalists. Neither side is complying. What is happening in the North is arms smuggling. My sources report that instead of demilitarizing, paramilitaries are building weapons arsenals that threaten national security. In short, given the right provocation, we might find ourselves involved in a full-scale civil war in Northern Ireland.''

''Who are these people?''

''Splinter groups who've become disenfranchised by the Peace Accord. The same people who import drugs into the cities are also bringing in weapons.''

''Drugs are the diversion?''

''Precisely.''

''Why didn't you tell me this before?''

For the first time the prime minister's face relaxed. ''You've a reputation, Neil. While I'm convinced you're the man for the job, I didn't think you'd accept if given the entire picture. Drugs are a dirty business and Northern Ireland is a cesspool. Men in your position can call their own shots at this point in their careers. No one in his right mind would choose Northern Ireland. Quite simply, there was no one else and I couldn't risk the chance that you would turn us down.''

''So, you assumed everything would simply unravel in time and by then I'd be in too deeply to back out?''

''I'm afraid so.''

''Where does Kate fit into all this?''

''She's become an important part of the equation. Her husband's brothers are very much involved in arms smuggling. We may need her help.''

Neil couldn't keep the expression of shock from his face. ''You can't believe Kate knows anything about this?''

The prime minister shrugged. ''Probably not, but we can't rule it out. That's where I need you.''

''I won't set her up.''

''What if she isn't the person you think she is? Her husband certainly wasn't. What if she's involved? Isn't that worth finding out?''

Neil could feel the blood leave his face. Never, since their first meeting, had he even considered such a thing.

''You said you hadn't allowed your relationship to become personal. Do you stand by that?''

He was slow in answering. ''That doesn't mean I'm going to feel comfortable selling her out.''

''That won't happen if she's as innocent as she appears.''

Neil hadn't prayed in a very long time. He found himself on the verge of a very brief prayer and wondered if it would help or hurt Kate Nolan. In the end he decided in favor of the drink the prime minister offered. They sat across from each other in silence facing the marvelous windows that overlooked Downing Street. Neither felt compelled to make conversation.

Twenty minutes later, the phone rang. The prime minister answered on the first ring. Neil straightened. The tension was unsupportable. What would she think when she saw him?

"Send her in. I'm expecting her."

Neil set down his drink, his gaze fixed on the door. His heartbeat accelerated.

She wore something green, a statement, perhaps, that despite her position, she was Irish.

"Welcome, Kate," the prime minister said. "Can I get you a drink?"

"Sherry, dry, if you have it."

"To the queen," he said after pouring her drink.

Neil suppressed a grin. He imagined that Kate had never in her life lifted her glass to the queen.

She did not pick up her glass. Instead she spoke to Neil. "I'm not sure why you're here."

"Perhaps I should ask you the same question."

She came right to the point. "I'm here for two reasons, the most important being Kevin. I've been told that his arrest was a sham." Her eyes, blue and cold, were fixed on Neil. "Is that true?"

"No," he said. "Kevin wasn't set up, if that's what you mean. His arrest was authentic. He was trafficking in cocaine. That's not something we see often."

"What about his sentence? Do we sentence sixteen-year-old boys to Long Kesh?"

The prime minister was silent.

"It isn't common," said Neil, "but neither is distribution of cocaine. We have a drug problem, Kate, but it isn't heroin or cocaine, not in Ireland. Ecstasy or cannabis are common, but not the hard drugs. Kevin is a troubled young man. A prison sentence for such a crime isn't unheard of.''

She stared at him, cool, lovely, angry. ''Are you using my son, Mr. Anderson?''

A great deal depended on his answer. He knew that. He also knew that a lie, now, with this woman, would come back to haunt him. Lifting his head, he met her stare. ''Yes,'' he said. ''By law, Kevin is an adult. He's agreed to act as an informant. I need him.''

''He was blackmailed.''

''Who is your source, Kate?''

Color flooded her cheeks. ''That's none of your business.''

''It could mean a great deal to Kevin if I knew.''

Her control broke. ''You don't care about Kevin.''

''I care about saving people's lives. I care about mothers like Mrs. Quinn who have sons and daughters who will be helped by cleaning up their streets. Kevin has committed a crime, Kate. Sorry or not, he's going to pay for it. Think of this as atonement.''

''He could die.''

''Who is your source?''

The prime minister leaned forward. ''No one will know, Kate. Your answers will be kept in strictest confidence.''

Her eyes flashed. ''I don't care about that. I care about Kevin. I care about my husband's investigation.''

Neil positioned himself in front of the prime minister, blocking Kate from his view. ''Who is your source?'' he repeated.

Kate shook her head, stood and walked to the window. She pulled aside the drape. Minutes ticked by. ''Dominick Nolan, my brother-in-law,'' she said at last.

"He visited my son at Tranquility House. Kevin trusts him. He's the one who most resembles Patrick."

Neil wasn't aware that he'd crossed the room or that his hand was on her shoulder. In his mind the prime minister was already dismissed. "Do *you* trust him?"

Her eyes blurred. She didn't answer.

His voice gentled, became personal, intimate. "Trust *me*, Kate."

"What about my husband's investigation? Should I trust you to tell me about that as well?"

The only sound in the room was the ticking of the huge grandfather clock. The tension was thick, ugly. Finally the prime minister cleared his throat. Pushing back his chair he walked around his desk to approach Kate. He studied her, unsmiling. "I have the greatest respect for you, Kate. If I could have spared you this I would."

"Don't spare me anything."

"Please believe me when I say we had no idea of any of this when we began the investigation of your husband's death."

She turned. "Go on."

Once again the prime minister cleared his throat and waved his hand to a wing chair. "Will you sit down? This will take some time."

Kate sat and folded her hands. Her skin was stretched tightly, her knuckles white and prominent.

"Patrick was very deeply involved in the Irish Republican Army."

"I know that," she said impatiently.

The two men exchanged looks.

The prime minister picked up a file on his desk and handed it to Kate. "Perhaps you should read the report on your own."

"I don't understand."

"There is some information here you may not be familiar with. It may be painful to you."

She looked down at the file in her lap. "May I have some time alone?"

"Of course." The prime minister's hand was on the doorknob. "Pick up the phone when you're finished."

Neil didn't move.

Kate looked pointedly at him.

"I'm staying," he said. "Don't try to convince me to leave."

She nodded, turned toward the light and opened the file.

Neil resumed his position at the window and waited. Ten minutes passed. Twenty. He would know the exact moment she finished, the moment she read his name at the bottom of the report.

Her gasp was harsh, choking. Neil turned to face his reckoning. Her hand was at her throat, her face bleached white like sheets drying in the summer sun. The blue of her eyes scorched him.

"All this time, you knew. It was you who investigated Patrick's murder."

"Yes."

"Why didn't you tell me?"

He shrugged, realized how pathetic an excuse the gesture was, and tried to explain. "At first, there was no reason. You were simply the wife of a terrorist. Later—"

"Later?"

The words came out, the rush of confession, the leaping to another step. "Later, I couldn't. I knew it would hurt you."

"Do you have any idea how this hurts me?"

"I'm sorry, Kate. I tried to protect you."

"That's a pitiful answer, Neil." She stood and walked toward him, the file open. "In your world, I suppose women need protection. But not in mine. I'm Irish. I saw my husband shot to death in front of me. I feared my children would be next. They do that, you know, murder children in front of their parents."

"Stop it, Kate."

"What could you possibly protect me from?"

Neil took the file from her, flitted through the photos, chose one and held it up.

"This."

She looked at the photo and dismissed it with the confidence of a woman who has never suffered an unfaithful husband. "Patrick was not a philanderer, Neil. There is nothing you could show me that would make me believe that."

"You didn't think he was a terrorist, either."

"I still don't."

Neil clasped his hands together. "I investigated this myself, Kate. I spent months verifying the information. I had no reason to falsify any of it."

"You're British and you're Special Forces. That's reason enough."

"Give me credit for some integrity, please."

"Why should I?"

"Because, damn it, I care for you."

Her hands clenched and her control broke. "How dare you say such a thing?" She pulled the file from his hands. "You don't know the first thing about caring for anyone." She picked up her handbag and coat. "Tell the prime minister that Robbie Finnigan is the biggest stumbling block to the peace process. Until he's removed we'll never have unbiased law enforcement in Northern Ireland.''

Neil frowned. ''Why not tell him yourself?''

''Because I'm going home. Don't call me, Neil. I want to be left alone.''

''I understand.''

At the door she turned to look at him one last time. Her eyes were wide, accusing. ''I doubt that very much.''

''Kate—'' He would have said more, wanted to say more, but she was gone and the copied file with her.

The knock on her door startled Kate. No one knocked in Ardara or in any another Irish village. Visitors called out from the yard, opened the door, stuck their heads inside and called out again. If there was no response they walked through the house searching the rooms for good measure. Kate knew to keep her bathroom door locked if she wanted privacy. Setting aside her report, she walked in stocking feet to the front door and opened it. The woman on the porch opened her arms and Kate, after her first mew of surprise, threw herself into them.

Finally she drew back, laughing. ''Maeve. I didn't expect you for at least another month.''

Maeve flipped back her waist-length red hair and sucked in her cheeks. ''I thought you needed me, darling.''

''I've never needed anyone more.'' She pulled her friend inside. ''Come in. Have you eaten?''

''I'm fine for food but I could use a drink. Have you anything decent?''

Kate felt almost giddy. ''I feel like wine, very decent, I think. Please, join me.''

"I'm yours, love. You needn't ask twice. Lead the way."

Deciding the occasion warranted something special, Kate selected a twelve-year-old merlot from Patrick's personal collection, held it up for Maeve's approval and poured it into her favorite Waterford. Maeve followed her into the living room. They sat across from each other on identical couches close to the blazing turf fire.

Maeve spoke first. "What in bloody hell is happening to you, Katie?"

The sound of her childhood name undid her. Tears spilled down her cheeks. Her hands shook. To avoid spilling the expensive wine, she set her glass on the coffee table.

"Good Lord." Maeve's eyes were wide with shock. "Is it as bad as all that?"

Kate nodded.

Maeve walked around the table and sat down beside her friend. "Tell me."

Pressing the back of her hand against her nose, Kate sniffed. "I don't know where to begin."

"Is it Kevin?"

Kate shrugged. "I thought so, until this morning." She searched for a tissue, blew her nose and tried to explain. "Have you ever been so sure of something, so sure that you would stake your very life on it, only to find that everything you believed was a lie?"

Maeve rubbed the lipstick from the rim of her glass. "This is about Patrick, isn't it?"

Kate looked up, surprised. "How did you know?"

"I didn't, not really. It was just a guess."

"They're saying Patrick was a terrorist." Her eyes filled. "That's not right, either. According to their report, he was more than a terrorist, he was an assassin, a murderer, no better than the men who killed him.''

''Do you believe that?''

''I don't know what to believe.''

''He was your husband for a very long time.''

Kate hesitated.

Maeve refilled her wineglass. ''Is there anything else?''

''No, not really.''

Maeve's eyes were green, light-struck, wise. ''Tell me, Kate.''

''There are photos of a woman.''

''Do you have them?''

Kate shrugged it off. ''It's ridiculous. Patrick loved me. I never doubted that, not once.''

Maeve was silent.

Kate's face clouded. ''There are a thousand reasons why Patrick was with her that may have nothing to do with infidelity.''

''Of course there are.''

Kate stared at her friend. ''I don't think I could bear it, Maeve, not even now, after all these years.''

Maeve folded her long legs beneath her, leaned forward and spoke earnestly. ''I know you, Kate. More than anyone I think, you could bear it. It might even make things easier for you.''

''How could that be?''

''It's been six years since Patrick's murder and you're still walking around like a corpse. For pity's sake, Katie, his clothes are still in your closet. Perhaps if you saw Patrick for who he was, a man with flaws instead of a saint, you could move on and find some happiness in this life.''

''I don't think it would make me happy to learn that my marriage was a lie.''

''It wasn't a lie. I have no doubt that Patrick loved you. You were his wife, the mother of his children. If there was anyone else, she certainly never took your place. Some men—'' She stopped.

''Go on.''

''I'm sorry. I've no business going on like this. I came to comfort you and I'm making you miserable and angry.''

Kate studied Maeve's lovely flushed face. ''Please finish.''

''No, Kate.''

''I think I've been horribly naive,'' Kate said quietly. ''I'd like you to finish what you were going to say.''

''It's just a theory. I've no evidence.''

''I've evidence enough for ten lifetimes. What I need are reasons. I've no experience, Maeve. Patrick was the only man in my life. You're different. Help me.''

Maeve sighed. ''Aye. I'm different.''

''I didn't mean—''

Maeve held up her hand. ''I know what you meant, Kate. I don't pretend to be a saint and I'm not offended. In my defense, I've never done anything to hurt anyone. In fact, I've gone to lengths to be sure no one was hurt. I don't know if I can help you. I know that men don't look at relationships the way women do. A man can sleep with a woman he finds attractive even if he doesn't love her, even if he has a wife at home whom he does love and has no intention of ever leaving. Having an affair or a mistress doesn't diminish the affection he has for his wife.''

''Are you telling me that Patrick—''

"I'm not *telling* you anything. I'm offering the possibility of an explanation."

Kate shook her head. "It isn't possible. I knew him better than anyone."

Eyes averted, Maeve, fidgeted with her wineglass. "Did you?"

"Do you want to see the file?"

"Good God! You actually walked away with a file?"

"Do you want to see her?"

Maeve swallowed. "Yes," she said, her voice huskier than usual.

Kate left the room.

Maeve closed her eyes and pressed her hands against her temples. Already she had gone through a considerable amount of wine. She felt Kate come back into the room. Opening her eyes, she took the cream-colored file from her grip and opened it. Drawing a deep, sustaining breath, she forced herself to look at the police photo and the woman seated beside Patrick Nolan.

Nineteen

Kevin was not familiar with the Falls. He couldn't remember ever visiting the house where his father grew up and where his uncles now lived. He'd never questioned that the relationship with his father's family began and ended in his own home. Now he knew that circumstance had everything to do with his mother. She wasn't comfortable in West Belfast. It was too dirty, too poor and too dangerous.

It was his first time away from Tranquility House. He kept his eyes on the ground, glancing up occasionally to be sure he was traveling in the right direction. Row after row of new brick buildings with colorfully painted doors did little to disguise the slumlike quality of the neighborhoods. Litter gathered in rain gutters, bars covered street-level windows and rusted debris lay in forgotten piles beside porches. Kevin thought of the lace curtains and cozy kitchens of Ardara, where peat fires smoked their friendly hazes and welcomes were warm and genuine. He hated Belfast. He hated Neil Anderson and, more than anyone, he hated himself.

A black taxi pulled up beside him. He walked faster. The window rolled down. "Kevin."

The voice was familiar. He turned and nearly tripped with relief. Uncle Liam. He would have called out but the man shook his head.

The door opened. "Climb in, lad."

Kevin scrambled over a pair of legs and fell into the middle of the back seat. Two men were in the back, two in front. Other than his uncle, they were all strangers. No one said a word. Kevin was very conscious of his own labored breathing. "Where are we going?" he asked at last.

Liam answered. "Settle in, lad. We'll be there soon."

Kevin was more nervous than frightened. He was with Liam. Nothing would happen to him.

Neil pulled out of the narrow space where he'd parked the nondescript car he was driving. He'd waited long enough. The taxi was a considerable distance ahead. He would not be observed. His hands clenched around the wheel. He'd made a mistake with Kevin. The boy looked more like a prep school student out for a Sunday stroll than a drug abuser. He was too clean, too innocent and much too young for the role thrust upon him. Whatever the lad's involvement in the drug world had been, it couldn't have been serious. He hoped to God that blood ran true and that Liam Nolan would protect his nephew.

He followed the taxi down the Springfield Road to the Monagh Bypass. He made a quick right on to the Glen Road away from the city toward Andersonstown. The streets were wider. Traffic had calmed. He dropped farther behind. The black taxi continued east and turned abruptly on to a small street where a group of young boys played football. Neil passed by the turn and doubled back. He drove slowly down the street. The taxi was parked halfway up on the footpath. No one was inside. Again, Neil turned, drove past the parked car, found a side street and parked in back of a lorry. He ached for a cigarette. Gritting his teeth, he resisted the urge and settled in for a wait.

Kevin looked around, careful not to make eye contact. He was seated beside Liam on a long L-shaped couch that faced a television screen. The conversation was filled with terms he knew nothing about. He felt awkward and very young, much younger than the grim, hard-jawed men all around him. He was obviously an outsider. No one would tell him anything. Deliberately he blocked out the voices on both sides of him. He knew he would have to bring something to Neil Anderson. He trusted Liam to supply him with information.

Somewhere in the conversation he was aware of his own name. The room was silent. Liam introduced him. "This is my nephew, Kevin Nolan."

No one said a word.

"Patrick's son," Liam finished.

The sudden buzz of conversation startled him.

"He'll be with us for a time," Liam explained.

The men had questions, questions they would voice after he'd gone. Kevin could see it in their eyes, cold, narrow, speculative. For the first time he was aware of details. Everyone was casually dressed, black leather jackets, windbreakers, denims. Only men were represented, all clean-shaven, unsmiling, purposeful. No one was high or out-of-control. Four men were hunched over a table quietly discussing what looked like an aerial map. Nothing had been exchanged. As far as he could tell, never once had drugs or money come into the conversation. Anderson would be disappointed. A burst of triumph surged through him. Perhaps this would be easier than he thought.

Liam stood, pulling Kevin up with him. "Come with me, lad. We'll have a snack in the kitchen."

Kevin followed him into a clean, brightly lit room furnished with a small wooden table and four chairs. Liam nodded toward a tray filled with biscuits, snacks and scones. "Help yourself," he said. He seated himself and spooned sugar into his milky tea.

Filling a small plate, Kevin sat across from him. "What am I doing here?"

"Working off your promise to the RUC."

"I'll have to tell him something."

Liam shrugged. "Tell him what you heard but describe no one, not even if he shows you photos."

"I heard enough but I didn't understand anything."

"Say there's a shipment coming in two MacReady lorries down the Crumlin Road at half past eleven on Tuesday next."

"Is it true?"

"Aye." Liam swallowed half his tea. "But it's only a front, to make him trust you. We'll give him a little to keep the rest in reserve."

"What kind will it be?"

Liam frowned. "What do you mean *what kind?* When did you become interested in weapons?"

"I thought you meant drugs."

"No," his uncle said slowly. "Drugs ruin a man, lad. I hope you're done with all that."

"Anderson won't be happy," Kevin protested. "He wants drugs."

Liam pulled another cup across the table and filled it for Kevin. "Trust me. He'll be happy with what you give him."

* * *

Neil opened his thermos and swigged down a healthy portion of steaming tea. Ten years in the desert had thinned his blood. He felt the cold. No one had gone in or come out of the house in over two hours. Once again he checked his watch. Was it his imagination or was time moving particularly slowly? Where in bloody hell was Kevin? What were they doing in there? His imagination soared. He felt heat in his fingers and ears, an indication of rising blood pressure. What was the matter with him? Breathing deeply, he deliberately quelled his fears. The lad was in no danger, not here, not this time. The meeting was a setup, designed to test Kevin and to put Neil off the track. Nothing he needed to know would take place tonight.

The door opened and Kevin walked out with Liam Nolan. They were alone. Together they climbed into the taxi. Neil slumped down, careful to keep his head hidden. Two more men left the house and joined them. Neil didn't recognize the driver. The taxi pulled away from the curb, circled and headed back down the street. Neil kept his eyes on his rearview mirror, waiting until the taxi disappeared around the bend before starting his car. Kevin looked unharmed and in good spirits. He would wait until tomorrow before contacting him.

Neil's hands shook. He couldn't insert the key into the ignition. Cursing, he tried again. This time it fit. Slowly he turned the car around and headed back toward the City Centre.

Maeve's laugh bordered on the hysterical. Kate didn't know whether it was her fourth glass of wine or the shock of reading the contents of the envelope she'd filched from the prime minister's office. "Are you all right, Maeve?" she asked anxiously.

"I'm drunk," her friend replied.

Kate frowned. "Shall I make up a bed for you?"

Maeve shook her head. "I'll manage. I'm not driving."

"You haven't said anything about the photos."

Maeve hugged herself and leaned over the table to inspect the pictures again. "There isn't much to see," she said slowly. "The woman's face is completely shadowed and so is Patrick's. It may not even be him."

"It's him."

"How can you tell for sure?"

"I know my husband. The way he holds his head, his fork." Her throat closed. She cleared it. "I know my husband," she repeated.

"Do you know the woman?" Maeve's voice was low and muffled, alcohol-thick.

Kate picked up the photo and studied it carefully. "No," she said at last, "but there's something about her—"

"What?"

"I can't put my finger on it." She handed the photo to Maeve. "What do you think?"

"About—?"

"Do they look like two people having an affair?"

"Oh, Kate," Maeve moaned. "How can anyone determine such a thing from a picture?"

"Look at them," Kate insisted.

Maeve looked. She hesitated. "They're eating," she said slowly. "It looks like they're drinking, too. I see wine on the table."

"What else?"

"Their faces are too dark, but their hands—" she stopped.

"Their hands—" Kate prompted her.

"They're not touching each other," Maeve finished.

Kate sighed. "No, they aren't."

"People have meals together, Kate. It doesn't mean they're having an affair."

"Look at the matches on the table."

"Why?"

"Look at the monogram. What does it say?"

Maeve squinted. "I can't make it out."

"Try," Kate insisted.

"It looks like the Lime Tree."

"Do you know the restaurant?"

"It's in Belfast, I think."

"Yes, it is, a lovely restaurant in Belfast."

"Well?"

"I was there for the first time last week."

"So?"

"Patrick was a regular patron."

"Is that a problem?"

Kate leaned forward, her eyes wide and earnest. "Don't you think it's odd, considering the amount of time Patrick and I spent in Belfast, that he never once took me to one of its finest restaurants, one that he frequented often?"

"I'm not sure that's important."

"He never even mentioned it."

"Is that unusual?"

"Patrick was a conversationalist, Maeve. There wasn't anything he didn't say or describe in great detail. It was very uncharacteristic of him not to even mention the name of a restaurant where the maître d' knows his name, enough to offer me condolences six years later."

Maeve's mouth, lovely, sultry, deliciously curved, tightened. "Leave it, Kate."

"What if I can't?"

"What good will come of it?"

"The truth."

Maeve snorted. "Truth, always the Holy Grail. What if it tears your family apart?"

Kate looked at her friend incredulously. "Look at my family, Maeve. Can it get any worse?"

The green eyes were very bright and filled with pity. "Don't test the waters, Katie. Leave this one alone. You've your children to think of. Patrick was a man, not the best, but certainly not the worst. Accept that and move on."

"Is that what you would do?"

"It is."

Kate leaned her head back against the cushions and closed her eyes. Six years ago she thought nothing could ever hurt her again.

The following Wednesday she stayed the night in the city. Seven o'clock found her at an impasse, clenching the telephone. Her wrist ached. Coming to a decision she punched in Neil Anderson's number. *Please be home,* she prayed silently.

He answered on the second ring. She relaxed her death grip on the receiver.

"Neil, this is Kate Nolan."

"Kate. How can I help you?"

"Can you meet me?"

"Of course. When?"

"Now."

"Are you in Belfast?"

"Yes."

"I'll be there in ten minutes."

"No. I'll come to you, and make it an hour."

"Done. Do you have my address?"

"Yes."

"I'll be waiting."

Kate replaced the receiver, walked into the bathroom and turned on the shower. She stared at her reflection in the mirror and winced. Pulling herself together, she stepped into the spray. A shower would revive her.

Her visit with Kevin had been a disaster. He was cocky and sarcastic, the Kevin she couldn't reach. Even Deirdre's wit and patience couldn't cut through his cheek. Her daughter was a love, too serious and cautious for a girl her age, but a rock of sanity. As much as Kate appreciated her, she knew she must not cling too closely. The child's experience bore little relation to normalcy. Time, the experts said, would take care of everything. Kate was beginning to doubt their judgment.

She was very close to succumbing to panic. For the first time since Patrick's death she doubted her ability to cope. Only her work kept her sane. Attending to the abused civil rights of the downtrodden of the Six Counties, she lost herself in their difficulties and avoided her own. Even her father's unfailing wry wit, which once had the ability to send her into peals of helpless laughter, couldn't lift her spirits. Kate was ashamed to admit it was Patrick's defection more than anything else, more than Kevin, that had claimed her spirit. Despite her brave proclamations to Neil and the prime minister she had grave doubts. It was impossible to read the report and not have them.

Kate combed her hair back allowing it to dry naturally and pulled on a pair of denims and a pullover.

Deciding against makeup, she smoothed balm over her lips, zipped up her boots, threw a blue leather jacket over her shoulders and stared at herself objectively in the mirror. A slim woman, obviously forty years old, with good teeth, large eyes surrounded with spidery laugh lines, a mouth defined by recent suffering and thick, fine hair stared back at her. Her only jewelry were the tiny hoops in her ears and the gold wedding band she had never removed. Kate frowned at her reflection. She was pale and plain and aging. No one looking at her scrubbed face and straight hair would ever accuse her of vanity.

Digging in her purse, she found her keys, locked the door of her room and ran down the stairs to her car. Neil lived near the City Centre. She was familiar with the streets around the government buildings. Ten minutes later she stood in front of his door and rang the bell.

He was dressed casually, khaki slacks and a plaid shirt open at the throat. It suited him. He seemed warmer, more approachable. Kate smiled.

"Please, come in," he said, ushering her into a large room with glossy wooden floors.

Kate looked around admiringly. "This is lovely."

"It's stark," Neil admitted. "I've kept it that way because I've never really considered it home."

"Where is home?"

"Nowhere, really. Things have been temporary for quite some time now."

Kate pointed to a photo in a silver frame. "Is this your daughter?"

"Yes. That's Erin. It was taken last year."

The child was lovely, blond and blue-eyed, without

the usual adolescent gawkiness that characterized most teenagers.

"Would you care for a drink?"

Kate nodded. "White wine would be very nice, if you have it."

He disappeared into the kitchen.

"Thank you for seeing me on such short notice."

He returned with two goblets filled with a delicate golden liquid.

Kate sipped hers tentatively. "Delicious," she pronounced.

His glance was probing, serious. "We didn't part on the best of terms the last time we met. I want to apologize for that. The circumstances were awkward."

Kate nodded. She sat down on the couch. "That's why I'm here, to apologize for accusing you of ulterior motives regarding Patrick's investigation."

He looked surprised. "No offense taken, Kate. Your reaction was perfectly normal." His smile lit up his face. "But I'm grateful if that's what brought you here."

She felt the heat flood her face. "I have another reason as well."

He grinned and sat down across from her. "I'm still grateful."

Kate twisted the wineglass in her hands. Her feelings were mixed. She felt comfortable here, secure and protected. What she had to say would destroy the mood. But it must be said. Finally she looked up. His eyes, gray and honest and very direct, were on her face. "I need your help."

"You shall have it," he said.

Kate bit her lip. "Just like that. No matter what?"

"No matter what."

"Why?" His answer would lead them into dangerous areas. But Kate no longer cared.

"Because I've never met anyone like you."

She stared at him, shocked. "You're not serious?"

"Never more."

"Will you explain that?"

"Not now."

"When?"

"After you tell me why you're here."

She drew a deep breath. "I want you to tell me everything you know about Patrick."

"My report is very complete." He hesitated, looked at her face and changed his mind. "Is there something in particular you want clarified?"

Six years had passed. Six years and the searing pain still had the power to cripple her. Damn Patrick. They'd had a life, children, careers. Why had he thrown it all away? "When did it all begin?"

"What are you referring to?" he asked cautiously.

"Oh, Neil." Kate didn't know whether to laugh or cry. "You're so very kind to me. I want to know when Patrick's involvement became more than defending his clients. After that we can talk about the woman or women, whichever it might be."

Neil looked embarrassed. "I would have spared you this."

She believed him. "I know but it's too late now. If you want to help me, tell me what you know."

A minute ticked by while he studied her face, gauging her capacity to endure. Finally he spoke. "Patrick joined the Provos before he left secondary school."

The gasp nearly strangled her but she refused to allow it to leave her throat, understanding, somehow, that if she did he would stop talking.

"He was a brilliant student, as you know," he continued. "They handpicked him, nurtured him, perhaps even guided him into and through his professional life. When he married you, his reputation was well established. Given his record, his talent was obvious. That's when he came under the scrutiny of Special Forces." His voice was toneless, articulate and completely without emotion. "After the Enniskillen bombing and the falter of the initial Peace Accord, operations were escalated. That's when the Belfast Brigade became exceptionally organized. Numbers were scaled down. Informants were ineffective. No one cracked under interrogation. Special Forces couldn't infiltrate. Patrick had risen to an executive level. All targets, all operations were overseen by him. He was an exceptional man. Unfortunately his talents were channeled in the wrong direction. For the last five years before his murder, he was responsible for all of the assassinations by the Belfast Brigade of the Irish Republican Army."

Kate listened in disbelief. This was Patrick he was describing, her Patrick. How could it possibly be? How could she not have known the man she'd married? "I can't believe it," she whispered. "I would have known. Surely I would have known." She appealed to him, the question begging for an answer. "How could I not have known?"

"He didn't want you to know," Neil replied. "Patrick was clever."

"Not clever enough to prevent his own murder."

"An inevitability for a man in his position."

"What do you mean?"

"The IRA isn't the only paramilitary group with clever leadership, Kate. For every man like Patrick, there will be one like him on the other side."

"What about the woman?" she asked.

"We don't know who she is. We don't believe she was ever involved in any IRA targets, therefore she wasn't important to us."

"In other words, she was Patrick's mistress."

Once again, he hesitated.

"Tell me, Neil."

"I believe so."

"Why?"

"On more than one occasion, they shared a room."

Kate's hands shook. She lifted the glass and wet her lips. Her stomach refused more. Her scope of vision narrowed. The room was going black and she couldn't find her breath.

Neil's hands were hard on her shoulders. His mouth was near her ear. "Kate. Are you all right?" Gently he eased her down until she lay flat on the couch. "Close your eyes," he said.

She heard him rummaging in her purse, felt him press the inhaler vial into the palm of her hand. "Breathe," he ordered.

She shook her head.

"For God's sake, Kate. Don't do this."

His voice was very far away. She didn't want to breathe. The sharpness would come back and with it the pain. She wanted it all to go away. *She* wanted to go away.

"Kevin needs you, Kate. Deirdre needs you. Stop this. Patrick was a man, a clever manipulative man. You made a mistake. You have two children. You're alive and he's dead. You have the best of the bargain."

His words pierced through her fog. Kevin and Deirdre. Kevin and Deirdre. Slowly she lifted the vial to her mouth, closed her lips around the head and squeezed.

Twenty

Later, much later, when the world had evened out again, when Kate could bear to open her eyes and sit and breathe and speak and think, when the searing hurt had settled into a dull ache, when once again Neil sat across from her, relief evident on his face, she came back to the question he had never answered. "How am I unlike anyone you've ever met before?"

He knew it wasn't the right time. He wanted no part of correcting Patrick Nolan's mistakes, but he also knew that she desperately needed reassurance. The only way to give it to her was to tell the truth.

"This is dangerous, Kate," he warned her. "But if you really want to know, I'll tell you."

She looked up at him through thickly feathered eyelashes. "Do you know that in the Irish language, the word *no* doesn't exist?"

His face changed, hardened. His eyes burned with an intensity she hadn't seen in a long time. Could it possibly mean what she thought? Please, she prayed silently, let it be so.

He crossed the distance between them to sit down beside her. Without warning or permission, he took her face between his hands and lowered his lips to hers.

His mouth was gentle, undemanding. Kate closed her eyes and gave herself up to the sweetness of it.

Too soon, he pulled away. "I think I've been in love with you since the first moment I saw you."

"Love?" She looked incredulous. "You love me?"

"What else would you call it?"

She pressed her hand so that it was flat against his chest. "I don't think I love you," she said, forcing the honesty from her lips. "I'm attracted to you. I like you, but love—" She shook her head. "I've never even considered the possibility."

"I know."

"You don't really know me."

"I know you, Kate. Not completely, but I know all that is necessary to have fallen in love with you. Any man in his right mind would love you. You're loyal and intelligent, generous and uncomplaining, a loving mother, a faithful wife." He sat back, not touching her.

She hadn't intended to push him away. The feel of a man's lips, his hands, after so many barren years was heaven.

She inched toward him. "Is this the way you normally make decisions, so quickly?"

He looked at her steadily. "I haven't made a decision, Kate. I'm simply telling you how I feel."

"I see." She felt deflated, presumptuous, embarrassed.

"There is your position to consider, and mine," he muttered under his breath.

"Of course."

He couldn't read her. Her eyes were veiled against him. Damn it, what was going on in her head? He'd just told her he loved her. "Kate—" he began, "I don't normally do things this way. I don't know how it's done."

She looked up quickly, a flash of blue, very bright, too bright, in the pale oval of her face.

Was it possible that he'd hurt her? He risked the question. ''What are you thinking?''

She shook her head.

He decided against caution. She would be the one to reject him. Gently he lifted her hand, worked open her clenched fingers and pressed her palm against his mouth. She shuddered. Emboldened, he ran his tongue from her palm to the inside of her wrist. She touched his cheek. Desire coursed through him. Threading his fingers through her hair, he pulled her head back and set his mouth on hers.

There was no gentleness in the kisses he pressed on her lips, her neck, her brow, the slope of her cheek, just heat and need and passion and a feeling that finally he knew what it was like to belong, to feel a woman beside him, around him, within him, to sense her presence, to care enough to please her, to protect her, to take her burdens for his own. He pressed her down on the couch. She looked up at him, blue eyes huge and trusting, dark hair splayed across the pillows. He saw the rise and fall of her chest and waited no longer.

He was conscious of the thinness of her, the faint blue veins under the pale skin of her breasts and the tight, toned muscles of her runner's body. She was small-boned but not fragile, shy but not self-conscious, inexperienced but willing. The feel of her beneath him, the taste of her skin, the slight weight of her breasts, the smooth silk of her legs undid him and he touched and kissed and stroked and moved with all the wonder and care of a man coming into love later than most and for the first time.

Kate sensed it and opened for him hungrily, completely, understanding that the differences between them might well be too much for this night to be repeated. It wasn't the physical satisfaction she missed. That had been rare, even when Patrick took his time to please her. It was the closeness she craved, the heat and muscle of a hair-rough body pressed against her own, the incredible intimacy of joining, the rising tension, harsh breathing, words, soft and low, muffled against her throat, the dizzy pleasure of lips on her breast and, finally, the moment of release, liquid warmth spreading through her, arms tightening, breath slowing and the even, steady drum of a heart beating in unison with hers. Secure in her expectations, anticipation rising, she closed her eyes.

She couldn't say when she first realized that nothing was the same. All at once they were upon her, sensations she'd never known her body was capable of feeling. Neil Anderson was not Patrick Nolan and lovemaking was as different as one man was from another. She welcomed it, the heat, the desire, the wanton urges of her newly awakened body demanding more and more until she felt it, the shattering moment where she no longer cared that her soul had been sold to a man that Patrick would have called *the enemy*.

Neil watched her breathe. Her sleep was deep, trusting. He was grateful for that. Whatever the future held he would remember this night and know there had been nothing held back between them. His arm ached. He would cut it off before he disturbed her. She would have her sleep. Instinct, and the dark bruises below her eyes, told him there had been little enough of that for her.

He must have slept as well. He woke to find her smiling at him.

"Hello," he said.

She blushed. "Thank you."

"The pleasure was mine." He lowered his head to her lips and lingered there.

"Ours," she said when she could speak again.

He nodded. "Ours."

Again she smiled. "Ours."

He watched her sit up, find her clothes and pull them on, wondering if she had any idea how lovely she was.

"I need to ask you about Kevin."

Neil's heart sank. He zipped up his trousers and waited.

"He's changed."

Neil frowned. "How?"

"Until now, he's been grateful for my visits and anxious to come home. When I saw him today, he was angry and sarcastic, just like he was before this whole thing blew up." She sat very still, her hands in her lap. "Has something happened?"

Neil tugged his shirt over his head. He would tell her. She had a right to know. "Kevin has been in contact with his uncles. I imagine they've convinced him that they have his interests at heart. More than likely his attitude has everything to do with his level of confidence. He feels invincible."

"Is that true?"

"Absolutely not."

"How can you be sure?"

"These are terrorists, Kate. They do what they have to do."

"Are you telling me that Kevin is in danger?"

"There is a risk. You knew that."

He watched her swallow. She was pale again and obviously terrified. Her hands shook and she concentrated to control her breathing.

"It can't be like that, Neil. What do we have to do to get him out of this?"

We, she'd said we. "As a matter of fact, I was thinking the very same thing."

The brightness in her eyes was worth his admission.

Quickly he moved to clarify his thought. "It has to be done carefully, Kate. Kevin has already been seen. I can't just pull him out. It would be too dangerous." He hesitated. "There's something else."

"What?"

"He still has the terms of a drug conviction to fulfill. He won't be sent home scot-free."

The light died in her eyes. "What will he have to do?"

"I don't know. I'm not experienced with this sort of thing. I'm sorry."

"Where do we go from here?"

"There's an arms shipment he told me about. His time and location are wrong, of course. A lad like Kevin would never be trusted with accurate information. I can make it seem that he's unreliable. He'll be pulled."

"What has an arms shipment to do with Kevin?"

"We're after the paramilitaries' weapons arsenal. Drugs are only a front. The same people are involved in both."

Her hand was at her throat. "My God. You have my son involved with paramilitary weapons? Kevin can't do that, Neil. He's a boy, not even a boy from the streets. He hasn't been raised like that."

"I realize that now. It was obvious the first time I sent him off by himself."

He watched her struggle to gather herself, to remain calm. Whatever was between them was forgotten for the moment.

"Won't it be obvious if you pull him out after only one attempt?"

"What else can I do, Kate?" Neil was feeling desperate. "We both want him out."

She stared at him, her face innocent of makeup, her eyes huge and hurt. "I have to trust you, Neil. There is no one else. I can't take much more. Please understand that if anything happens to my son, it will destroy me."

"What about us?"

She smiled. "This was lovely. Thank you."

He forced himself to speak calmly. "That's it?"

"Did you expect——" She stopped and started again. "Did you want something more?"

"You know damn well that I want something more."

Kate wet her lips. "What about who we are? I believe you called it *our positions*."

"We're beyond that and you know it."

"I'm a Catholic, Neil. This is Northern Ireland. I can't fraternize with a police officer. My credibility would be ruined."

"You're home is in the Republic. When this is over, that's where you'll be. I'm not Protestant, Kate. Religion hasn't been part of my life for a long time, but if that's important to you, it will be."

"This won't be over for years and years. We're not making any real progress. The sticking point for us is a new government, a new policing force. You could very well be out of a job if those demands are met."

"I'll take my chances," he said dryly. "Quite

frankly, if I never see Northern Ireland again, it won't disappoint me."

"Do you feel that way about all of Ireland?"

"Of course not."

"Our timing is poor."

"Better that than not at all."

Kate stood and stretched. "I have to think about this, Neil. I didn't expect it. There are so many unresolved matters."

"Such as?"

"Kevin, for one."

"I'm going to fix that."

"There's Patrick."

"He's dead." His words were honest, brutal, powerful.

"Not for me," she said. "Not yet."

"Why not?"

"Because I don't know the truth."

"I'll help you."

She turned to him eagerly. "Will you?"

He nodded. "It may not be what you think, Kate. There is the possibility you may be hurt very badly."

"Will you help me?" she repeated.

"Yes," he said wearily, wishing he had another choice.

Kate stood in front of the double doors that had served as a small upstairs office and retreat when Patrick was alive. This was the room Kate and the children had known not to disturb without permission. He had ordered sliding doors to separate it from their bedroom and close out the light when he worked late. Kate had never felt quite up to clearing it out, even down to the scattered papers on his desk and the heavy coats and parka in the closet. Someday, she had promised herself, when she could smell remnants of his scent without breaking down, she would organize and give away the last of his belongings. Weeks became months and months, years. She always seemed to find something else to do that could not be postponed. She refused to put it off any longer. Instinct told her the answers to her questions would be found in this room.

She stood in front of the closet, closed her eyes and opened the door. His coats were hung according to season, heavy wools first, lighter wools and windbreakers for spring and summer. So far, so good. She fingered a dark gray tweed, moved it across the rack so that a lighter gray wool was exposed. Suddenly it hit her, the faint, familiar smells of tobacco and aftershave, old leather and wool, Patrick's smells.

Kate picked up a sleeve, buried her face in it and inhaled. It was different, this time. Somehow it felt right to be standing in Patrick's closet with her cheek pressed against the sleeve of his coat. She smiled into the wool, running her hands down the expensive fabric, then inside over the lining. Humming to herself, Kate slipped her fingers inside the pocket and pulled out a slip of paper, a bookmaker's receipt. How odd. Patrick had been one of few Irishmen who had no interest in racing. Pencil marks hid some of the numbers. She flicked on the light, squinting to decipher the faded writing. It looked like a phone number, but there were too many digits.

On a hunch, Kate carried the paper downstairs to her study, opened the top drawer of the desk and pulled out her address book. 011 was an international code and 212 was the area code for numbers in the city of New York. She relaxed. Patrick knew people in New York.

He hadn't been specific about all aspects of his work but, to be fair, she had never shown much interest. She stared at the receipt and thought of the restaurant in Belfast. On an impulse, she picked up the phone and dialed the number. No answer, nor was there a machine. Slowly Kate replaced the receiver and looked at her watch. It was five hours earlier in New York, four o'clock in the morning. She would try again later.

Pocketing the receipt, Kate grabbed a jacket and locked the door behind her. Maeve would have a fresh perspective. She would beg a cup of tea from her friend.

Maeve answered the door in a multicolored Hawaiian sarong tied in a double knot around her tanned hips and a brief white spandex top. She had a half-finished martini in her hand. Kate stared at her in amazement. "It's ten o'clock in the morning and we've hail on the way."

Maeve shrugged her shoulders. "I've been on the treadmill. If I get cold, I'll change." She pulled Kate inside and closed the door. "Half of Ireland is drunk by this time of morning. You know that."

"Times have changed, Maeve. People are working now. Drink isn't such an important part of our lives."

Maeve shook back her red mane and snorted. "I'm too old to change and I'm not working."

Kate didn't take off her jacket. "I didn't come here to argue."

"Then don't criticize me." Maeve's tone was sharp. She looked at Kate and was instantly contrite. "I'm sorry, love. Pay no attention to me. I'm always a witch when I've had a few too many."

Kate followed her friend into the drawing room and slowly removed her jacket. "Is something troubling you, Maeve?"

Maeve's laugh was brittle. She sat down beside Kate

and crossed her legs beneath her. "I'm forty years old, single, childless and my prospects aren't at all good. On those rare occasions when I take stock of my life, I wonder what I've done with it." She lifted her glass and swallowed the last of her drink. "I've accomplished nothing, Kate, absolutely nothing."

"That isn't true," Kate protested. "You're an accomplished artist. Your work is wonderful and you're a dear friend. What would I do without you?"

Maeve's yellow-green eyes were very bright. "You're a love, Katie, but in the end, perhaps you won't think I've been such a dear friend."

"I don't understand."

"I'm gone most of the time and I'm close to inebriation when I am here. What kind of friend is that?"

"I don't remember your drinking that much, Maeve." Kate was obviously troubled.

"Let's not talk about me anymore," Maeve said. "Isn't today a workday?"

Kate smiled. "I should be working. Instead I came for a cup of tea and some conversation."

Maeve's hand flew to her lips. "God, I'm hopeless. Follow me into the kitchen and I'll brew a pot of Bewleys."

Ten minutes later, fortified with steaming cups of tea and a pot that promised more between them, the two women sat across from each other at Maeve's solid oaken table.

"Tell me your troubles, Katie," she began.

The urge to tell Maeve about Neil Anderson was strong, but she decided against it. Her own feelings regarding Neil weren't settled. Until they were she would wait. "I went into Patrick's room today to clean out his things," she began.

"Good," Maeve broke in. "It's about time."

"I found this." Kate reached into her pocket and pulled out the booking receipt. She handed it to Maeve.

"It's a booking receipt."

"It's also an international phone number."

Maeve squinted. "So it is." She returned the slip of paper to Kate.

"I called the number but no one answered."

"Why would you call?"

"I want to find the woman, Maeve." Kate's voice was tight, strained. "I must find her."

"What good will it do?"

"I need to know what her relationship was with my husband."

"Will it make you feel any differently about Patrick?"

"Yes."

Maeve sighed. "Whatever you find won't bring him back, Katie. Nor will it change anything at all. Why do this?"

"It will change everything."

"All right." Maeve lifted one perfectly shaped eyebrow. "Let's assume worst case. Suppose Patrick was unfaithful to you with this woman. Suppose she was his mistress. What will you do?"

Kate's mind was blank. She floundered for words. "I don't know. Talk to her, maybe."

"For what purpose?" Maeve persisted.

"Stop badgering me, Maeve. I don't know."

"Shall I tell you?"

Kate stared at her. "Please, do."

"You want to see her, to know if she's more attractive than you. You want to know if he promised her anything, if he was the same person with her that he was with you, if she was better in bed. Women always want to know those things.''

''You sound experienced.''

''God, I need a cigarette. Do you mind if I smoke?''

''As a matter of fact, I do.''

''Am I right?''

''Is it so wrong to want to know those things?'' Kate countered.

''I can answer them all for you.'' She ticked them off on her fingers. ''She will be attractive, but not more attractive. He won't have promised her anything. Their lovemaking will have been entirely different, but no better and he won't have been the devoted husband and father. Different needs will have been fulfilled. You will be terribly hurt and become embittered. You'll hate her and then you'll hate him. Is that what you want, Katie?''

''On the other hand, she could be a business acquaintance and all my worries will have been for nothing.'' She appealed to Maeve. ''Isn't that worth finding out?''

''You tell me. How will you feel if it's worst case?''

''I don't know. I'll solve that one when it happens.'' She looked thoughtfully at Maeve, at the thick red hair, the feline green eyes, the smooth tanned skin, and wondered how Ireland could have produced the sheer, beautiful, sultry, foreign quality of her. ''You would do it differently, wouldn't you?''

''Yes.''

''Why?''

''I don't believe in full disclosure.''

''Do you really believe it's better to live a lie?''

''It isn't a lie, Kate. It's simple omission. We don't need to know everything about the people we love. When we try for that kind of omniscience, they become diminished. Don't you see? No one can live up to the kind of scrutiny you're proposing.'' She was more earnest than Kate had ever seen her.

"I can," Kate said quietly.

Maeve stared at her. "Congratulations, Kate," she said tonelessly. "Let me know when they canonize you."

Kate held the telephone in her hand for a long time. Was Maeve right? Should she leave Patrick to his privacy or would the not knowing haunt her forever? Once again, she slowly punched in the numbers on the booking receipt. The phone rang once, twice, a long, single ring. She wasn't prepared for the woman's voice on the other end of the line.

"Hello," she stammered. "Can you please tell me the name of the party I've reached?"

"Who is calling?" the voice replied.

"My name is Kate Nolan. I found this phone number and wondered—"

There was a moment of silence, then a click and dial tone.

Frustrated, Kate replaced the receiver.

The voice wasn't right. The woman was too old, with the demeanor of a domestic. Impossible scenarios flitted through Kate's mind. Neil was a Special Forces investigator. He said he would help her. She would ask him to find the address through the phone number. He would know how to do that. She'd seen movies. Then she would book a morning flight to New York, find the address and knock on the door herself. She would book a room for the night just in case the person wasn't home. Deirdre was in school and Kevin was at Tranquility House. She would be home before anyone knew she had gone. Perhaps she would ask Maeve to go with her, Maeve who knew New York City as well as Kate knew Belfast.

Twenty-One

Deirdre waited on the corner where the Eglantine and Malone Roads crossed each other. Belfast was an orderly city. Traffic was heavy but, unlike Dublin, no one drove over the speed limit and no one crossed against traffic lights. A green-suited member of the RUC walked past her and nodded. She ignored him, pretending she hadn't noticed. Deirdre was angry with herself. She missed Peter. It was absurd. She hadn't known him very long, only a few weeks, really. But in that time he'd filled up her spare moments. It was odd, when she stopped to reflect, how much more she'd missed him than she had her own father. Not that Peter's exit from her life could ever come close to the wrenching pain she'd felt immediately after her father's murder. But Patrick Nolan had been devoted to his work. Sometimes he didn't come home for days and, when he did, he remained closeted in his study. Deirdre couldn't recall a time when she'd actually had a conversation with her father. It was different with Peter. He'd become part of her daily life.

She was having second thoughts about continuing her education at Queen's. Her mother had warned her against it. She'd tried to explain what it was like living in a city with a Protestant majority. Deirdre listened but hadn't believed. She'd chosen Queen's not only because of its reputation for excellence in the sciences, but because her mother worked in Belfast and it was close to home. She'd had no idea how she would feel as a member of a despised minority population. In the Republic only six percent of the entire population was Protestant. Because their numbers were so small, they were cultivated and appreciated. It was not the same for Catholics in the Six Counties. Deirdre did not have the words to describe the feelings of oppression and paranoia that followed her everywhere except areas heavily frequented by university students.

The coffee house was half-empty. Deirdre ordered a cappuccino and slid into the corner booth. She spread out her books, opened her *Ancient Civilisations* text, shook her hair over her face and settled in for a lengthy stay. History did not come easily to her, not like mathematics and physical science. Peter was the one with a gift for understanding the subtleties of politics, ancient or modern. She could have used his tutoring for her last exam.

"Hello, Deirdre." The voice came from a booth near the wall.

She turned, saw him in the flesh and couldn't stop the look of dismay that crossed her face.

His welcoming smile faded. "I saw you come in," he explained. "It seemed awkward not to say anything."

She nodded. "How are you?"

"Miserable," he confessed. "And you?"

"I'm busy," she said truthfully.

He frowned into his coffee.

"Wouldn't your grandmother like your business?" she asked.

Peter grinned. "Gran can't make a proper cup of coffee. Hers is strictly a tea shop. Besides, I had a late night and needed the extra caffeine.''

"How did you do on your exam?"

"Which one?"

"History, of course."

"Well enough. What about you?"

Deirdre groaned and the words spilled out. "I'm hopeless. It's so disappointing. I'm just not interested, Peter. How am I ever going to get through? I don't know things other people know and I don't care about Philip of Macedonia, Alexander the Great or Napolean."

He stood and walked around to where she sat. Pointing to the empty seat across from her, he asked, "Do you mind?"

She should turn him away. It would be better for both of them. "No," she said.

"Would you like to hear my theory?" he asked after he sat down.

"Do I have a choice?"

"You have a mental block," he continued, ignoring her question. "Somewhere, you decided it wasn't important to know why the Battle of Hastings changed the course of English history. Ever since then you were lost."

"How did you get to be so smart?"

Again he grinned, ignoring her sarcasm. "It's obvious. You have an excellent mind, almost legal in its ability to synthesize information. Your ineptness in the humanities makes no sense."

"What do you suggest I do about this so-called mental block?"

He thought a minute. "You could hire a tutor," he

said. "I know of an exceptional one who hires out at seven pounds an hour."

"I'm serious."

"Well then, my second suggestion is to read historical fiction."

"That's absurd."

"No, it makes perfect sense. Reading plot driven novels will stimulate your interest. You'll remember events, people and places when you come across them in texts if you've heard of them before."

"I don't know."

"Try it. You're Irish, Deirdre. We Irish love stories."

He'd surprised her. She didn't think Protestants considered themselves Irish.

"I don't have a great deal of time to read novels, Peter."

"We've the best writers in the world right here in Ireland. You're missing out on one of life's true pleasures."

"I've never seen you read a novel."

"I don't read when I'm with people. What would be the point in that?"

"Maybe I should hire a tutor." She frowned. "It's just that it costs money and I don't want to bother my mother with this just now."

"I'll help you."

"I don't think so, Peter."

He leaned forward, eyes intent on her face and spoke earnestly. "It wouldn't be the same as meeting socially. We'll discuss our studies, that's all."

She hesitated. Why not? No one could object, not if the intent was purely for purposes of raising her exam scores. "All right, but I won't be able to pay you much."

"We'll work that one out later."

Deirdre smiled. "I will pay you, Peter. I promise."

Kate answered on the second ring. "This is Kate Nolan."

"Hello, Kate. It's Neil."

They hadn't spoken since the night in his flat, over a week ago. "Hello, Neil," she said coolly.

"How are you?"

"I'm well, thank you."

"You left a message," he said after a moment of awkward silence.

"Yes. Could we meet?"

"Of course. Where?"

"Brennan's at noon."

"I'll be there."

Kate stared at the phone. She was strangely depressed. So much for his loving her. How could a man be in love and require no contact beyond a night of intimacy? She wanted no part of Neil Anderson's kind of love. But she did need him. She mustn't lose sight of that.

Brennan's, with its dark wood and smoky corners, was a perfect place for an illicit meeting. Not that his meeting with Kate was illicit, Neil assured himself. But he had a feeling she would rather no one knew about it.

He chose a secluded table at the back of the restaurant. He saw her before she saw him and his breath caught. What was there about a woman that made her stand out? She lit up the room as if she was the only one there. Spunky, fey, elegant. The words came to his mind. She filled his senses. He was conscious of smoky hair, clear, light-filled eyes, sharply defined bones, a walk that combined the sensual and athletic. Where had she been the last twenty years of his life? The question was rhetorical. She was Patrick's wife, Deirdre and Kevin's mother. Neil could have stared forever, but she'd seen him. Suddenly he was nervous. He stood and pulled out her chair. "Hello, Kate."

"Hello." She looked directly at him. "Have you ordered?"

"I waited for you."

She picked up the menu and glanced at the page. "I think I'll have the chicken salad and a Squash."

Neil couldn't begin to concentrate on food. "Is everything all right?"

"I'm not sure." Again she looked at him without blinking. "I was beginning to think our interlude existed only in my imagination. Were you ever going to call me again?"

He schooled his features into a polite mask. She'd shocked him. Neil couldn't remember the last time he'd experienced such an emotion. No woman of his acquaintance, no lady anyway, would have brought up such a subject. He made an instant decision to be just as straightforward. "Believe it or not, I've given it quite a bit of thought."

"Go on."

"You scare me, Kate," he said honestly. "I don't want to start what can't be finished."

"I don't understand."

"I'm forty-two years old and single. Brief affairs hold no appeal for me. I'm thinking about whom I want to wake up next to for the next thirty years. I see no point in involving myself in a situation that has all the potential for heartbreak."

She opened her mouth and closed it again without

saying anything. Then she wet her lips. "What about Kevin?"

"I'm working on it."

"Can you tell me what you've decided?"

"I'd rather not."

Kate sipped her water. He noticed that her hands shook. She was not as coolly collected as she appeared. "Can you tell me if he'll be safe?"

"I'll do my best, Kate. Believe that."

She nodded.

The waitress took their order, returned with their drinks and left them alone again.

"I need your help," Kate said, changing the subject.

Neil waited.

She pulled a slip of paper from her purse. "This is a New York City phone number. I want you to find the address of that number."

"Have you tried it?"

"Of course," she said impatiently.

"And?"

"A woman answered. She was probably a maid, a very discreet maid."

"I see."

"You did say you would help me."

Neil pocketed the number. "I'll help you, Kate, on one condition."

"What condition?"

"You won't leave the country without telling me first."

"Do you have any idea how arrogant you sound?"

Neil grinned. "You'll never catch a man by insulting him."

Her face flamed. "I have no desire to catch a man.

Besides, if he can't stomach the real me, I wouldn't want him anyway.''

"Thank you. It helps to be informed."

"I thought you didn't want to be involved in a situation with a potential for heartbreak."

"I've changed my mind. I've always been a risk taker."

"Well, I haven't," she snapped. "All I want is my address."

He sobered immediately. "This is illegal, you know."

"It's done all the time."

"Not by me."

She said nothing.

"What do you hope to gain by this, Kate? Whatever you find, it won't be pleasant. Patrick was involved in a great many things, none of which will delight you. Why not just leave it and move on?"

"I want to know if I've lived a lie."

"We all live lies."

"I don't."

He sighed. "And if you have?"

"I don't know," she said honestly.

He frowned. "Do you agree to my condition?"

"I have no choice."

"Of course you do."

"I don't see it that way, however, under the circumstances, yes, I agree."

"I was afraid of that," he muttered under his breath.

Neil was having a difficult time reining in his temper. The boy was obstinate and rude. Only the fact that he was Kate's son kept him from abandoning his mission. He tried a different approach. "Are you hungry?"

Kevin shrugged.

A beggar sat on a pile of newsprint in the shadow of a vendor's awning and held out a cup. Neil pulled out a coin from his pocket and dropped it in. "How does fish and chips sound?"

"I'd rather have a burger."

Neil looked around.

Kevin pointed to the McDonald's marquis on the corner of the next street.

Neil managed a smile. American-style hamburgers weren't among his preferred foods. He took another look at the boy's face and made a decision not at all consistent with what he was feeling. "Come along, then," he said.

When they were seated across from each other in the sterile, plastic-covered booth, Neil tried a different approach. "Will you leave Ardara when the time comes?"

"What?" Kevin looked confused.

"When you're grown and this is behind you."

"I hadn't thought about it."

"Surely you've considered university and what you'll do for the rest of your life."

Kevin shook his head. "I'm not much of a student," he offered, "not like Deirdre."

"A trade perhaps?"

"I don't think so. Mum would have an attack."

Neil bit into his fish sandwich managing the question and the chewing at the same time. "I can't imagine your mother having an attack over anything."

Kevin looked somewhere over Neil's shoulder, considering his answer. "She doesn't really," he agreed, "not usually. There was that one time when she picked me up from the RUC barracks in Belfast. You were there,'' he reminded Neil.

''I don't remember her losing her calm. It must have happened after you left.''

''I told her to leave me alone.'' Kevin grinned. ''It was my language she didn't like, and my tone.''

''I see.''

Kevin kept on talking. ''She pulled over to the side of the road, got out and started running.''

''What?'' Neil stopped chewing.

''She does that, you know, runs at every opportunity.''

Neil didn't know. He remembered her athletic stride, the toned muscles, the absence of fat. Kate was a runner. It wasn't important, or was it? Somehow, his perception of her changed, tilted slightly in another direction. What did it mean? Why did it pull him up short?

''How long has she been running?''

''Five years or so. She started up after my da died.''

He'd said *died,* not the harsh *murdered* or the benign *passed away.* Neil swallowed the last of his fish. Why was he obsessing like this? What difference did it make to know that Kevin thought of his father as dead and his mother and sister considered him murdered, or that Kate Nolan had passions that exorcised themselves through harsh physical exercise?

Kevin's next statement jarred Neil out of his reverie.

''I think I'd like to be an artist.''

Where had that come from? ''Really?'' He knew less than nothing about children. Instinct told him to listen, say little and encourage the boy to talk about himself.

''Aye.'' Kevin nodded. ''I'm good at animated figures, you know, the kind you see on the telly.''

Neil waited.

"I won a prize once, in primary school. There was a contest. I didn't want to enter but my da made me do it and I won. Someone mounted it and it was displayed in the community center for a month. Mum was so proud. She brought everyone she knew in the whole town of Sligo to see it." Kevin's eyes sparkled with the memory.

Neil was fascinated. He'd never seen that relaxed, happy look on the boy's face.

"Have you studied art?"

Kevin's face fell. "Not in school. Mine is a preparatory school, strictly academic. Art isn't considered an important subject."

Neil balled his napkin and aimed for the trash can. The paper ball rolled around the edges and tumbled in. "It occurs to me that you may not be going back to that school."

"Mum will make me. She's very set on it."

"She's also had quite a scare. Your mum isn't unreasonable, Kevin. You may be able to convince her to give your art a chance at one of the National Schools or, maybe when you're finished with traditional education. Perhaps an art academy would be a better choice."

Kevin's face reflected his disbelief. "Do you really think she would agree?"

"You know her better than I do. But there's always a chance, if you're clean and stay away from whatever it was that sent you into this spin."

"I can do that."

"Good."

Suddenly Kevin's face closed. "I should be getting back now."

"Would you like to get out of this, Kevin?"

"God, yes, but—"

"What?"

"What about my sentence?"

"Trust me."

The boy was no longer eating.

"Together we can get you out," Neil continued, "but it must be done carefully."

"I thought you said I was the only one who could get inside and tell you what was happening."

"I've changed my mind."

Kevin looked up. "Because of my mother?"

Neil's heart twisted. The lad was so very young. "No," he said shortly.

"Why, then?"

"Because it isn't right." Neil spread his hands. "Because I didn't have all the facts and, now that I do, I see that involving you isn't the right thing at all."

"What about catching the drug lords?"

"There will always be drug lords. Let someone else catch them."

"Won't you be in trouble?"

"No."

"May I think about it?"

"Why?"

Kevin hesitated.

"If this has to do with your uncles, Kevin, they'll make their own way. If they've done nothing wrong, nothing will happen to them."

"What if they have?"

Neil considered the question carefully. He'd made enormous strides with Kevin this afternoon. The wrong words would set him back to the place where they'd started. "That depends on them," he said honestly. "They'll face consequences just as you did. If they cooperate things will go easier for them. No one comes away from committing a crime without some trouble, lad. They're grown men. They know the odds. You needn't worry about them.'' He was about to add that they wouldn't worry about him if the circumstances were reversed, but he caught himself in time. He would lose the boy if he passed judgment on his father's family.

Kevin stood. ''I should be getting back. There's a meeting I'm required to attend.''

Neil knew when to back off. He picked up Kevin's jacket and his own and followed the boy out the door. They were silent on the drive back to Tranquility House. Kevin gave a terse ''goodbye,'' and hurried up the steps.

Neil watched him walk through the door. He'd done all he could do. Whether or not Kevin agreed, the boy would be out. It would go easier with his knowledge and cooperation, but it could be done without them. After their conversation he was more convinced than ever to pull the boy out of the entire mess. Now, if he could only convince Kate to give up her absurd quest.

Somehow, before he fully realized what was happening, Neil had become emotionally embroiled in a family situation that was not his own. All it needed was for Kate's daughter to suck him into something for which he wasn't prepared. He wasn't discounting the possibility. Stranger things had happened.

He picked up his mobile phone and dialed the number for directory assistance. ''Belfast Telegraph, please.'' He punched in the number, waited for someone to pick up the phone and ask for his contact. ''I need a favor, Danny. A shipment of arms is scheduled for the Ormeau Road tomorrow morning. It could be a rumor, but—'' He deliberately let the edge of his sentence hang.

"Someone will be on it."

"Be sure to include a photographer. The RUC will be out in full force."

"Consider it done."

Neil placed the next phone call directly to Robbie Finnigan. "A source informs me of an arms shipment down the Ormeau Road tomorrow morning."

"Is it legitimate?"

"I don't know."

"Who is the source?"

"I'd rather not say at the moment."

He heard the hesitation. His hand tightened on the phone.

"Is he reliable?"

"Yes."

"All right. We'll send our men out, but if this is a mistake, Neil, my head will be in a noose."

"No more than if you allow an IRA shipment to slip through your fingers."

"I see your point."

"It's your decision," Neil reminded him.

"And my responsibility."

"As you say."

"Very well. I'll do it. Where and when?"

Neil repeated what Kevin had told him.

Twenty-Two

"Deirdre doesn't know anything." Liam insisted, draining his lager. "Patrick made sure of that."

"Don't be naive," Dominick chided him. "She knows faces. Our Deirdre isn't stupid, Liam. All Geoffrey Clarke needs to know is that his son is diddling Patrick Nolan's daughter. He'll have the whole of the constabulary down on her. She'll talk if she's brought in. They all do."

Liam was offended. "It's our niece you're shaming with such talk. You can't think they would coerce her?"

"Why not?"

"She's not one of us, Dom. She's a university student. Her mother is the ombudsman for Northern Ireland. There are no grounds."

Dominick swore softly. "Keep your voice down. Do you want the whole bloody pub to know who you are?"

Liam laughed. "Do you think they don't know us, Dom? Now who's being naive?"

"The boy needs to go."

"You're using this as an excuse to take out another Protestant, to even the score for Patrick's death."

"What if I am?"

Liam threw his napkin down. "I won't have it, Dom. He's a boy. He's done nothing. For Christ sake, he isn't even a Loyalist. I'll go against you on this one. No one has the stomach for this kind of thing anymore. You'll be alone.''

''I've been alone before.''

Liam Nolan leaned across the table and fixed a cold blue stare on his younger brother. ''You aren't understanding me, Dom. What I'm saying is, I won't allow it. I'll stop you.''

Dominick took a long time to swallow the last of his ale. Then he wiped each finger with his napkin and finally crumpled it into a ball. ''How do you propose to do that?''

''I don't know yet. But I will do it.'' Liam's voice had the earnest quality of a vow. ''Never doubt it.''

Neil picked up the phone on the first ring. He'd waited half the morning for an answer and his patience ran thin. How long could it take to match up an address and telephone number? The woman on the other end gave him the street address and offered no apologies for the delay. Neil thanked her.

He pulled a map from his desk drawer and located Manhattan Island and then Third and Lexington. He didn't recognize the name, only the location, an upscale neighborhood not far from Central Park. Apartments were more than pricey. They were prohibitive. When it came to women, Patrick Nolan ran in expensive circles.

Kate would have to be told. He understood her well enough to know that she would not be dissuaded from following through with this. Neil cursed under his breath. Now was not the time for a jaunt to New York. It was Wednesday, the day Kate drove into Belfast. Resigning himself to the inevitable, Neil picked up the phone and punched in her mobile number.

"Can we meet?" he asked when he heard her voice.

She answered immediately, without hesitation or a single question. "Yes."

"In front of the city buildings, near the Victoria statue?"

"When?"

"Noon. I'll bring sandwiches."

"I'll be there."

She was late. Her cheeks were flushed and her normally smooth hair fell in a dark, slightly disheveled curtain around her face. She was a woman who stood out. Neil could never remember what she wore after he left her, only that it suited her.

"Sorry," she apologized. "I had a last-minute phone call."

He reached into the bag. "I brought turkey and roast beef. Which will you have?"

"One half of each."

He laughed, divided the sandwiches and pulled out two bottles of water, handing her one.

They sat on a stone bench facing the street. Neil watched her bite into her sandwich and wished for the impossible, a warm day, a man and woman with no agenda but to share company and a sandwich.

Kate slipped on dark glasses against the rare Irish sun, looked at him and stopped chewing. "I assume you have the address."

"Yes."

"Will you give it to me?"

Neil reached out and removed her sunglasses. "No."

He watched her upper lip tighten.

"I'm going with you," he said quietly.

"You don't know that I'm going."

Carefully he fitted the glasses over her ears and

pushed them up the bridge of her nose. "You're going."

She lifted the water bottle to her lips and tilted her head back to drink.

When she smiled his heart twisted.

"You're right," she said. "Actually I'm glad you'll be going with me. You have resources I know nothing about."

"I'm taking that as a compliment."

Kate shrugged.

"Have you been to America?" he asked.

"No, have you?"

"Yes. I'll book the flight and hotel."

She wanted to ask if they would have separate hotel rooms, but she hadn't the nerve. "Thank you," she said instead. "I'd like to leave as soon as possible."

"I also have a name, if you're interested."

"I am."

"The number is registered to a Maeve Murphy."

Stunned, Kate stared at him. Her face paled and when she spoke her voice sounded far away. "That's impossible."

"Why do you say that?"

"I know Maeve Murphy. She lives in Ardara."

He had to work not to laugh. "Murphy is the most common name in Ireland. Maeve isn't unusual, either."

"My Maeve Murphy lives in New York part of the year. She's a glass sculptor, a famous one."

Neil felt the beginning of an edge. A famous sculptor could afford Lexington and Third. "I'm sure it's a coincidence."

She did not appear convinced.

"Where is Maeve now?" he asked.

"In Ardara. I spoke with her yesterday. She's a very good friend."

"Did she know Patrick?"

Kate nodded. "They didn't get on. He thought she was overblown, gaudy. He didn't care for the friendship."

"His disapproval didn't stop you?"

"Of course it didn't. No one dictates my friends. I was Patrick's wife, not his child. He certainly had enough friends I didn't care for."

Neil needed a minute to gather his thoughts. He finished his sandwich, collected their trash and looked around for a bin. The questions he burned to ask weren't typical of picnic-lunch conversation. They would have to wait. He had work piling on his desk and a certain Maeve Murphy to check on.

He walked Kate back to her office in the commerce building, past the statue and the huge columns to the double oak door. "When shall I make the reservations?" he asked.

"I'll call you."

He couldn't read her expression. "I wouldn't do anything on your own, Kate."

"You haven't given me the address."

"You do have a name."

"Yes," she said thoughtfully.

"Don't do it, Kate," he warned her. "This is more complicated than you think. The woman could be dangerous. We know nothing yet. Give me a few days."

She smiled at him and held out her hand. "I'm very grateful to you, Neil. Thank you for lunch."

He nodded, attempted a smile and turned away. She frustrated him. He wanted to shake her. It shocked him, the depth of his feeling. Even Lydia at her worst hadn't engendered in him this kind of emotion. He remembered only a deep weariness, not the heat and fear that washed through him at the thought of Kate taking matters into her own hands.

Summer days were long in the north and Kate arrived in Ardara before dark. She'd had four hours to go over in her mind what she would do. She pulled into her driveway, her resolve firm. Hitching her purse over her shoulder, she grabbed her briefcase and walked up the porch steps. The door was open and her father stood on the other side, his arm raised in welcome.

Kate fixed a smile on her face. "Hello, Da."

"I've been waiting an age, Katie. Was the traffic bad?"

"Not too bad. Are you hungry?"

"I thought we could go out."

"Not tonight." She walked into the hall and dropped her purse and briefcase in the corner. "I'm tired and I've work to do. Why don't I make something for us?"

"You're always doin' that," John grumbled.

"I like it," Kate assured him. "Besides, there is something I'd like to discuss with you."

"Is it about Kevin?"

Kate shook her head. "Let me change clothes and I'll tell you about it. You can make a salad while you're waiting. Vegetables are in the refrigerator."

When she joined her father in the kitchen, a credible salad sat in a wooden bowl on the counter. She opened the refrigerator, pulled out a bottle of white wine and poured herself a glass. "I've orange and cherry soda, Da. Which would you like?"

He waved aside her offer and looked up from beneath bushy brows. "What's on your mind, Katie?"

She sipped her wine, pushed it away, climbed up on a bar stool, both hands cupping her chin. "It's about Patrick."

"Aye?"

He wasn't meeting her eyes.

"Is there anything you haven't told me?"

This time he did look at her, a level blue-eyed stare that was direct and uncomfortable. "What is this all about?"

She sighed and dove in. "According to police files, Patrick wasn't just a barrister who defended members of the IRA. He was heavily involved." She dug her nails into the palms of her hands. "He was an assassin, Da. He arranged for people to be murdered."

"How did you find out?"

"I demanded answers about the investigation." She laughed bitterly. "Now I wish I hadn't asked."

"It doesn't help to bury your head in the sand."

"There's more," she said. "There was a woman."

"I don't believe that," John said flatly.

Kate's mouth twisted. "Your reaction is the same as mine. It's easier to believe he was a murderer than a philanderer?"

"I know that Patrick loved you, Katie. It may have been the only truth he ever told you, but it was the truth. No one looking at the two of you together would believe that man didn't love you."

"Did you know about the other?"

"Aye. It wasn't difficult to figure out."

"My head *was* in the sand." She looked accusingly at her father. "Why didn't you tell me?"

"Ah, Katie, what good would it have done? He was your husband. Nothing you could have said would have changed him. It would only have caused terrible trouble in your marriage." He laid his hand on top of hers. "Would you have left him, lass, because of what I told you?"

She thought a minute, turning the question over in her mind. "I don't know," she said at last. "I'm not the same person I was six years ago."

"What are you going to do?"

She turned her hand over and gripped her father's. "I'm going to live, Da. I'm going to raise my children and begin again, without him. I'm going to tell Kevin and Deirdre the truth because they need to know that their father's murder wasn't a random act, that he brought it on himself, that people orchestrate their own destinies and that Patrick reaped what he sowed. They need to know that people in Ireland, normal people, aren't assassinated." She drew a deep breath. "I'm going to find out about the woman. It's killing me, Da. I'm ashamed to admit this, and may God forgive me, but at this moment I hate him more for the woman than for the blood on his hands."

Kate hesitated on the footpath in front of Maeve's house. She'd tried to phone but the answer machine was on and Maeve wasn't returning phone calls. Stiffening her resolve, Kate walked up the front steps and rang the bell. One minute passed, then two. She rang again. Still no answer. Where was she? Her message said nothing about returning to New York. Kate stuffed her hands into the pockets of her windbreaker and walked home.

The Aer Lingus flight out of Shannon Airport was only half full. Neil had booked them a window and a middle seat. The one nearest the aisle was empty. Kate hoped her anxiety didn't show. Until Patrick's death, flying never made her nervous. Now she worried about her children and how they would withstand the loss of both parents in the event of a plane crash.

She was very aware of Neil seated beside her, his legs filling up the space between his row and the one in front. She watched him flip through a magazine. His hands were competent and strong, the fingers wide, his nails neatly clipped. He was very attractive in his own quiet, unassuming way. Appreciation welled up inside of her. He was here with her for no reason other than he cared.

He looked at her and smiled encouragingly. She smiled back. He'd been against this trip from the beginning but not a word had been said since they'd boarded the plane. "Thank you," she said.

He didn't pretend to misunderstand. "You're welcome."

The engines roared. The ground speed increased. Kate closed her eyes and clutched the armrests. This part was the worst, not knowing if this massive flying machine would actually lift itself from the ground. She felt Neil's hand on hers, warm, reassuring, his thumb circling her palm.

His question wiped the fear from her brain, replacing it with tension of a completely different kind.

"Do you think there's a chance for us?"

"What do you mean?"

"It isn't a trick question, Kate."

She wet her lips. "You need to be more specific. What exactly is it that you want?"

"A companion, a friend, someone to share my life, a lover."

Her face flamed. "That's a tall order."

"Is it?" He looked beyond her, out the window. "We're in the air now."

Her eyes followed his gaze and widened. "You did that on purpose."

"Not entirely." Again he picked up his magazine.

His absorption angered her. Reaching over the armrest, she covered his page with her open hand. "Which part was *not entirely?*"

The beginning of a smile appeared at the corners of his mouth. "You are obviously nervous about flying. I meant to divert your attention away from the plane. The subject is one that is very much on my mind."

He was too direct. She looked away.

"I can wait," he offered, "if there's a chance."

She shook her head. "I don't know. I know it isn't enough but it's all I have right now. My mind is filled with other things." This time she looked at him. "Can you accept that?"

This time the smile was there, carving the laugh lines into his cheeks. "Perhaps I've missed something, but I don't believe you've given me a choice."

She stared at him curiously. "Do you ever get angry?"

"Frequently."

"Are you angry now?"

"No."

Kate had never been to New York City but she had been to London and the two were nothing alike. Here, horns blared at the slightest provocation. Traffic jammed at every corner barely waiting for the steady stream of jaywalkers to cross against the signals. Men and women of every color walked and jogged, gyrating through thick crowds, dressed in stylish suits, carrying briefcases and wearing tennis shoes. Vendors selling jewelry, watches and T-shirts hugged street corners. Music boomed, lights flashed and a hot, wet, gray heat hung over the vast concrete maze that was Manhattan.

She was both fascinated and repulsed. She could feel the pulsing energy, hear the loud voices, the unfamiliar accents, see the swiftly moving bodies of people on foot, all intent on going somewhere other than where they were. Odd smells assailed her nose, vapor rose from holes in the streets, lights lit the night and the shops, good Lord, the shops were like nothing she had ever seen.

Reminding herself of why she was here, Kate deliberately pushed the evocative displays to the back of her mind and looked at Neil. "Where are we staying?"

"There's a nice little hotel in the theater district. It's called the Helmsley. The rooms are small but charming and, best of all, it's quiet. The service is excellent, a rarity in this part of the world."

"Really?" Kate was curious. "Are Americans rude?"

"Only New Yorkers."

"You're not serious?"

"Not a bit."

She made a face. "I feel very naive."

The cabdriver pulled up in front of an entrance complete with moldings and an elaborately carved wooden door. Clusters of tiny white lights illuminated the entryway. Kate followed the emerald carpet to the registration desk. The lobby was alive with flower arrangements, pink, mauve, wine and celery, all artistically sculpted to fit into nooks and crannies in a tasteful display.

Neil handed her a key. "Your room is next door to

mine. I'm afraid there isn't much of a view, but we won't be here long enough for that to matter.''

The room was compact with antique furnishings, a well-stocked bar and comfortable queen-size bed. Kate closed the door behind her, dropped her overnight bag and flopped backward on the bed. The space between her stomach and chest burned. She wanted this finished and yet she was terrified. Worst case, she reminded herself. Nothing could be worse than worst case. What if Patrick had been having an affair? Would she survive? Of course. What if he'd been in love with the woman? Kate thought a minute, imagining intimate details of another woman with her husband. Yes, she decided. She could manage even that. She forced herself to delve even deeper. Was there anything she couldn't sort through, anything at all that would shock her into immobility or cause her to lose her mind? Did anything matter that much? Images flew through her mind. Patrick, her father, her brothers and sisters, her job, the children. Discarding one after another, she settled on the last. Her children. Only Deirdre and Kevin could irrevocably alter the course of her life. The rest was history. She was researching history, nothing more. Anything she would learn had already happened.

Kate picked up the phone and punched in Neil's room number. ''I'm ready now.''

His answer was measured, calm. ''All right. Give me ten minutes.''

She applied fresh lipstick and changed her blouse. Then she stared at herself in the mirror. What would someone think, seeing her for the first time? An average woman, tall enough, but fragile looking and small-boned. Another ten pounds wouldn't hurt at all. Her eyes, she decided, and her hair, fine and straight and thick, were her best features. Did she look forty-one? She had no idea. What did forty-one look like in the new millennium? Certainly not like the women in fashion magazines. Those women had no crow's-feet, no laugh lines, no shadows under their eyes and cheeks. The magical wand of airbrushing had completely eradicated the evidence of life's experience. Kate frowned. She didn't want that, or did she? Was perfection the current fashion and if so why, now, should it make a difference?

The knock on her door came sooner than she would have liked. She wasn't ready. Would she ever be ready? Summer in New York was too hot for a jacket. Kate picked up her purse and opened the door. Neil smiled and she relaxed.

"I made reservations for dinner," he said.

"Thank you."

In the lobby the doorman greeted them. "Would you like a taxi, sir?" he asked holding the door.

"No, thank you, we're walking."

Neil maintained a light, easy flow of conversation for the twenty minutes it took to reach their destination. Kate paid no attention. Her mind was on the interview to come.

Resting his arm lightly on her shoulder, Neil led her into a multistoried building with a blue-striped awning. A man in uniform barred their way. "May I help you?"

Neil pulled out his wallet and flipped it open. "Neil Anderson from Special Forces, London Division, for Maeve Murphy."

Without changing expression, the man stepped aside and pointed to the lift. "Fourth floor. I'll tell her you're here."

Kate watched the light panel change, second floor,

third, fourth. The movement stopped. The door opened and she stepped outside. Then she turned to Neil. "I'd rather do this myself," she said.

He shook his head. "I can't allow that."

"This is important to me, Neil."

"It could be dangerous."

"There's a café across the street. Wait for me there. Please."

He hesitated.

"Please."

He checked his watch. "I'll give you an hour. If you're not down by then, I'll come after you." He shook her slightly. "Do you understand, Kate? I *will* come after you."

She nodded and, on impulse, kissed his cheek.

He stepped back into the lift, his eyes on her face until the door closed between them.

The door to the flat was ajar. Kate knocked firmly. Familiar footsteps sounded in the hall and then Maeve Murphy stood in the entry, a vision in white capri pants and a black halter-top, red hair skinned away from her face and secured at the back of her head with a claw clip. Awed by the clothes, the hair and Maeve's strikingly beautiful bone structure, Kate could do no more than stare at the woman who had been her friend.

Maeve stepped aside. "Come in, Kate. I've been expecting you."

The flat was sophisticated, cut glass and severe, dramatic furniture, no window coverings, just a priceless view of the city. Without waiting for permission, Kate sat down on the fuchsia-colored sofa.

"Would you like a drink?" Maeve asked.

"Yes."

Maeve poured two glasses of whiskey, added water

to one, handed it to Kate and sat down across from her. She set the bottle on the table between them. "Where shall I start?"

"I want you to explain the relationship you had with my husband."

Maeve drained her glass and poured herself another drink. Settling back into the couch, she began. "In the beginning we worked together."

"And later?"

Her cheeks flushed. She raised defiant eyes to Kate's face. "Later, we were more than that."

"Were you lovers?"

"Kate, please."

"You're ashamed to say you slept with my husband, but you weren't ashamed to do it, were you?"

"All right, Kate. You win. We were lovers."

Twenty-Three

Kate gulped down her whiskey and reached for the bottle. She refilled her glass and lifted it to her lips.

"Easy, Kate," Maeve warned her. "I'll be wiping the floor with you before you know it."

The alcohol swam through Kate's brain. She had trouble forming the words. "You were my friend. How could you?"

"He was your husband," Maeve snapped back. "Why not ask, how could he?"

"I would if he were here. As it is, you're all I have. Believe me, it isn't my choice."

Maeve's eyes glistened. "So, sweet, gentle Katie has claws. I wouldn't have believed it."

"What would you believe, Maeve? That I would lay down, roll over and smile benignly while you fucked my husband?"

"Stop it, Kate. It wasn't like that."

"Tell me, Maeve." The pain had turned to fury. "Tell me what it was like."

Maeve fortified herself with another gulp of whiskey. "Ours was a business arrangement."

"I don't believe you."

"Watch yourself, Katie. I don't care what you believe. You're here because you want something from me. I would have been perfectly happy to let this lie with Patrick in his grave. As it is, the least you can be is civil.''

Kate stared at her incredulously. "Is it civility you want, Maeve, or is it forgiveness? I can give you the one but definitely not the other.''

"Civility will do.''

"All right. What kind of a business arrangement did you have with my husband?''

Maeve hesitated and then shrugged. "I suppose it no longer matters what I tell you. If you found me, others will as well. There will be no evidence. They tried the first time and it came to nothing.''

"They have the photograph," Kate reminded her.

"It's inconclusive. Even you didn't recognize me.'' Her forehead puckered. "How did you find me?''

"I showed you the phone number scribbled on a receipt.''

"Good God.''

"Tell me about your business.''

"I create documents, passports, birth certificates, credit reports, bank statements, anything and everything. I delete them as well.''

"In other words, you're a computer hack.''

"Yes.''

Kate's head felt thick and fuzzy. "Do you work for the IRA?''

Maeve laughed. "No one works for the IRA, Katie. It's not a corporation. One belongs because one believes.''

"And you believe?" Kate mocked her.

"Actually I do.''

"Is that all there was to it?''

"Leave it, Kate. Please.''

The burning pain twisting Kate's stomach was making its way to her lungs. Every breath was agony. "I can't," she said hoarsely. "I wish I could. You know I can't."

Maeve drew a deep breath. "I don't want to hurt you. You must believe that. What I had with Patrick was our own. It had nothing to do with you. He would never have left you or the children. I knew that. I never expected it."

"Did he love you?"

"We slept together. I wouldn't say what we had was love."

"Why not?"

Maeve bit her full, rust-colored lower lip. "There was no question of that between us. What we had was pure physical lust." She looked up quickly. "Neither of us meant for it to happen. Nothing was planned. Once it began—" She stopped.

The ringing in Kate's ears increased. "Go on."

"We couldn't stop." Maeve stared at her defiantly. "He suffered from terrible guilt. A whole part of his life he wasn't able to share with you. It haunted him."

"And you were there to assuage the haunting."

"Yes," Maeve answered softly. "There's no need for sarcasm."

"Did you love him?"

"That's none of your business."

Kate's eyes narrowed to thin slits of angry blue. "Everything about Patrick is my business. I was his wife. My children are his children."

"You didn't ask about Patrick, Katie. You asked about me."

The rebuke silenced her. Maeve's face blurred. First she was one, then two. Two noses, two mouths, four eyes. "Was he an assassin?" she asked at last.

"If you're asking me if he actually murdered, the answer is, no."

"Did he order murders?"

"Yes."

Kate stood. "I don't want you to come back to Ardara."

"I hadn't planned on it."

"Goodbye."

"Goodbye, Kate. I will miss you. Please, believe that."

Kate turned, her hand on the doorknob. There were so many things she wanted to say. Her tongue felt thick and strange in her mouth. Her head swam. In the end she said nothing. Turning the knob, she let herself out. She needed a bathroom. Vaguely she knew that she was supposed to do something, but what? Sliding her hand along the wall for balance, she moved slowly in the direction of the lift. A man came out of another door, looked at her and then looked again.

"Are you all right, miss?"

Kate nodded.

The man hesitated. Kate stared straight ahead and he moved on.

Her stomach cramped. She leaned against the wall. A rush of hurt welled up in her chest. Her eyes filled. Tears streamed down her cheeks. She hated Maeve, hated Patrick. Where was the lift? Blindly she wandered down the hall and turned a corner. Green lights blinked at her. Gratefully she pressed the down button. The doors opened. The elevator was empty. She stepped inside, pushed another button and waited for the familiar drop. In the lobby the doorman opened the door for her. She stumbled past him into the street. Where now?

It was raining, not a fine light misty Irish rain, but

hard hurting pellets that soaked her to the bone, plastering her blouse to her skin, her hair to her head. It was summer in New York City. She hadn't bothered with an umbrella. Kate lifted her purse over her head and ran aimlessly down the street through the puddles. The wet crept through her soles. Water dripped from the end of her nose. She ducked into a shelter and read the sign. *Flaherty's Pub*. She tested the words on her lips. *Flaherty's Pub*. It had a friendly sound. Making her way to the bar, Kate climbed up on a high stool. Her feet hung awkwardly. She looked around. One man sat at the other end of the bar. A few tables were occupied.

The bartender placed a napkin in front of her. "What'll you have, miss?"

She thought a minute. Better to not mix drinks. What had Maeve served her? "Glenfinnan whiskey," she said, "no ice, no water."

He nodded, poured the drink and set it in front of her. Her head ached. Her heart ached. She was cold. She wanted to go home. Downing the drink, she pushed aside the empty glass.

"Another?" asked the bartender.

She nodded.

He placed the glass on a clean napkin. "Get caught in the rain?"

"Yes." Once again she downed her drink.

"Where are you from?"

"Ireland."

"I knew it wasn't a British accent."

"God, no."

He laughed and glanced at her empty glass. "You might want to slow down. That's powerful stuff."

"Do you have a bathroom?"

He pointed toward the back. "In there."

Kate slung her purse over her shoulder and hopped off the chair. Her legs wobbled, bonelessly, under her weight. Embarrassed, she gripped the stool.

"Do you need a taxi, ma'am?"

"No, thank you. I need a bathroom." She cocked her head. "Why do you call it a bathroom? There's no bath inside, only a toilet."

"I don't know."

"You Americans have the oddest expressions."

He walked around the bar and held out his hand. "I'll help you."

Kate straightened and brushed away his hand. "I'll manage."

"I'll call a taxi when you come out."

She ignored him and pushed open the door to the ladies' room. At first she thought another woman was in the room with her. Then she realized it was her own reflection in the full-length mirror. Sinking down to the floor, legs splayed, she rested her head against the wall and stared at the new Kate Nolan. Huge circles bordered her eyes and black mascara streaks marked her cheeks. Her hair was hopeless, matted and lifeless, as if it were painted on her head. Her cheeks were pale as milk, her lips a sickly gray. Even her eyes looked ravaged and red-rimmed, watered down, as if all the tears and rain and anger had leeched the color from them.

Kate pulled at her wet blouse, attempting to tuck it back into the waist of her skirt. She could see the complete outline of her bra beneath the linen, the lace cups, the swell of her breasts. No wonder the bartender had been so friendly. The unexpected flash of humor surprised and comforted her. She wasn't past help if she could still laugh at herself. Leaning back against the door, she looked up, saw the bolt and slid it across the door. Bracing herself on the door handle she pulled herself to a standing position and bent over the sink. Bile, thick and bitter, rose in her throat. Her stomach heaved. Barely making it to the toilet, she threw up again and again, until her stomach was empty. Weak and trembling, she slid back down on the floor, leaned her head back and passed out.

Neil checked his watch. Where was Kate? He'd given her forty-five minutes and still she hadn't come out of the building. Could he have missed her? He frowned, glanced at his watch again, threw down two dollar bills and a handful of change and left the coffee shop.

The doorman recognized him. "Did you leave something behind, sir?"

"I'm here to pick up the woman I was with earlier."

"She left nearly an hour ago."

Neil tensed. "Do you happen to know where she went?"

"No, sir. I could call Miss Murphy and see if she knows."

"Don't bother." Neil pushed the elevator button. "I'll ask her myself."

Maeve answered the door immediately. "Good afternoon, Mr. Anderson. Please, come in."

Neil masked his surprise. "Have we met?"

"Kate told me a great deal about you." Her smile was no more than a grimace. "When we were still friends," she added.

He noticed the swollen, averted eyes. "I'm looking for Kate."

"She's gone."

"Do you know where?"

Maeve shook her head. "She was upset and very drunk. Kate isn't a drinker, Mr. Anderson. She had quite a bit of whiskey. I'm sorry but I don't know where she is."

"I take it your meeting was difficult."

The woman's laugh was harsh and bitter. "You might say that." She looked at him. "Do you know about me?"

"I do."

"Why haven't I been arrested?"

"The evidence is sketchy."

"I don't believe you."

"That's your prerogative."

"Please, tell me the truth."

Neil thought of his career, his promise to the prime minister and the entire complicated mess that was Northern Ireland politics. Then he looked at the puffy eyes and ravaged expression on Maeve Murphy's face and made his decision. "No one wants this investigation resurrected. The peace process has been sabotaged too many times. News of Patrick Nolan's IRA involvement serves no purpose. In short, Miss Murphy, we're trying very hard to sweep all of this under the carpet. You happen to be one of the beneficiaries of that philosophy."

"I see."

"Is there anything else you want to know?"

"No," she whispered.

Neil felt sorry for her. "Stay in New York, Miss Murphy."

"Yes."

"Where do you think Kate might go if she were distressed?"

"Home, Mr. Anderson. Kate always goes home."

In the end, he decided to walk back to the hotel and wait in her room.

Four hours and twelve cups of coffee later, he was a wreck. For the first time in his life, Neil was at a loss. Kate was a stranger to New York. She knew no one in the city. Mugging was always a possibility, especially if she'd been drinking. Another hour, he promised himself. He would give her another hour before notifying the police.

It was nearly nine when he heard the key in the lock. He'd left only one lamp on. Relief and anger flooded him at the same time. His words were harsh, accusing. "Where in bloody hell have you been?"

She stared at him mutely. He flicked on another light, took one look at her and started forward, gripping her arms above the elbows. "Good God! What happened to you?"

She stared at him with wide, expressionless eyes.

Neil forced himself to speak gently. "Are you injured, Kate? Do you need a doctor?"

She shook her head.

"Tell me what happened."

She pressed her palm flat against his chest and, once again, shook her head. "I want to sleep," she said in a strange, raspy voice. "I want to sleep and then I want to go home."

"We're leaving tomorrow."

"No." She hovered on the brink of hysteria. "I want to go to the airport tonight, after I sleep. I want to go right away. I need to go home, to Ardara."

"We can do that."

She broke away from him and crawled on top of the bed. Gently he sat down beside her and removed her shoes. Her hose were filthy and torn. He studied her face. Her eyes were closed, her mouth slightly open. Her breathing was even. She smelled like perfume and whiskey and vomit. Carefully, he unzipped her skirt and eased it down and off. Then he unbuttoned her blouse, working it from her shoulders and waist. Slipping his hand under the elastic of her panty hose, he pulled them off and threw them in the trash. In the bathroom he soaked a washcloth in warm water, unwrapped a bar of soap and carried it back into the bedroom. She didn't move when he cleaned her face, her neck, her chest, hands and finally her feet. He pulled up the blankets and covered her.

When he'd finished, Neil stared down at her anguished face. He couldn't leave her. Unlacing his shoes, he stretched out on the bed, on top of the covers and closed his eyes. The day had been one of the longest of his life.

Kate awakened slowly. She kept her eyes closed. An unfamiliar heaviness pinned her down. Something was wrong. Her head pounded relentlessly and her mind refused to focus. She'd felt like this before for months, no, it was years, after Patrick died, coming awake in the early hours of dawn, knowing instinctively that nothing would ever be the same again, but still too fuzzy to remember why. Then the flash of memory, the edge of pain and the long, endless hours until she could sleep again.

Experimentally she opened one eye and then the other. She was in an unfamiliar room. The curtains were pulled against the light. She couldn't tell what time it was. She felt cocooned, her arms trapped against her sides. A sharp pain shot through her left temple, and her mouth and throat were cotton-dry. Shifting slightly, she turned her head and opened her eyes. Recognition hit her full force. For fifteen years she'd awakened with a man's arms wrapped around her. It wasn't something a woman forgot. But this wasn't Patrick, it was Neil. Neil was the man she was pressed against. Neil had stayed the night in her room, in her bed. She waited for the disapproval she was sure would resurrect itself if she gave it some time. Neither happened. She was tired, so very tired. Burrowing her head against his chest, she gave herself up to the fatigue and slept.

It was late morning when she woke again. This time she was alone. The pain in her head was gone. Grateful to be spared Neil's questions, she swung her legs over the bed and headed for the bathroom. Turning on the tap, she bent down and drank until the raw burn in her throat subsided. She wiped her mouth with the back of her hand and straightened. Her reflection in the mirror shocked her. Hastily she shed her slip and panties, turned on the shower tap and stepped into the tub. The mist was hot and fine and satisfying. She tilted her head back. The spray ran down her cheeks and chin. Kate soaped her breasts, her belly and back, her legs, the hard to reach spaces between each toe and then she shampooed her hair. Fifteen minutes later, warm, scrubbed clean and towel-wrapped, she sat down on the floor in front of the long mirror and contemplated the last twenty-four hours in the logical, straightforward manner that had cemented her professional reputation.

She had lost two things. No, she amended; she'd never really had them. Patrick had never been a loyal, loving husband and Maeve had never been her friend, not by true definition. The man she loved and believed in had never existed. Maeve, the woman she confided in, had come from Patrick's bed to Kate's kitchen table. It was ludicrous, really, all that had escaped her. She thought back to all the nights she'd spent alone, to her ignorance of her husband's schedule and whereabouts, to the odd phone calls and hushed meetings where the silence was thick with tension and resentment and the conversation stilted if she interrupted, to the business trips where she wasn't invited. Not that he could have taken her with him, she rationalized. It was too dangerous and she had the children. Yet, he'd taken Maeve.

She fed on her hurt, creating ludicrous, imaginary scenarios. It was a tactic she used often to dull the pain. Imagine the worst and, for the most part, it never happened. Her husband, the man she loved more than life, had preferred another woman. It was Maeve who had accompanied him. It wasn't too dangerous for Maeve and she wasn't burdened with Patrick's children.

Kate twisted the edge of her towel. The pain was new and raw as if the events had happened yesterday instead of six years ago. She felt furious, betrayed, shaken, a woman on the edge of her nerves, unsure of how to go on, wondering if she could swim from the bottom into the light. She had no experience with deceit. It had never occurred to her that her own husband, Patrick Nolan, as close to a legend as a contemporary man could be, had walked in it, fed on it every waking moment of his adult life.

What was real? Kate asked herself. Were there moments when he was hers alone, when the life they'd created was enough? Did Patrick ever long to be an ordinary man with nothing more on his mind than rising interest rates? She untied the towel and looked at her naked body. She was nothing like Maeve. What had he seen in her, a too-thin woman, all eyes and legs and sensible hair?

The questions tumbled over each other, each one leading to another more twisted than the one before. She would have liked to ask him. She would have liked him to be alive, to do what? *Kill him.* The words slipped into her consciousness before she could screen them and push them away, thoughts unworthy of saintly Kate Nolan, Patrick's widow. The Kate Nolan she knew would never have formulated such an uncharitable thought.

"I hate you, Patrick Nolan," she said out loud. "I'm glad you're dead." Immediately she felt better.

A knock on the door startled her. She didn't get up. "Yes."

"It's Neil. I wondered if you'd like breakfast."

"No, thank you."

She felt his presence and his hesitation. Why didn't he go away?

"Please open the door, Kate."

"I'm not dressed."

"I won't come in. I just want to see you."

Reluctantly Kate retied the towel and padded to the door on bare feet. She opened it a crack and peeked through. Neil held out a tray with a pot of tea, milk and sugar, two sugary pastries and a single cup and saucer. She opened the door wider.

"I thought you might like some privacy this morning," he said.

She took the tray. "Thank you, Neil. You're very thoughtful."

"Are you all right, Kate?"

"I need to sort out a few things. Would you mind if I met you this afternoon at the airport?"

He looked as if he were about to speak, but then changed his mind. "Of course not."

She drank the tea but could only manage a bite of pastry. Then she crawled back into bed, pulled the covers over her shoulders and closed her eyes. Kate recognized her need for sleep. She was no stranger to emotional shock. Her body reacted by shutting down until her mind was ready to deal with the mess that was her life.

John O'Donnell had a bad feeling. It wasn't something he could put his finger on. He just knew. He'd felt this way ever since his visit with Kevin the day before. The boy was confused and for the first time in the lad's sixteen years, his grandfather couldn't reach him. Their conversation had been stilted and formal, a disappointment for John, a chore for Kevin. When had he lost the lad? John racked his brain to remember an event, a moment. There were none. Somewhere the boy had shifted his thinking and John despaired of getting him back on the right track. Tranquility House didn't seem to be accomplishing much. Kevin was still sullen, still defiant and, it seemed to John, still without the slightest hint of remorse or feeling of responsibility for what he'd done.

John thought back to his own children. They were different than children today, or were they? Had he ever really known his the way he knew Kevin and Deirdre? His life had been a round of work and chores and the quest for enough sleep to begin the cycle over again. He'd had no time for his children. They were Eileen's responsibilities. Eileen with her sharp tongue and her quick hands and her penchant for criticism had screamed and slapped her children into submission. Not once had he stepped in, hesitant to intrude, assuming that child rearing was a woman's business. In retrospect, he would do it differently if only he could go back. He thought of Kate and the others. There was no going back, but there was Kevin. He wouldn't give up on Kevin. Perhaps hearing the truth about his father and his uncles would bring him around. He would go back tomorrow. Tomorrow their conversation would be nothing like today. Tomorrow he would tell Kevin what he knew about the Nolans. He would show him that living the hate-infested life his uncles lived cut a man off before his time, made him bitter and twisted with little left for personal happiness. Liam and Dominick were bachelors, men married to a dead cause. Patrick had paid the ultimate price. John would show Kevin there was more to life than paranoia and secrecy, interrupted nights and directionless lives. He would make the lad listen. Kevin was a good boy. He would come around.

Twenty-Four

Gerry Donovan rubbed his grizzled chin. He stood with one foot on the edge of a straight-backed chair and the other on the ground. His eyes were blank, focused on some point outside the window of the small room where six men sporting the blue denims and black jackets of the organization stood around him waiting deferentially. Donovan's world was West Belfast. He'd joined the guerillas thirty-three years earlier, after the barricade of the city. In the seventies he'd orchestrated and led the daring escape from Long Kesh, the largest, most successful escape of the century where one hundred seventeen prisoners climbed out of an underground tunnel to freedom.

Times had changed. There were only forty or so left in the Belfast Division of the Irish Republican Army. The group was close-knit. Leadership was passed down within families or came from within the ranks of Sinn Fein, the political wing representing the Nationalist party. The officer commanding headed the structure. Then came the Belfast Brigade Command, ten men, give or take a few, headed by three Sinn Fein officials. Next in line was the command staff, responsible for supplying all weapons, the engineering staff for constructing bombs, the finance staff for securing funds and the internal security unit for exposing and eliminating informers. The groupings were no more than two or three men each, operating like a family rather than a military structure. Everyone knew everyone else. In Belfast it was impossible to breach the security of the IRA.

Donovan was a third generation revolutionary. Like his father and grandfather, he lived to see his country free from British Rule at whatever the cost. There wasn't a male member of his family who hadn't done time in Long Kesh. The Peace Accord did not interest him nor did democracy or compromise if it included Protestants. It was immaterial to him that the IRA was no longer popular. He wanted Ireland ruled by the Irish. His reputation as the craftiest, most audacious terrorist on the RUC's wanted list was secure. As leader of the Internal Security Unit, he'd grown accustomed to killing. It was the price of freedom. It no longer disturbed him. He couldn't remember a time when it had. Still, something about Dominick Nolan's logic bothered him. Taking a man's life had to have some purpose. Nothing would be gained by assassinating Peter Clarke. Nolan's reasoning was filled with holes.

Using a quick hand signal, Gerry emptied the room. He waited until the last of his men had filed out before turning to Dominick. The two men measured each other for long minutes. Finally Gerry spoke. "What's this all about?"

It never occurred to Dominick to lie. "He's Clarke's son. We'll never have another opportunity like this."

"Why should we do it at all? The RUC will be on us like maggots on rot."

Dominick's blue eyes glittered. "We should do it for Patrick."

"Patrick's been gone a long time, lad. I'm not sure

he would want us to risk this. He was never one to
enforce 'an-eye-for-an-eye' unless it made good
sense.''

''Patrick was the best friend you ever had.''

Gerry's right hand closed into a fist. ''I don't need
you to tell me that.''

Dominick pressed him. ''How can you let this pass?
Geoffrey Clarke was in on the murder. You know that.
It's in the file.''

''We're not discussing Clarke. It's his son you want
us to take out. Jesus, Dom, the boy's nineteen years
old.''

''How old was Timmy when he died, or Danny Mc-
Carthy or Max or Sean?''

Gerry shook his head. ''They were involved. This
boy isn't. Besides, things have changed. No one will
put this one through.''

Dominick knew the way he worded his answer would
mean everything. He began slowly, calmly, as if such
a request were an everyday occurrence. ''I don't think
we should wait for a consensus,'' he said softly. ''If we
do this on our own it will go more easily. Fewer will
be involved. The risk will be less.''

''Are you suggesting we take out the son of a constable without permission?''

''No. What I'm saying is, we should go straight to
the top.''

''The lads won't like your going over their heads,
Dom.''

''We'll get the okay from Tom. That's good enough
for me.'' Dominick willed his voice to remain neutral.
''What about you?''

Gerry waited a full ten seconds before answering. He
recognized his own fallibility. Too many killings had

jaded him. He couldn't trust his own judgment. He would rely on those above him. "If the officer commanding agrees, I'm in," he said at last.

Dominick released his breath and shook off his anger. How in bloody hell was anyone to get anything done if an assassin like Gerry Donovan had reservations? "I'll be in touch," he said shortly and left the room.

Gerry stayed behind for a good ten more minutes. Dominick's loyalty was irrefutable but he was a hothead, nothing at all like his older brothers, Liam and Patrick. Gerry's instincts told him there was more involved than a vengeance killing. He wasn't about to let Dominick relay Tom McGinnis's message second hand. He would contact the officer commanding himself, even if it meant breaking the chain of command. Taking out a nineteen-year-old university student who happened to be a constable's son was a serious matter.

"Are you bloody daft?" Tom McGinnis leaned over the scarred table of his favorite pub and pointed an angry finger at Dominick. "We're not butchers. You're in the wrong organization, lad, if you think I'd allow something like this."

"We've done it before, and for less."

"We agreed to a ceasefire after the Good Friday Agreement and we've kept our bargain."

"People have died."

McGinnis shook his head. His full, pocked face was very red. "Not on my watch and not by my order. We're not terrorists, Dominick. Sinn Fein is trying to do something here. There's no sympathy for a guerilla force, not today. Catholics are working, attending university, landing skilled jobs. They don't need us to fight their battles anymore.''

''Are you saying we should tuck our tails between our legs and slink away?''

The older man shrugged and emptied his Stout. ''Maybe so. It's comforting to lay your head on a pillow and know you've nothing to be afraid of.''

''What about Patrick?''

McGinnis's eyes narrowed. ''Patrick wouldn't have wanted the boy dead.''

''Patrick was my brother. I knew him better than anyone.''

''What about his wife?''

Dominick snorted derisively. ''Kate? She knew nothing about him.''

''She arranged for a reopening of the investigation,'' McGinnis said. ''She's got the prime minister's ear.''

''How do you know?''

''We have our sources.''

''Has she found anything?''

McGinnis looked up.

''I mean anything we don't know,'' Dominick amended.

McGinnis turned his empty glass around on the table, leaving wet ring marks. ''She knows about Maeve.''

Dominick swore. ''Damn the woman. Can't she leave it alone?''

''She was his wife,'' McGinnis reminded him. ''Without her we wouldn't know who was responsible for Patrick's murder. Don't underestimate Kate Nolan.''

This time it was Dominick who leaned forward, earnest rage darkening the blue of his eyes. ''What will we do with those names, Tom? Is it all to be for nothing?''

"Whatever we do will not include the murder of an innocent boy." McGinnis pushed his chair away from the table and stood. "That's my final decision. You won't be changing my mind, Dominick. Leave it." He hesitated. "Don't be thinking to do this one on your own. We won't be backing you. The charge will be murder. You'll be a criminal doing hard time, not a prisoner of war. The screws will be treating you differently. You'll have no terms, no way of commuting your sentence. You're a young man, Dominick. Why not think of a life for yourself, a trade, a family? Get on with it."

He waited for Dominick to say something. When it didn't happen, he laid a heavy hand on his shoulder. "I'll be seeing you, lad," he said and left the pub.

Dominick stared broodingly at the wall in front of him. Tom McGinnis's word was law with both Sinn Fein and what was left of the IRA. Yet he had as much as acknowledged there was no longer any place or reason for violence in the New Northern Ireland. The IRA and other paramilitary organizations were obsolete. Perhaps Tom McGinnis was obsolete as well.

Gerry threw a half crown to the newsboy on the corner and picked up his morning paper. Tucking it under his arm, he walked into the tea shop, ordered a pot and sat down at a table in the corner facing the door. He unwrapped his paper, glanced at the headlines and his face blanched. Tom McGinnis, scion of the Belfast IRA for more than a decade, was found dead in his Clonard home last night, presumably of natural causes. An autopsy was scheduled for later today. More details would be forthcoming.

Tom, wily, audacious and thorough, hadn't been

more than fifty. No one had been groomed to take his place. What would they all do now? Gerry wondered. He thought back to his conversation with Dominick. The lad would be getting nothing from Tom, and the rest of them would be too confused to agree on anything. It looked as if Peter Clarke would be reprieved. Gerry wasn't sorry. Killing innocents didn't appeal to him. He always insisted on knowing the culpability of his target. It helped him concentrate on the deed, not the person.

Dominick was obsessed. That could be the only explanation for this single-minded nonsense. Liam looked up from his computer and stared at this brother in disgust. "You can't be serious. You actually crashed Geoffrey Clarke's birthday dinner?"

"I did."

"Why would you do such a thing?"

"Because I wanted to see the swaggering bastard, that's why. I wanted to see if I could get in."

"You're a danger to yourself, Dominick. Crashing a man's birthday when he's surrounded by family and friends is a sign of sickness, not to mention dangerous."

Dominick leaned against the doorframe. "No one knew me."

"You were lucky."

"We owe it to Patrick to take the boy out, Liam." Dominick's eyes burned feverishly bright.

"No."

"Why not?"

"Murder holds no appeal for me."

"Since when?"

Liam sighed. "I'm no killer, Dom. You know that.

Nothing like this has been ordered for a long time. Tom is dead. Let things lie for a while.''

"Don't pretend to be a saint. You were one of us, too, in the thick of it.''

"Only when there was a purpose and no other way.''

Dominick pushed away from the wall. "I'll do it myself.''

Liam shook his head. "No, you won't.''

Dominick's eyes narrowed. "You can't stop me.''

"Aye. I can.''

"Will you be informing on your own flesh and blood, Liam?''

"Deirdre is my flesh and blood, too,'' Liam countered. "You seem to be forgetting that.''

"Deirdre is fraternizing with the enemy.''

"She doesn't see it that way.''

Dominick frowned. "What do you know about how she sees it? Have you been talking to her about this?'' His voice roughened. "So help me, Liam, if you've—''

Liam rose, a tall man, taller and thicker than his younger brother, with the same black hair and vivid blue eyes. "Don't be threatening me, Dominick. I told you I'd stop you. I'll do it my way, no matter if it suits you or not.''

With a strangled curse, Dominick flung himself out of the room.

Liam rubbed the furrow between his eyebrows and shook his head. He had never known Dom to behave so strangely, so irrationally. He was always the cool one, collected and sane, a man who looked at all the angles before making a decision. It was almost as if someone else had taken possession of his brother's body. Blood or not, he could not allow Dominick to carry out his macabre foolishness. He made a single phone call, wrote the information he needed on a slip of paper, lifted his jacket from its hook on the wall, walked through the kitchen and out the back door.

The boy answered the door on Liam's first knock. His look of surprise was replaced by wariness.

"May I help you?" he asked politely.

"Do you remember me, lad?"

The boy nodded.

"I need to speak with you. Will you invite me in?" Liam saw the hesitation. "It's important."

Peter stepped aside. "I'm sorry. Please, come in."

"You're in danger," Liam said bluntly when he was safely inside. "Is there somewhere you can go for a bit?"

"It's the middle of the term." Peter looked skeptical. "What is this all about?"

"It's your life I'm talking about."

Peter whitened. "I don't understand."

"My brother knows your father was involved in covering up the investigation of the execution of Patrick Nolan."

"It isn't true."

Liam said nothing.

"What does that have to do with me?"

"Dominick wants to even the score."

A voice came from behind him. "What's going on?"

Liam winced and turned to face his niece framed in a doorway.

"What are you talking about?" she asked.

"How long have you been here, Deirdre?"

"An hour or so. Peter is helping me with a class. What's happening, Uncle Liam?"

Liam sighed. "I didn't want you involved in this, lass. I'm sorry."

Deirdre looked first at her uncle and then at Peter. "Will someone please tell me what's happening?"

Uninvited, Liam sat down on the nearest chair. There was no avoiding it. She had to know. "Geoffrey Clarke, Peter's father, was one of the men involved in the cover-up of the murder of your father."

Deirdre gasped. "No."

Liam hurried to explain. "He wasn't in on the killing, just the investigation."

"What does that mean?" she asked.

"It isn't so unusual," he admitted. "People protect their own. We all do."

Deirdre sat down. To Liam it looked as if the blood had completely left her body, so white and spent was her face. Her question surprised him.

"Why was my father targeted?"

Liam heard the tick of a clock. Somewhere outside the window, a bird trilled and, in the Mews, the quiet, upscale streets surrounding Queen's, he heard the faint sound of an impatient hand on a horn. "Patrick had a gift for getting men acquitted for their crimes," he said quietly.

She came back quickly as if the subject wasn't new to her, as if she'd taken the time to think about it. "So did Martin Walsh and Michael Whelan. They worked with him and continued to do the same work for years after. Why was it my father who was killed?"

Liam was silent for long minutes. He hated his role in all of this. He shouldn't be the one to tell her. He didn't know who he was angrier with, Kate, for protecting her children from what was real, or Dominick for creating the entire mess in the first place. "Your father believed in a united Ireland and equal rights and opportunities for Catholics," he said at last. "He was frustrated by the lack of progress. That frustration led him to the IRA."

"My father was in the IRA?"

Liam nodded. "He was a very important member because of his education and his ability to influence people."

"The IRA is illegal. They're terrorists. How could my father be involved with an illegal organization? He was a barrister. He believed in the law."

"I don't know how he rationalized it, lass."

Her question was pointed, accusing. "Are you in the IRA, Uncle Liam?"

He leaned forward, elbows on his knees. The admission was difficult for him. "I am."

Her cry tore at his heart. "How can you be? They're killers."

"No one has killed in years, Deirdre. We don't sanction murder anymore. Believe me."

She turned the subject. "Why is Peter in danger? Why doesn't Uncle Dominick go after the men who actually killed my father?"

"Dominick never got over your father's murder. He wants to blame someone. We don't know who actually came into your house that day. The investigation wasn't conclusive. Peter is a logical target because of Geoffrey Clarke. Dominick recognized his name as soon as I did."

"You just said murder was no longer sanctioned."

Liam sighed. "Dominick is not himself. I don't believe he would actually carry out his threat, but—" He hesitated. "He needs time to sort it through, to cool down a bit."

Deirdre's hand was at her throat. She raised frightened eyes to her friend's face. "This is my fault," she whispered. "It's because of me that he recognized you." Panic hurried her words. "You'll have to go away. Please, Peter. You don't know what it's like." Threading her fingers through her hair she lifted the weight of it off the sides of her face. "I can't do this again. You must know that I can't do this again." She appealed to Liam. "What can we do?"

"Leave for a while. See nothing of each other. Allow Dominick to find another cause."

"Will he do that?" Peter was clearly skeptical. "Suppose I'm gone for a month, or two, or even three. Will he forget or will I have to relocate forever?"

"It won't be as long as that," Liam assured him.

Peter shook his head. "This is absurd. I won't do it. I refuse to let anyone do this to me." He threw back his head and looked at Liam. "I appreciate the warning, Mr. Nolan, but I'll take my chances."

"No, Peter," Deirdre pleaded.

Liam ignored her. "Informing on my brother won't help you, lad. He's done nothing. The Special Provisions Act has been remanded. It's no longer legal to arrest Catholics because they *might* be dangerous."

"I have no intention of informing on your brother. What if someone retaliated against Deirdre?"

Liam stood. "You're a good lad. I came here to warn you. I've done that. Whatever you do now, my conscience is clean." He appealed to Deirdre. "Do me a favor, lass, and stay away from Peter. It's dangerous for you and it won't help him."

She wouldn't look at him. "This is my fault. I won't leave him to deal with it alone. We're in this together."

Liam swore, caught himself and tried again. "Think

of your mother, Dee. She's already suffered more than
most people.''

Deirdre was silent.

"Will you call her?''

She nodded. "I'll call her, Uncle Liam.''

"You'll tell her what I said.''

"I'll tell her.''

Liam breathed a sigh of relief. Kate would convince
Deirdre to be reasonable. He would rely on Kate to take
care of Patrick's daughter.

Deirdre checked her watch comparing it, once again,
with the clock above the display case in the coffee bar.
Peter was nearly thirty minutes late. It was very unlike
him. She rubbed the worry lines from her forehead.
Liam's warning the day before had left her with a serious case of paranoia. He was probably delayed for a
very good reason that had nothing to do with Dominick
Nolan. Most likely he had car trouble or someone
stopped by to chat. Perhaps he had a phone call. She
fingered the keypad of her mobile phone. No voice
messages. Again she looked at the clock. She would
wait ten more minutes before checking his flat.

Two minutes passed. Three. Deirdre hitched the strap
of her backpack over one shoulder and left the coffee
shop. The lovely cobbled streets and brick buildings
surrounding Queen's soothed her spirits. There was
something about academia that put things into perspective, erased boundaries, brought people together in an
atmosphere of cooperation. The Mews was like that.
Peter's flat was on the south end on University Road.
She climbed the stairs, lifted the brass knocker and
pounded twice on the yellow door. She heard movement inside, footsteps, rustling. She knocked again. Still

no answer. Peter had given her a key, insurance for an early arrival and poor weather. She opened the door and stepped into the entry. "Peter," she called out. "It's Deirdre. Are you home?"

His voice, muffled and strange, came from the kitchen. "Stay where you are. I'll be with you in a minute."

Frustrated, she sat down. What was the matter with him? Normally she would have walked right in. Wasn't that what one did when one had a key?

When he finally joined her, she was shocked to see him so pale. "Are you ill, Peter? Do you need a doctor?"

"I'll be fine in a day or so, but I don't want you to catch it. You should leave, Dee."

"Not on your life." She shook her head vehemently. "I'll make you soup and tea. I'll read to you. That's what friends are for."

"No," he said, too forcefully. "You must leave. I can't have you here, now."

She frowned. Maybe it was something else entirely. A thought occurred to her. "Have you someone here, Peter, another girl, maybe? Is that what this is all about?"

He exploded. "Of course not. What would I want with another girl? I can't explain right now. Please, leave. I'll call you later."

She crossed her arms. "You're being ridiculous. I won't leave without an explanation."

He took her arm and pulled her from the chair. "You'll probably hate me forever, but I really can't do this now. I'm throwing you out, Dee. There's nothing more to say."

She began to struggle. "What's the matter with you,

Peter? I've never seen you like this. You need a doctor. I'm going to ring your parents.''

''Don't.'' His face tightened. ''Just go home. Please.''

She pulled away from him and stamped her foot. Fury had replaced her worry. ''No,'' she shouted.

He cursed. ''What am I going to do with you? Why won't you trust me?''

Deirdre looked over his shoulder and froze.

Peter turned and groaned. A man in a black balaclava pointed a gun directly at them. Another stood behind him.

She recognized the blue eyes and leanly muscled build of the man in front immediately. ''Uncle Dominick,'' she whispered.

The other man spoke quickly. ''You're mistaken.''

Deirdre stared at the man she was sure was her uncle. She wasn't mistaken. Somewhere underneath the black clothes was Dominick and he was here for Peter. Her heart pounded. She backed away. ''I'll be leaving now,'' she said.

''I'm afraid not, lass.'' The same man spoke. ''You'll both be coming with us.''

Deirdre panicked. ''Don't do this, Uncle Dominick.''

''Easy, lass,'' said the spokesman. ''Nothing will happen if you do what I tell you. Come along now. Don't be making this difficult for us.''

Deirdre's eyes flicked from one black mask to the other. Then she looked at the guns and the years rolled back. The man who was not her uncle spoke quietly, soothingly. He was saying something. What was it? Why did he sound so familiar? He started toward her. She backed away, small whimpering sounds coming from inside her throat. He reached for her arm, clamping down hard above the elbow. The pressure of his fingers, his smell, the panic stealing her breath was all so achingly familiar. Deirdre opened her mouth and began to scream, loudly, hysterically, the sound filling the small flat, rooting the three men to the floor, rendering them clumsy and slow to react.

"Shut up." The man lifted his right hand.

The blow came down hard on her temple and she fell, unconscious, to the floor.

The man who never spoke, cried out for the first time. He shouted a single, hoarse, "No!" and leaped forward cradling the girl in his arms. "What in bloody hell are you doing?" he said in the same hoarse voice.

"She was hysterical. Someone could have come in at any time. Let's go. I'll take the lad. You carry the girl and take your mask off," he ordered. "I'll blindfold the boy." He pulled a handkerchief from his pocket, tied it around Peter's face and ripped off his own mask. "We'll not be getting far with these."

Dominick felt for Deirdre's pulse, found it and sighed gratefully. He pulled the balaclava from his head, stuffed it into his pocket and hoisted his niece over his shoulder. "Say your prayers. If she's hurt, you'll be paying for the rest of your life."

"The RUC will be looking for the boy, not a Catholic girl."

"It isn't the RUC I'm worried about. It's the girl's mother."

"This is your brain-child, lad. I won't be the only one answering up."

Twenty-Five

Kate was silent for most of the seven-hour flight back to Belfast. Neil instinctively knew not to press her. She needed time to process what she'd learned. Loss was never easy and Kate had lost more than her share in a few short hours. He followed her out of the plane and left her waiting on the footpath while he picked up his car from the overnight car park. The drive back to her lodgings was equally silent. Neil walked her to the door, squeezed her arm and told her he would be in touch.

"I think I'll go home to Ardara for a while," she said wearily.

"Good idea."

"Promise me you'll see to Kevin."

"He's my first priority."

She smiled, her first in two days. "Thank you."

He had no more than walked back to his car and strapped himself inside when she ran out of the B & B after him. Her face was white and he could see that her breathing was difficult and erratic.

He set his brake, opened the door and walked toward her. She clung to him, her words mixed with strangled gasps for air. "Deirdre is at the Royal Victoria Hospital. She's in a coma and Dominick has kidnapped Kevin."

"Get in the car."

"How did it happen?" he asked when they were on the road.

Kate shook her head. Her breathing had resumed with help from her inhaler. "I don't know. The message from the hospital was on my machine. My father is there and Liam, Deirdre's uncle."

Alarm bells sounded in Neil's brain. He pulled a light from the back seat of the car, fastened it to the hood and turned on the siren. Cars pulled over to the sides of the road. He increased his speed and within minutes pulled into the emergency car park of the Royal Victoria. He dropped Kate at the entrance and then looked for a space to park.

John O'Donnell clutched his daughter's icy hands. "Thank God, you've come."

Liam Nolan and a boy near her daughter's age rose from their chairs.

"Where's Deirdre?" Kate asked.

"She's in Intensive Care," said John. "Liam brought her in last night. When you couldn't be reached, he called me."

Kate looked at her brother-in-law. "What happened? Where's Kevin?"

Liam didn't mince words. "Deirdre was knocked unconscious from a blow to the head. However, it is the doctor's opinion that it wasn't serious. Something else is keeping her from waking up, something emotional."

Kate pushed the hair back behind her ears and sat down in the row of seats facing the ICU. Something wasn't right. "Where is my son and what does all this have to do with you, Liam?"

Neil walked down the hallway. He stood beside her.

Liam frowned. "What is this? What are you doing here?"

"This is Neil Anderson," Kate said. "He brought me here."

Neil did not offer his hand.

The boy stepped forward. "I'm Peter Clarke. Perhaps I should explain."

Clarke. The Protestant from Queen's. Kate waited.

"I was helping Deirdre with her history class when Mr. Nolan came to warn me that I was a paramilitary target."

Kate frowned. "Why would you be an IRA target?"

Peter drew a deep breath. "My father was part of the cover-up of the investigation of your husband's murder. His name is Geoffrey Clarke. He's an RUC constable."

Kate drew a deep shuddering breath. "I see. What does this have to do with Deirdre?"

"She was with me when they came."

"Who?"

"Dominick Nolan and another man. They were in masks," the boy continued, "but she called him by name. At first she tried to convince him to go away but then something happened."

Kate's hands clenched. She dug her nails into her palms. "Go on."

"I don't know why she reacted the way she did. They were quite polite, actually. But she started to scream and wouldn't stop." Peter swallowed and waited a moment before continuing. "The other man panicked. He hit her. She was knocked unconscious. I'm not sure exactly what happened after that. I was blindfolded. They drove us somewhere. The next thing I knew, Mr. Nolan came and made them release us. He brought us here."

Kate looked at Liam. "What about Kevin?"

Neil interrupted. "Most likely he's outside the country with Dominick. He took the lad out from under their noses at Tranquility House."

Liam blanched and spread his hands. "I swear to you, Kate, I didn't know. I had no idea Dom would actually go through with this. Something's wrong with him, but he won't harm Kevin. I know he won't."

Again Neil pressed him. "But you knew Peter was a target."

"Aye."

"Why didn't you call the police?"

Liam stared at him. "Are you mad? We don't call the police on one of our own. Nothing in our experience with the RUC would lead us in that direction."

"Do you still feel that way?"

Liam shrugged.

"Peter could have died and Kevin is missing. You would have been an accessory. Peter is still in danger now that he's our only witness."

"The boy saw nothing. He can't identify Dominick. But if it comes to that, he's not your only witness. Do you understand my meaning?" Liam looked Neil directly in the eye.

"It won't be easy for you."

Liam grimaced. "You don't know the half of it."

Kate rubbed her arms. "I'm going to find the doctor and then I'm going in to see my daughter." She laid her hand on Neil's arm. "Please find my son."

"You know I will. Keep your mobile phone on."

She watched him walk through the automatic doors into the drizzle of the car park.

"You're very friendly all of a sudden," her father remarked.

"I'll explain later. First I want to speak with Deirdre's doctor."

John frowned. "The doctor is a woman, a very young woman. Perhaps we should ask for someone with more experience."

"Why?"

"I'm not sure she's qualified."

Kate exploded. "Of course she's qualified, Da. If she weren't, she wouldn't be here. What difference does it make if she's female or young? This is a hospital. If someone has a question there are enough others out there who can help. What's the matter with you? This is the twenty-first century. I can't believe you would judge someone on the basis of her sex. Do you think I'm not qualified to do my job because I'm not a man?"

"Hold on, Katie. I meant no offense to you or your sex. My concern is for Deirdre. All I'm suggesting is that we consult with someone who has more experience in these emotional coma things."

Her eyes filled. "I'm sorry, Da," she whispered. "It's been a difficult two days."

John's thick eyebrows drew together. "Did you find what you were looking for in New York City?"

She laughed bitterly. "More than I was ready for. I'll explain later. Now, I need to find out about Deirdre."

Dr. Shannon Fahey was young and lovely and intelligent. "We've done all we can, Mrs. Nolan," she assured Kate. "The next twenty-four hours are crucial. Deirdre's tests have all come back. She's extremely healthy."

"Except that she's unconscious," Kate reminded her.

"I'm so sorry I have nothing more positive to report to you."

They were sitting across from each other in the hospital cafeteria nursing two cups of tepid tea.

Kate rubbed the furrow in the middle of her forehead. "If nothing is physically wrong with her, why won't she wake up?"

Dr. Fahey shook her head. "I can't answer that. Modern medicine has progressed only so far. Some theorize that a coma is the mind's way of shutting out something that is too painful to bear. Perhaps your daughter has suffered a trauma she's unable to deal with."

"How long does something like this last?"

Again the doctor shook her head. "I don't know. I'm sorry."

"Is there anything I can do?"

"Talk to her. Remind her of her life."

"Will she hear me?"

"Research has shown that brain activity continues during comatose states. We believe that people remain aware of their surroundings at some level. It's very likely that Deirdre will respond to your voice." She reached across the table and squeezed Kate's hand. "It can be a slow process, Mrs. Nolan. Don't give up. Your daughter is young and healthy. All the odds are with her."

"I'd like to see her now."

Deirdre's hair, dark with a hint of fire, was splayed across the pillow. Kate twisted a strand around her fingers. It was clean and shiny straight. Deirdre was always so particular about her hygiene. In better days Kate had teased her about the number of showers she had taken in a day and the towel she wrapped like a turban around her head. She looked no more than asleep, her chest rising and falling with every even breath. Even her skin looked healthy, except for the bruise darkening her left temple.

Kate bit her lip. Dr. Fahey said to talk. She cleared her throat. "Hello, love. Dr. Fahey says you aren't hurt at all. That's very good, don't you think? She says you're healthy and there's no reason for you to be here. I know you don't want to miss your classes, Dee. You hate falling behind. That nice young man outside in the waiting room is very concerned. He's all right, by the way. Actually you may have saved his life. Liam might not have interfered if you hadn't been involved." She couldn't go on like this. It was ridiculous. This wasn't what she wanted to say. She tried again. "Please wake up, Deirdre," she began. "I don't think I can go through much more. You and Kevin are more important to me than anything. I can't bear any more losses. I know it hasn't been easy for you, but this is such a small part of what your life will be. I'm sorry that your father did what he did. I didn't know. Maybe that was my fault. Maybe I didn't want to know. I'm certainly paying a price for my ignorance. Nevertheless, I'm not giving up. I'm going to live, Dee, and so are you. We're going to live like normal, good people and we're going to create happy lives for ourselves. You have the world ahead of you. You're educated and lovely. People love you, more than you know. Your brother needs you, Dee, and so do I. You can't imagine how much we need you. Please, wake up." She was crying now, the tears streaming down her face. Resting her forehead against the side bar of the hospital bed, she closed her eyes and prayed.

Neil hadn't intended to visit Deirdre. His hope had been to catch Kate before she left the hospital. He'd missed the mother but something drew him to the daughter's room. Deirdre was a mystery to him. Kate had described her often but recent developments had given Neil an entirely different picture of Deirdre Nolan. She was of slight build. Neil could see the lines of her body beneath the blanket. Her features were very like her mother's, delicate and clearly defined. Her hair was dark with a touch of copper. Long eyelashes curled against her cheeks and Neil could see from the length and shape of her eyelids that her eyes were large. They would be light, of course. Both parents were blue-eyed. She was eighteen, but looked much younger lying there so pale and still under the bed covering. This was Kate's child. Protectiveness surged through him. Somehow, he would right this. Kevin would go home and Deirdre would heal. He would be there to make sure of it.

Reaching across the bar, he lifted the girl's hand and held it between both of his. "Wake up, Deirdre. Your mother needs you. Wake up. I promise you everything will be all right."

Had her fingers tightened around his hand, or was it his imagination? Neil couldn't tell. Gently he squeezed. She squeezed back. "Deirdre," he said gently, "wake up."

Again he squeezed. Again, the slight pressure against his hand. He touched her cheek. Her head moved slightly. Eyelashes fluttered. His heart pounded. "That's it, love," he said. "Take your time."

Slowly, ever so slowly, her lids slid back, revealing large, startlingly blue eyes. She stared at him for a long time. "Who are you?" she managed at last.

"Neil Anderson."

He watched as she processed his information, fitting into whatever memory she had of his name. Then she looked around. "Where am I?"

"This is the Royal Victoria Hospital. You've been unconscious for nearly a day now."

She frowned. "Where is Peter?"

"I imagine he's at home with his parents."

She sighed. "That's all right then."

"He has you to thank."

She looked at him, neither agreeing nor disagreeing. "Is my mother here?"

"She was along with your grandfather and your uncle."

Her eyes clouded. "My uncle?"

"Liam Nolan. He brought you here."

"I don't remember."

Neil pulled up a chair and sat. "What do you remember, Deirdre?"

She wet her lips. "I'm thirsty."

Neil looked around, found a paper cup and filled it at the sink. Then he slid his arm behind her head and lifted her to an upright position. She drained the cup.

"Thank you."

"Can you tell me anything about what happened that day?"

"I don't think—" Again her eyelids fluttered. "I'm so tired."

Disappointed, Neil smoothed the blanket over her. "Go to sleep, Deirdre. The next time you wake up, your mother will be here."

Neil left the hospital wondering whether he'd done the right thing by notifying the nursing staff of Deirdre's revival. By the number of hospital staff and the complicated machinery entering her room, it didn't look as if she would get much sleep.

Kate, who had borne everything remarkably well, broke down in tears when he called her. ''Thank God,'' she sobbed. ''Oh, Neil, I'm so grateful. I don't know what I would have done if Deirdre—''

''She's going to be all right, love. You can relax a bit now.''

''Whatever did you do?''

''I'm not sure,'' Neil confessed. ''I was looking for you. When I couldn't find you I decided to check on Deirdre. I told her that everything would be all right. She seemed to understand. More than likely, it was nothing I did. She was ready.''

''Thank you.''

''There is something else.'' He hesitated.

''Go on.''

''Dominick has been linked to Tom McGinnis's death. He's a suspect.''

''The newspapers say that Tom died of natural causes.''

''The autopsy revealed differently.''

''What does this mean?''

''Dominick Nolan is a very dangerous man. He hasn't much to lose. We must be very careful. Peter Clarke is under police protection. I think it would be a good idea for Deirdre.''

Her voice was tight and strained. ''What about Kevin?''

Neil relaxed. He should have known Kate would be sensible when it came to her children. ''I'll be in touch. Come to the hospital and stay with Deirdre. I'll take care of Kevin.''

Twenty-Six

Liam Nolan shook his head. "It's too dangerous. Dominick isn't stupid. After what I've done, he won't be trusting me."

Neil leaned back in his chair and thought. Liam had agreed to meet him at a pub near the edge of the harbor. He sat across from him, his eyes narrowed and suspicious. "From what you've told us, there is no real proof that Dominick kidnapped Peter Clarke. The boy was blindfolded. Deirdre believes she recognized the man in the mask as her uncle but no court will convict a man on that kind of evidence. Your interfering in his plans for Peter didn't put Dominick in any danger. The McGinnis murder is different."

Neil could see the light dawn in Liam's eyes. "In other words, I might go so far as to prevent my brother from kidnapping the son of a constable as long as no one is implicated, but I wouldn't betray him to the police for something that would put him away."

"Precisely."

Liam shook his head. "You're right about that, Mr. Anderson. I can't do it. Dominick is my brother. Betraying him is like betraying myself."

Neil changed his strategy. "Your brother is on a crash course, Liam. He's not going to stop here. You said that he's not himself. Perhaps he isn't. Do you want more innocent people killed and the Peace Accord compromised because Dominick has gone off the deep end?''

"He'll go to prison."

"Yes," said Neil, "he will. But he won't be the target of a Special Forces Team. They don't ask a man if he'll come along nicely. Dead or alive it's all the same to them."

Liam paled. "Will you speak for him?"

"Only if he surrenders. Tom McGinnis was IRA. There won't be much sympathy in the courts for him."

Liam hesitated.

"You'll be helping him if you can get him to turn himself in."

"Dominick won't do that."

"Then we have no choice."

Liam sighed. "I'll think on it."

"We don't have much time."

Liam's thoughts turned to Kevin. His nephew, black-haired, blue-eyed, young, his lean adolescent body as thin and long as a deer rifle, a carbon copy of all who carried the Nolan name, caused him a sharp pang of regret. It was too late for Dominick, but not for Kevin and, perhaps, not too late for Liam as well.

There was no death penalty in Northern Ireland. Prison wasn't forever, not like dying. Nothing was as bad as dying and Dominick was anticipating his demise as surely as if he were standing out in the streets with an Uzi crying, "Shoot me."

"All right," he said, not bothering to hide his reluctance. "I'll do it, for Kevin's sake."

"Have you any idea where Dominick might be?"

"Aye."

"I won't tell you what to say to him. You know him. You'll have to work that one out yourself."

Liam shook his head. "This isn't going to be easy no matter how much we plan it. Dominick is my brother. He knows me. It won't be easy to fool him."

Neil's gaze was steady, level, icy. "Under normal circumstances, I might agree with you, but you've done this before. I'm not worried about your ability to keep yourself tight under fire."

Minutes ticked by, long, intense minutes where the two men, one who lived outside the law and the other sworn to uphold it, measured each other. It was Liam who spoke first. "I've done things I'm not proud of. I admit it. And so have you, Mr. Anderson. The difference is I was never paid nor protected by the government because of my position." He smiled slightly. "What have you to say to that?"

Neil's gaze never wavered. "I'll admit to my share of things I'm not proud of, however, killing isn't one of them."

"You've never killed a man?"

Neil shook his head. "Not by arrangement. We Brits frown on that sort of thing."

Liam snorted. "You haven't been in Northern Ireland very long. You Brits thrive on killing the Irish and you've been doing it for eight hundred years. Have you ever read the Penal Laws, Mr. Anderson?"

"I seem to recall they were rescinded a while ago," Neil said dryly.

"Rescinded my bollocks!" Liam's face was red. "We had a bloody revolution and gained our independence. That's when they were rescinded in the Republic, never here, in the North. History wasn't your subject, was it, Mr. Anderson?"

"I'm ashamed to say that I don't know very much Irish history," Neil said quietly.

"I wouldn't have expected you to," Liam fired back. "No Brit knows Irish history because they all believe that nothing of historical significance happened outside of England. Answer this for me. Isn't it strange how we Irish all know English history?"

"It makes sense," said Neil. "I believe the two are interwoven."

"My point exactly," replied Liam triumphantly. "We know yours but you don't bother learning ours."

"I think that gives you a definite advantage. What do you think?"

"I think you're all arrogant sons of bitches."

Neil grinned and held out his hand. "I can live with that."

Surprised, Liam blinked, and then stretched out his hand to grip Neil's.

"I suppose you really are out of the common way, but then you're not a real Brit, are you?"

"Excuse me?"

"I heard that you hailed from Wales."

"I was born and raised in Swansea."

"That's all right then," Liam said, smiling reluctantly. "The Welsh have been treated nearly as poorly as the Irish."

Neil hated to disturb the camaraderie that had so suddenly and unexpectedly cropped up between the two of them, an officer of the law and a member of the Irish Republican Army. This was new for Neil, cooperating with a self-proclaimed terrorist.

He stood. "One more thing. The movement of weapons that you leaked through Kevin. Is it authentic?"

This time it was Liam who grinned. "Not entirely."

"I'm counting on it being a sham." He added, "For Kevin's sake."

"I don't understand."

"If Kevin is seen as an unreliable witness, he'll be pulled out and sentenced differently. It's what he and his mother want."

"The weapons will be shipped. But the route will be changed," offered Liam.

Neil waited.

"I won't be giving you that information, Mr. Anderson. Murder I won't go along with, but I'm not for giving up all our leverage. No one would be listening to Sinn Fein if it weren't for the IRA. When we Nationalists get what we need the same as everyone else, we'll demilitarize. Not before."

"Someone must go first."

"It won't be us."

"Fair enough. As long as Kevin looks like he isn't trusted, it suits my purposes." He walked to the door. "I'll wait for you to reach me. I want to know what's happening before it happens. At all times I want to know where Kevin is. Do I make myself clear, Mr. Nolan?"

"Perfectly clear, Mr. Anderson."

Kate pulled into the only empty space in the hospital parking lot, decided she was too close to the neighboring car's passenger door, backed out and reentered. A painful crunching noise and the sudden impact froze her into immobility. "Dear God, not again," she moaned. This time her insurance surely would cancel her.

Backing out again, she maneuvered her Volvo into the spot at a dead center position and climbed out of the car. The side panel of the sporty Rover she had been

trying to avoid was seriously crushed. She closed her
eyes, leaned against the side of her Volvo and gave
herself up to self-pity mixed in with an unusual dose
of temper. Why this? Hadn't she enough on her plate?
If she were to compose a résumé of her problems, a
daughter so traumatized she'd fallen into a coma, a son
caught selling drugs, a husband who'd planned assassinations, who'd cheated with her best friend and was
murdered for his pains, no one would believe her. She
must have done something dreadful when she was
young; something so terrible she could no longer remember what it was because she'd blotted it out. That
was it. Retribution. She was Catholic. All Catholics believed in retribution. It was a fact of life, like mortal
and venial sin, novenas, no meat on Friday, no divorce,
no birth control and Purgatory. A thought occurred to
her. Thank God Patrick was dead. Otherwise she would
have to divorce him or join half of Ireland and live in
sin.

The thought cheered her. Suddenly she felt stirrings
of positive energy. Deirdre was recovering and surely
Neil was sorting out Kevin's mess. Maeve had fled to
New York and Patrick— No, she wouldn't go there.
Not yet.

Once again, she looked at the dented Rover. Her
Volvo was barely scratched. Summoning new reserves,
Kate reached into her purse, pulled out a notepad, scribbled a brief message and her phone number and placed
it under the windshield wiper. Immediately she felt better. It was an unfortunate incident, but it was only a
car. If the owner was unreasonable, she would offer to
trade places with him, his life for hers. The absurdity
of her reasoning struck her. She laughed out loud. She

was still smiling when she opened the door to Deirdre's room and stepped inside.

The sight of her daughter sitting up in bed reading a magazine as if nothing more had happened to her than a scraped knee stopped Kate short. She stood quietly in the shadow of the door unable to do more than stare in grateful appreciation that her child's resilience had overcome her demons.

"Hello, love," she called out softly.

Deirdre looked up and smiled. "Hello, Mum. Where have you been?"

Kate closed the door and pulled a chair from the corner to a place beside Deirdre's bed. "I've taken Grandda to his hotel."

Deirdre's smile faded. "How is Kevin?"

"Kevin's going to be fine, Deirdre. I have a good feeling that we're all going to be together again soon."

"How can that be?"

"I'll explain later. Right now I want you to tell me what happened to you."

Deirdre twisted the fringe of the blanket between her fingers.

"Peter gave me his version. But I think there's more to it, isn't there?"

Deirdre looked up guiltily. "I wasn't going to see him anymore, Mum, but I really needed the help in history and he volunteered."

"Good Lord, Dee. Whatever gave you the idea that you shouldn't see him? He's a perfectly nice boy."

"He's a Protestant," Deirdre sat flatly.

"Is something wrong with that?"

Deirdre looked confused. "You told me to be careful."

"Yes, I did. I would give you that advice about any

boy. The fact that the two of you are living in a city where Catholics and Protestants don't usually mingle makes it more difficult. But I never meant for you to believe you couldn't be friendly with someone of a different religious affiliation. I'm sorry if I gave you that impression.''

''You were right,'' Deirdre said, her voice low. ''Because of me, Peter was nearly hurt.''

''That isn't quite right, Deirdre. None of this is because of you or Peter. Your fathers are responsible. Because of who they were and what they did, you and your friend were held accountable.''

Deirdre looked directly at her mother. ''What happens now?''

''We go on.''

''What about Uncle Dominick?''

Kate's face hardened. ''Dominick behaved foolishly. I'm afraid he'll have to pay for that.''

''I'm the only one who knew it was him.''

Kate lifted her daughter's hand from the bed cover and held it between both of her own. ''Dominick is IRA, Deirdre. This aborted kidnapping of Peter is a very small thing compared to what he's done. I'm afraid he's a suspect in the murder of Tom McGinnis. That's what the charge will be when they arrest him. You won't be involved at all.''

Deirdre was silent for a long time. Finally she spoke. ''Tell me about Da.''

Kate chose her words carefully. How much to tell? How much to leave out? ''What would you like to know?''

''I figured most of it out a while ago. People aren't murdered the way he was without cause. The reasons you and Grandda gave made no sense to me. Liam told me the rest.''

Kate sighed.

"He didn't want to," Deirdre hurried on, "but when he came to warn Peter, I asked him and he told me."

Kate nodded.

"I'm glad he told me, Mum. It cleared up some things for me."

"I don't understand."

Deirdre's cheeks were flushed. Her forehead wrinkled in concentration. "The man in the mask with Uncle Dominick was the same man who came for Da. He was in our house that night."

Kate paled. "That's impossible, Dee. The men who murdered your father weren't IRA. They were Loyalist paramilitaries."

"It was the same man," Deirdre insisted. "I recognized his voice and his eyes. He's the same one, Mum. I know it."

Kate could barely swallow. "Do you know what you're saying?"

Deirdre nodded. "Da was killed by his own."

"But why?"

"Perhaps we should tell Mr. Anderson."

"Yes," Kate replied absently. Questions crowded her mind. Who, among his own people, would have wanted Patrick dead? Patrick was a rarity, a barrister from the Falls. A man loyal to his roots, Patrick gave them his knowledge, his money, his loyalty. How would anyone have benefited from such a loss? Perhaps Neil would know.

Deirdre's words resurfaced. "How do you know Mr. Anderson?" Kate asked.

"He was here when I woke up. I heard his voice. He

talked for a long time. In the beginning I was too tired to pay attention, but then he talked about you and how much you needed me to be well and healthy. I believed him,'' she said simply. ''He seems like a very good man.''

Kate wet her lips. ''He is a good man.''

''Is he a Protestant?''

''No, but he's an Englishman, which is even worse.'' Deirdre laughed. ''You sound like Grandda.''

Kate smiled. ''Don't be cruel. I was teasing.''

''I think he likes you, Mum.''

''Yes, he does.''

Deirdre looked surprised. ''Have you been seeing him socially?''

''Not really.''

''It's all right, Mum. You've been a widow for a long time.''

Kate shook her head. ''It's more complicated than that. I'm not sure about anything right now. Learning about your da was a shock and this business with Kevin has been dreadful. Right now I want to go home, dig a hole in the sand and crawl into it.''

Deirdre held out her arms. ''Poor Mum. Everything will turn out the way it's supposed to. You'll see.''

Kate hugged her daughter fiercely. ''How did you get to be so smart?''

''I had a wonderful role model.''

''Bless you for that, Dee,'' her mother whispered.

Twenty-Seven

Thoughts of Dominick dominated Liam on his drive north. There was something not quite right about his brother. Most of the time he appeared completely normal, but occasionally his behavior veered into the irrational, even the unbalanced. The Peter Clarke situation was an example. Liam didn't know what to make of it. His instincts told him to cut a wide, clear path as far away from his brother as possible.

The seaport town of Portstewart was lovely and clean with cozy tearooms, souvenir shops, a boardwalk, air thickly scented with salt spray and curbstones painted red white and blue, Loyalist colors. Dominick had chosen this location, rabidly Protestant, because it was completely devoid of sentiment for the IRA and the last place anyone would look for one of its members.

The beach cottage stood apart, a lonely structure on the blip of a variegated shore. Of indiscriminate color, two stories with three gables and a large empty porch, its walls had been scoured and worn by sand and wind, salt and sea. The yard appeared deserted and shades covered the windows. The only evidence of life was a thin line of smoke from the chimney.

Liam pulled into the gravel driveway and turned off the ignition. He walked around to the back door. A tricycle and several hand tools lay rusted and forgotten in the yard. The steps leading to the door were as weathered as the house but in better repair.

He knocked loudly. Minutes passed. He looked around, knocked again and walked inside. The house was dim and sparsely furnished. The air was still and empty as if no one had breathed it in for some time. The floorboards creaked under Liam's feet. He walked through the back room, the kitchen, down a long hallway and up a flight of steep, uncarpeted stairs into a small bedroom, stark and severely appointed enough for a monastery. Dominick sat in the single straight-backed chair, his hands quiet in his lap. Kevin sat on the floor, his back to the wall.

"Hello, Liam," he said softly.

Liam nodded, looked around for a place to sit and found none.

Dominick turned his gaze on his brother. "What brings you here?"

"You're a suspect in Tom McGinnis's murder."

"How did you find out that interesting bit of information?"

"It's already news."

Dominick shifted his eyes to another spot in the room. "Tom died of natural causes. It wasn't murder."

"According to the autopsy, he was murdered."

"Ah, the autopsy." Dominick grinned. "Modern forensics certainly changes the picture, doesn't it?"

"Did you do it?"

"Let's just say I was instrumental in helping him along."

Kevin swallowed a gasp.

Liam released his breath. "What are you doing to yourself, Dom?"

"How is Deirdre?"

''Time will tell.''

Dominick lit a cigarette, blew the smoke into a circle above his head. ''What are you really doing here, lad?''

''Anderson sent me to convince you to turn yourself in. He said if you gave him the information he needed, he could help you. Your sentence could be lighter.''

Dominick's eyes narrowed and a muscle twitched at the corner of his mouth. ''Did he now?''

''Aye.''

''So, Kevin, you think I should turn myself in? Give myself up to an English court with Protestant judges and lawyers and hope they do well by me?''

''Special Forces will be looking for you, Uncle Dominick. I don't want you to die.''

''Bless you, lad. Everyone dies. It's simply a matter of when.''

''You're not old enough to die.''

''No,'' said his uncle. ''I'm not.''

Liam swore. His voice rose. ''Damn it. Are you bloody insane, Dom?''

A flash of anger broke through the younger man's calm. ''What's it to you, Liam? You're the one who freed Peter. We would have been home free without you.''

''There's no proof you had anything to do with Peter Clarke. You were wearing a mask.''

''Deirdre knows.''

Liam shook his head angrily. ''She didn't see you. No jury will convict on such flimsy evidence.''

''I won't give them a chance.''

''They have you on the McGinnis murder, Dom. You'll be a marked man. Even the Republic won't keep you.''

''I'll take my chances.''

"Have it your way." Liam stood. "I'll be going and I'm taking Kevin."

Dominick's gaze slid from his brother to his nephew. "Kevin stays with me. I'll return him later."

Liam froze. Fear slowed his heart. It was an effort to breathe. Seconds passed. One minute. Two. Finally his heart resumed its regular rhythm. "Kevin's expected back."

Dominick's voice was sharp, edgy. "When did you become such a rule follower, Liam?"

"When you went over the edge." his brother shot back. "Come along, Kevin. We're finished here."

"Stay where you are, lad," ordered Dominick. "We don't want this to get ugly."

"I'm taking the boy, Dom."

Dominick reached into his pocket and pulled out a pistol. He leveled it at his brother. "Kevin stays with me."

"Do you expect me to believe that you would use that on us, Dom?" Liam scoffed.

Dominick laughed and the frightening, unbalanced sound of it stopped the blood flow in Liam's veins.

"I'm a desperate man," said Dominick.

"Don't do this, Dom," Liam pleaded. "For God's sake. He's Patrick's son."

"Patrick." Dominick's voice carried a tender, regretful note and for a minute, Liam thought he'd reconsidered. But then he shook it off and his face hardened again. "He's my only chance. Without him I'll be on the queen's dole for the next thirty years."

"You'll add kidnapping to the rest of your charges," Liam said.

"Nothing's worse than murder."

"Haven't you done enough to Kate?"

"There's truth to that, Liam," Dominick said. "More than you know."

Neither man noticed that Kevin was no longer sitting on the floor. "What have you done to my mother?" he demanded.

"Leave it, Kevin," Liam warned him and turned back to his brother. "Go now, Dominick, while we're here."

Kevin walked across the room to stand beside Dominick. His hands were clenched. "Tell me what you've done to my mother."

Sanity returned to Dominick. "Settle yourself, lad. It was no more than an expression. I meant nothing more than what was kept from her when your father was alive."

Relieved, Liam sighed. "Let's go, Kevin."

"Kevin stays."

Liam was frantic. "Be reasonable. You can't hide the boy. They'll be looking for him. You'll be better off alone."

Dominick's hand tightened on the gun. "I won't hurt him as long as he's cooperative. He'll have a bit of coin to call his mother when I've crossed the border."

Liam started forward.

"Stay back, Liam," Dominick said softly. "I said I wouldn't hurt Kevin. I'll do what I must with you. I haven't forgotten that you betrayed me."

"For Christ sake, Dom. I did it to save you."

"I'm not saved, am I, Liam?"

"I didn't know you'd murdered Tom McGinnis."

"You know it now."

"Aye." Liam backed away. "But I don't know you, Dom. Something's happened to you. You're not my brother."

"I imagine there's more than a bit of relief in that knowledge, isn't there, Liam?"

"I pity you."

"Save it, lad," Dominick said, "and give my regards to Kate. Tell her I'll return her son when I'm safely out of the Six Counties."

"Take me instead," Liam said.

"Don't be a wanker, Liam. You're not important enough. Special Forces will have us marked, trussed and sewn up in body bags before the cocks crow. Now, the lad here is different. They'll be using kid gloves with our Kevin." He smiled engagingly at Kevin. "You don't mind helping out your uncle, do you, lad?"

Liam held his breath, praying that the boy would say nothing to antagonize Dominick.

Kevin swallowed and shook his head.

Liam relaxed and gave himself up to the inevitable. "Do you want me to wait until you've gone?" he asked.

"Not at all. I want you to drive back to Belfast immediately and tell Neil Anderson that I've got Kevin and if he wants him back in one piece, he's to allow me to leave Northern Ireland with the papers you'll supply for me."

"Is that all?"

"Aye." Dominick ran his free hand through his thick hair, a habit carried over from childhood. "I've no demands, if that's what you mean."

"Where will you go?"

"Immediately or in the end?"

"In the end."

Dominick shrugged. "I've no real plans. Away from Ireland, I think. I've no real stomach for the place anymore."

Liam nodded. "Take care of the lad, Dom. Don't take risks."

Dominick nodded. "Go along with you, now. The traffic home is a bugger."

Liam held out his hand to Kevin. When the boy took it, he pulled him into his arms for a hard, brief hug. "Take care of yourself, Kevin. Be smart," he said, pulling away and walking quickly out of the room, down the hall, out the back to the car parked in the gravel driveway.

Neil Anderson swore. His eyes blazed black and the pencil he carried snapped in his hand. He walked to the window, pushed the blinds aside and stared out at the rainy world that was Belfast. He waited a full five minutes, enough time for the white-hot rage consuming him to settle a bit, before addressing Liam.

"I didn't think he would use Kevin. Was there no other way?"

"You should know the answer to that," Liam replied patiently. "If there was any possibility of taking Kevin with me, I would have. He's my nephew, my blood."

"I could accuse you and your brother of orchestrating this between you."

"I wanted no part of it," Liam reminded him. "I told you Dominick isn't himself."

"Would he harm his own nephew?"

"I don't know."

"Good Lord." Neil passed his hand over his face. "How am I going to tell Kate?"

Liam remained silent.

"My instincts are good, Nolan. I don't believe you're part of this. What I want from you now is information. How unstable is your brother?"

"I don't understand."

"Will he harm the boy if we go after him?"

"I don't know."

"Would he have harmed you?"

"Possibly. That's why I left without Kevin. I can't predict what Dominick will do. He's feeling trapped. Trapped animals strike."

Neil sighed. "It doesn't matter. We've no choice but to go after him, now more than ever. Any suggestions as to how I should break this news to the boy's mother?"

"Tell her the truth, straightaway. Don't lie to her. Kate doesn't beat about the bush. She'll forgive anything except a lie."

Neil's glance was curious, speculative. "Did your brother know that?"

Liam nodded. "He knew Katie better than anyone. But he had trouble measuring up, if you know what I mean."

Neil most definitely knew what he meant. He was feeling a bit overwhelmed himself. He picked up his jacket. "She'll be at the hospital."

Liam nodded. "Better to get it over with."

Neil pulled into the hospital car park, set the brake and walked through the door of the Royal Victoria Hospital.

The smile Kate gave him when he entered Deirdre's room turned his heart inside out. She held out her hand and he went straight to her. She looked younger, more relaxed than he'd ever seen her. This was what she must have been like before worry and tragedy had etched the wariness around her eyes.

"How is the patient?" he asked.

Deirdre smiled shyly. "Much better. Thank you for everything you've done."

"I'm pleased that it worked out the way it did. Peter's a good lad and very worried about you."

Deirdre blushed. "He's a good friend."

"When will you go home?"

"The doctor says tomorrow if I feel strong enough." She turned impossibly blue eyes on her mother. "I feel strong enough now."

"Another day won't hurt you," said a voice from the door.

Deirdre's face lit up. "Grandda. Did you come back all the way from Ardara?"

John O'Donnell walked across the room and caught his granddaughter in a tight embrace. "I came when I heard you were hurt. I'd walk to the moon to see you, lass. You know that."

Deirdre clung to him for a long time. Laughing, she finally pulled away. "I'm fine, Grandda. Really I am. Thanks to Uncle Liam."

John's eyebrows drew together over eyes as blue as his granddaughter's. "It's glad I am to hear that the Nolan brothers are good for something."

"Da," Kate broke in hurriedly. "I don't think you've officially met Neil Anderson."

John straightened and offered his hand. "Pleased to meet you," he said stiffly.

Neil smiled and shook the older man's hand. "The pleasure is mine. I've heard a great deal about you from your grandson. He admires you very much."

"Does he now?"

"Absolutely."

John began to thaw a bit and a glint of humor appeared in his eye. "Did you ever hear what happened to the B-Specials, Mr. Anderson, the last time they were seen in Belfast?''

''I can't say that I have.''

''You don't say.'' John stroked his chin. ''I would have thought, in your line of work, you would have heard the story.''

''Tell me now.''

''No, Da,'' Kate protested. ''Neil hasn't the time right now. He just stopped in to see Deirdre. I'll walk him out while you, two, visit.''

''Goodbye, Mr. Anderson. We'll have a bit of craic and a pint or two the next time.''

''Was he speaking English?'' Neil asked when the door closed behind them.

''Craic means conversation and you must know what a pint is. Surely they have them in England.''

''Craic, conversation.'' Neil shook his head. ''I never would have guessed.''

''It really was lovely of you to check on Deirdre.''

Neil took her arm. ''This isn't a social call, Kate. I wish it was. I'm afraid I have bad news.''

Kate whitened and swayed. Neil reached out to grip her arm.

''What is it?'' she whispered.

''Liam believes that Dominick intends to leave Ireland for a safer haven.''

''Is he taking Kevin?''

He could hear the hysteria in her voice and spoke deliberately, calmly. ''I don't believe he intends to harm Kevin. Neither does Liam. We're going after him, Kate. As we speak there are checkpoints at all the border crossings. We're covering every square inch of land. I'm going in myself. We'll find him, Kate. I promise you.''

She was pale and mute and obviously terrified. Neil recognized shock when he saw it. Sliding one arm around her waist and the other behind her legs, he lifted her into his arms and carried her into an empty room. Gently he eased her down on the bed and slid a pillow behind her head. Then he pulled the blanket up over her shoulders and pressed the red attendant's button. A nurse appeared.

"Mrs. Nolan has had some difficult news," he explained. "Is there anything you can do for her?"

Immediately the woman moved to the bed and felt Kate's pulse. "I'll find a doctor," she said and left the room.

Kate's eyelids fluttered. "I'm all right," she said. "You shouldn't be here. I want you to find my son."

"Right now you're the one I'm worried about."

Kate sat up. "Dominick won't harm Kevin. He's using him, that's all."

"I'll wait with you until the doctor comes."

"Do you have any idea where he's gone?"

"No. However, I'm sure Liam does." Neil lifted Kate's hand and kissed it. "I'll find him, Kate. I promise you I'll find him."

"I believe you."

Twenty-Eight

Neil marked another x on the map and retraced the route Dominick had taken with his finger. The man was an amateur. The trail was direct and obvious, almost as if Dominick wanted to be found. An ambush was a possibility but one that Neil discarded quickly. At this point Dominick's motive was to leave Ireland, nothing more. What Kevin's role would be and for how long his uncle would keep him, Neil could only speculate. The boy had no passport with him. It would take several days to manufacture one for him, and Maeve, the IRA's counterfeit document specialist, was in New York and not likely to want any more involvement with the Nolans. Neil didn't believe Dominick would take Kevin out of Ireland.

Liam had suggested the Strabane checkpoint into Donegal. It was farther north and too far west of Newry, the usual exit point, to be suspect. Neil had his own misgivings over Liam's contributions. Dominick was his brother and because of Kevin's abduction there was no longer any hope for clemency. Fortunately Neil hadn't needed anything more than the briefest of initial direction. He sent Liam home and proceeded with only a staff of two agents, James McElroy and Douglas Hartwell, both experienced, silent and purposeful.

After picking up a trail at Strabane, they followed

Dominick to a series of safe houses in Spiddal, cottages used by members of the IRA while on the run. The only question was which one. The town was in the middle of the Gaeltacht, an Irish-speaking strip of land on the coast of Galway, heavily infested with tourists in the spring and summer, a condition for which Neil was grateful. Three strangers with grim, watchful expressions who ate all their meals out and had little to say to one another would be more obvious to the suspicious natives than a signpost advertising their presence. He had no doubt that the locals would be sympathetic to the Nolans over three British government agents unless, of course, they knew about Kevin.

The Irish loved children. Unlike the English who delegated the care of their children to nannies on nearly every occasion, the Irish included theirs in every aspect of their lives. Even the pubs with pool tables and television, soft drinks, bright lights and popular music were geared to families.

Neil sat at a corner table and nursed his lager. Feeling the need for solitude, he had begged off dinner with his colleagues and wandered into what was obviously the local pub. He wondered what his daughter would think of this. Erin, with her cool sophistication, her preference for American fast food, shopping malls and hip-hop music, would more than likely scoff at the idea of girls dancing together and boys arm-wrestling for coppers. Their last visit had not been a success. She was bored with nearly all his suggestions, spoke in monosyllables the entire weekend and requested to be sent home early. In essence, she was very like Lydia. He couldn't help comparing her with Deirdre and then immediately chastised himself. Erin was thirteen years old, typical of her age. He should be comparing her with Kevin who was also often sullen and unappreciative.

The waitress, a sturdy young woman with apple cheeks, stopped at his table. "Would you like anything else?" she asked in English.

"Are you serving sandwiches?"

"Only until two. Can I interest you in steamed mussels and brown bread? We're famous for both."

Suddenly Neil was hungry. "Bring them on."

"Would you care for another lager?"

"I'll have one when you bring the mussels."

She moved away. The door opened and a lean, black-haired man walked in and looked around.

Neil tensed and looked away, keeping the man in his peripheral vision. His eyes would be blue. Blood ran true among the Nolans. The resemblance was uncanny. Except for about two stone, the man could be Liam or even Kevin in twenty years. There was no doubt the man was Dominick Nolan. He was alone.

He walked to the bar, sat down on a stool and spoke to the barman. The man leaned in close to Dominick. Neil felt the hair lift on the back of his neck. Something was wrong. They were too casual, too careful not to look in his direction. The barmaid came with his mussels, blocking his view. When she moved away, Dominick was gone.

Neil reached into his pocket for a twenty-pound note, slid it under his untouched plate and left the pub. There was no sign of Dominick. A white vehicle turned the corner at the end of the road. Neil ran for his car. Reaching for his mobile phone, he flipped it open, pressed the single digit that would connect him to Hartwell and backed out of the car park.

The connection was immediate. "Nolan's here," he

said tersely, "just leaving Mulvaney's Pub in a white auto, traveling east on the Coast Road. He's alone. I didn't get the make of the car or the plates. Can you follow me?"

Hartwell's answer was clipped, regretful. "We're at a restaurant at the north end of town. Give us ten minutes."

Neil swore under his breath.

"Sorry, mate."

"It can't be helped. Do your best."

During the summer, days were fifteen hours long in the West and the light was good. Still, Neil saw no sign of a white car. Local families inhabited the small cottages clustered along the road. He'd checked them out and they were all legitimate. There was no way of knowing if they harbored IRA activists, but he doubted it. Safe houses would not be those with children. It was too dangerous. Children could not be counted on to keep secrets.

Neil could feel the rise in his blood pressure. Keeping his cool was essential. Because of Kate, he was too close to this one. Kevin was too important. He began to doubt his ability to see this through.

What was he missing? Where could they be? A fork in the road stopped him. To the right, tire tracks marked freshly turned earth. To the left, was dry gravel. He was about to veer right when he changed his mind. Setting the brake, he opened the door, stepped out on to the road and reached down to scoop up a handful of dirt. Frowning he stared at the mix of dirt and gravel in his hand. The gravel dribbling through his fingers was dry, yet the dirt with the patterned tire tracks was wet.

An innocuous, gray automobile pulled up behind him

and stopped. Simultaneously McElroy and Hartwell stepped out of the car and walked toward him.

"Where do we go from here?" McElroy asked.

Neil pointed to the ground. "What do you make of this patch of dirt?"

"It looks like tire tracks," Hartwell volunteered.

"Where did the dirt come from?" McElroy asked.

Neil stared thoughtfully at the ground. "From anywhere, I suppose. It's an Irish road."

McElroy shook his head. "The road is gravel, like the other one. This is only the spot with earth and yet there's gravel beneath. It looks deliberate as if someone raked it across and drove over it."

Neil smiled. "You're brilliant, McElroy. We'll take the left fork. I've a hunch our man is headed in that direction."

Connemara, or the Burren, was a desolate, windswept bogland, unlike any other part of Ireland. The terrain was flat and golden with silver lakes, some the size of puddles, others as large as glaciers, dotting the landscape as far as the eye could see. This was Connaught, the province where, four hundred years before, Cromwell had banished what was left of the massacred Irish population. It wasn't the Ireland of the guide books but it had a severe beauty of its own.

Neil credited sheer luck with what happened next. Out of the dozens of narrow, unpaved roads leading to nowhere at all, he happened upon the one he was looking for. At the end of a dirt-carved road which curved treacherously several times before ending abruptly, stood an unappealing dwelling that was little more than a flimsy shack. There was no sign of a white car. He killed the engine quickly, but it was too late. He saw movement behind the pulled curtain. Dominick knew they had him.

Slowly Neil pulled out his gun and released the safety. They were out of range for most firearms but one could never be too sure. McElroy and Hartwell had stopped behind him. He signaled them to remain in their vehicle. Then he opened the door. Using it as a shield, he crouched behind it and spoke into a bullhorn. "Send the boy out, Nolan."

There was no answer. Neil hadn't expected one. Again he lifted the horn to his lips. "This is Neil Anderson, Special Forces Investigator. We know you're in there. Come out with your hands up."

Again, no answer.

Neil picked up his telephone, dialed Belfast and waited for the connection. It came quickly. "We have him," he said, "and he's not responding. I believe the boy is with him." He pulled out a map and unfolded it. "We're about thirty kilometers south of Galway. A chopper would be helpful if you can spare one." His hand tightened on the phone.

"Good God. Well done. Do you have it on tape?" He waited.

"Charles, this is Kate Nolan's son. I don't think you'll get an argument on this one."

Hartwell was looking through binoculars. He hand-signaled Neil, acknowledged his nod and began a half run to the other side of the dwelling. Shots rang out and he hit the dirt.

Neil flipped off his mobile phone and stuffed it into his pocket. McElroy was beside him. "Anything positive?"

"Martin Crosse has confessed to the murder of Tom McGinnis."

"Is Nolan in the clear?"

"He was there."

"Where does that leave us?"

"He's an accessory, not the murderer. That gives us some leverage in dealing with him. Maybe he'll be open to a bargain."

"He's shooting at us, Neil."

"He's afraid. I'm going to try to talk to him."

McElroy shrugged. "It's your funeral. I'll cover you as far as I can. Shall I call for backup?"

"Not until I get the boy out of there." Neil lifted the bullhorn to his lips. "Hold your fire. I'm coming in to make you an offer."

"Call your man off," shouted a voice from the house.

Neil punched in Hartwell's mobile number. "Hold your position," he said. "I'm going in."

Stuffing the gun back into his belt, he cautiously moved toward the house, his mind forwarding to every possible scenario. Dominick had nothing to lose and everything to gain by listening to an offer. He was outnumbered with no possibility of escape. His only options were surrender or die resisting arrest. Neil took comfort in the knowledge that neither his nor Kevin's death would benefit Dominick.

Encouraged by the silence, Neil stopped in front of the house and knocked. Kevin opened the door. Relief was instant and intense. The boy was unharmed. Neil stepped inside and Dominick, gun raised, walked into the light.

"There's no need for a gun," Neil said.

"I'll be the judge of that."

"Let the boy go. You have me."

Dominick's mouth twisted into a half smile. "Not a chance. What's your offer?"

Neil hadn't expected him to agree. "Amnesty in this case and reluctant accessory status in the murder of Tom McGinnis. Crosse confessed."

"There was nothing reluctant about it, mate. It was my idea. He wouldn't go along with the Clarke kidnapping."

"No one knows that."

"You do."

"We make deals all the time."

"When the circumstances are right?"

Neil nodded. "Yes."

Dominick waved the gun.

Neil held his breath.

"You must want our Kevin here very badly."

"He's just a boy. The risks are enormous."

Dominick glanced at his nephew. "Are you just a boy, Kevin, lad? Why don't we tell the man what sixteen-year-old boys do in the Falls?"

"Uncle Dominick," Kevin pleaded. "Listen to him. You aren't getting out of this one."

Dominick's voice was very soft. "Maybe you won't be getting out of this one either, lad."

Kevin's cheeks paled and he looked away.

"You'll get seven years, less maybe with good behavior."

Dominick laughed. "So, you really think seven years is a good deal?"

"I do."

"Have you ever been to prison, Mr. Anderson?"

"No."

"Seven years is a long time."

"Death is longer. You'll be a free man and Tom McGinnis will still be dead."

"You do have a way of turning a phrase, Mr. Anderson."

Neil's phone rang.

Dominick tensed. "What's that?"

"My phone. I'd like to answer it."

Once again, Dominick lifted the gun and aimed it at Neil. "By all means."

Slowly, with one hand, Neil reached into his coat pocket and pulled out his phone. "Anderson, here," he said. "What is it?"

McElroy's voice filled his ear.

"That's impossible," Neil said flatly.

Again McElroy repeated his incredible information, this time including the source.

For the first time in his career, Neil blanked. Deliberately he kept McElroy on the phone, stalling for time. When his conversation was no longer believable, he ended it abruptly.

"Trouble?" Dominick asked innocently.

"Let the boy go, Nolan," he said.

"What about our deal?"

"We'll work it out when Kevin leaves."

"There isn't anything you can't say in front of my nephew. Kevin is family."

Against his will, the words came out. "Family means a great deal to you, doesn't it, Nolan?"

Dominick's eyes glittered. "It does."

"Send the boy out."

"No."

"I don't think you want him to hear this."

"Be careful, Anderson," Dominick warned.

"Send the boy away."

Dominick considered his nephew. Kevin sat at the table as silent and still as a corpse. "What do you have to say about all this, Kevin, lad? Is it time to leave your uncle?"

Kevin said nothing.

"Answer me, lad." Dominick's tone was ugly, menacing.

"It doesn't matter," replied Kevin.

"There now. You have your answer, Anderson. Kevin doesn't want to leave. Say whatever you will."

"Very well. Martin Crosse confessed to more than one murder. He named his accessories to that one as well. In case you wondered, you were not left out."

"Martin and I have done a number of eliminations together. We were at war."

"This one was much more personal in nature. Do I have to spell it out?"

Dominick's hand shot out and knocked aside the chair. "Wait outside, Kevin," he ordered. "Stay by the door."

"Wait!" Neil held up his hand. "My men won't know him from you. Let me call them."

Dominick held out his hand. "Give me the phone."

Neil handed it over.

Dominick flipped it open and gave it to Kevin. "You call."

Neil nodded. "It's programmed," he said to the boy. "Not to worry. Just punch the number five. You'll get through."

Kevin's hand shook. Almost immediately a voice responded. Lifting the phone to his ear, Kevin identified himself. "I'm coming out," he said. "Mr. Anderson will be staying."

Kevin threw Neil a last desperate look before slamming the door behind him.

Neil closed his eyes and waited, one second, two, five, ten. Slowly he unclenched his hands. McElroy and Hartwell had received the message.

"Now," said Dominick softly, "we're alone."

"I can't offer you amnesty any longer. Crosse's confession of your brother's assassination is too big. It has political ramifications. The prime minister is involved."

"Are you telling me I should kill you now and be done with it?"

Neil shrugged. "In all honesty, I don't see that my death would do you any good. If I were in your shoes, I might take a hostage in the hope of leaving the country. It's a chance."

Dominick's eyebrow quirked diabolically over one blue eye. "You surprise me, Anderson."

"How so?"

"Your honesty is unusual. I don't remember anyone ever volunteering to become a hostage."

"If the choice is between death and abduction, it's the lesser of two evils."

Dominick laughed. "Perhaps not."

"Why did you do it?"

"Do what?"

"Murder your own brother."

"I didn't intend to. That was never the plan. I thought we'd shake him up a bit. He was going careful on us. Somehow, before we got there, the plan changed. I still don't know why. I wasn't in on it. It wasn't official. No one knew but Crosse and Kelly."

Neil interrupted. "Joe Kelly."

"Aye. It turned my stomach but I couldn't say anything, not to the Provos or anyone. They would have killed us.''

''He was your brother. How could you live with it?''

''What was the alternative?''

Oddly enough, Neil understood. He had his own demons, many that had not been exorcised, but rather pushed away into the corners of his memory to be taken out and relived in bad moments. ''What will you do now?''

''That depends. Will this be made public?''

''Yes.''

Dominick sighed. Reaching down, he righted the chair he'd upset and sat down. ''Do you ever get tired of it all, Anderson?''

''Yes.''

''How do you go on?''

''Retirement comes early, for good reason.''

''I'm tired,'' Dominick volunteered. ''I simply want the whole bloody mess to go away.''

''Why did you target Peter Clarke?''

''Blackmail. Geoffrey Clarke arranged for Loyalist paramilitaries to take the blame for Patrick's death. Clarke has three other children. I knew he'd be less willing to blow the whistle on us if he thought the others would go the way of Peter.''

''After all this time, he isn't in a position to say anything.''

Dominick shrugged. ''One never knows. Kate had the investigation reopened. I didn't want to take any chances. I thought Clarke needed reminding.''

''Tell me you wouldn't have murdered the boy.''

Dominick shook his head. ''Despite all this, you're still a Boy Scout, aren't you, Anderson?''

''Not really.''

"We would have killed him."

Neil was disgusted. "God help you."

"I doubt if He wastes much time thinking of me."

Neil waited. They had run out of conversation. Dominick's next words surprised him.

"I can't go back to Belfast with the world knowing I was responsible for Patrick's murder."

"I agree."

"Even in prison, I wouldn't last long."

"What do you suggest?"

"Would you mind turning around, Mr. Anderson?"

Neil hesitated.

Dominick laughed. "I won't shoot you."

Slowly Neil turned so that his back was to Dominick. Minutes passed. He heard a click and wondered at it. The sound registered at the exact moment he heard the shot. Turning, he saw Dominick with his head thrown back and blood pouring from his throat.

The door crashed open and Kevin burst into the room. "Mr. Anderson," he screamed, "Neil."

Neil shook his head.

Kevin stared, first at his uncle and then at Neil. "Thank God," he whispered before flinging himself against the police officer and wrapping his arms around him.

"It's all over, lad," Neil managed to say before the boy broke down into shuddering sobs.

Twenty-Nine

Kate woke to the blare of her alarm. Groggily she groped for the familiar feel of the clock on her nightstand, managed the snooze button and signed with relief. Her throat felt like sandpaper. Wearily she opened one eye, glanced at the time and groaned. It was nearly seven and she'd had two hours of sleep, at the most. The ache, never far from the center of her stomach, hit with full force. She curled into a fetal position and pulled the covers over her head.

Would she ever feel normal again? When would she awaken without the weight of betrayal or fear of nausea? Would life ever work with the smooth symmetry of her younger years? She rolled over and tentatively stretched her legs. Not that her life had ever *really* worked smoothly. She just thought it had. Reality was that she had lived a fantasy.

Slowly she worked her legs over the side of the bed, slid off the mattress and stood, swaying slightly. When she felt balanced enough to walk, she padded down the hall to Deirdre's room and peeked inside. Deirdre was sleeping the same way she had as a little girl, on her stomach, one arm thrown over her head with her face tucked into the crook of her elbow. Deirdre was safely home. Kate breathed a silent thank you, closed the door and walked back to her own room. If only she could say the same about Kevin.

Until yesterday, Neil had reported regularly on Kevin's whereabouts. Yesterday evening all communication had stopped. Kate was terrified. Her appetite had completely deserted her. Work was no longer a possibility. She spent her hours silently pacing from one room to the next. Occasionally when claustrophobia set in, she would pull on sweats, lace her running shoes and cover the miles between Ardara and the Coast Road in record time.

Oddly enough it was in her worst moments that she appreciated the beauty all around her, hills wet with mist, peat bogs dark and rich and mysterious, ripe with memories of creatures whose thundering steps had pressed them into existence eons ago, a west-facing cliff, the ocean rolling in below it, valleys smooth and gently rounded, bowls of green, a green purer, richer and more vibrant than any that existed outside of Ireland. This was why those who left moved to cities, London, New York, Boston, Chicago. They couldn't bear to live in a country nowhere near as lovely as Ireland.

What if Kevin were to miss all of this? What if he never experienced the joys of adulthood, the choices, the freedom, the challenge of responsibility? The horror of it stopped her in midthought, her mind refusing to follow its natural inclination. If only Neil would call. She felt her eyes swell. Pressing her fingers against her lids, she willed the tears back.

"Katie?" John O'Donnell's voice called from downstairs.

She leaned over the banister. "Shh. Deirdre's sleeping."

"It's going on eight o'clock," said her father. "She'll sleep away the day."

"She needs the rest, Da. Please, lower your voice."

It was too late. A yawning Deirdre emerged from her room. "Good morning," she said. "Did I hear Grandda's voice?"

"You did, lass," he called from the bottom of the stairs. "I came over for a bite of breakfast."

Deirdre looked at her mother. "Are you in the mood to cook, or shall I?"

"I'll do it. Let me dress first." Kate called down to her father. "Start the tea. I'll be down in a minute."

Deirdre smiled at her mother. "Don't worry. I was nearly awake. Have you heard anything from Kevin?"

Kate shook her head. "Neil hasn't called since yesterday."

Deirdre's smile faded. "Oh my God, Mum. Isn't there anything we can do?"

"I don't think so, Deirdre. I have no idea where Dominick might go. Liam knows but he won't tell me. He thinks it's dangerous and that I should leave everything to the authorities."

"He's right. After all, what could you do?"

Kate thought a minute. "I could talk to Kevin, perhaps calm him a bit. He's bound to be terrified."

"Is there anyone else who knows?"

"I don't think so. There—" She stopped, her tongue stumbling over the name, Maeve. "I can't think of anyone who would tell me what Liam won't."

"We'll have to trust Mr. Anderson." She crossed the hall and hugged her mother. "Hurry and dress. Grandda will be restless."

In a way, her father was a blessing, thought Kate.

His blustering manner and absurd suggestions had the effect of reorienting her.

"Why do you think he isn't calling us?" John fumed, tapping his fingers on the wooden table.

Kate passed him the buttered toast. "I don't know."

"It's possible there's no phone reception," said Deirdre.

John's face brightened. "You've hit it on the head, Dee." He slapped his knee. "Did you hear her, Katie. There's no reception."

"I did," said Katie, throwing her daughter a grateful look.

"I always said Dominick Nolan was a bad sort," said her father, between mouthfuls of egg. "He's sneaky, not a bit like Patrick and Liam."

Kate looked down at her untouched plate and felt the bile rise in her throat. "I wouldn't say that Patrick and Liam were patterns of virtue."

She felt two pairs of eyes staring at her. "Well, it's true," she said defensively.

"Patrick was Deirdre's father, Katie," her father remonstrated.

"Thank God she's nothing like him."

"Mum!" Deirdre's eyes were wide with shock. "I've never heard you say anything negative about Da in my life."

"She won't again," her grandfather reassured her.

Kate pressed her fork into her napkin first horizontally and then vertically. She liked the way the lines crisscrossed in an orderly fashion. She liked her life orderly. She'd planned it that way. Damn Patrick.

Had anything between them been real? When she scrutinized their marriage, really looked at it, brought it out under the magnifying glass, held it up to the light and polished it, they'd had little in common beyond the children. She loved travel, exploring museums and restored castles. He preferred beach vacations when he could be persuaded to leave home. He liked reading deep, political commentaries. She was a fan of escapist fiction. He'd hated the heat. Their bed had been a battle zone with Patrick throwing off the covers while she burrowed under down and flannel. Kate hoped he was in a particularly hot place in hell.

"Patrick was a murderer," she said deliberately, "a murderer, a liar and a cheater." She looked up at Deirdre. "If you know that, if you hear it from me, you'll manage when you hear it from others. And you will hear it, Deirdre. This isn't over yet. When Neil arrests Dominick, everything will come out. I want you to be prepared for it. It won't be easy, but if you can come up with a strategy for bearing the rumors, it will at least be tolerable. Do you understand me?"

Deirdre's eyes were bright with tears. One spilled over and rolled down her cheek. She nodded. "This is really awful, isn't it?"

For once John was silent.

Kate shook her head. "The past is awful. The present isn't. Neither is the future. We'll get beyond this."

"What about Kevin?"

Fear, desperate and all consuming closed around Kate's heart. "I don't—"

John held up his hand. "Listen."

Through the frozen silence, Kate heard it, the sound of an car coming up the long driveway. She leaped up from the table, raced through the door and out into the day. Kevin, framed by the sea and the new light of a milky sun, climbed out of Neil's car and ran toward her.

Later, when the heightened emotions of seeing her son alive and eager and safely walking up the footpath of his own home, had faded, Kate would relive this moment in her mind, the impact of his ropey young body when he threw himself into her arms, the smell of his hair, the soft down on his cheeks, the rapid beating of his heart, the hard, hurting pressure of his hands on her back, the swelling of her own heart, so that it seemed too large for her chest.

She was aware of Deirdre and her father behind her, of Neil standing before her, grinning, but her focus was Kevin, all arms and legs and lean young body, black hair, blue eyes, blurred now with tears. She clung to him, lifting her head to kiss his cheeks, his chin, his forehead, pulling his head down to her shoulder. She tasted dirt and salt and skin. She inhaled the smoky turf smell of him. Pulling him closer, into the safety of her arms, she pressed his head down on her shoulder. For the first time in years he made no attempt to resist her, allowing the mother part of her, the instinctive protective pull of parent to child, to envelop him. She felt warm wet streaks against her cheeks, his tears or hers? She didn't know, didn't care. "There, there, love," she crooned. "It's all right now. Everything is all right now."

Too soon he left her embrace to be smothered first by his sister and then his grandfather, their welcomes no less enthusiastic than Kate's. So absorbed was she in her family's reunion, that she nearly missed Neil's exit. He had turned on the ignition and was backing down the road, when she ran after him, signaling him to stop. He rolled down the window and waited for her.

"You're not leaving?" she asked when she'd caught up with him.

"I'll call you tomorrow. The four of you need this time to yourselves. I don't want to intrude."

She straightened, her hands on her hips. "Come back with me this instant. I want to know what happened."

Neil's face was grim. "It's not pretty, Kate. Dominick shot himself."

"Dear God." Her hand was at her throat. "Please tell me Kevin wasn't there."

"He was outside. But he ran in when he heard the shot. He was afraid I had been killed. I managed to get him out as soon as possible, but he saw Dominick."

"No."

"He's a brave lad, Kate. There's plenty of steel in him. He handled himself well. You can be proud of him. I'm sure he'll be all right. He wasn't in the room when I told Dominick we knew about his role in Patrick's death."

"Deirdre knows. It isn't right for her to know and for Kevin to be kept in the dark. Both of them are his children."

"Do whatever you think is best."

She hesitated. "Neil."

"Yes."

"Thank you."

"I'll call you tomorrow."

"Are you sure you won't stay?"

He shook his head. "Not this time. Kevin needs to be with family. I imagine he's seen enough of me for a while."

"How can I ever thank you?"

"I'll think of a way."

She heard the laugh in his voice and laughed back. How easy it was. "I'm sure you will. Don't stay away too long."

"Do you mean that?"

She tilted her head to one side and considered his question. "Actually I do," she said.

"I won't disappoint you."

She watched him drive away. A small, ridiculous kernel of fear cropped up in her mind. What if all this was too much for him? What if he thought seriously about everything and came to the conclusion that two needy children and the widow of a terrorist was more than he was willing to take on? What would she do without him?

The familiar self-preservation mode she had cultivated rose like shackles around her. Self-doubt, her most serious flaw, had a way of crushing her confidence, of dousing her with a healthy portion of reality. Oddly enough it was Maeve's words she thought of. *I've never been sorry to see a man go, Kate. If he doesn't realize what he has in me, he isn't worth having.* Incredibly she would miss Maeve. She already missed her, more than she missed Patrick.

They waited for her on the porch, her family, holding back questions, wondering where they would go now. They weren't complete without her. It pleased her, this codependency among the four of them. For this moment it seemed a tremendous responsibility, one she would gladly hold on to forever. She hooked arms with her children and kissed her son. "I'm sure you're famished. What would you like to eat?"

Kevin laughed. "The world falls apart and Mum still wants to know what to cook."

"Lucky for you," his mother retorted. "The refrigerator's full."

"When has it ever not been full?" Deirdre asked.

"After Kevin and his friends come home after school," said Kate.

"You didn't really mind, did you, Mum?" Kevin's expression was worried. Kate thought of the rough-and-tumble innocence of those lost days and nearly broke down. What she wouldn't give for them again. "No, love," she said.

"What happens now?" John asked when they were seated around the sunlit kitchen table.

"What do you mean?" Kate buttered a second piece of toast. Her appetite had miraculously returned.

"Will Kevin continue here at school? Does he have anything left to do in Belfast?"

"I don't know." She looked at Kevin. "Do you?"

He shook his head. "I haven't been back to Belfast, not since Neil found me. He didn't say anything."

"Well then," said his mother bracingly. "We'll wait and see. No one's going anywhere. As far as school, perhaps we can talk about that after Kevin rests a bit."

"I'm not really tired, but I will take a shower." He stood, his throat working. "I'm glad to be back."

Deirdre stood and ran around the table to hug her brother. "Oh, Kevin. We're so glad to have you here."

Kevin's arms enfolded her. "I've made a mess of things, Dee. I wish I could take everything back."

"Everyone wishes he could take something back," Deirdre murmured into his shoulder. "Experience isn't wasted. It always has a purpose."

Kevin tugged on her hair. "How did you turn out to be so serene?"

She stared at him. "You're joking? I had the perfect role model. When have you ever seen Mum in a state?"

Kevin threw his mother a conspiratorial look. "She's had her moments."

Deirdre shook her head. "Not when I'm around."

"I have a way of provoking her."

"Stop it," Kate protested. "You have me sounding like an ogre. Go upstairs and take your shower. I'm sure if you try you might even sleep a bit."

Kevin stopped at the foot of the stairs. "I didn't say goodbye to Neil."

"I said if for you. He understood."

Kevin hesitated. "Will you be seeing him again?"

Kate felt the heat rise in her cheeks. She lifted her head. "I hope so."

"I'm glad," said her son, surprising her.

Soon after, Deirdre followed her brother up the stairs Kate was left alone with her father.

"You're quiet this morning, Da. Is everything all right?"

Her father sighed and drummed his thick fingers on the table. "I'm a simple man, Katie, and I won't be beating around the bush."

"If you did, the shock of it might kill me."

"Now, there you go. That's exactly what I mean." John's brow wrinkled. "You've changed, Katie. You have a tongue on you that's new. And what of this Neil fellow? Are you stepping out with him, Kate?"

She swallowed a smile. "No one steps out anymore Da. They stay in."

"Mind that tongue, lass. It's your father to whom you're speaking."

"Don't disapprove of me, Da. I like Neil very much Is that so bad?"

"He's not Irish."

"He's Welsh."

"Is he Catholic?"

"Not anymore." Better to get it all out. "He's divorced with a daughter."

John groaned.

Suddenly Kate was angry. "Did you really believe I would live the rest of my life alone? Is that what you want for me?"

"Of course not."

"At my age, do you think I'm going to find someone who hasn't been married?"

"I hoped you would find someone like you."

"A widower?"

"Aye."

"How many widowers in their early forties do you think are out there, Da?"

John scratched his chin. He looked embarrassed. "I haven't really thought it through."

Kate's anger dissipated suddenly, without warning, leaving her flat and empty. She pressed her fingers against her temples. "Never mind. It doesn't matter. More than likely nothing will come of it anyway."

"Have a bit of faith, Katie. You're a fine, attractive woman. A man would be a fool to look the other way when you're taken with him. Neil Anderson doesn't appear foolish."

"I thought you didn't like him."

"I never said that. I merely wondered if he was right for you, that's all."

"I don't know if he's right. We're not there yet."

"I'd hurry up a bit if I was you, Katie. You're not getting any younger."

"You're incredible, Da. You really are."

He knocked on the door tentatively as if unsure of his welcome. She liked the casualness of him, khaki slacks and a slate-blue shirt that turned the gray of his eyes to pure silver. He looked young and relaxed.

"Come in," she said holding the door open for him.

He sat across from her at the wooden table, gleaming and sweetly scented of orange polish. "I thought you would never come back to Belfast," he confessed.

"I wanted to wait until Kevin decided what to do."

"Has he made any decisions?"

"Art school." Kate shook her head. "I never would have guessed. He said you told him to appeal to me."

Neil grinned. "There is no harm in asking."

"I'm amazed at what I never noticed. It's a lowering thought." Her lip quivered. "There's a great deal for him to work through."

"You're a marvelous mother, Kate."

"Thank you."

"What about Deirdre. Has she gone back to Belfast?"

"Not yet. I'm trying to persuade her to transfer to Galway or Dublin. Belfast is difficult and will be for some time."

"Any luck?"

"Some. We'll see."

They sat in silence until it became awkward.

"Can I get you anything?" she asked.

"Tea would be splendid."

"What happens now?" she asked after she poured the tea.

"What do you mean?"

"Is your job finished in Belfast?"

"That depends on you."

Courage, Kate, courage. "I don't understand."

He leaned forward and took her hands in his. "I've fallen in love with you, Kate. I don't know what you're like in the morning or what part of the paper you read first. I don't even know how you like your coffee or your eggs or whether you read or visit the theater. I do know that you're a woman of tremendous character, educated, warm, loyal and beautiful, a woman I'd be a fool not to pursue. Maybe, if things work out, we could make it permanent. I don't need bells and whistles. I need a partnership that endures.''

She pulled her hands away. ''That's a dreadful proposal. No wonder your wife found someone else.''

He stiffened. ''That's a terrible thing to say.''

''So was your declaration.''

He shook his head, bewildered. ''I don't understand.''

Her eyes flashed dangerously. ''You aren't the least bit romantic. A woman wants to be told she's swept a man off his feet. She wants the words, lovely, romantic words telling her she's the love of his life, that he's never felt this way before, that this love is different. She wants him to look at her and hear bells and whistles.'' Her voice rose. ''I want bells and whistles. I don't want a partnership. I want to be loved desperately, giddily.''

He stared at her.

''Say something,'' she demanded.

''Are you in love with me?''

''Yes,'' she snapped, angry at her own admission.

His lips twitched. ''I was being so very careful not to scare you away.''

''What?''

''I thought you needed more time after this mess with Patrick. I believed the best way to approach you was slowly, showing up with an invitation now and then, allowing you to grow accustomed to me, becoming better acquainted with your children.'' He laughed, a low, deep chuckle that made her heart beat faster.

''I don't need any more time,'' she whispered. ''I don't want you to go away, ever.''

He reached for her, pulling her out of the chair and into his arms, brushing the hair away from her forehead, his lips against her cheek murmuring the words, romantic and passionate, words that worked their way into her heart, soothing her ego, easing her bruised soul, words leaving no doubt that, in his eyes, she was more than he'd ever dreamed of finding.

Later, they sat on the long couch that faced the window, the one with a view of the Atlantic. ''I was worried that you would say no, or that it was too soon.''

''Too soon? I've been alone for six years.''

''Not really,'' he said gently. ''Until a few days ago, Patrick was still with you. I'm still a bit worried that I'm meeting you on the rebound, but I've decided to take my chances. I'm going to do this right, Kate. I'm going to woo you and your children and even your father, if I have to.''

''How will you do that?''

''Through old-fashioned courtship, dinners out, the cinema, an occasional play, the opera, a weekend away, family holidays.''

''It sounds lovely.''

''Is it what you want?''

He looked very earnest sitting there with hair falling over his forehead. She would have taken him bald or any way at all, but she was ever so grateful for his full head of hair and his lean tight stomach and the way his cheeks creased when he laughed. It was a shallow sentiment, she knew, and she was more than a little ashamed to admit that appearance was important to her, but admitting it or not made it no less true. "Yes," she said. "I want it very much."

He released his breath. "Thank God."

She traced the line of his nose with her finger and pressed a soft kiss on the corner of his lips. Dare she say it? Yes. With this man she could say anything without fear. But she would not tell him of her life with Patrick, or her suspicions, the absences, the emptiness, the frustrated anger. She would rise to a new level of expectation. What had he called her, a woman of tremendous character, warm, loyal and beautiful? And why not? Wasn't it possible that she *was* all those things? That a different woman could rise up because of a different man? Wasn't everyone a myriad of parts, each one waiting for the right circumstances to emerge?

Gently she touched his ear with her tongue, smiling when he shivered. "We're not all that young anymore, you know."

"We're not that old, either." He replied.

"Old enough to know what we want."

"Absolutely."

"Do you believe in long courtships?"

He pulled away to look at her. "Do you?" he asked cautiously.

"No."

The laugh started in his eyes. "Is that a proposal?"

"Yes."

"I've never had a woman propose to me."

"You never will again."

"In that case, I should probably accept."

"Most definitely."

"I do."

Kate smiled. "Those are lovely words. They'll come in handy quite soon."

"Are we officially engaged?"

"We are."

"Thank God," he said for the second time that morning.

USA TODAY **Bestselling Author**

ANNE STUART

For Sophie Davis, turning Stonegate Farm into a quaint country inn is the fulfillment of a lifelong dream. She doesn't even mind that the farm was the scene of a grisly murder twenty years earlier....

When a stranger moves in next to the farm, Sophie believes the sense of peace she has created is threatened. Because there's something different about John Smith. It's clear he's come to Colby, Vermont, for a reason...and that reason has something to do with Sophie and Stonegate Farm.

Now her dream is becoming a nightmare. Who is John Smith? Why does his very presence make Sophie feel so completely out of control? And why is she beginning to suspect that this mysterious stranger will put in jeopardy everything she's dreamed of—maybe even her life?

STILL LAKE

"A master at creating chilling atmosphere."
—*Library Journal*

Available the first week of August 2002 wherever paperbacks are sold!
Visit us at www.mirabooks.com

MAS908

Will fate give him a second chance?

CANDACE CAMP

With his life in ruins, Richard, Duke of Cleybourne,
returns to his country estate to deal with a tragic loss.
His quiet respite is suddenly interrupted by the arrival
of the feisty, flame-haired Jessica Maitland.

Fate and a raging snowstorm bring together an odd
assortment of guests at Cleybourne Castle. And when
murder strikes, Richard and Jessica must catch
a killer and unravel a dark mystery, even as they are
plunged into the most passionate *mystery* of all—
the secrets of the hidden heart.

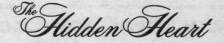

The Hidden Heart

**Available the first week of August 2002
wherever paperbacks are sold!**

MIRA®

Visit us at www.mirabooks.com

MCC922